BAD LUCK CHARLIE

THE DRAGON MAGE BOOK 1

SCOTT BARON

Being a fish out of water is tough,
but that's how you evolve.
– Kumail Nanjiani

CHAPTER ONE

"Starboard heat shield seven is gone!" Charlie called out as calmly as he could over the din of their ship more or less tearing apart. He was going to carry out his duties like a professional if it was the last thing he'd do, and the way things were going, it was starting to look like it might be.

"Copy that," Captain Reynard bellowed over the noise. "Gaspari, redirect the primary debris shield to cover as much of starboard seven as possible. Pull power from wherever you have to!"

Rika Gaspari, his second-in-command, began frantically throwing switches, inverting the power flows, her hands a blur of activity as she carried out her orders. The ship's rattling lessened, but did not cease.

"Still low on power, Captain. The atmosphere has some powerful radiologic properties that are wreaking havoc with our phase shielding. I don't know if it's going to be enough."

"Then pull power from life support."

"Sir? Won't we need that?" Charlie asked as he struggled to keep the engines from redlining into critical and blowing them all to hell.

"Not if we don't survive atmospheric entry. First things first. Right now, getting down in one piece is the highest priority," the captain replied.

Rika did as she was ordered. A moment later the crew felt the ever-present breeze of recirculating air that moved about them cease. It was something they were so familiar with that they didn't even notice its presence until it was abruptly gone.

"Done, Captain," Gaspari announced, her close-cropped hair sticking to her damp forehead. "Twenty seconds until we clear the exosphere."

"Copy that. Jamal, are you suited up?" the captain asked over internal comms.

"Affirmative, Captain," he replied. "Prepped and standing by with backup fire suppression."

The chief of security and emergency services had geared up the moment things began to sway out of parameters, which was just before they were unceremoniously sucked through a massive wormhole and spat out Lord knew where. His foresight was a good thing. It was looking like things were about to get a whole lot worse.

The ship bucked and tossed, its hull glowing bright orange as the edges of the strange world's atmosphere pummeled it with brutal intensity. It was a rough ride in command. Captain Reynard knew the rest of his crew were being subjected to a vicious beating in their compartments. He just hoped they had strapped in. They launched with twenty-four living crew aboard, and he planned to keep it that way.

The command module's power flickered and dimmed.

"Losing primary power," Gaspari said.

"I see it," Charlie replied, already in motion, rushing from his seat to the door to the adjacent engineering compartment just off the bridge.

His team in main engineering down below would keep the

reactors powered up. It was his job to keep that power flowing to the controls during flight.

Smoke greeted him as he manually opened the door with the backup access crank tucked into the wall panel.

"We got a fire?" Reynard asked, sniffing the air.

"Negative, Captain. Just some blown circuits and overloaded wires," Charlie replied as he stuck his head in and surveyed the damage.

The room was small, just row upon row of circuit racks and relays. A harness chair sat in front of a work bench, never before used. Of course, for the maiden flight of the ship, why would it have been?

"The damage looks relatively minimal," Charlie informed them. "Give me a couple of minutes and I'll have it sorted."

"We don't have a couple of minutes."

"I'm on it. Let me know when the main control power surges normalize and level out."

Without another word, he slid through the narrow gap he'd opened in the door and set to work. The blown circuits were the easiest to repair, and, luckily, the most vital as well. The smoldering wires nearby, while important, were not crucial to staying aloft.

"Powering off navs and switching your panels to emergency reserve. Nobody touch anything until I say so. We're already maxing the load," he yelled out through the door.

Melted circuits went flying, his nimble fingers quickly replacing them with the backups stored in neatly arranged cases mounted to the wall nearby. A mere thirty seconds after he began, he called out to the others once more.

"Okay, we're good. It's powered back up. Test the system."

Captain Reynard feathered the controls. The ship responded as well as could be expected given the circumstances.

"Controls are functional. Gaspari, how are secondary navs and telemetry?"

"We're limping, but it should be enough," she replied.

"Okay, we're good. Get out of there, Charlie."

"Just a sec, Captain. I need to swap a few wires and reroute some of this charge so we don't fry everything if there's another power surge. It'll just take me a minute."

"Can it wait?"

"It can, but it shouldn't."

"All right, then. But be quick. We may have to make a much more abrupt landing than would be ideal."

"Believe me, the last place I want to be is stuck in here," he replied, setting to work.

He had just replaced the first of the failing wires when the ship bucked and slammed him into the wall, the emergency protocols sealing the re-powered door shut with him inside. He frantically clawed for the crank handle, but the turbulence was too much. Miraculously, he was thrown backwards—right into the harness chair. The back of the chair, that is.

Gotta get strapped in, he realized with a desperate grunt as his body switched from weightless to crushing Gs as the ship lurched and dove.

Charlie slammed into the ceiling with a rude crunch, held weightless a moment, hovering just out of reach of anything from which to push off, then was thrown to the floor, pinned by the G-force.

The pressure relented for a moment, allowing him to breathe. Charlie ignored the pain racking his body and dragged himself into the harness chair and strapped in snugly, and not a moment too soon, as the ship flipped upside down, then plummeted in a tight spiral.

Stuck in the memory foam chair, Charlie cried out, then fell silent as the pressure of the mounting G-force drove the blood from his head, rendering him unconscious.

He wouldn't remember the crash. But he would never forget the aftermath, nor the folly that had led up to it.

CHAPTER TWO

It was six months prior, and Charlie Gault had already been working on billionaire Brockton Millbury's top-secret *Asbrú* project for nearly five years when the call came in.

"Chuck?" a voice asked over his portable comms unit.

"Hey, Vickie," he replied, smoothly merging with the vehicles around him.

Only one person ever called him Chuck, despite the many times he made it known he did not really like the nickname, and that person was Vickie Rogers, the head of the entire R&D team spearheading the eccentric visionary's project.

"You sitting down, Chuck?"

"I'm driving, Vickie, so I would certainly hope so."

"You could be using an auto-pilot for all I know," she replied. "But that's unimportant."

Anything not on Vickie's agenda was deemed unimportant, and that included time off, weekends, and even vacations.

"You sound agitated. Is everything all right?" he asked, staring out the window, pleasantly distracted by the passing scenery as his vehicle effortlessly lifted off, flowing smoothly with the few other permitted conveyances in the air.

He was, in fact, using his auto-pilot, but he wouldn't tell her as much.

"It's time," she said, barely containing her excitement. "Tests have come back, and the Einstein-Rosen stabilizer works."

"We know it works, Vickie. We've known for over a year. The question is, can we maintain a stable enough field to allow for safe transit? That's the tricky bit. The distance between the Earth and Mr. Millbury's test facility orbiting Mars is no small matter. The device has to be able to sustain for all thirty-three point nine million miles."

"Which will be covered in a flash."

"In theory. None of this has been real-world tested for those power parameters."

"But, Chuck, the prototype skiff just made the moon jump."

Charlie audibly gasped. He knew it was possible, the bending of space to allow for rapid transit from one point to another, but their energy sources were simply not powerful enough to allow much more than a several thousand-mile hop. It was impressive, but it would not alter the course of human history. At least, not yet. Their work could change that, one day.

"That wasn't scheduled," he said. "First space trials aren't even slated until two years from now. It's still in the experimental phase."

"I know. But Mr. Millbury himself green-lit the test."

"He's a dilettante, not a scientist. He should have waited."

"He's a genius, Chuck, and he's our boss. If he wants an early test, we give him an early test."

Charlie sighed. He knew how this would go. Protest would be useless. It would be just like every other time the billionaire had a whim. Charlie and his team would whir into action like the residents of a kicked anthill, frantically tweaking ops parameters and pulling seventy-two-hour engineering brainstorming sessions to meet the new goals their patron had just pulled out of his ass.

An ideal work environment, it was not.

"Okay, so we know the unit works on short hops. Christ, I can't believe he went and did that," he groaned. "How much did it drain the reactor? We'll need that data if we're going to figure load requirements for the longer jump."

A brief silence hung in the air.

"All of it," she finally replied.

"All? It drained the whole core? That's impossible."

"Nope. Apparently, it's very possible, as we've just learned. The fusion core is cold as ice."

Draining a battery was one thing, but actually sucking the life out of a nuclear fusion reactor was—up until today, at least—impossible. Charlie put on his best game face and stayed calm.

Treat it like just another glitch to work through, Charlie. Don't freak out, he silently told himself, taking a deep breath and counting to three before speaking.

"So, once again, it seems we are faced with the power problem," he said, managing to sound relatively calm. "Only now, our only test reactor is toast. Think he'll spring for a new one?"

"We have other reactors, Chuck. Bigger ones."

He knew what she was speaking of, he just couldn't believe she was saying it.

"Those are supposed to power the ship, Vickie. We've been working on that thing for nearly five years. You can't just go and steal our work for Millbury's impulses."

"Relax. We're not going to strip them out of your ship, Chuck. Your pet project is safe. The *Asbrú* will remain intact."

"Good, becau—"

"We're going to run the next test *with* the ship."

Charlie fell silent. They couldn't be serious, could they? Taking hundreds of billions of dollars worth of research and work and turning it into a science experiment? It was folly. Madness.

And just the sort of thing his quirky employer would do.

He sighed, resigned to his project's unfortunate fate.

"All right," he finally said, knowing it was a fight he simply could not win. "When do I have to deliver it? I've got to warn you, the ship still needs a lot of work and a proper shake-out to get any bugs out of the systems."

"You'll have plenty of time to shake them out."

"I'm sorry, that sounded like you said *I* would be doing it."

"That's right, Chuck. You've been promoted. You're no longer design lead. You're now the official specialist for engineering and flight ops. Congratulations."

"You know I don't fly, Vickie. Space and me, we don't get along."

"It's a great honor to be one of the first humans to travel utilizing this tech, and you were a key designer. You should be excited, not pouting like a little baby."

"I don't do space flights. That was made clear when I signed on to this project."

Silence hung icily over the open line.

Finally, she spoke. "You do realize what this will do to you? To your career?"

"I'll have to find another job. Maybe I'll teach, this time," he replied.

"You won't, you know. You'll be blacklisted from every major research facility, shunned from reputable universities. Is that what you want?"

"He wouldn't do that," Charlie said, only half believing himself.

"He wants this badly, Charles, so yes, he would."

She had called him Charles. Suddenly, he realized just how deep the shit he was standing in truly was. If forced to estimate, he'd have said roughly eyeball level. And rising.

He had some savings, sure, but not nearly enough to become an unemployed, and, far worse, *unemployable,* man. A choice would have to be made, and his options were either bad or worse.

When the *Asbrú* launched six months later for what was only supposed to be a short test flight of its main drive and reactor systems, it left Earth carrying a greatly reduced crew, but enough to run some smaller experiments in the shake-out process.

Charlie, miserable and still a little queasy from launch, found his reluctant ass planted firmly in the engineering and ops seat within the command module. The captain's second-in-command flashed him a look.

"I know you don't like space flight, but I'm glad you're with us, Charlie."

"Thanks, Rika."

They'd worked well together in the months leading up to that day, and he felt confident he could trust not just her abilities as the Captain's Number One, but her counsel as a friend as well. She'd helped get him over his crushing fear of flight. And now he was in her hands.

"Okay, everybody," the captain said over comms. "The countdown has started. Full systems test in one minute. This will just be a power test in orbit. Yang, are all of your gadgets and test samples good?"

"Yes, Captain," Winnifred, 'Winnie' Yang replied. "The critters are caged up and secure. We're all buttoned up and ready to go."

"How about you, Mr. Quick? I hope we won't need your services, but are you set to go?"

"Yes Captain, standing by."

"All right, then, everyone sit tight and let the computers do their thing. This is automated and should take less than two minutes to cycle through."

What Captain Reynard didn't know was that a lone microcircuit was about to fail in the most spectacular manner. A fluke of poor quality control, caused by a rather embarrassing oversight, had allowed it to slip into the mix. It was a tiny thing, but it was enough.

"Five. Four. Three. Two. One," Captain Reynard counted down.

Nothing happened.

Then their reality spun and went to shit, pausing to hit the fan on the way for good measure.

"What the hell's going on?" Gaspari managed to utter through the forces assailing her, before vomiting on the deck.

Charlie knew. It was obvious to him. Obvious and horrifying.

"Shut it down! Shut down the power systems!"

But it was too late.

The ship had torn a hole in space, a massive wormhole that had formed in a flash.

"We're being pulled in!" Charlie shouted as the ship spun on its axis and lurched toward the gaping maw.

"Give me full power, all engines! Get us free fro––" Captain Reynard tried to say.

The ship was swallowed whole before he could finish his thought, then was abruptly spat out unceremoniously on the other side of the wormhole, somewhere very far away, just as the space anomaly vanished in a flash.

"Status?" the captain barked over the warning sirens.

"Life support operational. Drive systems online but losing power. Navs are all shot to hell," Gaspari said.

"What hit us, Charlie?"

"It-it was an unstable Einstein-Rosen bridge," he said, shell-shocked. "I think we somehow tore open a wormhole. It shouldn't have even been possible. We should be dead. But for whatever reason, the same malfunction that got us here also protected us."

"From what?"

"From being turned inside out and boiled down to jelly," he replied.

"Captain, we're being pulled in toward a gravitational field," Gaspari said. "Something is reeling us in."

"Visuals. On all monitors."

"Aye, Captain," she replied.

The screens flickered on for a moment before going black, but it was enough. It was a huge, round shape. An object with immense gravitational pull.

"Buckle up, everyone, this is going to get bumpy," Captain Reynard barked over ship-wide comms.

"What was that?" Charlie asked.

"It looked like a planet."

Charlie strapped in tight and wondered what colossal design flaw had escaped notice. What the hell had managed to go so wrong for things to come to this.

The answer might have surprised him.

CHAPTER THREE

The strangest of things can cause a domino-effect disaster. Faulty materials, improper securing of load-bearing connections, or, in this case, human error of the most negligent variety. And it was such a very *human* folly that caused the whole thing.

"C'mon, Johnny, no one will know," the coverall-wearing clean room tech said, attempting her very best to show at least some of her feminine shape through the bulky over suit.

"Arlene, are you nuts? You're going to get us both fired," Jonathan replied.

He scanned the bustling lab, hoping none of the busy staff had overheard her propositioning him. Their affair was a secret. Not only because having relations with coworkers within the same department was against company policy, but also because Arlene was married to a giant of a man who just so happened to also be the HR manager.

If anything became public, it would be her husband deciding his employment fate. The man would not, however, lay a finger on him. Of that, Jonathan was sure. Arlene had bitched about his passive nature enough times by now for him to know that, despite his intimidating size, he possessed a weak spine.

He was also, Johnny learned, surprisingly under-endowed for a man of his enormity. Sometimes, nature played funny little jokes, it seemed.

"Nothing's going to happen," she said, brushing her rear firmly against him as she slipped past, carrying a tray of high-density data chips to the destruction chute. Another batch had microfractures in the still-cooling circuit underlay, and, while they were structurally sound enough to support the data and power lattices embedded upon and within, the minuscule imperfections caused the flows to be out of parameters.

They disposed of thousands of dollars worth of imperfect material every day. A cost of doing business in this zero-tolerance industry. And these particular chips were highly specialized, on order for yet another top-secret project for some billionaire playboy, rumor had it.

The chips clattered to their doom down the chute, and Arlene walked by him again. Her look was sensual fire. Jonathan worried his growing erection might become noticeable despite his bulky clean suit.

"Five minutes. The decon showers," she whispered, gently groping him as she passed. The showers were the one place on the level where there was no video surveillance. A response to the threat of potential lawsuits should images of naked workers getting a Silkwood shower ever be leaked.

They'd be totally alone, and despite common sense screaming at him, it was tempting. He could feel the pressure in his pants rapidly growing, sapping his IQ and self-preservation instinct with every pulse.

"Don't do it, Johnny," he mumbled to himself, attempting to put work—and job security—before animal urges.

Four minutes later he watched as Arlene walked from her

work station. He might have withstood the hormonal onslaught had she not briefly turned and looked back at him. The raw want in her eyes shot straight to his groin, sending another flush of endorphins through his body.

"Well, just this one time," he rationalized, tidying his workstation and quickly crossing the room.

"Where you off to, Cooke?"

It was Bill Turling. Not his boss, thank God, just another lab employee. One who happened to be a stickler for rules, though. In the schoolyard, he would have been the kid who narced on the other kids for eating candy bars between classes.

"Taking a leak, Bill," he replied. "Why? You want to watch?" Johnathan knew any allusions to anything remotely homoerotic would shut the man down immediately. *How sad*, he thought, *that he keeps himself closeted in an era where sexual orientation was unimportant to nearly everyone.*

He guessed Bill had come from one of those overly religious households that deemed anything outside their myopic world view to be a sin. It was too bad, really. Everyone in the lab knew, nobody cared, and Johnathan knew for a fact that at least one of his male coworkers found Bill kind of cute.

But no one plays matchmaker for narcs.

"Suit yourself, Billy boy," he said with a forced laugh. The man would ask no further questions, at least not for a while, and Johnathan had somewhere to be.

"What took you so long?" Arlene said, pulling at the zippers of his suit, while already halfway out of her own.

"Bill," he replied.

"Ugh. That guy," she groaned, yanking Johnathan's clean suit down to his knees. "Come on, we don't have much time," she said, spinning her back to him.

Johnathan obliged, quite vigorously at that, and five minutes later, the pair left the decon shower area––a few minutes apart––casually making their way back to their workstations.

Arlene was still in somewhat of an afterglow daze when she delivered the next tray into the destruction chute, while carefully depositing each of the chips from the other tray into small Mylar pouches, flooding them with neutral gas, then sealing them to be shipped out for installation.

What her sex-addled brain failed to notice was that she had destroyed the wrong chips.

After lunch, she finally noticed her mistake. The trays she used to sort the good from bad were reversed at her workstation. Had she done that?

A panic flooded her body. What if she was found out? They'd review the security camera footage. Her *husband* would review the footage. What would he see? They'd been careful, heading off to the shower area separately, but were they discreet enough?

Doubt flooded her mind. Johnathan had been right. She could get them both fired. And worse, she could give her husband grounds for divorce of a nature that would even preclude alimony. She doubted he'd have the spine to do it, but if he wanted to, he could not only fire her, but leave her penniless as well.

It was only a handful of bad units that were mistakenly sent out, she rationalized. And there were triple redundancies in all of those high-tech systems these days, anyway, so it probably wouldn't make the least bit of difference.

Her panic subsided. *Yes*, she thought. *That makes sense. It'll be fine.*

Arlene put the whole thing out of her head and got back to work, the burst of adrenaline slowly fading from her body.

Twenty-three months later, thousands of miles away in the depths of space, a multi-billion-dollar spaceship would power up all of its systems, massive amounts of energy passing through the meticulously constructed vessel. There were backups and redundancies, and backups to those, but within each of them, a handful of data chips lay waiting. Waiting like a shark in deep water, invisible, but ready to strike at any moment.

CHAPTER FOUR

Nearly eight months before their disastrous mission, Charlie and his pilot friend put another of their employer's toys through its paces. The ground shook slightly, a low rumble jostling the cup of coffee resting on the small folding table at Charlie's side. Another series of ripples spread across the surface, like a small pond in a storm. Then another.

"You okay up there?" he asked over his comms headset as he scanned the readouts whizzing by on his data terminal.

"Why wouldn't I be okay?" Rika asked from the pilot's seat of the towering mech. "You making a crack about my driving?"

Charlie wasn't, and even if he were, he knew better than to mouth off to the particularly strong-willed woman while she was operating a nearly three-story-tall survey and maintenance mech as she ran it through its paces.

"Of course not. You're a great pilot."

Rika smiled, amused. "Good save, Charlie," she said, then continued walking the giant machine down the testing path. "Hey, take a look at the left knee servos, would ya? I'm feeling a little bit of stiffness in the joint."

Charlie began typing in a series of diagnostics commands, pulling up detailed schematics of the machine. Calling it a giant robot would be a misnomer, since it was technically a human operating it. Nevertheless, it was a bipedal work of wonder, and arguably the most technologically advanced––and costliest–– mech ever built. And he would know, having designed a good portion of the machine's engineering.

"Joint appears to be functioning within parameters," he replied.

"Well, it feels like it's got arthritis," she shot back. "Balance feels off."

"Hang on," Charlie said, pulling up a wider frame of the mech's schematics. "I think I see the problem. It's a lag in one of the relays in the lower back area, right where the pivot would translate to an unexpected transfer of force through the endoskeleton. That'd put more pressure on that side. Give me a minute to see if I can't adjust it from here."

"Copy that, standing by," Rika replied, bringing the mech to a halt.

The plan for the day was to have it run through a full course of exercises to work out any bugs in the system. Bugs like the one they had just found. While Charlie was proud of the device, he griped in private that making the massive machine in a human shape had put it at a huge disadvantage from the get-go. Walking on two legs simply wasn't the most efficient way to ambulate something that large.

His boss, however, had other ideas. And when Brockton Millbury had an idea, oh boy, you had better watch out. He was a brilliant man, no one would argue against that, but he was also more than a little bit of a dreamer, and his exceptional wealth afforded him the ability to demand the unusual––and often impulsive––of his team.

A forty-five-foot-tall mech was just that sort of whimsical

creation. A crazy design, napkin-sketched late one night, now made reality by a team of talented men and women.

And a huge bankroll.

When the difficulties and weaknesses of the design idea were pointed out, he had told his minions he had the utmost faith in them. Then left them to get to it, the hastily jotted drawing that looked like something designed by a comic-loving kid acting as their lone starting point.

The design would go through many iterations, of course, losing the most impractical aspects––like folding in on itself to transform into a plane. It did actually wind up being designed to fold, but into a boxy and protective travel configuration, designed for ease of loading into transport craft.

It had taken quite some time to construct, even with the enormous amount of money thrown at it, but at long last, a fully functional version was up and running. It may have lacked the racing stripe awesomeness of Brockton Millbury's original concept, but Charlie had made sure it had more than a few bells and whistles.

"Hey, while I'm running these systems mods from here, how about you give the surveying and digging apparatus a quick run-through again?"

"On it," Rika replied, flipping a series of switches in the console.

Most systems were touchscreen operated, but Charlie had thought it wise to equip the mech with manually activated switches as well, just in case. Everyone had such confidence in the rapidly growing power of computers these days, but he still possessed a healthy bit of skepticism. A 'what if?' mentality that had served him well over the years.

The gripping hands of the mech spun and locked out, the wrist joints pivoting and retracting the hands as digging tools slid into place one by one. It was a cool toy his boss had ordered created, but that didn't mean it couldn't also be a functional one.

Drill heads and jackhammer bits cycled through, each powering on, running a test activation, then returning to their home nestled within the mech's arms.

"All good, Charlie," Rika reported, returning the hands to their original configuration. "How's it going down there?"

"Still working on it."

"Maybe you should swap out with me for a while. It might be faster from in here."

"Rika, you know I'm a crap pilot," he said with a little chuckle.

"Hey, I've seen you on the simulators. You're not that bad."

"Simulators are far different from the real thing. It's the wobbling around as it walks that throws me off. Doesn't feel right, ya know?" he said. "Hang on, I think this should do the trick."

Charlie punched a series of commands into the keyboard, adjusting the tolerances in the troublesome relay. The red lights on the screen turned green one by one.

"Okay, that should be it. Give it a go."

The mech took a few lurching steps.

"Yeah, that's much better. Thanks, Charlie."

"You got it. Now let's finish the run-through and grab some lunch. I'm starving."

He was on his third serving of chicken pot pie when Rika gave him the look.

"What? I'm hungry. And I like pot pie."

"You really don't stray from your comfort foods, do you?"

"I like what I like."

She rolled her eyes. "Oh, so adventurous."

"Hey, you can go eat all that weird stuff. Me? I'll stick to the staples."

"In abundance, apparently."

"I said I was hungry. It was a busy morning."

"Yeah, but you're eating like a powerlifter, Charlie, and all you did today was push buttons and run diagnostics."

"The brain burns calories too," he replied. "And besides, I'm in pretty good shape."

He patted his belly––which was not large by any means––for emphasis. He had always been athletic, and during his stint of military life all those years ago he even had an actual six-pack. Now, however, with a sedentary job, a layer of softness had taken up residence on his frame.

"I'm not saying you're fat, Charlie. Just, you may want to slow it down a little," she said with a chuckle. "Unless you want to join me for a few circuits on the O-Course."

He groaned at the thought. The obstacle course had been a part of his daily life when he first went through his military intake years prior. That was before reality set in and he realized he'd never be a mission tech or ops engineer with the elite squads running emergency missions around the globe.

When he returned to the facility many years later, it had recently been bought by his billionaire employer. The government had been selling off underutilized facilities when they found themselves in need of money, and his boss had picked it up for a song. And so it was that Charlie wound up back at his repurposed old base with the task of overseeing the design, engineering, and construction of Mr. Millbury's new toys. It was a sweet job, and what better place to do so than from the enormous facility, purchased as is, complete with its own obstacle course still intact.

He couldn't help himself when he first arrived, and muscle memory kicked in when he gave the O-Course a nostalgic little run-through upon arriving at the facility he had thought he'd never see again.

The next day his entire body ached everywhere. *That* was unexpected, and he briefly thought about making the O-Course a part of his daily routine once more, but then work got heavy and his plans shifted. He could always start again next week, he'd tell himself. And besides, he worked a desk job. There was no rush.

Or so he thought.

CHAPTER FIVE

The towering mech raced through its paces, relatively nimble for a machine that size, though it would periodically sound the stability parameter warning alarm. Keeping it balanced on two feet was an ongoing challenge despite the automatic gait moderation gyros.

Charlie deftly maneuvered the mech around a series of lower obstacles, narrowly avoiding the *Do Not Step* items at the lower edge of his field of vision as they illuminated on his heads-up display.

"Faster, Charlie. Clock's ticking," Rika said over the pilot's cabin speaker.

"I know, I know," he grumbled, increasing his pace as he neared the most difficult portion of the sequence.

Walking, and even running a bit, were becoming easier, but approaching the water obstacle required not only speed, but also timing, trajectory planning, and agility, should he hope to stick the landing on the other side and not stumble and fall back with a splash as he'd done so many times before.

The mech turned at his command and began moving with increasing speed, its massive feet thundering on the ground as it approached the reflecting pool. Charlie knew the correct angle he had to launch at, as well as the speed, and even which foot to lead with. It was putting all of that together while strapped into the cockpit of a man-shaped machine that was the hard part.

He feathered the controls as he approached the edge at speed.

Come on, Charlie. You can do this, he assured himself.

Ten steps to go.

Six.

Three.

He pulled the controls, applying a little body English from his seat as the mech leapt into the air, willing it to follow the trajectory he had set for it. Amazingly, it seemed that––for once––it was working.

Two enormous feet landed firmly on the other side of the water, the lengthy expanse cleared in a single bound. Warning lights flashed as the machine began teetering, first to the left, then backward toward the water.

Oh no you don't. Not this time.

Charlie pivoted the knees and threw the arms forward at an angle, counteracting the balance irregularity. One by one the red lights dimmed until the mech was standing upright and secure on the far shore. Charlie allowed himself a little victorious grin, then quickly headed off to the final series of maneuvers.

Four minutes later, he powered down and unstrapped from his seat.

"Not bad, Gault. Not bad at all."

"Thanks, Rika," he replied, hopping from the gimbal-mounted simulation chair.

"Finally stuck the water landing."

"That one's been a consistent problem for me."

"I've seen," she said with a grin. "Repeatedly, in fact. You've really improved these last few months."

"Thanks to your help."

"Hey, I only gave advice. You're the one who built the thing."

"I'm just a small part in a big machine that built it. And you need to give yourself more credit. Engineering know-how only goes so far. A pilot's input proved invaluable in resolving those last few maneuverability issues."

Rika took a long sip from her electrolyte bottle. "So?" she asked quizzically.

"No way," Charlie replied before she could finish her thought.

"Oh, come on, Charlie. Aren't you even a little bit curious?"

"Curious enough to crash Mr. Millbury's new space robot? I'll take a hard pass, thank you very much."

"It was only a little tumble last time, and it didn't damage anything. A little paint, and no one even noticed. That thing's built tough as nails," she replied.

"Nope. I'll leave the piloting to you. A simulation is one thing, but sitting in the pilot seat of a multi-billion-dollar machine, then having it topple over, is not something I want to repeat."

It had been one of the very early iterations of the mech that Charlie had his mishap with, and there had been no real damage caused. Hell, the machine was so sturdily built it would take quite a lot more than merely falling over to cause any damage to it. But Charlie had bruised something else in the process, and pride took a lot more to repair than a few nuts and bolts.

"Come on," Rika said, heading for the door. "If you're gonna chicken shit out of giving the actual mech a real whirl, then you owe me a solid hour, mister."

"Ugh, can't we skip it today?" he groaned.

"Nope. You've already dropped eight kilos since we got here. That's an excellent start—"

"With you kicking my ass regularly, it's no surprise."

"Hey, like it or not, you've been stuck on the flight crew, and the captain will not be amused if his engineer passes out or, heaven forbid, has an embolism because of the extra weight he's carrying around."

"I won't die. I promise."

"You say that, and going weightless in space will be fine, but the Gs you'll pull during launch are no cakewalk, and despite our simulations and data from the moon test, we really don't know all of the pressures a jump from Earth to Mars will put on our bodies."

Charlie picked up his bag and followed her out the door. "Fine. Let's get this over with," he grumbled.

She shot him a good-natured smile. "Excellent. I have some agility drills and plyometrics lined up for you today."

"Oh, lucky me," he said with a pained laugh as the mission's second-in-command led him toward another torturous workout.

Since Charlie had been abruptly added to the flight roster, Rika had taken it upon herself to get the lone non-compliant crew member in shape for the voyage. At first it was an effort even getting him through the most simple of workouts, but the soft man hadn't always been that way, and the old muscles were quickly making a return. Now, if only she could help him shed those years of junk food that were hiding them.

Every day they would train, and every day he would gripe and moan about it. But beneath that complaining, Charlie was actually kind of glad to see his old self returning. Not only that, he had made a new friend in the process. One he was glad would have his back when he reluctantly made his trip to the stars.

CHAPTER SIX

"Ground Control to Major Tom," Charlie joked over his comms as he slid into the brand-new memory foam harness seat in the command module. It was so new, it even had *the smell*, he noted.

"What was that?" Rika asked, swiveling to look at him with her piercing gaze.

"Just an old song, is all."

"Why were you singing it over ship's comms? We're about to launch."

"I know. It's just that it has to do with––"

"Good morning, team," Captain Reynard interrupted as he entered the bridge of the new ship with an air of unbridled joy. A new ship. *His* new ship.

"To be continued," Charlie said with a wink.

The captain took a stroll through the gleaming consoles of the heart of the vessel.

"So, how are we looking, Gaspari?" he asked as he slid into his command seat.

"Everything is green across the board, Captain," she replied, crisp and professional. "Supplies are stowed and secured, all systems check clear, and the rest of the crew have taken their stations."

"Excellent. And how are flight controls, Gault?"

"Looking good, Captain," Charlie replied. "There did seem to be a slight fluctuation in the dampeners, but nothing out of parameters."

"So we're good to go, Charlie?"

"Affirmative, sir."

"All right, then. Let's fire her up and give her a run, shall we?"

"Aye, aye, sir," Charlie said, then powered up the engines and began his careful monitoring of the critical flight systems.

He was going into space, and he was not thrilled about it.

The prior week had been one for atmospheric tests, followed by a dry-run just outside the atmosphere. Charlie had been spared those flights, his presence only needed when the mission-critical engineering and flight systems were brought online.

The earlier tests had gone off without a hitch. The ship flew easily in the atmosphere, even gliding with its fixed wings for several hundred miles as it descended during a power loss simulation.

Outside of the atmosphere, she maneuvered just as steadily, easily entering and exiting the planet's exosphere repeatedly with no ill effects. When he reviewed the data from the tests, Charlie knew the time would soon be upon him. The time he would have no choice but to fly in space.

Some would kill for the opportunity, and he supposed he could understand the desire, objectively. Subjectively, however, he found the idea horrifying and unnecessarily dangerous. Like skydiving. Taking risks he could avoid was something Charlie was resolutely opposed to.

With the advances being made with artificial intelligence studies, it looked like humanity might not even *need* to be the ones flying off into the cosmos for much longer. At least, not if the rumor mill was accurate. A functional AI could be up and running within a decade, and if that happened, it would only be a matter of time before they became integral to everyday life.

Dangerous jobs could be handled by machines, ones not afraid of losing life or limb, and exploration could be carried out by far smarter and far less fragile beings than himself. Unfortunately, *that* sort of thing was decades, if not centuries, away. Thus, Charlie found himself sweating in his flight suit as the ship rumbled into the skies.

It took several minutes to reach orbit, but when they finally did, and the rattling and shaking stopped, Charlie actually found the brief moment of weightlessness before the artificial gravity generators kicked in to be surprisingly tranquil and terror-free.

"What're you thinking, Charlie?" Rika asked, catching a glimpse of his expression.

"Um, I was just, uh––"

"Yeah, pretty cool, huh?" she said. "I remember my first time in space. You always remember your first time."

"Well, I––"

He felt his body suddenly become heavy, squishing down deep into his foam seat.

"Hang on," he grunted, fiddling with a few settings on his screen.

The pressure eased up, and gravity settled in to just slightly less than Earth normal.

"Sorry," he said. "It shouldn't have done that."

"Glitch?" the captain asked, one eyebrow high and askew.

"Nothing to worry about, Captain. I must have transposed a digit when setting the gravity prior to launch."

"All right, then," the captain replied. "Gaspari, confirm readiness of all crew, then prepare for phase one of the experiments."

"Aye, aye, Captain."

Within a minute the entire crew had sounded off their status. All were good to go. With that, the next steps could begin.

"This is your captain speaking," Reynard said over ship-wide comms. "We've settled into a low orbit around the Earth following a successful launch and atmospheric exit sequence. We're now going to begin powering up all drive and power systems in preparation for the next propulsion tests. No jump will take place. This is only a localized test. You may all begin your tests." He keyed off the comms and turned to his engineering chief.

"Okay, Charlie, the ball's in your court. Fire up your systems, and let's see what this baby can do."

"Aye, aye, Captain," he replied, setting to work carefully activating each of the sequestered systems. In just under ten minutes all were in the green and fully online. "That should be it, Captain. We are ready to begin."

He most certainly did not want to begin, but at this point there wasn't really a choice anymore.

"Great work, team. I want you all to know just how proud I am of you," Reynard said. "Let's get this show on the road. Gaspari, prepare to transfer full power to all systems. Once we've established that baseline reading, and if there are no fluctuations, we'll begin."

She shifted power dampers, feeding each system the raw energy they craved.

"Done, Captain. All looks normal."

"Great. Then we might as well give her a go. Let's start off with a simple orbital flight. Impulse power only, Charlie."

"Aye, Captain," he said, keying the engines. "Ready, Rika."

"Got it," she replied, steering them into an effortless loop of the globe, the craft easily maneuvering around the planet below.

"How's it looking, Gault?"

"All good, Captain."

"Okay, then. Gaspari, set a course for just past the moon, and open her up."

"Captain? We're only supposed to be doing orbital testing today."

"We're not jumping. Just giving her a proper shake-out. You heard me. Full power, Rika."

"Uh, aye, aye, Captain," Rika said, flashing a slightly concerned look at the engineering chief. "How are power levels?" she asked.

"Looking stable," Charlie replied, his knuckles transitioning to an even whiter shade as he gripped the arms of his seat. "All energy cells are within parameters. You're good to go."

She gave him a little nod and punched a command into her console.

"I know you don't like space flight, but I'm glad you're with us, Charlie."

"Thanks, Rika."

She was a fantastic pilot, and he knew, logically, that they were in good hands. It was just a little trip to the moon and back, that was all. Nevertheless, his stomach was in knots when the countdown hit zero.

Things went horribly wrong moments later, and their next desperate minutes would be filled with panic and chaos. Chaos that would end with their ship plummeting toward a strange, alien world.

"Starboard heat shield seven is gone!" Charlie called out as calmly as he could manage over the din of their ship tearing apart. He was going to carry out his duties like a professional if it was the last thing he'd do.

CHAPTER SEVEN

At least the atmosphere isn't toxic, Charlie thought as he crawled from the crumpled wreckage of their ship.

When he woke, still strapped to the firmly bolted seat in the engineering compartment adjacent the command center, he felt a dry breeze blowing on his face. He found it odd that the ship's air-con systems would be blowing hot and arid. Then his fuzzy head began to clear.

We were going down, he remembered as the fog lifted. *We were going to crash.*

And crash they had. He hadn't been conscious for it, of course, having blacked out from the crushing G-forces, but the ship had most definitely wound up on the surface of the odd planet they'd seen when the vid screens briefly flickered to life before giving up the ghost.

Also giving away their unfortunate circumstance was the long tear in the hull of the ship that was letting light and fresh air into his otherwise sealed engineering center. The light filtering in, he noted, was somewhat orange in color.

Charlie panicked for a moment, scrambling to find an emergency oxygen mask. Then the realization set in. He was breathing, and had been for some time while unconscious. If the air was going to kill him, it would have done it long before now.

He craned his neck and peered out the ragged hole, squinting at the bright light from the twin stars in the sky.

Those are two suns. One red, one yellow. That makes orange, he mused, still in shock as he began unbuckling from his crash harness. *That means it was all real. What we saw before—*

Charlie shook his head, clearing it, then ran a quick self-assessment. "Snap out of it, Charlie," he said to himself, the sound of his voice in the otherwise silent confines of the damaged space bringing him back to reality. "Okay, self-check. Any injuries?"

He moved his arms and legs, took deep breaths, carefully turned his head side to side. Everything seemed in working order. He had been shaken up, but the walls of the small room had created a highly-reinforced, impact-resistant nook. It wasn't designed for that purpose, but if he ever got out of this mess, he was damn sure going to thank the team member who drew up the specs.

Charlie tried the control panel, but power was fluctuating. Somewhere, a great many lines had been severed. As head of flight ops and engineering, it would be incumbent upon him to get them working and see his crew back to space. If that was even a possibility, that is. First things first. Get to the others.

"Anyone out there?" he yelled at the closed door, pounding his fist on the cold metal.

There was no reply.

"Okay, then. We do this the shitty way," he griped as he swung the manual release lever from its nook and began cranking.

The door, while not bent, was reluctant to open. But Charlie had gotten into decent shape, thanks to Rika's insistence. With a bit of work, an opening slowly appeared as the door slid into its frame.

Of course. Damage to the panel covering where it retracts. The door's fine, but the track isn't, he reasoned. *No matter. Just need to get it open enough to squeeze out.*

At long last a gap large enough to accommodate his frame had opened. Charlie sucked in his stomach as far as he could and slid out into the command center.

"Shit," was all he managed in the way of articulate speech when he saw the state of things.

Where his little side compartment was relatively intact, the command center was torn to bits, gaping holes in the hull providing unplanned windows to the outside world where massive rocks had punched through the metal. Judging by the lay of the ship, most, if not all of the lower levels were either destroyed upon landing, or were now trapped beneath the surface of the desert they had plowed into.

"Captain?" he said, searching for the man with a plan for every situation.

His seat was gone, the snapped metal bolts that had held it in place jutting from the crumpled floor like so many broken toothpicks. A drying pool of red had leaked out from beneath the boulder embedded in the rear wall. Charlie knew where the captain had gone, and he would not be coming back.

"Charlie?" a confused voice asked.

"Rika! Where are you?"

"I'm over––I don't know where I am."

Charlie vaulted a mangled section of control console to where her voice had emanated. He saw a foot sticking out from beneath an impossibly jumbled mass of electronics, all torn free and deposited against the bulkhead, G-force the likely culprit.

"Hang on, I'm coming. Are you injured? Can you feel your arms and legs?"

"I-I'm not totally sure, Charlie. I can't see."

"You're stuck under a bunch of––" He didn't want to say wreckage. "Look, just breathe slow and easy. I'll get you out of there, but I need to move slowly so nothing shifts and lands on you. Do you understand?"

"Yeah. I'll just lay here, then," she said with a pained little laugh. "Not like I was going anywhere anyway."

He worked as fast as he safely could, tracing back bent pieces of superstructure to ensure moving them wouldn't cause the whole mess to shift and collapse. After nearly a half hour, he was looking his friend in the eye. She was banged up, but intact.

"Hey," he said.

"Hey."

"So, give me about five more minutes, then you should be able to slide out."

"Don't rush on my account."

He continued his work, untangling wires, moving chunks of metal and composite until at long last, Rika Gaspari was free.

She sat up slowly, shook the dust from her hair, and surveyed the scene.

"We are so fucked," she said with a sigh. "Where's the captain?"

Charlie didn't say anything. He simply pointed.

"Oh," she said, softly.

A hot breeze coursed through the holes in the ship, whipping up little dust swirls within the confined space. It was reddish, Charlie noted. They could almost be on Mars.

Almost.

"We're not in our own solar system anymore, are we?" he said, already knowing the answer.

"You saw the same thing I did," Rika replied, "and you know the science as well, if not better, than I do. That was an Einstein-Rosen bridge. A wormhole. Jesus, we actually got sucked down a wormhole, Charlie."

"I know. And did you see the suns?"

"Yeah. Two of them, one red, one yellow. Binary stars."

"Judging by the orange light in this place, I'd say that's a fair assessment," he confirmed. "I don't know about radiation," he said. "The readings on my exposure band are in the safe range, but I think there may be stuff we've never encountered before. Wavelengths we didn't ever plan on testing for. But I suppose that's the least of our concerns at the moment."

"What about the others?" she said, rising to her feet. "Have you made contact with any of them?"

"No. You're the first, but judging by what I can see of the way the ship came in, I think we lost most of the lower lab spaces on impact."

Rika looked outside and realized he was right. The ship was sitting on its belly, and far too close to the ground for its normal mass.

"We need to assess the damage. See what we can repair. If Cargo Bay One is intact, then the mech might be all right. We could use it to dig us out. Once we––"

"Rika, the ship's a loss. We're stuck here," he said, sinking to the floor.

Rika took a deep breath and let the reality of the situation set in, then straightened her back and set her mind to dealing with their utterly novel circumstances. This was one emergency her training hadn't covered.

"Fine," she said, more to herself than Charlie. "Then our only objective now is survival on this alien world. The sooner we accept that, the better off we'll be."

"But they'll look for us, right?" he asked, holding on to a tiny thread of hope.

"How, Charlie? You know this was a rushed trial. And even if they could get another ship built and launched, we have no idea how we even got here. We weren't even supposed to do anything more than a simple orbital test. And if they did manage to locate us, it would still be months, if not years, before a ship was ready, even at breakneck speed."

"Shit."

"Hey, but at least the air is breathable, so there's that going for us. Food, water, and shelter are the next steps, once we search for other survivors."

"You're right. I don't know what I was thinking," he said glumly.

"You were thinking you wanted to go home," Rika said, fixing him with a reassuring look. "And I do too, but since that's not an option, we're in improvise mode. Now come on. We've got to pull it together and make the best of the situation. Let's get moving and see if anyone else made it. I don't have any idea how long we have until nightfall, or how long the night even is on this planet, and we need to do this in daylight if we can. Power is spotty, and the lights may not hold."

"I'll grab the portables," Charlie said, finally getting his head in the game.

"Good. I'll grab the emergency tool kit and we'll get started."

A few minutes later, the duo began the arduous task of finding survivors, as well as those not so fortunate.

CHAPTER EIGHT

"Watch the wall on the right," Rika called back over her shoulder as they slid into the next compartment. "See that conduit?"

"Yeah," Charlie replied. "Power routing to sub-section twelve."

"Exactly. Best not touch it."

Charlie had been taking note of active and dead systems as they moved through the craft. He helped design and build the ship, and on an alien world in a distant solar system, at least *this* was something he had a modicum of control over.

"That system is powered down, Rika. It's tied to the scan array we climbed over on the way out of the command module. No juice to any of it. Something knocked that whole section of the ship out, including the backups."

She eyed the dangling conduit. "Still, steer clear anyway, just in case."

The pair made their way through the compartment, stepping over the equipment and supplies, all of it torn free and scattered like debris from an over-zealous birthday kid's piñata, smashed to bits during the crash. Fortunately, there were no flight stations in that room.

If there had been, the occupants would have been torn to shreds.

"The hull's caved in up ahead. We should cross to the other side and see about accessing the lower levels," Rika said, shining her powerful flashlight down the pitch-black corridor leading away from the crumpled section of the ship.

Charlie nodded his agreement and followed her lead. Chivalry be damned, Rika was taking charge and settling in to her unexpected promotion as best she could. With the captain dead, the weight of the mission, and the welfare of its crew, was now squarely on her shoulders.

Her light danced along the rippled walls, the force of the impact having caused even the durable metal sheeting to contort, despite the robust core framework of the craft. Stepping through an airlock door stuck two-thirds open, Rika surveyed the storage units still intact and made a beeline for one of them.

She quickly forced the powered-down lock open with a piece of metal.

"What're you doing?" Charlie asked.

"We need to collect supplies as we go. Basics only at this point. Food, hydration packs, medical supplies," she said, stuffing a small first aid kit into a salvaged bag, along with some emergency ration bars that survived the impact. Several had been crushed and torn open, but she swept them into the bag as well.

"Hey, those are open."

"I know. No time to be finicky about food, Charlie. A little dirt won't kill you. At least, I hope it won't. In any case, I think that'll be the least of our worries. Now keep your eyes open and grab anything remotely edible. I'm going to pop up ahead into the next section and see if the access ladder to the next deck is intact. Hopefully the others are just trapped down there, but I think you may have been right about the lowest levels."

Charlie swallowed hard. Those people would have been torn to shreds when the belly of the ship ripped apart during their violent landing.

"Of course. Yeah," he managed. "I'll, uh..."

Rika grabbed him by the shoulders. "Take a deep breath. We'll get through this. I need you to focus now, okay? Food. Water. Med supplies. Keep looking. I'll be back in a few minutes."

She pressed the slowly flashing light next to the heavy door at the far end of the room and waited. The mechanism strained and squealed, but there was still power to the unit, and it finally ground open.

"Door systems are on a different circuit, broken down by level and compartment cluster," Charlie noted. "I may be able to cross-patch and get us some lights."

Rika was glad to see her friend start to break free from the shock that had slowly taken hold as the reality of their situation sank in. He was nowhere near one hundred percent, but the old Charlie––the brilliant engineer––was slowly coming back.

"Great. See what you can do," she said, then stepped through the doorway into the darkness.

Charlie took a deep breath and did his best to drive the creeping fear from his mind. Then he forced his hands to get to work, systematically digging through every single storage space that would hold useful materials. Even the damaged and torn Mylar pouches containing various edible materials went into his bag.

Rika was right. The ship originally had ample supplies, but after the crash, how much of that cache had survived was anyone's guess.

. . .

"Ow! Sonofabitch!"

"You okay in there?" Rika called into the narrow space between the bulkhead and the interior engineering pod.

"Yeah," Charlie said, rubbing his head and checking his fingers for blood. Clean. "I just banged my head again."

"Well, be careful. I don't want to have to go crawling in there to pull you out."

Charlie hadn't so much volunteered to squeeze into the tight confines of the service space as had no choice. He was the ship's engineer, and as brilliant as Rika may have been, this was his area of expertise. She'd fly the ship, and he would keep it running.

The reactor was undamaged, it seemed, but while it was in emergency standby mode, streaming out just a trickle of electricity to keep systems active, the battery backups and many links between systems were physically severed from the areas they were supposed to service.

As a result, they had been stumbling around in the dark for hours, manually forcing open the doors they were able when the power to those units had been cut. Unfortunately, this was time-consuming and tedious, not to mention a massive drain on their energy now that the initial surge of adrenaline had worn off.

The ship had been designed to have sections seal themselves and remain autonomous from the rest of the craft in the event of a depressurization. In such circumstances, the conduits and miles of wires running through the craft would have remained intact, the only issue being that of the lack of pressure.

A crash landing, however, had never even been considered during the spitball sessions when they troubleshot potential emergencies and how to design redundant systems to handle them. For all of their abundant caution, *this* was something they were not prepared for.

Much as he hated the thought, it was actually Charlie's idea that he could try to run a temporary bypass of whichever systems were still powered up to divert precious electricity to select segments of the ship one at a time. It was insanely labor-intensive, with Charlie constantly climbing back and forth through the ship.

First he would power up one section with a lengthy bypass, often involving great lengths of salvaged wire to trickle the charge to the correct circuits if their native boards were fried, then on to the next. It was tedious, but he managed.

Over and over, he managed.

Despite his efforts, the main lights were still out in much of the ship, and most of the emergency lighting systems had also overloaded during their tumble through the wormhole and subsequent impact with the alien world. Charlie had managed to find a few workarounds, though, restoring a fraction of the lights in several previously black compartments.

Lighting was good. What it revealed, however, was not.

"That's Keisha," Rika said, identifying their crewmate from the engagement ring on the hand that hadn't been crushed by equipment wrenched free in the crash.

"We should——"

"We'll come back for her," Rika said, moving on to the next compartment. "There's nothing to do for her, but there may be others we can still help."

She was right, of course.

"Hang on. If I can get the crew's onboard locators working, we can at least know where to look," Charlie said, hurrying back to a previously scavenged compartment. "Wireless comms are totally shot. That system was in the lower section of the ship. But the real-time locator will at least tell us where everyone is on board."

"Just no way to talk to them and no way to know if they're alive."

"Nope. That part we'll have to do the old-fashioned way," he said. "But at least we'll have a roadmap where to look. Otherwise, with all these systems down and power so spotty—not to mention all of the unstable sections that might just collapse on us—it could take us days to find them."

Rika thought on it a moment, then gave a quick nod. "You're right. Efficiency over raw speed. Let's implement that plan immediately."

"You're the captain," he replied, and began the backtrack to the nearest terminal.

He hadn't been the one to design that particular system, so he only hoped his idea would work in practice as well as in theory. Fifteen minutes later, they were on the hunt, map of locator signals in hand. They'd find something. The only question remaining was what.

CHAPTER NINE

Several dead bodies and a pair of rather banged-up survivors dragged to the surface later, Rika and Charlie were finding themselves facing growing frustration as they delved further into the ruined interior.

Rika attempted to thread a portable camera on a length of pipe into the dark and distant chambers, but it simply wouldn't reach.

"We need a better plan," she noted. "We can't just go cutting through stuff to get into an area that may or may not contain survivors. We'll diminish the structural stability of this thing, and it's already beat to hell and shaky as it is."

"Agreed. If we start cutting, there's a very real possibility we may unintentionally destabilize something that is actually holding other somethings in place."

"You have quite a way with words, Charlie," Rika said with a grim little chuckle. "But the point is well taken."

She took a small comms unit from her pocket and keyed it on.

"Anyone read me? Anyone at all?"

Silence.

"I told you, Rika, the comms system was routed through the belly of the ship, and that got crushed, then dragged and scattered in a bazillion pieces. On their own, our comms units aren't even as useful as the EVA suit walkie talkies. At least those operate on their own frequency with stand-alone transmitters and receivers."

"Which doesn't help us, since no one on board would have any reason to carry one of those things around with them."

"Obviously," he replied.

"I wonder if I might be able to reach the mech. If I can get it fired up, I could use its mining attachments to pull free the sections we can't get clear access to from the inside."

"But it'll take forever to even reach the thing. You saw the damage," Charlie pointed out.

An idea flashed through his mind. *That's kinda crazy, but what if—?*

"Charlie, you okay? You got really quiet on me all of a sudden."

He turned and met her with an excited gaze.

"The mech. I think I have an idea that might just make this search-and-rescue operation a whole lot easier. But it's going to require us passing through the mid-level starboard labs."

Rika blanched slightly. They had already assessed that area. The three crew members assigned that station had been securely strapped in upon impact. That didn't prevent the lone oxygen cylinder whose anchors had torn free during the crash from pinballing around the room. The devastation was quite horrific.

"Is there another way?" she asked.

"Not if we want to get this done in time. The parts I need are easiest accessed through that pod. Believe me, if there were another way—"

"Forget it. Let's just get this over with," Rika said, putting on her captain's face and steeling her nerves. "This is going to suck."

About that, she was certainly right.

They had managed to avoid most of the blood and bits of their friends splattered across the room, with the exception of the red smear on Charlie's pant leg from where he bumped into a sticky-slick table.

"Oh, God," he said as he desperately tried to rub the blood from his clothes with a clean piece of absorbent lab material salvaged from a bin.

"Forget about it, Charlie. We haven't got the time. You can deal with that later."

"Yes, of course. You're right," he said, shaken. "Come on, we're almost there."

Avoiding any further encounters with the remains of his crewmates, Charlie managed to lead them into the research lab's storage bay. There were no flight chairs in that pod, so no crew had been present during the crash. Ironically, the room full of dangerous equipment and tools had come through largely undamaged, its contents remaining firmly stowed.

Had anyone been in that area, they would likely have fared better than the rest of the crew.

"Here it is," Charlie said, pulling a small, wheeled rover from its storage bin.

Rika was nonplussed.

"Uh, that's not exactly my mech, Charlie."

He looked at the small survey rover in his hands.

"What? No, of course not."

"You said my mech. You said you had an idea."

"I do. Just not using your mech. It was the inspiration, is all."

Rika sat on the metal floor, exhausted and annoyed. "Seriously, Charlie? We just walked through *that*," she said, gesturing to the other room, "and all you have is this little remote-controlled dune buggy toy?"

He stared at her silently while her own words hung in the air.

"What?"

"Say it again."

"The part about your remote-controlled toy?"

"Uh-huh."

She felt her ire rising, then it hit her. "Holy shit. Remote control. Damn, now that *is* clever."

A broad smile lit up his face.

"How long for you to get something operational?" she asked.

"I think I should be able to tweak a few of the control units from the rover and get them jury-rigged into something that should do the trick in an hour, maybe."

"Will it be able to navigate around the debris?"

"That's the plan."

"What about the tighter spots?"

"Taken into account. I'll have to be a little creative, but using a few existing devices, I think I can get us something that will be able to access pretty much everywhere there's a signal."

"Then you'd better get to it. People could be hurt. Trapped," she said. "What can I do to help?"

"Start loading the crew locator signal readouts into your handheld. I'm going to install a proximity upload unit so it can read the device directly without our needing to input everything by hand."

"On it."

The two of them worked in near silence for the better part of an hour as Charlie's hands moved in a blur of activity. He was building something. Engineering. Problem-solving. This was where he excelled, and it seemed as if his state of shock and accompanying malaise were a thing of the past.

The small rover on its own could access most places by

means of its regular drive systems, but there would be obstacles, as Rika had noted. But Charlie had a plan. An audacious one, but one that should do the trick.

A half dozen small mechanized soil sampling units lay in pieces as he fabricated a makeshift mounting system for the armature to ride on the rover's back. Wires were jutting out all over the place, but ever the engineer, Charlie soon had them all tied off and tidy, not leaving much of anything to snag on random debris.

The six mechanized scooping and sampling arms cannibalized from other machinery were soon mounted atop the small, wheeled device, their arms tucked tightly into the sides until they would need to be deployed. Charlie powered it on and held his breath.

A series of beeps sounded out, then the readout on the remote in his hand flashed to life.

"We've got it!" he shouted.

With a feathering of the joystick, he maneuvered the breadbox-sized unit forward in a slow roll.

"Good so far, Charlie. What about the arms?"

"Should be good to go," he replied, keying in an activation sequence on the remote.

The six arms extended out slowly, their digging and sampling tips all slowly pressing down on the ground until the rover raised up in the air. It was two limbs short of arachnid, but Charlie's improvised search-and-rescue drone was up and walking––albeit slowly––successfully.

He steered it toward a storage container he had been digging through for supplies and managed to successfully maneuver it into a climb, mounting, crossing, and descending from the box relatively smoothly.

"How's the readout?" Rika asked.

"Looking good," he replied. "All of the crew location signals are showing on the remote, and I've overlaid each level's floor plan into your handheld as well," he said, showing her the display on the remote, which now showed not only a series of blinking dots, but a framework map of the ship's compartments.

"Nice work," she said. "You've just saved us hours and hours of time."

"That was the plan," he noted.

"Yeah, it was. Now let's get a move on and put that thing to work. We've got a crew to find."

They were both energized by the turn of events, and once they had crossed through the carnage wasteland of the adjacent pod, they began their rescue operation in earnest, hoping for the best, but preparing themselves for the worst.

CHAPTER TEN

Seven people.

Of a crew of two dozen, seven had survived the crash, and of those, only two were unscathed.

With his wits returning following the utter shock of the initial horror, Charlie's medic training from his early days before he decided to pursue an engineering and sciences path finally kicked in.

His skills, while out of practice, nevertheless proved quite helpful, and with the ample supplies from the salvaged first aid kits, he had managed to patch up the least serious of the little band of survivors' injuries as best he could.

Jamal had been pinned under a support beam when they found him. He was playing it tough, but Charlie knew the man had internal injuries. For all that muscle and power, without proper medical care, their head of security and disaster response wouldn't last the week.

Others had suffered broken limbs, which he set and splinted, as well as a variety of lacerations he sealed with medical adhesive when he could, and somewhat ugly sutures when he couldn't. By the time he had patched up their hurt, he was exhausted, emotionally as well as physically.

Still, he wished he had more patients to treat. Hurt was better than the alternative the others had suffered.

The lowermost lab spaces had, as they had feared, been utterly obliterated in an instant, they verified. Judging by the angle of impact, the belly had been destroyed immediately.

He hated to think what had happened to those people's bodies. The ones they hadn't found in the wreckage.

At least they didn't suffer, Charlie comforted himself. *The others weren't so lucky.*

"Charlie?"

It was Winnie Yang. The bandage wrapped around her head bore a small blossom of red, and her arm was wrapped in a makeshift splint, but her injuries had been relatively minor, all things considered. Compared to the rest of her teammates, she was in great shape. Compared to them, she was alive.

She had been up a few levels in her quarters rather than down below in the research lab when the crash occurred. She was always a little chilly, and running to get her lucky scarf had saved her life.

Perhaps it really was a good luck charm, Charlie mused.

Trapped on an alien world, time would tell if the survivors were actually the fortunate ones.

"Yeah, what's up, Winnie? Are you okay?" he replied.

"I-I think so, Charlie," she said, unable to take her eyes off of the row of bodies covered by tarps and whatever else they could find to keep them out of the elements until they could provide a proper burial. "I was thinking about the rats. Their containers were reinforced plastic, and boxes that size can withstand a lot of force without breaking. Do you think they might have survived?"

Charlie shared a quick look with Rika. Winnie was in shock and on the verge.

"Hey, you know what? They might have," he replied, cautiously. "The labs were torn open, but if they fell out, sure, I suppose they could have survived."

"We should look for them, then."

"Uh, we simply don't have the resources to do that, Winnie. People are hurt, and there's limited food and water to burn through searching for them."

"But they'd be useful to test local plant life to see if it's edible or not."

"Oh, you want them for experiments," he said, humoring her.

"What? Did you think I was getting sentimental about my rodents? They're tools, Charlie, and we could use every tool we can salvage."

"Still, finding those tiny boxes in that trail of debris, well, it's going to have to be a lower priority."

"But don't you see the value they could provide?"

"Sure I do," he said, seeing where this was going. "I'll tell you what. Tomorrow, I'll head down the debris path from our crash and see what I can find, okay?"

"Thanks, Charlie."

"You got it. Now try and get some rest."

Charlie would be true to his word and keep his eyes open for her little friends, but higher on the list of priorities was seeing if there were any traces of the thing she wanted to use them to test in the first place. Food and water.

They had crashed in a barren desert area, the red rocks and dry dirt finding their way into every nook and cranny. Charlie just hoped there wasn't any irritant in the soil.

He and Rika set to work, forcing their weary bodies into action once more, gathering up shelter materials, creating a windbreak at the entrance to the section of the crippled ship they had determined to be safe enough to serve as housing for the night. They had no idea exactly how cold it would get that night in the desert-like environment, but they took no chances, arranging their salvaged sleeping bags and other warmth-saving layers close by should they need them.

Charlie gathered whatever crude kindling they had and set to stacking them to form a basic blaze to help warm the group.

"No fire," Jamal said, fighting to keep the pain from showing on his face. "We don't know what's out there."

"You actually think there's aliens?" Charlie asked.

"I have no idea, Charlie. What I do know is it is always better to assume the worst, even when you're hoping for the best. Keeps you from unpleasant surprises."

"And disappointment," Rika added.

"That sounds more like dating advice than a survival tip," Jamal said with a pained grin.

"Aren't they one and the same?" she replied.

"Ow. Don't make me laugh."

"Sorry, Jamal."

"It's all good," he said, forcing the grimace from his face.

Charlie looked at the huddled survivors. The corpses wouldn't be suffering from the cold, but the rest of their motley group very well might.

"Okay, then, no fire. We started to gather up whatever rations and water were readily accessible. But there wasn't much. Saving crew was the priority."

"Appreciated."

"I'll grab what we have and hand them out. We'll eat while there's still light, then I'll make a trip into the powered sections to find what more we can salvage."

He handed each of the survivors a little something to eat from their sparse supplies, then hurried off, ready to once again search through the wreckage.

"Let me help," Rika offered.

"Thanks. I'm glad at least one body besides mine is intact."

"You really know how to flatter a girl, Charlie."

"I didn't mean it like that."

"I know, I'm just fuckin' with ya. It's been a long day, you know."

"Tell me about it."

Quietly, the two dug through the wreckage of the once-great ship for whatever additional food they could salvage. Laden with their meager booty, they soon returned to the others.

The suns were getting lower in the blue sky, the light spectrum shifting to a more normal, Earth-like shade as the red star dipped beneath the horizon, leaving them awash in the yellow light of the remaining sun. The survivors ate in silence until that sun, too, slid lower and lower, leaving them in darkness.

The wounded huddled together, sharing warmth. Charlie felt an arm wrap across his chest as the welcome heat of Rika played big spoon to his little one. He was unconscious in minutes.

The survivors all slept soundly that night, despite their situation. The stress and exhaustion of the ordeal had drained them completely. The next day, however, there would be little time for rest. It would be the beginning of the next stage of their scenario.

The one where they figured out how to survive.

CHAPTER ELEVEN

There had been no sign of vegetation of any sort as far as the eye could see, which was discouraging, to say the least. But as Charlie began the slow walk backtracking the debris trail strewn along the rut the ship had carved into the desert soil, he noticed one interesting detail.

The soil at the bottom of the trench was damp.

Damp means liquid water, he noted with a pleased grin. It looked like they might not die so quickly after all.

As for other resources, however, they might not be so fortunate. There was no sign of plant or animal life whatsoever, and the barren landscape stretched as far as the eye could see. There were occasional formations of rocks, long ago forced into unusual angles by the geological shifts far beneath the planet's crust, though some seemed almost unnaturally positioned, as if an even greater force had abruptly thrown them into place.

Those might provide decent shelter, Charlie hoped as he strayed from his path to examine the nearest pile.

Upon closer inspection, the rocks seemed almost as if they'd once been part of a building, though in that desert wasteland, that was simply impossible. Nevertheless, the lines of their bulk were clean more often than not, a few pieces even fitting together where cracks looked very much like seams.

Whatever their origin, some shady respite could be provided by their mass if need be, though the wrecked ship was serving that purpose well enough for the time being.

"Okay, chalk up one more potential resource, should we need it," he noted, then trudged back to the deep rut carved by their ship.

Much of the debris was either shredded, shattered, or ground to useless bits, the sheer mass of the craft effectively pulverizing all that was unfortunate enough to be beneath it as it slid to a stop. Some debris, however, had been thrown free, and Charlie was thrilled to find several snack bars someone had tucked away in their workspace, along with vacuum-sealed pouches of lab gear.

It wasn't high-tech equipment, but the plastic sheeting used to cordon off experiment areas was even more valuable than other equipment with what he had in mind.

"Now I just need some containers," he muttered, digging through a fairly dense cluster of debris. "That and some IV tubing from a med kit should work," he said, pulling up a piece of hull covering what seemed to be a sizable pile of wreckage.

"Fuck!" he shouted, falling back on his ass as he scrambled backward. His stomach heaved, but having nothing to discharge but a lone and long-digested nutrient bar, he vomited no more than a thin stream of bile.

A leg was in that pile. A leg, and nothing more. The rest of the body was nowhere to be seen.

Wiping his mouth with the back of his hand, Charlie pulled himself together and slowly climbed back to his feet, his eyes locked on the bright white bone where the leg had been torn free, mid-femur. It was a smaller limb. Possibly Kim, or maybe Inez.

"Don't think about that. This is survival 101. Just scavenge and keep moving," he told himself, the sound of his own voice mildly comforting in the silence of the barren landscape. "Don't let *anything* keep you from the three basics. Food. Water. Shelter."

It was easy enough to tell himself that, but he feared his dreams would now be prominently featuring the detached limbs of his former friends.

Charlie dug through the remaining debris in the area, careful to be sure there were no other body parts waiting to surprise him. Luck was on his side, and by the time he turned to head back to the others, no other limbs had presented themselves.

He walked past the leg, arms full of plastic sheeting, tubing, and a few dented drawers salvaged from a ruined shelving unit, but turned and looked back at the remains and paused.

I can't just leave it like that. Charlie dropped his haul to the ground and doubled back.

Pulling free a nearby fluttering scrap of insulation and using it to gather up the leg, he then dug a small trench in the red soil, in which he placed the remains. Charlie quickly covered them with a small mound.

He didn't bother making a marker. The whole debris-scattered area was a graveyard, of sorts.

"I wish I knew who you were so I could say something about you. Some last words, or rites, or whatever. Hell, I don't even know if you were religious." He shuddered, talking to a dead woman. "Anyway, I hope your end was a quick one and you felt no pain." He stared at the small mound of damp, disturbed soil a long while. "Okay, then. That's it, I guess. Rest in peace."

Charlie bent and gathered the collected materials up in his arms once more and began trekking back toward the others. He really hadn't walked very far, since he had set off just after dawn, when the red sun had peeked over the horizon, but the yellow one had now joined its twin, their combined rays rapidly heating the air.

"Did you have any luck finding my rats?" Winnie asked as Charlie trudged back into their makeshift camp.

"No. Sorry."

"It's okay. After this long, they probably died of exposure anyway."

"I really am sorry, Winnie."

"It happens."

"How about finding any food or water?" Rika asked.

"A few nutrient bars is all. I'll look for more next time I'm out."

"I meant indigenous resources. Was there anything we might be able to use?"

"Not really. There's no sign of vegetation or animal life anywhere. But I did find this," he said, dumping his haul on the ground.

"Plastic sheeting, some tubes, a few busted drawers? Charlie, what are we supposed to do with all this junk? We need food. And even more importantly, we need water."

"I know. That's where this all comes in handy." He opened a roll of clear plastic and laid it out beside a length of tubing and a metal drawer. "There's moisture not too far down in the soil. I saw it in the bottom of the trench the ship carved when it crashed."

"That doesn't help us. We can't suck water from dirt."

"No, but with these two suns, I bet we'll have some success with a solar still."

"A what?"

"A solar still," Charlie repeated. "Something my grandpa taught me when he took me camping as a kid. He said if I was ever stranded somewhere, I should know how to make water out of nothing. I thought he was wasting my time back then. I mean, everyone knew you just filled your bottles before you went camping. But he was old-school. Loved that living-off-the-land thing."

"You haven't answered how this junk will get us water."

"Simple, really. You know how there's condensation on your windows early in the morning?"

"Yeah."

"Well, it's like that, only instead of a window, we're using this plastic sheeting."

"But that's a negligible amount of water."

"From a window, yes. But we're going to dig a series of holes deep enough to reach the damp soil. That's our water source. Then we place one of these drawers in the bottom to act as a catch basin. We run the tube from the bottom of the drawer out of the hole––that's our straw, letting us get to the water without disassembling the still––and then we stretch out the plastic over the hole and seal the edges with dirt and rocks."

"Hang on. So we use the evaporation of the moisture in the soil as a water source?"

"Yeah. The plastic will catch the condensation as the suns rise and heat up the ground. It's like evaporative distillation. All we need to do is put a small rock in the middle of the plastic to make it drip downhill."

"Right into the catch basin," she finished for him.

"Exactly."

Rika smiled approvingly. "Not bad."

"One more thing," Charlie said.

"What?"

"We need to have everyone save their urine."

"I am *not* drinking piss, Charlie."

"Not to drink. To recapture the water by evaporation. It's like the waste reprocessing systems on the ship, only a far cruder version. Nevertheless, we can reclaim the water many times over if we're diligent about it."

"But that's not only gross, it's also not going to last."

"I know. This is little more than a Band-Aid, when we need a whole lot more. But at least it should buy us some time."

Rika mulled over his plan, then looked at the injured crew lying out in the warm air.

"It's a good idea, Charlie. But I think for now, we need to get everyone out of the sun and conserve energy and water."

"Agreed. Once the first sun sets, the temperature will drop, and we'll be able to dig a bunch of solar still holes. Then tomorrow, before first light, we'll head out to do a more thorough salvage to see what we can find. If we're lucky, we'll have some more food, and maybe even meds before the second sun gets too high and heats things up."

Rika gave him an appreciative smile as they helped the others into the shade.

"You know something, Charlie? For a guy who had absolutely no desire to come on this mission, you're proving to be something of a godsend. Our very own Robinson Crusoe."

Charlie just smiled and continued sorting through the salvaged supplies. A small pang of guilt twisted in his gut at her comment, though, just for a moment. It was silly, after all. Anyone would feel the same in his shoes. But still, with the thoughts flashing through his mind, he couldn't help feeling a little like a traitor.

Even knowing what the crew was faced with, if given a choice, he wondered if he'd just as soon leave them all behind if he could be back home on Earth.

CHAPTER TWELVE

"What about that one?" Rika asked.

Charlie came to a halt, the jury-rigged sled they had formed out of a piece of the ship's hull, a few lengths of wire, and padding from one of the flight chairs, settling into the disturbed soil of the crash trench.

He looked where she was pointing. The corner of a storage locker was poking out of the loose soil. Another night with winds like they'd experienced the prior day and it might have been totally hidden from sight.

"Good eyes, Rika. That looks relatively intact, from what I can see," he said, rushing to start digging it out.

"Hey, slow down."

"But there might be useful stuff in here."

"I know, but we should talk about what else might be buried around here."

"You don't mean––"

"Bodies, Charlie. I'm talking about our friends."

"Oh," he said, his digging hands slowing their pace. "Right."

"Yeah," she said, softly. "Look, we may not find any, but you just need to be aware of what may be under there. Under anywhere, for that matter."

"Trust me, I know. I mean, I didn't say anything, but I already found a leg yesterday."

"A leg? Whose?" she asked.

"I couldn't tell. It was severed mid-femur. A woman, from the look of it."

"Inez, maybe?"

"I don't know. The point is, I've already stumbled upon bits, so I can handle it. But what about you?"

"Charlie, I'm a seasoned pilot, and second-in-command on this mission. I've seen a lot of things, and just because I have a double-x chromosome, it doesn't mean I'm going to puke at the sight of any more death."

He hadn't mentioned his reaction the previous day, and he had no intention of doing so now.

"Okay. Right. Let's get back to it, then," he said, then began digging with renewed vigor, though wary of what unpleasantness he might uncover.

"What did you do with it?" she asked as she saw the storage locker's form become more visible with every scoop of his hands. "The leg, I mean."

"I buried it."

Rika nodded once in grim approval, but didn't say anything further for several minutes, until the locker doors were finally dug out and exposed. She tried the handle and found it unwilling to open.

"Come on!" she yelled, yanking the doors hard, but the keypad remained dark, and the locker's contents remained untouchable. "Dammit!" she blurted in frustration, punching down, the door ringing with a hollow clang.

"Hang on, you'll just break your hand doing that."

"I know. I'm getting really pissed off, is all."

Charlie thought a moment. "You know, I've got something

that just might do the trick," he said, digging in the small pack of tools he'd salvaged. After a little searching through the unorganized mess, he pulled out a small bypass device with alligator clips and a voltmeter.

"There's no power, Charlie. You can't run a bypass without power."

"You mean there's no power *yet*," he replied with a knowing grin.

He turned and began rummaging through the equipment and supplies they had loaded onto the sled he'd been pulling until he found what he was looking for.

"You can't use a spectrometer to open a lock."

"It's actually a *hybrid mass* spectrometer. And no, you can't. But this beauty runs on its own rechargeable power cell," he said as he unfastened the housing. "And if I were to tap into that power cell and feed a line into the access panel on the locker—"

"You'd be able to power up a bypass sequence."

"More or less. I'd have used the mediscanner, but we didn't find its recharging cradle to go with it, so I don't know exactly how many uses we'll get out of it. Gotta save 'em and make them count."

Rika set to work opening the protective panel on the locker's face, tucking a length of metal beneath the narrow opening and prying hard when her makeshift ratchet stripped a bolt.

"Careful. I wouldn't want to have to patch you up, too."

"Then you'd be the only beast of burden around here," she joked.

"Well, to be fair, I am kind of hoping the others will heal up enough to lend a hand. Their injuries are bad, but not life-threatening."

"Except Jamal," she said.

"Yeah," he sighed. "Except Jamal."

Putting all of her weight onto the length of metal, Rika bounced on its end one last time, using every inch of leverage to force the metal apart. The panel groaned and squealed, like an angry animal having its meal stolen from it, until finally, with a sudden pop, the lone, reticent bolt snapped free. She tumbled to the ground, landing square on her ass with a dusty *whump.*

"You okay?"

"Yeah, I'm fine, just had to try. One more reason to thank Grandma for these genes. A nice bit of cushioning," she said with a wry grin as she dusted herself off.

Charlie's expert fingers found their way inside the workings of the mechanism, his small alligator clips locking into place on the appropriate terminals. He then ran a separate lead to the exposed power cell of the spectrometer.

"Okay, here goes nothing."

He flipped the relay switch, sending a charge to the locking mechanism. The display panel flickered, then streamed a series of numbers. Moments later, the latch could be heard sliding free with a faint click.

"Now, let's hope this wasn't a toilet paper locker," he said as he gripped the handle.

"It wouldn't be in a locked one. Unless it's TP made of gold or something."

"Yes, Rika, I know. That was a joke."

He noted the amused crinkling at the corners of her eyes.

"Oh, ha-ha. I'll remember that if there actually *is* gold TP in here." He yanked hard. After a moment, the grit-filled hinges finally gave way, allowing the door to swing open.

"Holy shit," Rika gasped.

"You said it."

"Uh, what should we do with that?" she asked, looking at the rifle, machine guns, and pair of pistols nestled firmly in their storage racks.

"We take them with us," he said, gathering up the boxes of ammunition and adding them to his sled along with the weapons. "I hope to hell we won't need them, but better to have them and not need them than to need them and not have them, right?"

Rika dug farther into the locker's contents, pulling out an extendable baton, a can of what appeared to be pepper spray, and a few dozen pairs of zip-tie handcuffs. "Jamal came prepared, I'll give him that."

"But for what? I mean, the odds of finding little green men on a simple test flight to the moon were pretty much zero."

"I know. But like you said, better to have them and not need them, right?"

"A man after my own heart," he replied. "But this isn't going to help us with our immediate problems. The solar stills should be producing enough for bare-minimum survival hydration, but we need more than that. Anything else useful in there?"

"Actually, this might be," she said, holding up a tub of post-workout protein powder.

"Excellent. All we need is a whole ton of water to mix it in."

"Still, better than nothing, right? At the very least, people can eat a spoonful here and there for nutrition."

"And with only a sip of water to wash it down," he said with a shudder. "But you're right. It's better than nothing."

Charlie rose to his feet and scanned the vast expanse surrounding them. The twin suns had risen quite high in the sky, and while the rays didn't seem to be enough to cause serious damage, the two of them were beginning to get a decent sunburn.

"Come on, let's head back."

"I think we should keep going. We need supplies, Charlie."

"Yeah, but the sun is getting intense."

"Hey, I'm in command now, so I say we keep going."

"Rika, this isn't the time to be stubborn. If we use up all our energy now, we'll be of no use to anyone."

She thought about his point a moment. "I agree, to an extent, at least. So, we keep going for another half hour. *Then* we turn back."

"Thank you, oh fearless leader."

"I'm more of a benevolent dictator," she said with a chuckle. "Now come on, let's get a move-on."

They made fair time, but with the discovery they came upon after only fifteen minutes, she found herself wishing she'd heeded his advice.

"We should bury them," Charlie said, staring at the broken bodies of their friends, lying motionless in the red soil where they'd landed. "We can do it on our own. The others don't need to know about this. We can just say we never found them."

"Yeah," Rika agreed, swallowing hard. "I-I'll cover them up until we've made a grave."

Charlie began digging, while she threw a tarp over the broken bodies of their crewmates. Two of them, to be exact, though with the jumble of limbs, they almost wondered if a third might be in there somewhere.

They'd been thrown clear of the crash. If the impact itself had not killed them, the rapid deceleration as they hit the ground certainly had.

Their shoes even came off, Charlie found himself noting, morbidly. *That's how you know it's a bad accident.*

They worked in silence, piling up the red soil until a shallow grave lay empty.

"I'll do it," Charlie said, sliding the twisted bodies into a hole.

They then piled the dirt until a little mound was the only sign of anything amiss in the wasteland.

"I should say something," Rika muttered. "But I don't know what to..." She trailed off.

"It's okay," Charlie comforted. "I'll do it."

He proceeded to give the eulogy he'd had building in his head since he buried an unidentified leg the day prior. This time he had names to put with the remains, their uniforms making the identities clear enough. He kept it brief, then, without further ceremony, turned the sled around and began heading back.

"Let's walk topside out of the trench on the way back. I think we've pretty much picked over everything down here, don't you think?"

"Whatever," Rika replied. "Let's just get out of here."

The pair trudged along the torn ground of the crashed ship's final landing, scavenging bits and pieces from time to time, but, fortunately, not encountering any further bodies.

They both knew they'd have many more to bury once they returned to the others. The living needed it, and the dead deserved it.

Sunburned, exhausted, and covered in red soil, Rika and Charlie set down their loads and sipped from the solar stills as soon as they reached their camp. The makeshift devices had worked, and even in the heat, a mouthful of hot water had never tasted better.

Despite their aching bodies, they then set back to work, digging holes away from the camp and moving remains. By nightfall, all of the dead were buried.

Charlie finally lay his weary body down to rest a bit, while Rika decided to make a quick run into the belly of their ship. Looking at the mounds of freshly dug soil, he couldn't help but wonder how long it would be until the rest of them joined their fallen shipmates.

CHAPTER THIRTEEN

It was hard work, moving through the interior of the wrecked ship nearest the top cargo bay, but the interior lights were mostly functional, thanks to Charlie's clever rerouting. Even so, Rika carried a portable light as well as a backup. She had no desire to be stuck in the belly of the beast in the dark. Especially if the hull shifted and she had to make a quick escape.

Hazards abounded as she plodded along, and much of her time was spent crawling through narrow spaces while avoiding jagged bits of metal and other debris that could cause all manner of unpleasantness if she wasn't careful.

It was dangerous, but she pushed on, slowly squeezing past toppled equipment blocking the starboard corridors as she edged her way even farther inside.

While some of the passageways in the section were intact and passable, far more were either entirely collapsed, or dangerously near. That meant Rika had to be particularly careful as she maneuvered her way through the tangled mess. Even with Charlie's remote-controlled rover, it had been a bit of a chore scoping out a suitable––and safe––route.

The lower levels had been much easier to access during the

rescue attempt, and, as that had been where the bulk of the crew was located when the event occurred, that was where they had aimed all of their search-and-rescue efforts.

Now that the survivors were accounted for, the ship's second-in-command was trying to access something other than crew and supplies. Something that could prove quite valuable, if it was indeed still functional.

The giant mech was pretty damn solid, designed to operate in both the vacuum of space as well as the hostile environmental conditions of Mars. In its travel configuration, its systems were even more robustly protected. She just hoped the electromagnetic clamps holding it in place hadn't failed during the crash.

Rika jammed her small pry-bar into the airlock door separating sections of the corridor and pulled hard. The buckled hull had thrown off the alignment all throughout the ship, and there were several seemingly intact doors that she felt likely wouldn't open without blasting charges or a plasma cutter. This one, however, had some give to it.

"That's more like it," she grunted as the door began to slowly creak open, reluctantly giving up its treasures to the determined woman.

"Oh, fuck," she said as she squeezed inside.

The mech was intact, as she had hoped, and the mag clamps had indeed held it in place during the crash. It was the rest of the equipment that had not fared so well.

The power cell storage racks had ripped from the walls. Their bolts appeared to have snapped free, sent flying like the hastily discarded buttons popped from the male stripper's shirt she'd seen in that show in Vegas years ago.

The units had been thrown all over the place and had battered the compartment, destroying the recharge dock and trickle lines keeping the mech on standby for the flight.

The main power cells themselves had been removed from

the machine for the voyage. It had been deemed safer to store them separately, re-installing them upon arrival. Unfortunately, their steel housings were all bent to hell. There was no chance of them fitting into their cradles in the mech's massive body. Even with a healthy amount of elbow grease, there was no chance they'd be able to bend them back to straight.

Rika checked over the metal casings carefully.

"At least there are no ruptures." She sighed with relief. A broken cell would mean contamination of the area, and she still wanted to have a better look at her baby.

She climbed up the side of the mech, popping open the pilot's access hatch and sliding down the ladder into the belly of the machine. Everything was intact, and the internal backups had kept all systems in low-power standby mode.

"Do you have anything left for me?" she wondered aloud, flipping a series of switches on the pilot's console.

The mech silently powered to life, its displays illuminating with diagnostic readouts and status updates. The bipedal craft was in perfect condition, it seemed. Perfect but for one little problem. It lacked even the power to shift from its storage and travel configuration to its proper form.

There was just enough juice to power the internal computers, but nothing to make the thing move.

Rika reluctantly powered down, sitting quietly in her pilot's seat a long moment before climbing back out of the machine and sealing it up again. It had been a good idea. If she had been able to get the power cells loaded and fire it up, the mech would have made the search for resources so much easier. And finding water? Hell, digging was one of the things it was designed for.

But that was not to be the case. They were stuck searching on foot and digging by hand, it seemed, and that was going to suck.

"Sorry, big guy. I was hoping to take you for a spin," she said, then left the silent machine in its final resting place. The mag clamps would eventually lose power, like the rest of the ship, as its damaged systems continued to short out. But even freed of the restraints, the massive mech would not be going anywhere.

Rika cleared her head and set back to work. There were some other supplies in the cargo bay, however, and she made quick time in gathering what could be of use to the survivors. She then slung the laden sack over her shoulder and crawled out through the half-open doors and headed back to the surface.

"Any luck?" Charlie asked as his exhausted friend climbed out of their wrecked ship.

"I found some supplies," she replied, dropping the duffle onto the ground with a dusty thud. "But the mech's power cells were damaged. It's not going anywhere."

"Damaged? How bad?" Charlie asked, sitting up.

"Don't worry, they're intact and not leaking. Just all bent up. There's no way to get them loaded in, so I'm afraid we have a perfectly-intact mech but still no way to use it."

"Just our luck," he grumbled.

"Tell me about it."

"At least you were able to reach the upper cargo bay."

"It wasn't easy, let me tell you. I had to squeeze past tumbled gear and shimmy down a partially collapsed corridor just to reach the access door, which only opened about halfway, even with a pry bar."

"So salvaging anything of any size isn't an option."

"Not from that section of the ship. Too much work, and too risky."

"How about shelter? Anywhere look stable enough to use?"

Rika thought about it a moment. "Well, I think we may be able to set up somewhere on the mid port levels, but we'll need to give them a more thorough going over before we risk moving anyone back inside. Too many structural issues going on, and I don't want to risk a collapse trapping us all in there if something goes wrong."

"Wonderful," he said with a defeated sigh.

Charlie lay back down and stared up into the vast sky. Tomorrow would be a new day, and he hoped it would bring some better news. For now, however, sleep was a priority, and he soon drifted off into a sound slumber.

CHAPTER FOURTEEN

Morning greeted them with clear, rose-colored skies and a slight breeze.

Charlie ran a systems diagnostic on the medical scanner as the injured crew slowly roused with the rising red sun. He knew by now he'd have about two hours before the sun's yellow twin would crest the horizon, their combined rays casting a faint orange tint to the barren plain.

"We should head out toward those rock formations today, Charlie," Rika said as she chewed a nutrient bar. "They're the only things not flat and dirt out here. I figure they're worth taking a closer look at. Who knows? We may get lucky."

"Sounds like as good plan as any."

"Thanks for the vote of confidence," she said, stretching out the kinks from a bad night's sleep. "I'm going to get us some extra water for the trek. We'll head out as soon as we check on the others."

"I can do it. Besides, I'm the one trained to use the med scanner, anyway."

"All right. Get to it, then meet me in command. I want to

have another look in daylight, and we have a few things to discuss before we head out."

Charlie gathered up the scanner and some supplies and made his way through the waking survivors, performing a basic medical analysis of each, while distributing breakfast rations from their stores along with small containers of water.

They had accumulated a surprising amount via the solar stills, but nevertheless, water was strictly rationed on the dusty planet. The small containers into which he had siphoned the prior day's production were far from full, and that would need to be addressed sooner rather than later. For now, however, getting the crew healthy was priority one.

Winnie's injuries, while undoubtedly debilitating, were not critical. Her broken arm had been properly set, confirmed by the med scanner, and the blow to her head did not appear to have caused any lasting damage beyond a decent concussion and a sore neck.

Sven Jurgensson, the man in charge of logging and organizing the ship's supplies, was in worse shape. While he looked relatively uninjured to the naked eye, the device in Charlie's hand revealed a subdural hematoma pressing on his brain. The small leak had self-sealed, and the pressure was gradually decreasing as his body reabsorbed the fluid. In their current location and with such limited resources, it was all he could ask for.

They kept him safely covered in the shade of the ship, where the dazed man refused food, but at least was coherent enough to drink water. He was a big man, and a few days without a meal wouldn't kill him. A few days without fluids would.

Rika was right about moving back inside the ship for shelter. The craft was terribly damaged from the crash, its walkways were unstable, and liable to shift or even give way without warning. While Rika and Charlie were in good enough condition to avoid the dangers, the rest of the survivors could not possibly move fast enough to stay clear of hazards. In fact, with their injuries, most, if not all, would have to be carried anyway.

"Hold still, Omid," Charlie said as he passed the handheld scanner over the shallow-breathing rocket scientist's chest.

"How bad is it, Charlie?"

"If you'd hold still, I could get a better reading and tell you."

"Sorry. It just hurts to breathe," he said, tugging on the tight wrap Charlie had placed around his torso.

"I know it does. That's because you've got a flail chest, and that shit hurts."

"Flail chest?"

"It means several adjacent ribs are broken in a way that lets them free-float with your chest as you breathe. It's one of the most painful types of rib breaks."

"I noticed. And this wrap is killing me."

"Stop tugging at it, Omid. Bad as it feels, the pressure of that wrap against the broken section is actually *reducing* the pain."

"You've got to be kidding me. You mean it could be worse?"

"Yep. Now hold still, I've only got so much battery on this thing."

Charlie passed the scanner over the ailing man's chest, then, once he had a full set of readings, continued over the rest of his body.

"Okay, all done. You can squirm now, though I'd advise against it."

"So what's it say, Charlie? Am I going to be okay?"

"I think so. You bruised some organs, which is hardly surprising given the broken ribs, but there seems to be no internal bleeding."

"Great. How long until I'm able to walk?"

"You could try now, but it would hurt like a sonofabitch. Just rest. Rika and I have things under control."

Omid let out a pained sigh. "Okay. I'll just lay here, then. Doctor's orders."

"You do that," Charlie said with a little laugh. "You'll heal, just give it time."

He rose to his feet and made his way to the heavily bandaged particle physicist lying on a makeshift cot. Both of her legs were splinted, as well as her left arm, which was held in place against her torso with a heavy swathe.

"How you feeling, Siobhan?"

"Not running any marathons," she said, managing a forced smile. An avid runner, her shattered legs were almost worse than death in her eyes.

"I know this sucks, but we'll get through it," he said, not sure if he believed his own words. "Rika and I salvaged some goodies. I didn't find much of your gear, at least not that was intact, but I did score this med scanner."

"I don't need that to tell me my legs are fucked."

"Such language, Doctor Stewart," he said with an amused grin as he passed the device over her heavily wrapped legs.

"I'm Scotch-Irish, Charlie. I learned to swear before I learned to walk."

"Noted. Well, you'll be pleased to know that, while you are well and proper fucked––"

"We pronounce it 'fooked,' by the way."

"Okay, you're fooked, but it looks like the bone ends are aligned, so given time, your legs should heal up okay."

"We don't have any cast material."

"No, we don't. So when Rika and I get back from our next salvage run, we'll see if we can find something that'll do the trick well enough. I was thinking we could heat the memory foam from one of the seats until it becomes extremely pliable. Then we wrap your legs. It won't be totally rigid, but if it holds form when it cools, it should keep stuff in place and protect you from further injury."

"Won't my legs burn from the heat?"

"We have some scraps from a damaged EVA suit we can use. We'll pull the heat-reflecting outer layer and make a sort of under-cast bandage. It'll feel warm, no doubt, but it shouldn't burn."

"Pretty ingenious, Charlie. And here I always took you for more of a follower. I misjudged you."

"Nah, I don't *want* to be doing all of this, but there's no one else to do it."

"Well, I appreciate it." She shifted her gaze, looking past him into the sky. "A binary star system. And a breathable atmosphere to boot. I never in a million years would have thought I'd be standing––um, *lying* on an alien world like this. We were paving the way for *future* generations, you know? It wasn't supposed to be us out here."

"And yet, here we are."

"Yep."

"At least we haven't been cooked by radiation," he said.

"With the wave spectrum of these stars, along with the basic look of this world and its breathable atmosphere, I think we're safe. We may burn a little faster, and who knows what skin cancers we may get in thirty years, but for the short term we should be okay."

Charlie gave her a long drink from the water container and left a nutrient bar at her side. "I'll do what I can to find some pain meds, but medical took a serious hit when we crashed. Most of the facility is gone."

"I appreciate it, Charlie."

He flashed her a warm smile, then walked to where Rika was squatting beside Jamal's motionless form. She looked up at him with a pained expression. He knew before she said a word.

Charlie rested his hand on her shoulder. "We should bury him with the others."

Rika nodded once, stoic, but hurting. The two then covered

his body and slid him onto their sled, pulling him away from the survivors to join the ranks of their buried dead.

CHAPTER FIFTEEN

Charlie and Rika sat quietly in the ship's ruined command center. Rika had done another check on the comms systems, confirming their demise. At least they were out of earshot of the rest of the crew. It would be a quiet place for them to discuss the dire nature of their situation without unnecessarily stressing the others.

"They have good reason to be stressed," Charlie had noted.

"We all do, but there's no need to unduly increase it if we can help it. I mean, Siobhan is so on edge I think she's about ready to take someone's head off. And it's not for want of pain meds."

"Nah, it's a different kind of pain. Being forced into a sedentary role when you're used to being active, it can drive you batty."

"Well, her legs are both shattered. It's going to take a long time of her sitting on her duff before she walks again, let alone runs."

"I know," Charlie said. "And believe me, I know how she must be climbing the walls. Did I ever tell you about the time I got a stress fracture in my shin?"

"Not that I recall," Rika said.

"I was in high school. I used to run a *lot* back then. So one day, during cross-country practice, my shin started hurting. I ignored it and kept running. Stuff like that happens when you're an athlete, right? And teenagers think they're invincible anyway."

"So you just kept going."

"Precisely. So about a week later it still hurt, but worse. My coach said, 'Run it off, it's just shin splints.'"

"Let me guess. It wasn't."

"That's cheating. I already told you I had a stress fracture. But at that point I didn't know, so I just did what my coach said and kept running. Eight, nine, ten miles a day, the tiny crack growing until finally it hurt to even walk. My mom took me to get a bone scan, and the doctor said if I'd kept running the tibia would have split vertically. I'd have had one leg over an inch shorter than the other."

"Yikes. That must've really hurt."

"Oh, yeah. But you know what was far worse? When the doc told me I couldn't run for nine months."

"But bones heal way faster than that."

"I know. But because it was vertical, they couldn't just break it clean and put a cast on me. Instead, I had to walk around with no cast and no visible reason I couldn't run. From ten miles a day to zero. Couldn't even jump rope or anything. As a kid that active, you can imagine how hard it was."

"Probably even more so for your poor parents. I mean, a teen stuck in the house with all that energy and nowhere to spend it?"

"Yeah, it was not ideal, to say the least."

"So what wound up happening?"

Charlie took a swig from his canteen and climbed to his feet.

"I drove myself and everyone around me nuts until it healed enough for me to at least start riding a bike. But what I'm saying is, I know how Siobhan is feeling, and unfortunately, there's nothing we can do to help alleviate it. And that's coming from someone who's been there."

He walked to the airlock door and slid an empty pack over his shoulder.

"We should get cracking. Jamal was hurt beyond our ability to help, but the others should mend. But even with one less mouth to feed, we're still going to run out of food eventually, and, I for one, have no desire to recreate the Donner Party's little adventure."

Rika grabbed her pack and joined him, following the corridor back to the orange-lit sky of the strange world.

"I'll grab the sled," she said, trotting off to retrieve the makeshift load bearer.

"Okay, I'll pull us some water from the solar stills. Enough for a few hours' trek at least."

"Sounds good. Meet back here in five."

Charlie nodded, and the two went their separate ways. In just a few short minutes, another day of mind-numbing labor would begin, starting with a long walk in a dusty wasteland.

A group of explorers, the Donner party ran out of food and ate each other in the American midwest (somewhere in Nevada)

CHAPTER SIXTEEN

The winds had been light the prior day, and as a result, the shifting mounds that had begun to cover smaller items had blown clear. Reflection from the metal parts littering the debris field were everywhere, like an exploded disco ball.

The gouge carved by the *Asbrú*'s crash was a jigsaw puzzle of destruction, filled with exposed bits of the ruined craft, torn free as its belly slid along the hard ground.

Most of the storage compartments in the lower rear of the ship had been completely destroyed, ripped apart on impact. Unfortunately, that was where the majority of their foodstuffs had been located.

As this was to be a relatively short test run, the *Asbrú* hadn't even been loaded with anywhere near her full capacity of the assorted freeze-dried and vacuum-sealed meals. There was more than enough for the slimmed-down crew for a lengthy voyage, should it be required, but nowhere near what the stranded men and women would need to feed them for more than a few months.

And that was if those supplies hadn't been shredded and flung to the wind.

Charlie and Rika were both painfully aware of their increasingly poor outlook for survival.

"If we don't find at least some of those pods, we're going to have to go on stricter rationing," Charlie grumbled as they trudged along the ship's debris trail.

"I know," Rika said. "In fact, I was thinking it might be a wise idea to do it anyway. Even if we had all of our supplies, we have no idea how long we'll be stuck here, or if there is any native vegetation or even, I don't know, algae or something for nutrition."

"I'll pass on algae, thanks," Charlie said, crinkling his nose.

"If we have to resort to Winnie's dead rats, you'll thank me if we find algae," she shot back.

"Dead rats?"

"Yeah. Protein is protein. And anyway, by the time we find them, they'll probably be rat jerky anyway."

Charlie felt a hot flash of bile in his throat and gagged a little.

"Sorry. I forgot how sensitive you were about food."

"It's okay," he said, taking a sip of water and wiping his lips. "It's just, I'm really not an adventurous eater, ya know?"

"That I do," she replied with a grin. "But if things don't improve, and I mean dramatically, you may find yourself needing to get over that issue sooner than later."

The duo trudged along, digging through what appeared to be debris-dense areas as they pulled their sled behind them, hoping to find anything worth salvaging.

Two hours had passed when Charlie suggested a break from the heat of the sun. Rika was more than glad to take him up on the suggestion, and in short order, he rigged a temporary sun shade for them from bits of metal and plastic gathered from the debris field. Seated comfortably in the shade, they surveyed what they'd managed to dig up so far. It wasn't much.

"So, we've got a roll of duct tape, four intact containers we can use for water storage, a few smaller canteen-sized ones, and a few drained but seemingly undamaged battery packs, though we'll have to see if we can find a way to get them charged on a trickle feed once we get back to the ship."

"Don't forget the food," Rika said.

"Of course. And one slightly worse-for-wear case of freeze-dried beef stroganoff," Charlie added. "That's really gonna suck without enough water to properly reconstitute it."

"And if you eat it dry, it'll absorb the moisture in your gut and leave you all plugged up. A food cork, of sorts," Rika joked.

"That is downright nasty, Rika."

"But true."

"Well, yeah. True, but still, nasty."

The corners of her eyes crinkled slightly, glad for the moment of levity breaking up the stress of their otherwise oppressively difficult situation. Charlie dug through a few plastic containers holding sealed pouches with a variety of seeds in them. They had once been carefully cataloged and organized, but after the crash, they were a jumble of tiny, vacuum-sealed pouches that grew Lord knew what.

"What do you think? These look like apple seeds to you?" Charlie asked, holding up a pouch to the light.

"Could be," Rika said, scoping out the seeds.

"Great. All we need now is about three years and a few hundred gallons of water and we'll be rolling in apples."

"If we can find any of the hydroponics equipment, we could maybe try to set up a small greenhouse. Use more of your solar stills to generate enough water to maybe grow *something*."

"It's a great idea, but you know those were stored in the ship's belly, right along with the rest of the experiment equipment for our little voyage. And all of that is strewn over a few miles of desert, so I pretty seriously doubt we're going to find any of it intact enough to use."

Rika's shoulders slumped slightly.

"Hey, but it was a really good idea," Charlie quickly added. "I mean, who knows? Maybe we'll get lucky, right? Never say never."

She smiled. "I appreciate the pep talk. Or the attempt at one, anyway. But you're right, we're pretty well screwed on the food-growing front. Though maybe if we can somehow get the scanning arrays up we'll be able to see if there's anything resembling foliage beyond the line of sight out here."

"Well, the reactor core is intact, so given enough time to scrap together parts, I think I should be able to power up the unit––that is, if it wasn't too badly damaged in the crash. But we can make fixing it a priority. Not like we have any other pressing obligations, right? And the plasma cutter seemed to be undamaged, so once I rig a power source for it, we should also be able to use it on thicker pieces so we can build some proper shelter. No telling how long the weather on this planet will stay favorable."

"Good point. For all we know it could get much colder, or hotter for that matter. I suppose worst-case scenario, we use the EVA suits. We've got plenty of 'em stored in the ship, and almost all of them are intact, so those can be an emergency source of insulation if the weather starts to really shift on us."

"You think we'll really live long enough to see that, though?" Charlie asked, fixing her with a sad look.

"You know what? I do. And so should you. We need to keep our spirits up. If not just for us, then for the others. It's going to be a while before they're healed up enough to help us, so for now, as long as we're acting as nursemaids, we need to set the tone."

Charlie digested her words, the sage advice well-taken despite their desperate situation.

"You're right, Rika. Sorry I was being a downer."

"No, you've got every reason to be down, but right now, we simply can't afford it."

She climbed up to her feet and brushed the sandy red soil from her hands. "Come on, let's get back to it. I thought I saw something in the distance. We should check it out."

With that, they folded up their sun shade, loaded it onto the sled with the other salvage, and started walking beneath the glaring gaze of the world's twin suns.

CHAPTER SEVENTEEN

The larger rocky formations dotting the landscape were far more distant than it had seemed when Charlie and Rika set out on foot to get a better look at what appeared to be the nearest one.

The nearest turned out to be almost two miles away, and the others were easily several times that distance.

"You okay?" he asked, offering a water container to his companion.

"I'm good," Rika replied.

"You should hydrate. It's getting warmer."

"We need to conserve our water."

"What we need is for us to not pass out from dehydration. The others are resting. We're exerting ourselves. Besides, if we find more plastic sheeting, I can put together a few more solar stills when we get back."

Reluctantly, she took the container.

"Atta girl."

They walked in silence for a while, saving their energy as much as they were deep in thought. There were mountains far off in the distance. From the look of them--at least what they could see from so far away—they spanned across the entire horizon three hundred sixty degrees. It looked as if they almost curved all the way around them.

Of course, it would have been easy to survey the area from space and map the exact terrain, but they had crashed blind. All they knew of the terrain was what was in front of them.

"Charlie? Does that look like something moving?" Rika asked, pointing to an area fifty meters from the rapidly nearing pile of rocks.

It did kind of look like something was moving. Blowing in the wind.

"Debris, maybe?"

"You think?"

"Something light could have blown this far when it was windy."

"We'll find out soon enough."

Soon enough turned out to be nearly fifteen minutes of slow walking, the sled dragging behind them with the soft sound of soil grinding along its bottom.

"Holy shit. That's a plant!" Charlie exclaimed as they grew closer.

They picked up their pace, rushing to the discovery. A small cluster of thin, tan shoots were jutting up from the ground, waving in the gentle breeze.

"Vegetation, Charlie! Do you know what this means? There's got to be water close by."

"That, or they live off of the sparse moisture the way we've been doing."

Rika knelt in the dirt. "Give me something to dig with."

He handed her the knife they'd salvaged from Jamal's locker.

"Thanks," she said, carefully removing soil from the plant, digging deeper and deeper as she explored, searching for water. What she found was not what she expected, but something that had the potential to drastically alter their odds of survival just the same.

"Is that a potato?" Charlie asked as she pulled a small tuber from the ground.

"It looks sort of like one, doesn't it?" She brushed the dirt free and sniffed the beige lump. "You think it's safe?"

"No idea," Charlie replied. "Here, let me try something."

He took the potato-looking plant and wiped an area clean, then made a small cut in it. A milky sap began to form at the site of the incision, which he dripped on a clean spot of his exposed forearm

"What are you doing?"

"Testing to see if it's poison or not."

"By rubbing it on yourself?"

"It's like the old allergy tests. The inner arm is a very sensitive area, so if there's going to be any reaction, that's the most likely place a test would show it."

Rika stared at his arm expectantly. "So, um, how long, exactly, until we know if it's going to make your arm fall off?"

"I can't say for sure, but twenty minutes should suffice, I'd think."

"Okay, let's start the clock." She took the tuber back from him and studied it, turning it over and over in her hands. "It looks so normal. So Earth-like. And yet, here we are, Lord knows how far from home, and the first ever proof of alien life is a potato." She fixed it with a fierce gaze. "Take me to your leader!" she demanded of the tuber.

Charlie burst out laughing, and Rika, too, soon found herself caught up in his mirthful delight.

"Oh man, thanks for that," he said a minute later, wiping his tearing eyes. "I really needed a good laugh." He held up the plant by its stalk. "I am Charlie Gault, man of Earth. If you're not toxic and good eating, how about taking us meet your friends, if not your leader? Hello? Anyone?"

"You're ridiculous, Charlie."

"My most endearing trait, and it takes one to know one," he said, his spirits restored. "Well, since we have to wait a bit to see if my arm falls off, let's keep looking. This little guy is a super positive sign. Now let's just hope there's more vegetation growing around here, and who knows? Maybe we'll even get lucky and find some water."

"Let's leave the sled here. Canteens only. We'll be coming this way on the way back, and there's no sense dragging that extra weight along. The rocks are only about a quarter mile away."

"Sounds like a plan," Charlie said, dropping the straps to the sled on the ground. "Come on, then. Let's go see if this walk will bear any more pleasant surprises."

They covered the potato-thing and left it on the sled, then set a course for the jumble of rocks nearby. As they approached, they found the ground was much more uneven than the rest of the area.

"I'm glad we left the sled," Charlie said. "Dragging it across this would've sucked."

"It's weird, isn't it? This doesn't look like normal geologic activity to me. What do you think?"

"You're right. It feels odd. Like, things were picked up and smashed into the ground, then yanked up again. But that's impossible. Look at the size of some of these stones."

Rika ran her hand over the first one they came to. "I don't know. Feel this. It's so smooth. Geometric. How could it be natural?"

"I don't know, but no one would build in a wasteland like this," he said, gesturing at the stones, most of them buried in sand and debris.

"Maybe, but couldn't it have been a long time ago?"

A flashing light caught his eye in the distance. A shimmer.

That's gotta be a mirage, he reasoned.

"Charlie? Earth to Charlie."

Rika followed his gaze.

"Water!" she shouted, bolting for the apparition.

"Rika, wait. It's probably just the heat waves making it look like—"

She dove to the ground, splashing the water over her face.

"Or, maybe it actually *is* water," he said, hustling over to join her. There was an odd shimmer to the water. Something more than just the dual suns' reflections. "Don't drink any until I test it. We don't know if it's safe."

Rika smiled, rivulets running down her hair, the dust washed from her face.

Huh. Must've been mostly the red dust, Charlie mused, noting her healthy skin. *Looked like she was pretty sunburned earlier.*

He turned his attention to the small pool. It was perhaps three feet across and only a few inches deep. How it hadn't merely evaporated in the arid environment was a mystery.

I wonder.

Charlie took the medical scanner from the small pouch on his hip. In their haste to depart after burying Jamal, he had forgotten to leave it behind at their camp. That oversight might now bear unexpected fruit.

"What are you doing, Charlie?" Rika asked as she dipped her compact materials analyzer into the pool.

"I'm changing the settings to treat the soil as flesh, and this water as blood."

"Can you even do that?"

"Well, not really, but sort of. I just have an idea, but I need something that can see through the ground to do it. We don't have any geological survey equipment, so I'm making do with what we've got."

A green light sprang to life on Rika's analyzer, and the display churned out a stream of information.

"It's water, and aside from a somewhat high mineral content, it's perfectly safe." With great relish, she leaned down and took a big gulp from the pool. "Oh my God, that's what I'm talking about!"

"So nothing unusual?"

"No. Why?"

Charlie looked again at the odd shimmer to the water. "Nothing. Never mind."

Rika filled their containers until the pool was nearly entirely empty. "Shame, we could have used more than this, but it'll have to suffice," she said, swirling the filled containers.

While she carefully collected as much as their vessels would carry, Charlie had been fine-tuning the med scanner. The readings were all over the place, as if the machine was intentionally keeping him from dialing in to the settings he desired. But Charlie was persistent. A brief flicker lit his screen, then vanished.

"Gotcha!"

He knew he was close, and with a few minute adjustments, he found himself with an incredibly faint, but tangible, reading.

"What've you got, Charlie?" Rika asked.

Her skin really does look better, he noted.

"I think this is dialed in," he replied, bending over and sticking his left hand in the remains of the pool of water.

A faint tingle could be felt, then was gone as fast as it had come. He took his hand out and looked at it compared to his other.

The sunburn is gone. It wasn't just the dirt washing off. This water made the burn fade almost immediately.

"You okay, Charlie?"

"Yeah," he said, more than a little distracted. The implications were staggering. "I finally got this working, I think."

"So what does it do, exactly?"

"It's like a high-tech dowsing rod. Only this one is set to penetrate the soil to seek out water as if it were flowing through a vein." The pool was still nearly empty. Based on his readings, it would take weeks, if not months for it to slowly fill again.

"What are you saying, Charlie?"

"I'm saying, there's a teeny, tiny leaching flow of water deep under the surface. You'd never find it if you didn't know where to look. But thanks to blind luck, we did. And there's more water somewhere around here, Rika, and this baby's going to take us to it."

CHAPTER EIGHTEEN

"Help me dig."

Charlie had walked like a drunk on a beach, following the beeps and chirps of a metal detector in his quest for shiny, only he held a modified med scanner, and Charlie was stone sober.

After following a weaving path through tumbled rocks the size of small cars—losing the signal a few times along the way—they had arrived at an impassable mound of shattered stone, the base of which was deeply buried under windswept sands.

"It says it's here, Rika. Look at the readings! There's water in here," he said, his hands digging deep into the soil. His left hand was quickly dirty again, but there was no doubt, the waters had somehow healed his sunburn. He found himself wondering what else they could do.

We might even be able to help the others.

"Less daydreaming, more digging," Rika joked, nudging him with her elbow.

"Sorry. I was just thinking, this water has a strange effect, don't you think?"

"How so?" she grunted, pulling aside a large armload and shoving it away from the stone.

"You were filling the containers. Look at your hands."

"What about them?"

"The sunburn. It's gone."

"No, it isn't, just loo––" Rika paused, gasping as she studied her hands. "How is this possible?"

"I don't know, but it did the same to my hand. And how are you feeling?"

"I feel––I feel pretty great, actually."

"You drank some. I think whatever it did on the outside, it did to your insides as well."

"The Fountain of Youth? In deep space?"

"Maybe not quite that, but the effects are incontrovertible. Maybe it's something in the soil. Maybe it's being exposed to the dual suns' rays. I don't know, but the scanner shows a larger body of water somewhere under these rocks, and if we can get to it, I have hopes we can maybe use it to help heal our crew."

"You think it could fix broken bones?"

"Who knows what properties it has? Sunburn's pretty minor, after all. But even if that's as much as it can do to help our bodies heal, it's still doing amazing things. And at the very least, we could sure as hell use the hydration, in any case."

Rika began digging with renewed vigor, the soil falling aside as they burrowed deeper and deeper toward the long-buried rocks.

"Look at the color," she said. "The dirt is darker."

"Moisture. We're getting close."

They continued, pulling with both hands until they finally reached the hard mass of a buried stone. Its surface was cool. More importantly, it was damp. The pair made quick work digging out its perimeter.

It was an irregular shard, no more than perhaps a half meter at its widest, tapering down to a smaller end, which had apparently fallen from height, the weight driving it into the ground.

"I can feel a breeze," Rika said, running her fingers along the topmost edge, where a gap had been exposed. "You think we can move this thing?"

"Together? Yeah, we might. But look how it's situated. If we pull and pivot at the same time, it might flop back and rest against the other rocks. That'd take a whole lot less effort."

"Then stop yapping and give me a hand," she said, wedging her fingers into the narrow space.

Charlie put his shoulder up against hers and added his strength to the equation.

"Okay, on three."

"Screw three. Just pull!" Rika commanded, the muscles in her arms straining with the effort.

Charlie pulled with all his might as well, and the heavy stone did budge, but not nearly as far as they'd hoped. He repositioned, bracing his foot against the adjacent rock's uneven face and tried again, pushing with the powerful muscles in his legs as well as his arms.

Slowly, the stone began to pivot.

"It's working. Keep going!" Rika urged.

They pulled even harder, fingertips turning white from the effort. With a soft grating of stone on soil, the rocky obstacle pivoted free at last, releasing a gust of cool, wet air. The opening was tight. One meter high and less than half that in width.

"We can fit," Rika said, slipping through the gap. A light popped on inside the opening. "Come on, Charlie! You've got to see this!"

Charlie shoved his upper body through the gap, scraping his elbows as he forced his way into the space. "What the hell?" he gasped upon seeing where he stood.

They were in a long passageway with flat stones lining the floor, longer, arched ones curving overhead. Every four meters or so, perfectly carved sconces adorned the buckled walls, long vacant their illumination. The walls themselves bore designs in the stone, looking as if the smooth lines had been a natural part of the rock rather than carved.

"This is..." Words failed him.

"This is proof of intelligent alien life," Rika said, breathless, her eyes aglow with excitement.

"Something happened here, Rika. Something bad. A civilization is gone. What could have done that?"

"It might have just been time, for all we know. But look," she said, turning off her light.

"Hey, what are you doing?"

"Give it a second, your eyes will adjust."

Sure enough, they did, and that was when Charlie saw it. "There's light up ahead."

"Yep. I saw it when I first crawled in. Super-faint, but something's illuminating whatever's around the bend down there."

Charlie felt a flash of hesitation course through his veins. A moment of fight-or-flight. *This is stupid. I just survived a spaceship crash on an alien world. What more could I possibly have to be afraid of?*

"Come on, Rika. Let's go see what surprises our alien friends left for us."

CHAPTER NINETEEN

The subterranean cistern was vast, the vaulted ceiling miraculously intact despite a spiderweb of cracks from whatever cataclysm had ravished the surface many years prior. Light reflected off of the pale stone, a radiant glow spread across the chamber by the iridescent, silent waters.

A power was present. Far more than the tiny puddle they had found above, its contents thinned and weakened over hundreds of meters of slow filtration through tiny fractures in the stone beneath the wasteland's surface. In this place, the true potency of the waters was readily felt.

Charlie crouched low and gingerly placed his right hand beneath the calm surface.

"Do you think that's a good idea?"

"We've both already touched it. I don't think it's going to hurt us."

Rika, though she agreed with him, nevertheless placed her scanner into the water.

"It's pure. Perfect."

"I know," he replied. "Can you feel it, though? There's something to this place."

Without thinking, Charlie slid from the shore into the glowing pool, the dirt and aches of their ordeal washing away in an instant.

"Oh my God," he gasped. "Rika, you have to come in."

She didn't require any further motivation, and was, in fact, already out of her boots when she took his invitation and stepped into the water. Her body felt alive, her skin tingling with energy as the waters stripped her of dirt and pain.

"It–it's amazing," she managed to say. "I can feel my muscles unknotting. And my sunburn, it's gone."

"I know," Charlie replied, his eyes wide with amazement, reflecting the water's faint glow. "There's some compound in this that doesn't show on our scanners. Maybe a topical analgesic combined with, what? Something that triggers cellular regeneration? The science is beyond me."

"We need samples. This could change medicine!" Rika blurted before the reality of their situation reared its head once again. "Oh yeah, we're stranded on an alien planet and no one knows we're here."

"I've been thinking about that," Charlie said. "What if we could figure out what exactly caused the phenomenon?"

"You mean wormhole."

"Tomato, tomahto. What I'm saying is, the drive control systems and power cells are located in the top of the ship. It may take a hell of a long time, but now that we aren't going to die of dehydration, perhaps we'll be able to backtrack the glitch and reverse engineer it."

"That ship will never fly again and you know it."

"Obviously. But we don't need to fly. We just need to get a message home."

Rika pondered for a moment. It was an incredibly long shot, but as good as the waters had her feeling, she was beginning to think maybe it just might be possible now that their deaths seemed less imminent.

"Maybe, Charlie. Maybe. But for the moment, we really should get some of this back for the others. It's *so* much more potent than what we found in that little pool."

"I agree. Unfortunately, we filled all of our containers back on the sled, but we can empty the one we were carrying with us and fill it with this water. We'll drink our fill before heading back, anyway."

"Sounds like a plan," she said, swimming lazily to the smooth stone shore.

Charlie followed, enjoying the feel of the water on his body one last moment before their trek back through the dust and grime.

"Here," Rika said, offering her hand, pulling him up from the water.

The two bumped into one another, standing close, face-to-face. Charlie could feel the heat of her body, radiating through their wet clothes. Impulsively, she pulled him in and kissed him, and much to her pleasure, Charlie kissed her back.

"Whoa," she said. "I don't know what came over me."

"Me either," he replied, cheeks flushed.

"I'm sorry, I didn't mean to––"

"It's okay. I-I mean, it must be the water. It makes *everything* feel good."

"Yeah. We, uh, should probably, uh, get going," Rika blurted. She made no move to leave.

"Uh, okay, if you want," Charlie replied after an uncertain pause.

Rika stared at him a long moment, gears turning. "You're right. We've been gone long enough." With that, she turned and headed for the passageway to the surface.

Stupid, Charlie! What were you thinking? 'Okay, if you want?' My God, way to kill the moment, idiot. He silently kicked himself, then poured out what remained in his container and refilled it with the pool's rejuvenating waters. "Hey, Rika. Wait up!"

They crawled back to the surface, drying off quickly in the heat of the afternoon suns, the dry air wicking the moisture from them in no time.

"We should keep this from the elements," Charlie said. "Even with that much water, we don't know how long it'll have to last us."

"Agreed. Let's slide the rock back in place and pack dirt over it to seal the cracks. Now that we know where it is, we can pretty easily find this particular pile of rocks and dig it up as needed."

"Yeah. And maybe we can rig something less heavy when we have a chance. Like a pair of plastic sheets to seal the entrance. That'd be a whole lot easier to move, especially if you consider that we may be here a very long time."

"That's a good plan, Charlie," Rika said, a teasing hint of the curiosity and warmth she'd shown in the cavern flashing in her eyes. "You know, you're really thriving in this," she said, gesturing at the wasteland surrounding them.

"Just trying to keep us alive, is all."

"Well, you're doing a good job. Stepping up. Not everyone would, you know. Most would fall apart from the pressure."

"Don't worry, I'm falling apart on the *inside*," he joked.

"Somehow I doubt it."

Again, with that look.

"Okay, enough pep talk. Let's get back and put some of that water to work. I know you're as curious as I am to see how it will affect more serious injuries."

"You know me so well," he said with a laugh, his spirits higher than they'd been in days. Maybe even longer. It had been a while since he'd felt so good. "Lead the way, madam," he said with a little bow and a flourish.

"Why, thank you, good sir," she replied with a warm smile, and took the lead for the long trek back.

CHAPTER TWENTY

It had been a surprisingly short walk, with Rika and Charlie quickly covering the distance from the hidden cistern to where they had left the sled in no time. Their spirits as well as their bodies were humming with good energy.

They retrieved the sled and trekked back toward the others. Charlie's skin had remained unharmed, even before his dip in the healing pool, so he deemed the potato *likely* to be edible. They'd experiment further with the lone tuber upon their return to camp.

Loaded on the sled were a few semi-functional pieces of diagnostic and scanning equipment, which, while pretty banged up, Charlie hoped to salvage for parts. Also weighing down the sled were several containers of the restorative water, one of which happened to be particularly potent. Despite the load, Charlie's legs felt great.

"Hey, Rika."

"Yeah, Charlie?"

"Do you think all of those other piles of rocks could be ruins?"

She looked out across the barren expanse, small––

depending on distance—clusters of stone dotting the landscape. With the red sun falling lower on the horizon, the mysterious mounds seemed to somehow stand out as the spectrum shifted.

"I don't know. Maybe? I mean, given what we now know, it seems highly likely there were other stone buildings at one time or another, so could those others be ruins from long ago? I don't see why not."

"Wild," Charlie said with an appreciative whistle. "We not only met our first alien—"

"I shall call him Mr. Tuber," Rika joked.

"Yes, Mr. Tuber. And then we found an alien swimming pool."

"I really doubt that was a swimming pool."

"I know, but just go with it, okay?"

Rika laughed, and a warm happiness filled Charlie's heart.

"You know what?" he said. "I'm starting to have a good feeling about our odds out here."

A shadow fell over them, moving quickly past.

"What the hell?" Rika said, looking skyward.

A strange craft with a smooth bottom shell and no visible means of propulsion glided over their heads, dropping down toward their crashed ship. The vessel was forty meters long, thirty wide, and twenty tall, with the front only slightly more tapered than the rear.

It made no sound as it flew by.

"Charlie! Aliens!"

"I see them," he replied, suddenly very much not sporting the good feelings of moments prior. "But what's driving that thing? There's no wake. No thrusters. I can't see any engine systems at all."

"I don't know. But they're actual aliens, Charlie!"

He looked closely as the ship dropped lower near their camp a mile ahead. As the dust rose, it seemed as if there was a faint orange glow surrounding the ship.

My eyes aren't that good. How did I see that? Charlie wondered. Maybe it was simply that the water's healing properties that had given him better than 20/20 vision. In any case, the odd craft had settled down into a low hover just beside their ruined ship.

"We've got to get back," he said. "Come on!"

The two wasted no time, running as fast as they could while still staying relatively out of sight, ducking behind small rock piles until they were able to cross the crashed ship's debris field and trench, placing their ruined vessel's mass between themselves and the aliens as they approached.

Out of sight, blocked by the wreck, they picked up their pace, the sled bumping behind them, until they reached their ship's crumpled hull. Then they listened, silently, but there was no sound to be heard around the ruined craft's bulk.

"We should go see what they're doing," Rika urged. "Our friends may need us."

"We won't do them any good if the bad guys catch us too."

"We don't know they're bad. We don't know the first thing about them," she said, making for the front of their ship. "I'm going to take a look."

"Rika, wait!" Charlie hissed. "We should wait until dark."

She looked at the lone, yellow orb still in the sky. "Dark is nearly two hours from now. There's no time."

Dammit, he grumbled, then followed as she crept toward the bow.

"They look almost human," Rika said.

Indeed, the beings were bipedal, and human in build. They wore a patchwork assortment of iridescent clothing bundled with coarser fabrics, almost as if they'd dressed themselves from a pile of castoff materials.

Their hair seemed to have a greenish tint to it, which went with the distinctly green tone to their skin. Their ears, Charlie noted, were rather elongated and somewhat pointed.

"They're kinda like dark elves," he said.

"Dark what?"

"Elves. I'm not saying they are. Just that's sort of what they look like."

A pained voice cried out, and the nearest of the alien elf creatures turned to investigate.

"That was Siobhan. I'm going to see what's happening."

"Rika, wait! We should wait until dark."

"They may be hurting our friends, Charlie. I won't sit back and wait around."

"It's not tactically sound. It's almost dark, just wait that little bit."

"Sorry, Charlie," she said, her gaze lingering just a moment longer, then she turned and darted around the ship, crouching behind a stack of supply crates they'd been using for a windbreak.

She surveyed the scene and made a choice. It was not one that Charlie approved of.

"I am unarmed," she said loudly, rising from behind her cover. "I am Rika Gaspari, acting commander of this crew. We mean you no harm. We have come to your world by accident and are stranded. We are a peaceful race. Will you help us?"

What is she thinking? There's no way to know if they're hostile or—

A pair of the green-tinged aliens rushed for her, grabbing her arms firmly and dragging her to the camp with the others. A third alien, a large one clothed in an even more hideous hodgepodge of patterns, made for the front of the ship.

Shit!

Charlie scrambled backward, but there was nowhere to run, and nothing to hide behind. The alien would round the ship in less than a minute.

Think, Charlie!

His eyes darted left and right. The debris was too small for cover. There was, however, a rut at the side of the ship where it had settled upon landing.

If I could squeeze in there and pull some soil on top of myself—

He wasted no more time thinking and set right to work acting, diving into the small rut and frantically pulling dirt on top of himself. He only hoped it would be enough.

CHAPTER TWENTY-ONE

Charlie hated the feel of the dry, red soil creeping into every nook and cranny, but he remained mostly buried for nearly two hours in his impromptu hiding place, pressed against the ship's hull. It was uncomfortable and claustrophobic, but he waited until he was absolutely sure the threat had passed.

After the first few minutes of discomfort he tried to slow his breathing like a Zen master, only to realize it was hard to do with a mound of dirt pressing down on top of him, and a Zen master he was not. It was a long wait.

Finally, as the yellow sun set below the horizon, he dug himself out and slid free of what had begun to feel uncomfortably akin to a self-made shallow grave. The greenish aliens were nowhere in sight.

Charlie pulled the tools and lone tuber from his pocket and left them in the divot against the hull so he could move more quietly and freely, then crept silently around to the front of the ship, dropping to the dirt and belly crawling the last few meters.

Carefully, and ever so slowly, he peered around the curvature of the wrecked craft where the dirt met the hull. It was a good thing he did, because one of the oddly clothed aliens was looking in that direction. A pair of eyes hidden at ground level, however, didn't catch his attention.

Charlie slid back slowly, then made his way to the rear of the wreck in a crouch, just in case prying eyes were watching from another direction. He dropped down into the trench dug by the craft and quietly scrambled his way up to the other side. The alien ship was still there, silently hovering inches from the ground on what appeared to be a thin cushion of some sort of glowing golden energy, barely visible to the eye.

A dozen of the tall alien elf-looking creatures had camped out in a small group beside their craft. Most had shed several layers of their patchwork clothing in the heat. Their underlying outfits were actually quite clean and orderly, the outer garments apparently mere protective gear.

Shit. Where's Rika? Charlie wondered as he scanned the area. He could hear occasional sounds of human chatter, but the survivors were held somewhere just out of his line of sight. A cry broke the quiet, Omid's voice clear through the dry air.

"Leave her alone! Can't you see she is injured," Omid yelled. With his broken ribs, it must have been incredibly painful.

"I'll be okay," Siobhan said, but Charlie could hear the effort in her voice. Whatever was going on, she was working hard to keep the agony of her broken legs in check.

That settled it. The aliens were not warm and fuzzy types, and his crew, his *friends*, needed help.

Charlie slid on his belly, clearing the corner of the ship and slowly inching along the shadowy spot where the ship's hull and the ground met.

If I can just get behind those crates, I'll be able to see what's going on. And hopefully find out where the hell they're holding Rika.

An opening appeared in the hull of the alien ship, and a well-dressed man stepped out onto the red soil. He wore no overcloaks, and his clothing was different than the others.

Cleaner. Not patchwork, and made of what appeared to be fine fabric.

His hair was pulled into a loose ponytail, and his figure was adorned with a variety of jewelry and baubles on his hands and wrists. The others lowered their heads in respect as he passed, surveying the site.

Okay, I know that look. He's gotta be their captain. Charlie increased his pace, while the others were distracted by their leader. *Better.* He breathed a little sigh of relief as he moved behind the crates for a better view, safely blocked from the elf creatures' scanning eyes.

Their leader pulled a small ring from a pouch on his belt and slid it onto his slender finger. The others seemed to lean in with anticipation as he held out his hand and muttered something guttural.

Orange flames leapt to life atop an upturned piece of wreckage.

How did he do that? I didn't see a beam. Must've been outside the visible spectrum, Charlie mused as he watched the man slip the ring back into the pouch on his belt.

The others quickly set to work, laying out meat from some sort of animal and piercing it with long skewers, then positioning them on a hastily arranged rack so the flesh was just above the flames. The smell was amazing, and Charlie's mouth watered involuntarily as the aroma wafted into his nostrils.

His attention quickly shifted when Rika, gagged and hands bound with a fine cord, was yanked to her feet from behind the wreckage she'd apparently been sitting against. Even from a distance, Charlie could see the bruising on her face. She was a tough one, but he couldn't help wonder how much it would take to make her crack.

Of course, they were castaways on an alien world with nothing of value and no strategic intel to conceal, so it was a very real possibility they were beating her for no reason at all. Their rough treatment of the injured crew only served to reinforce that belief.

The captain ran his fingers down her cheek, and Charlie could see the hate in her eyes. If she weren't gagged, the offending digits would have likely been bitten clean off, but Rika was at their mercy. And mercy was something the aliens did not appear to have.

The captain said something in a sing-song language, nodding toward his captive. Two of his men snapped to attention and roughly manhandled her into the gaping maw of the waiting ship. Charlie didn't know what he was going to do, only that he had to act.

His eyes fell on a pile of salvaged equipment. The aliens seemed to have little interest in what he'd managed to recover, and even the bag of weapons had gone unnoticed. Charlie smiled to himself. If he was going to die on a strange world a bazillion miles from home, at least he'd do it in style.

He really had no desire for that ending, though. He hoped a significant show of force, and perhaps a hostage or two, would land him the freedom of his crewmates.

Darting from cover to cover as best he could, hiding behind wreckage and debris, Charlie did his best to avoid the illumination cast by the strange fire, which, so far as he could tell, wasn't actually burning anything. In any case, it would put him in shadow, and hopefully decrease the elflings' night vision, though he had no idea how good the aliens' eyesight was.

Omid saw movement at the edge of their camp, locking eyes with Charlie as he crept toward the weapons cache. Wisely, the injured man kept silent. Charlie saw the others as well. Siobhan had been dragged there with the others, dumped in a heap, undoubtedly jostling her broken limbs out of alignment. Sven was there too, lying beside Winnie, the poor man dazed, but at least conscious, which was an improvement.

With careful hands, Charlie quietly pulled the bag of Jamal's deadly wares from its resting place. He glanced warily at the aliens, but they were preoccupied with their food.

Eat up, you bastards. Just you wait, he quietly said to himself as he slipped behind a twisted piece of hull and began gearing up.

It had been a long time since his service days, but it took him only a moment to figure out how to properly load the unfamiliar rifle and chamber a round as quietly as possible. It was a very different model than any he'd trained on all those years ago, but undoubtedly just as deadly.

After a moment's reflection, he decided to add a pistol to the mix as well, slipping on Jamal's tactical vest and stuffing the pockets with extra magazines. The machine guns and all of their ammo he then stored in a dented cargo container. He could get them later if needed, but he only had two hands, so carrying them would be foolish excess.

Of course, he hoped none of that would be necessary, but he was becoming a firm believer in the benefits of having something and not needing it rather than needing it and not having it.

The collapsible baton slid into a nice holster conveniently mounted on the side of the vest, and he stuffed another pocket with several zip-tie cuffs for good measure. Cuffing the aliens wasn't the plan, but he never knew if he'd need to improvise.

Charlie took a deep breath and checked his holstered pistol and slung his rifle.

Okay. Be bold. Shock and awe. They don't know that you don't know what you're doing.

Pep talk over, Charlie stood and rolled his shoulders. Then, without further delay, he stepped out into the firelight.

"Okay, you green bastards. Put your hands in the air!"

The aliens looked up from their meals calmly, sizing up the strangely clad man who appeared to be threatening them with a strange metal pipe. One even laughed.

"I'm serious! You are all in a world of shit, and I'm the goddamn plumber!"

"What does that even mean, Charlie?" Siobhan said with a pained laugh.

"I don't know. But we're taking over."

The aliens' eyes darted to his side. It was a fraction of a second, but he saw the look and spun. The captain was standing not more than three meters away, what looked like a small set of brass knuckles slid over his fingers.

"Tell me you did not bring knucks to a gun fight." Charlie laughed, his confidence growing by the second. "You aren't as scary as I'd tho––"

The alien held up his suddenly glowing hand and barked a phrase, though Charlie couldn't quite make it out through the electric pain flashing through his body as he was abruptly flung through the air.

He slammed roughly into a pile of debris and slumped to the ground, very much unconscious.

CHAPTER TWENTY-TWO

Charlie woke with a pounding headache that hurt almost as bad as the rest of his body. Whatever he'd been shot with, it had done quite a number on him from head to toe.

He sat up, sliding his aching back along the smooth wall of the––

What is this? A cell? he wondered as his eyes slowly focused on his surroundings.

There were a pair of low cots, and what appeared to be some sort of toilet mechanism, though its means of operation was unclear. No light source was visible, but a low yellow glow illuminated the room.

The doorway seemed to have been left wide open, as was the small window on the wall. Judging by the faint red glow coming in from outside, he'd been unconscious all the way until sunrise. He just wished it had been a less violently induced slumber.

"Hey, you okay?" a man's voice asked from his left.

"Yeah, I think so. My head's killing me, though," Charlie said, sluggishly.

"Not surprising. Most people no survive a full blast of Captain Tür's slaap. You must be strong species."

"I wasn't slapped. I was knocked the fuck out by some weird energy thing."

"No, not slap. *Slaap.* Is for to power focus when using spells."

"Why do you talk like that?" Charlie asked, turning to the man beside him. "And what do you mean, '*spells*?' Oh. Shit" he gasped as his cellmate moved closer.

"What is shit?" the creature asked, his wrinkled blue skin jiggling over his large frame as his twin eyestalks twisted for a better look at the odd little pink being beside him. He stood just over six feet tall, but aside from a basic man shape, he was most definitely not human.

"Uh, nothing," Charlie quickly covered. "I was just, I mean, you're the first alien my entire race has ever spoken with. Well, if you don't count those green fuckers who zapped me with that thing––that *slaap*."

"Not say this loud," he hissed. "Tslavars give hurt if hearing you speak bad of them."

"I'm sorry, but what's a Tslavar?"

"The others. Ones who take us."

"Ah, the green elf-looking dudes. Gotcha." Charlie rubbed his temples slowly. It was going from bad to worse. "And what species are you?" he asked.

"Me Bantoon," the blue man said, proudly thumping his chest. "Me called Tuktuk."

"Well, it's nice to meet you, Tuktuk. I'm Charlie. My race are called humans."

"Oomans."

"Yeah, close enough. But how do you speak English all the way out here in, well, wherever we are?"

"Oh, me no speak Eengleesh. Is translate spell. All slave trader use for to make us have communication. Only, spell is expensive, and we slave, so they use low one. Cheap kind. Not good, but at least we may talking, though they cancel when they want to speak to each other private-like."

"You keep saying spells. Like magic or some shit."

"Of course. What else would it be?"

"I'm sorry, but that's ridiculous. I believe in science, not hocus-pocus."

"Science. Is type of power?"

"I suppose you could say that. Einstein would."

"Is he visla, this Einstein?"

"He's a scientist. One of the greatest."

"And is this hocus-pocoos a spell?"

"What? No. I mean, yes, but not for real. It's magician stuff."

"Magician?"

"Like a wizard. A powerful magic person in stories."

"Aah, like visla."

"Which is?"

"Visla is highest power spell person. Above even emmik, and far above mester."

"I assume these are some sort of power rankings?"

"In manner of speak."

"And the guy who zapped me? What's his rank? Grand Poobah?"

"Oh, Captain Tür not power man. Him use slaap that is powered."

"That brass knuckle thing? That's his weapon, then?"

"Yes, was made strong with spells by his employer, the powerful Emmik Yanna Sok."

"And that's who we'll be taken to?"

"Possibly, if we no sold off first."

"Well, maybe he's more evolved than his servant."

"Oh, Emmik Sok is no man. Is woman. *Strong* woman."

"Ah," Charlie said. "You know, there was a woman with me, as well. A short-haired one. Strong. Feisty. I saw the captain take her on board before I was captured. Do you have any idea where she is? Are there other cells nearby?" He rose unsteadily to his feet and tried to pass through what appeared to be their open door, only to be thrown backward, a hot pain in his neck.

Charlie reached up, his fingers discovering a thin metal band sealed around his neck. So far as he could tell, there was no seam. Looking closely at Tuktuk, he realized the blue man was wearing one as well, though it was largely shrouded in folds of blue flesh. From what he could see, some sort of faintly glowing runes were engraved on the surface.

"Goddamn wireless fence," he grumbled, pulling on the band. "Now I know how the dogs felt."

"The what?"

"Nothing. I was just saying this zap collar reminds me of the ones my folks used on our dogs as a kid," he said, tugging harder.

"No, Charlee. No pull. Spell will knock you down again."

"It's electricity, not a spell."

"Not sure what is electricity, but collars are made with power. Control slaves."

"Well, that's just great," Charlie grumbled, letting go as he felt a tingle building in his pulling fingers. "Are there others on board? Maybe people you talk to? I need to know what happened to Rika. The female. My friend."

Tuktuk looked around as if to ensure there were no prying eyes or ears in the cell, but they were quite alone.

"There are others, yes. And sometime we talk when Tslavar are not around. I hear that one you speak of was combative. A fighter. Give one of Tslavar bleeding nose before she knocked down."

"Is she all right?" Charlie asked, a surge of angry adrenaline clearing his head.

"Don't know. They try to wipe her. To make her loyal, but spells no working. Is very unusual. Both of you, very unusual."

Charlie realized there was one thing the two of them had in

common. They had both very recently had their fill of the mysterious healing waters from the secret cavern.

Might that stuff be negating some of the effects of whatever these elf bastards are trying to do to her? And maybe that's why the slaap only stunned me. Charlie noted the ache in his body was already decreasing.

"Tuktuk, how long have you been a prisoner here?"

"Two months," he answered. "I was taken when my ship go out of fuel. Stranded. Was stupid. Wife said to fill power cells, but Tuktuk no listen. She must worrying about me." A sadness drifted across his visage.

"I'm sorry, man. Really, I am. But maybe we can help each other. Maybe we can find a way to get out of this place. A way to rescue Rika and the others."

"Is no use."

"You don't know until you try," Charlie said, climbing to his feet and slowly edging toward the open cell door.

When he got close, an abrupt tingling in his neck told him the device was about to trigger. *Okay, so there's the boundary,* he noted. He then paced to the window. It was too small for a man to fit through, so they had apparently used a much smaller repelling charge in it, and the restraint band only tingled a little. Lined up outside, Charlie could see his shipmates, all lined up on the dirt, looking exhausted and worse for wear.

Locking me up and smacking my friends? These bastards are going to pay, he promised himself, then set to work planning his escape.

CHAPTER TWENTY-THREE

"What is this useless refuse?" Saur spat, the wiry Tslavar second-in-command angrily shoving over the scanning equipment piled on Charlie's retrieved salvage sled. "So many pieces. And the material is inelegant. Crude, even."

"The off-worlders claim it is powerful in its own regard," Captain Tür said as he walked through the organized mounds, casually kicking over the painstakingly salvaged instruments and makeshift survival gear.

From the nearby ship, Charlie was pained to see his and Rika's carefully gathered water containers go flying, their precious contents gurgling out into the sand.

"I have seen no such sign of potency, however. These beings are no better than hoarders of junk," the green man grumbled.

"I'm inclined to agree with you, Saur. I had hoped for perhaps some worth to be found in their flesh, but even in that regard, only two of their number have any resale value to us. These others will cost more to heal than they'd fetch at market."

A dozen of the slave traders' crew were digging through the ship's remains, searching for anything they might be able to sell or trade. A pile of possibilities was amassing in the survivors' camp area, though the green men had no idea what any of their booty was actually used for.

"What are they doing?" Charlie asked, watching them through his cell's small window from the nearby slave trader ship. "They're just dumping random things in a pile."

"Standard way of thing being done, it is," Tuktuk said. "Is all money they seek. Trade or sale, it no matter so long as value."

"But they're leaving the useful equipment inside. They've only taken out a bunch of broken junk." Charlie realized what was happening. "They really don't understand technology, do they?"

"Technoggy? Is not a word I know."

"Even with the translation software?"

"What is software?"

"The program that makes whatever they're using to let us understand one another function."

"Ah, is spell, then."

"No, technology."

"Makes thing happen without me doing? Sound like spell to Tuktuk."

Charlie sighed. There seemed to be no point in arguing semantics with the blue humanoid.

"You said they seek profit," he mused, watching the Tslavar work team hauling devices they didn't understand out of the ship and placing them in piles based on appearance alone. It seemed they valued aesthetics over function, placing sleek but benign machines together, while bulkier and far more powerful ones were arranged in a separate group. "Tell me, Tuktuk, it looks like they're sorting our machinery for--"

"What is masheenry?"

"Those things," Charlie said, pointing.

Tuktuk's eyestalks swiveled as he looked over the strange containers and boxes with shiny, colored bits and filaments jutting out where they were smashed open. Wires and lights, seen by eyes unfamiliar with them.

"You said they're all about making a profit, right? So, will they load our gear onto this ship to sell elsewhere?"

"If value."

Excellent. And if they really don't know what our gear does, maybe they'll bring along something I can actually use. The plasma cutter isn't self-powered, and it needs its tanks, but it should be easy to jury-rig with a battery cell from a number of other devices. And with that, we could cut our way out of this place.

Unfortunately for Charlie, the cutter was a fairly bulky piece of equipment, and odds were the unfamiliar aliens wouldn't have the first idea how to dismantle it to bring along. Judging by the gear they'd amassed so far, he thought that assessment was a likely one.

For the better part of the day the Tslavar stacked up piles of broken equipment. Captain Tür sorted through the potential salvage with disgust. Almost none of it seemed to have much value to his untrained eyes. Strange magic that he could not figure out how to use.

Charlie wondered if he should try to convince them to let him help select items of value in hopes of secreting aboard something that might help him free Rika and the others. But no one came to see him all day, save the lone collar-wearing slave who brought them a cup of water and plate of surprisingly flavorful porridge of some sort.

She was, Charlie noted, a stocky being with thick hair and a curvy, rather human shape. That, however, was where the similarities ended. Her orange-hued skin was definitely other-worldly.

"I'm Charlie, and this is Tuktuk. What's your name?" he asked as the woman stopped short of the invisible door barrier and slid a pair of hovering trays into their cell.

Now that's a neat trick, he noted.

The orange girl looked as if she was about to speak, but the runes on the slender band around her neck began to glow. She quickly turned and walked away.

"She no talk now. Used to talk much. Share news. Tslavars no like, so now she have make-quiet spell on her. Talking cause much pain."

Charlie found the idea quite offensive. "Bastards," he muttered. "But at least they feed us pretty well."

"You think this good?" Tuktuk asked as he ate his portion, seemingly offended.

"Not bad, for prison food."

Tuktuk snorted a laugh. "Is amateur. I far greater cook. But they no let Tuktuk in kitchen. Say I fill others' heads with nonsense."

"You?" Charlie said with a little laugh. "No offense, but you're not the most subversive of speakers."

"Is just bad translation spell."

"Oh?"

"Yes. Back on my world, I great speaker. I poet."

"A poet?" he said, eyeing the blue man. "You? Really?"

"Yes, really. Among my people, many say I quite articulate."

"I'll take your word for it," he replied, taking a sip from his cup. "Eww, this is *not* tasty."

"Tslavar no use good spells for slave water. Us get cheap stuff."

"I wish they'd let us have the water we found. It was delicious, I tell you, but those assholes kicked the containers over. Such a waste."

The alien looked at him curiously, a strange look on his face. "You say you find water here?"

"Yeah, a tiny puddle in the desert," Charlie said, a bit unsettled by the alien's sudden interest. "But we drained it all, so there's none left."

He didn't know why he felt the need to hide the continued

existence of their discovery, but given all that had happened in the past twelve hours, Charlie thought it wise to play his cards close to the vest.

"Is impossible," Tuktuk said. "No water in Balamar Wasteland. Not for hundreds of years."

"Well, we found some, but it wasn't much."

"You no understand, Charlee. Much bad magic here. Great visla killed in wartimes. When Visla Balamar die, his whole realm made desert."

That would explain the stone structures, he realized. *So they actually were buildings. But some war wiped them out hundreds of years ago.*

"It must've been some fluke, then. Just condensation in the rocks or something," Charlie said, keeping the glowing cistern secret for the time being.

Shouting erupted outside.

"That's Omid!" He dropped his food and rushed to the window.

He couldn't see all that was happening, but from his vantage point he was afforded a clear view of his injured crewmates being roughly dragged together next to the piles of gear.

"What the hell are they doing?"

Tuktuk leaned in and looked out the window. "Sorting. Determining value."

"They intend to sell us, then?"

"Of course. But them injured."

"So? They'll heal. I treated them, splinted their breaks."

"No understand this word. Splinting?"

"Helping a bone heal."

"Then why they not healed?"

"Well, it takes time for bones to set and regrow."

"No, does not. Spell bind break immediate-like. But very pricey."

A sinking feeling hit Charlie's stomach, along with a horrible realization. "They're weighing the value of their lives versus the cost to heal them?"

Tuktuk didn't bother answering the obvious.

Captain Tür reached into one of the pouches on his belt and slid the slaap over his fingers.

"No!" Charlie shouted against the muffling field covering the window. "They're getting better! I can help treat them! Don't—"

"Hokta!"

The guttural word and accompanying blast of deadly energy from the alien's hand cut him off. Captain Tür repeated the process three more times, until Winnie, Omid, Sven, and Siobhan lay dead on the red soil. The elf-looking alien then directed his men which salvage to bring to the ship and walked away, leaving the bodies to the elements.

CHAPTER TWENTY-FOUR

The red sun had dipped toward the horizon, the light shifting gradually from orange to yellow as its paler twin remained high in the sky. The Tslavar workers had discarded most of the salvage, then loaded the remaining bits and bobs they thought might fetch some coin onto their ship.

Locked inside the vessel, Charlie was beside himself with grief, but as the hours passed, his pain rapidly shifted to a growing anger.

"How long until they let us out of these cells?" he asked from his cot. "They can't keep us in here forever."

"No sure," Tuktuk replied. "Depending how far fly to next planet. Maybe gather more slaves, maybe go to sell us."

That got Charlie's attention.

"Another planet? But this ship doesn't have anything that remotely looks like a space drive system. In fact, I didn't see any visible propulsion means on this ship at all. Maybe it has atmospheric capabilities, but how would it even break out of the exosphere?"

"I not understand all the words, but Tuktuk believe meaning

is clear. This ship is fast. Very strong. Has many Drook on board."

"What's a Drook?"

"Is spell caster. Person of power. Mesters, even emmik, sometimes."

"Mesters are like wizards, right? But what's an emmik?"

"Is more powerful than mester. Only below visla, but for visla, death is preferred to being slave. But many emmik and mester captured in battles. Wars lost. Them become slave. Get collar, like this, but much more stronger. Keep them from using magic. Them only able to cast specific spells."

"Wait a minute. You're saying this ship is powered by a bunch of shackled wizards, casting spells for propulsion like a bunch of hamsters on a wheel?"

"What is hamster?

"It's a small animal that runs nowhere on a wheel for hours and hours. An analogy for expending energy but accomplishing nothing."

"But we go somewhere. Drook race that have power to make fly, and Captain Tür have many Drook on his ship. Even backups, for to if should badness happen."

"Yeah, sorry, I'm calling bullshit on that one," Charlie said. "There's got to be a logical, scientific explanation. Like the slaap, for example. It looks like a voice-activated weapon, but that doesn't make it magic."

"Is made work by power user. You see."

"I saw a man with a gun, even if it didn't look like one I'd ever seen before."

"You strange man, Charlee. No believe what you see. It always been this way. Power to fly, power to fight, power to heal, this is how is across this galaxy. Each solar system gives different power."

"Wait, that's like some Clark Kent stuff, there. The sun gives you all powers?"

"Oh, not. Of course, no."

"Whew, for a minute there I was thinking--"

"Only *some* have powers. Vast majority just normal people. Only very few born with them. Rest of us pay power people for them help us. Charge devices, do work at houses, that sort of thing."

"You're saying these people run your planets? Your whole world uses this 'magic' instead of technology? Instead of science?"

"I thinked you say science was like magic."

"Well, it seems that way sometimes, but it's just science in the end. There's even an old Earth saying: '*Any sufficiently advanced technology is indistinguishable from magic.*'"

"Strange talking. You say it magic, then it is not. Seems obvious."

Charlie noticed a nearly imperceptible vibration in the ship, traveling up the floor to his hard cot. There was no sound, no sensation beyond that, but something was definitely happening.

"You feel that?"

"Feel what?"

"That vibration."

"Is nothing. We leaving now."

Charlie jumped to his feet and went to the window. Though he felt no G-forces from liftoff, the ship, indeed, was airborne, rapidly ascending into the sky. The force field across the window opening prevented any wind or loss of pressure, but visually, it was just a hole in the ship's hull. It was hard to ignore the sensation that he was about to be sucked out at any minute.

Higher and higher the ship soared, until the wreck site below was just a speck. That's when Charlie saw the reality of their situation.

"Sonofa--" he muttered. "Of all the places to crash."

From what he could tell, Tuktuk had been telling the truth about Visla Balamar and his great war. The desert wasteland he'd been toiling in was no more than fifty miles across, a shallow red crater where something had taken place. Something awful, by the look of it.

It wasn't a ring of mountains bordering the dusty, red desert. A blast had forced the soil and stones to the periphery. And Charlie had somehow crashed right in the center of it.

"It's so green," he said, eyes darting across the vast expanse of lush forests and clear lakes spanning the planet. "And you say Balamar's place was like that, too?"

"Oh, it were *much* nicer. Him *very* powerful visla. Was great healer and loved by many. Even spoke with *Zomoki* and other creatures. Many fought on his side during war. Was much good man."

"So what happened? You said everyone liked this guy."

"Not every. Many visla and emmik who very bad want to take from Balamar. Steal him powers."

"Wait, they wanted to steal his power source."

"In manner of talking. But Balamar wise. Him spend much power create way to tap source and create more power. Him said to found way to heal even a visla like him. To no die. Was secret. A rumor. But bad men want for themselves."

"So they did what tyrants have done since forever when they find someone stronger than they are. They joined forces."

"Exactly. Even then, was too great power them to overcome. Finally them decide if they can not tap the flow, no one can. Them spend years storing powers, then hours casting worst spell. Take turns, use many Ootaki, building bigger and bigger until finally they overwhelm even Visla Balamar."

"The crater."

"Yes. Was terrible spell, and them not expect it to do so much destroy. Power flow was destroyed along with Visla Balamar. Along with millions of people."

"That's horrific," Charlie said.

A jolt knocked him to his cot.

"What was that?"

"We leave air shell. Guess we going to another world now."

"That was us passing through the atmosphere?" Charlie said, moving back to the window. Sure enough, they were in space, and the only thing keeping him from dying in the vacuum was some invisible barrier over the window.

"Ship should not have bumped. Captain Tür will be angry with the Drooks on duty. Maybe punish."

"For a little turbulence powering through the atmosphere? Hell, where I'm from, anyone would be thrilled for so smooth a flight."

"No Captain. Him very particu--"

The blue man's eyes went wide on their stalks.

Charlie turned to see Captain Tür himself standing outside his cell, watching him with an appraising eye.

"Your people are most unusual," he said, ignoring Tuktuk and casually walking into the room, untouched by the force field blocking the door. "Your craft. So cumbersome. So inelegant. And absolutely full of useless clutter and debris."

Charlie noted he could understand the lithe elfish man clearly. *Sonofabitch uses the good tech for himself, I see.*

"You saw it in less than perfect condition. We crashed," Charlie replied. "It was a very rough landing."

"Yes, I am aware. I wonder, however, where were your Drooks? We searched the vessel and found no sign of them."

"We use engines. Fuel. Reactors. That's how we power our ship. Or did, before we crashed, anyway."

"Pity. A fresh clutch of Drooks would fetch a sizable price in this system. All told, your salvage was quite pitiful, but now that you're awake again, I was hoping at least you might at least have some worth."

"I'm not for sale. You can't just take people and force them into slavery."

At this Captain Tür laughed, though the edge in his eyes was anything but friendly.

"I can do whatever I please. And now, what I please is to see how much value is in your pink hide."

Without warning he uttered a phrase and blasted Charlie with his slaap. Charlie tried to dodge, but he wasn't quick enough, the blast sending him flying across the small cell into the wall. It wasn't a powerful blow this time, but it still stung something fierce.

Charlie climbed back to his feet, a small trickle of blood running down his temple. He glared at the alien with undisguised hatred.

"Hmm. Resilient, at least. And decently quick on your feet. I may have use for you yet," Tür said, then walked out the door.

"Wait. What about the other crew? My shipmate, when can I see her?"

"She will be assessed further. Perhaps she has value as well. If not, at least she can gain us some coin as a meal for the Zomoki at the Buru Markets."

The green alien turned and was gone.

"What's the matter, Tuktuk?" Charlie asked, wiping the blood from his head. The cut was tiny, he felt, but the head was vascular, and it certainly did tend to bleed.

"Did you not hear? They are taking us to the Buru Markets on Gilea. There most are sold for hard labor."

"Well, then. We'll just have to see about getting ourselves free first."

CHAPTER TWENTY-FIVE

Interstellar travel aboard a "magic"-powered ship was not something Charlie ever thought he'd be a part of, but as they traveled farther into space, he found himself marveling at the strange technology, whatever it was. Call it magic, call it science, it didn't matter, so long as he didn't suffocate or freeze to death in the inky void.

As they distanced themselves from the verdant world on whose lone desert Charlie had managed to crash, he got a better look at the solar system in which they'd arrived so unexpectedly. It was exhilarating despite the ordeal.

Planets and their moons flew past as they moved at an incredible rate of speed. The suns at the center were a red dwarf and a yellow dwarf, each reasonably sized and locked in proximity by each other's pull.

The yellow sun burned brighter, but that was to be expected, as red dwarfs typically had far less mass than other stars, as well as a greatly lowered rate at which they used their hydrogen stores. The orange glow of the combined stars was beautiful, and it reached all the way to the farthest of the dozen planets Charlie had managed to count.

"We're moving so fast," he marveled. "Yet the ship doesn't even vibrate. There's not even a hum."

"Me tell you, Captain Tür have many Drook pushing ship. Very fast, but we go much more faster when out of system. Then we jump, most likely."

"Faster?"

"Oh, yes. Is only because of closeness of suns we cannot go full speed yet. Powers of them make Drooks weaker."

"Is this some sort of Kryptonite thing?" Charlie joked.

"What is Kiptoneet?"

"Nothing. Just a thing from home. There's a guy, and he has all these powers, but if he comes across a piece of his former planet, it saps his power."

"Oh, then no, is not Kiptoneet."

"Didn't think so."

"Is sun that lower power, not piece of planet."

"Seriously?"

"Drooks almost always from blue sun system. Blue make them develop push and pull powers more than others. That why blue systems first to be invaded. Drooks valuable. Very powerful, but not in war-make way."

Charlie found himself almost wanting to believe the odd creature's stories, at least part of them. Maybe there really were fuel sources in solar systems with blue stars. Blue giants burned at over twenty thousand Kelvin. Blue supergiants could hit forty. There was a theory that even hotter suns were out there, blasting out radiation so intense it even surpassed blue and ultraviolet, but they had never actually been observed.

Solar radiation. He mulled over the possibilities. *Well, I suppose certain materials could absorb the rays and be used as a fuel source. Earth digs up liquefied dinosaurs and radioactive rocks, after all. These Drooks are probably the ones who know how to refine it, is all.* He looked at the blue-skinned alien sharing his cell. *My guess is my buddy Tuktuk, here, is just some hick who believes every tall tale he's told.*

"Hey, Tuktuk. What about other kinds of stars?" he asked, wanting to test a theory. "Do they have powers too?"

"Oh, yes. Red suns are very, very old. Slow fire in them. Longevity. Them give deep, life fix power."

"Like healing?"

"Yes, and for to make things change shape."

"What, like turning a man into a dog?"

"Do not know what dog, but most powerful of vislas from red system could make change, yes."

"And you've seen this?"

"Seen? Of course not. Power men that strong no come to my world. But cousin have friend who know man who have turned into fooshkar when offended a visla."

"A friend of a friend knew a guy..." Charlie sighed. "Okay, cool. I see how it is. And I suppose yellow and white suns work differently as well."

"You learning fast, Charlee."

"Yeah, well, Mama didn't raise no fool."

Charlie lay back on his cot and stared at the strangely illuminated ceiling, pondering what he could possibly do in the depths of space to make the situation better.

Rika's locked up somewhere, we're in the middle of nowhere, and even if we could get free, I have absolutely no idea how to operate this tech. It's all based on mythology and bullshit, though I'd love to know the science behind it. These guys are light years ahead of us in propulsion tech and shielding design, he thought, looking out the invisible window. *For now, I guess I just watch and learn.*

He lay down on his bunk and closed his eyes, exhausted from his ordeals. Soon, he was drifting off into a shallow sleep.

CHAPTER TWENTY-SIX

"Charlee," Tuktuk said. "Charlee, you hear me?"

Charlie woke from his slumber. He was groggy, but the exhausted edge was gone, at least.

"Yeah, what's up?"

"Your head," Tuktuk said. "I look to help cleaning where you cut, but it already healing."

Charlie sat up and ran his fingers gently over the area he'd injured when Captain Tür flung him into the bulkhead.

"Huh, still working, I see."

"You *power* man?" Tuktuk asked, his eyes going wide on their stalks.

"Nah. It must be the water."

"Water? What you mean?"

"Oh, just when we were exploring that desert, there was this weird water, is all."

"There no water in Balamar Wasteland, Charlee. Everyone know this. Me tell you so."

"Then it must've been one hell of a mirage."

"Mirage?"

"Illusion. But this one was wet, and it made my skin heal."

Tuktuk gasped. "The *Flow*?"

"The what, now?"

"Me tell you, but you no listen. The legend. Gone when Visla Balamar destroyed. Him tap into something bigly, make to pull and store power in water. Them say that why he live so long. Why he so strong."

"Well, I don't know about anything like that," Charlie said.

This guy sure is worked up about this Flow stuff, he was musing just as the lights to their cell abruptly grew bright as Captain Tür and his right-hand man, Saur, stormed into the cell.

"You are to come with me," Tür demanded. If Charlie had any thoughts of resistance, the look on Saur's face made him think twice. He could heal fast, but probably not fast enough.

The two led him down a corridor. It was his first look at the ship outside his cell, and the rest of the craft was devoid of any signs of technology. Smooth walls, gently glowing ceilings, and doors that, while apparently open, made the collar around his neck tingle if he strayed too close.

A soft chanting came from one room, and as they passed it, Charlie saw a dozen men and women, all of them with a faint, glowing blue tint to their skin, sitting in a circle. They appeared to be in a trance as they repeated the same words over and over again.

Floramar Ivanti Necctu, he silently repeated to himself. *Not a very catchy tune.*

"Hey, what's with the kumbaya people?" Charlie asked, leaning in toward the door. He received a jolt to his collar that sent him sprawling to the floor, the clatter breaking the concentration of one of the chanting women.

The ship lurched a moment before she regained her composure and began chanting once more.

Okay, now that was weird.

"Do not do that again," Saur growled. "Ever."

"Okay, okay. Don't make fun of the sing-along. Got it."

They turned left, following a curving passage until they reached a small room with two seats and a table.

That looks an awful lot like an interrogation room, Charlie noted.

"You will sit," Captain Tür said.

Charlie obliged.

"Would you like refreshment?" Tür asked, sliding a cup of water in front of him. He watched Charlie glance at the beverage but not drink it with curiosity, then poured another and slid it in front of his prisoner, swapping cups and drinking deep.

"It is not poison, I assure you," he said. "I know the water provided our guests can sometimes be less-than refreshing."

"Oh, I'm a guest now?"

"Of course you are," Tür said. "We merely got off on the wrong foot. A misunderstanding. I'm sure you understand, it can be so tiring in the Balamar Wasteland. Even the best of us get cranky at times."

"If you call blasting me with that thing cranky, then yes. Very cranky."

"But we are rested now, and refreshed. A nice drink of water makes all the difference, does it not?"

"I suppose," Charlie replied. *These guys are all about water all of a sudden. They must've been eavesdropping in our cell. They heard everything, and this was so important to them they took me away from Tuktuk to talk about it. Which means—*

"You must have had a difficult time out there," Captain Tür continued in his nicest voice. "And with limited supplies, that could be difficult, I'm sure."

"It was," Charlie answered. "But we were making do."

"I noticed you dug holes in search of fluids. But tell me—"

Aw, hell. Here it comes.

"Tell me, Charlie. Did you happen to find water out in that desolate place?"

Captain Tür was doing his best to appear totally at ease.

Disinterested, even. But the underlying desire driving him was impossible to entirely conceal.

"Uh, well, there was some water out there," he said.

Tür almost jumped at the words. "Oh, how interesting," he managed to say in a relatively calm tone. "And was there anything *unusual* about this water?"

He knows. Not what we found, but something, Charlie realized. *I'm going to have to play this very carefully.*

He shrugged as nonchalantly as he could. "Well, it was kind of iridescent, I suppose. And when I got it on my skin, it made the sunburn go away."

"Sir! It has to be!" Saur blurted.

"Refrain from outbursts, please. You'll frighten our guest."

"Apologies, Captain."

The intimidating man turned back to Charlie. "I'm sorry for my lieutenant's enthusiasm. It's just such a rarity, finding a water source in the desert. It would make stopping there so much less of an ordeal. Tell me, could you show me where it was if we went back?"

"I could try to find it again, sure," Charlie said. "But it was a pretty vast desert, and it might be hard to--"

"Saur, turn us around--"

"But it wouldn't matter," Charlie continued. "It was only a tiny little puddle, and we drained it completely when we found it."

He could have sworn the captain took a little step back from him when he heard that.

"Oh, I see. And, did you drink that water?" Tür asked, his hand slowly creeping toward the pouch he kept his slaap in.

"Drink it? Oh no, of course not," he lied. "We didn't know if it was poison or not. I just got some on my skin when we were gathering it up, is all."

I hope he buys that, Charlie thought, while trying to maintain his best innocent face. The one he perfected as a boy when his mother would come home to find something disassembled on the floor. Of course, she *knew* it was him, and she was angry, but she humored her son. He had a knack for repairing things. He just had to take them apart first to figure out how they worked.

The green-hued alien's shoulders relaxed ever so slightly.

"Probably for the best. One should be careful in the wasteland," he said. "But you say you emptied the pool."

"Puddle, really. Not much there."

"Puddle, then. You filled containers?"

"Yeah, brought them back to camp to analyze and see if they were safe to drink."

"And did any of the others touch the waters?"

"Nope, just me," he said, casually omitting his impromptu swim with Rika in the water-filled cistern.

A smile began to grow on Captain Tür's face. "So they are still there."

He turned to Saur, ignoring his "guest."

"It splashed his skin. Saur, it would explain this one's resilience."

"He did not drink it, but even so, is it worth the risk?"

"He is weak. Unpowered. Just look," he said turning to Charlie. He realized the human was listening. *"San ovusk,"* he said with a dismissive wave of his hand.

Charlie suddenly found himself unable to understand the aliens.

So, that's the command to shut off the translation software. 'San ovusk.' That may come in handy, he thought, tucking away the alien word for another time. The two Tslavar continued to speak in front of him, but he couldn't make out a word of it.

"If I may speak freely, sir. If he came in contact with the water, he is unpredictable. It makes him a risky cargo. I believe it is best to get rid of him at the next planet."

"Perhaps. But first we return to Balamar Wasteland and collect the waters. Do you realize, Saur, that no one has seen a drop since the great war? It was thought destroyed. And he claims to have several containers full? We will be rich beyond our wildest dreams."

"I know, sir. But perhaps we should unload him first. Sell him to a Zomoki breeder for chum."

"I've made up my mind, Saur. I appreciate your counsel, as always, but this one may be of use to us yet." He turned to Charlie. *"Impezu ovusk."*

I understood those words. They sounded different than that other gibberish. It must be a base coding language. Not their native tongue. 'Impezu ovusk,' he silently repeated to himself.

"We are going to return to your ship to gather more salvage. Perhaps when we are there, we will even bring the water containers on board and complete the tests you were running for you. Where did you say you hid them?" Tür asked, buttery-smooth.

"Oh, I didn't hide them," Charlie replied. "They were sitting on the sled your goons dragged back to our camp when you ransacked the place. It'd be great to get some of our supplies, sure, but the water is long gone."

"Gone, you say?"

"Yeah, I saw it happen. Don't you remember?" Charlie asked, relishing what was coming next. "Actually, it was you who did it, if I remember correctly. You kicked the containers over before brutalizing my friends. It all drained out into the sand."

If the alien weren't already green, he would have turned that color.

"If legend is true, it doesn't evaporate," Saur said.

"But it certainly did soak down into the ground," Charlie muttered.

The slave ship's commander's shoulders slumped slightly.

"It is lost to the sands, Saur," Captain Tür said quietly. "It was there, right under our noses. The find of a lifetime. And we lost it. By our own hands, no less." He took one final glance at

Charlie, sighed, then turned to his aide. "We're done. Take him back."

The wiry alien roughly hauled Charlie to his feet and hauled him unceremoniously out of the room and tossed him back in his cell.

"That went well," Charlie said with a laugh, then settled into his bunk for a long flight to who-knew-where.

CHAPTER TWENTY-SEVEN

Two days of their deep space voyage through the blackness between solar systems had passed. Charlie couldn't even guess the rate of travel at which they were moving, but to pass from solar system to solar system so swiftly, he knew full well it was far beyond anything humanity could have dreamed of.

Tuktuk apparently had one thing right: Captain Tür had spared no expense on procuring enough Drooks to get his ship moving at ridiculous speed. Whatever the tech was they used to achieve that end, Charlie had to admit they certainly did their job well.

Apparently, there was an even faster way to travel. A warp, or jump, or something of that sort, but it was prohibitively expensive to use with any regularity, and the captain seemed to be all about saving his coin.

Charlie woke on the third day to a faint blue glow coming in through the window. At first he thought it was some sort of work light or display reflecting through the opening, but he didn't have the opportunity to look before the Tslavar toughs came and dragged him and Tuktuk out of their cell and brought them to the ship's store rooms.

It was only after the work boss had directed them to pick up the large containers fitted with shoulder straps and marched them out of the ship that Charlie realized the astonishing reality. They had landed.

"Holy shit," he gasped. "This is *another* world."

"You saying this as if never happen," Tuktuk said, craning his eyestalks to get a better look at the bustling marketplace they and the other slaves were being herded toward.

"It *doesn't* ever happen, Tuktuk. At least, not on my world."

"You people not have strong magic, do they, Charlee?"

"Enough with the magic talk, already. Let's just say we have different tech and leave it at that, okay?"

"Fine. Your tech-magic is no very good strong."

"Seriously?" Charlie grumbled.

The blue giant illuminating the sky was a marvel to behold. The intensely burning ball of helium within a hydrogen plasma envelope had once been a red dwarf before entering the blue giant phase of its dwindling life.

The sun's rays felt strange on Charlie's skin. Not as though it was burning, exactly, but the spectrum was simply so different from what he was accustomed, his body didn't know how to react.

Tuktuk, however, being a blue-skinned being, seemed to revel in the warm glow. His load almost seemed to lighten on his shoulders.

"You okay, man?" he asked his happy blue friend.

"Very okay. Feels good to have sun on my skin."

"I've never seen a blue sun before. I mean, not like this. They're incredibly rare, you know."

"Is weaker than my home, but feel good. And blue not rare, though power people from blue sun worlds are much rarer than others. Almost everyone just normal person, like Tuktuk. Just want to live our lives."

As if he heard their conversation, the Tslavar leading their procession shouted for them to keep up, then muttered a few words that Charlie couldn't quite hear. The resulting shock from his collar, however, he didn't miss.

"Ow!"

"Keep moving. If you fall behind again you will receive a much less gentle reminder."

"He calls that gentle?"

"For Tslavar, yes. We lucky he no make us shock until we no move. But, of course, they need us for to carrying supplies, and no moving make us bad for that job."

"Great, so the one thing that's our saving grace is we can carry stuff for them. Lovely."

Charlie made a point to stick with the other collar-wearing slaves as they moved through the marketplace. Despite his circumstances, he couldn't help but marvel at all that was going on around him.

This is incredible. Actual aliens. A shit-ton of them, too. Charlie only wished he were on this world as a tourist and not a beast of burden. There was so much to see, so many different species of aliens to discover, and Tuktuk was happy to be his guide.

"Hey, how about that one? What's that kind called?" Charlie asked, pointing at an extremely pale alien with thick black hair. The man was wiry and relaxed, yet radiated an unstated strength. He was wearing a light material in the heat of the blue sun, and what appeared to be small spinal ridges made a slight bumped impression through his tunic, the only real oddity to his otherwise humanoid appearance.

"Oh, him Wampeh. You no want get too close to Wampeh. They typically bad mood people," Tuktuk said, unconsciously veering farther from the pale alien.

"What's up, Tuk? You okay?" he asked, noting his friend's discomfort.

"Yes. Is just that some Wampeh sometimes have strange

people from them. Known to hurt power people for take their blood."

"I'm sorry, they what, now?"

"Is rare. Very, very rare, but them come from black hyper-giant place. That why they so pale. But power there very strange for different species. Even among other Wampeh, they anomaly. They sometimes power-taker."

It was then that Charlie noticed the Tslavar leading them through the marketplace had also observed the Wampeh, and his slaap was already on his hand, held casually, but ready for rapid deployment if needed.

Damn. The guy doesn't seem to be bothering anyone, but if it got him *spooked.* Charlie may have been a foreigner to the strange world, but he was not stupid.

"I have no idea how any of that works, my friend, but I'll take your word for it," he said, steering well clear of the pale man.

Apparently, the Wampeh had drawn the attention of others, and not scrutiny of the good kind, Charlie noted as they plunged into the depths of the tents and stalls. Everyone gave the intimidating man a wide berth, but wary eyes were continuously on him. It felt like one of those old movies where prison yard toughs circled the new guy, waiting to see who'd be the first to test his mettle.

Charlie turned and kept up with the others. Whatever befell the pale man would happen with or without him watching, and he had no desire of another zap from that collar for holding up the others. He looked back one final time, wondering what would happen to the man, then trotted off.

Not my problem.

CHAPTER TWENTY-EIGHT

The sights and smells––often incredible, though occasionally not in a good way––left Charlie feeling akin to a kid in a candy shop. Sure, he was a beast of burden at the moment, but he was actually walking through an alien bazaar. The first human ever to do so. The thought made him once again wonder where Rika was. She'd be amazed at the cacophonous marketplace.

It had been several days, and they still had not let him see her. When they headed back to the ship, he'd see if he could get any information from the other slaves in their little group. For now, however, he just tried to keep up.

They walked for another ten minutes or so, until the Tslavar leading them stopped outside a small tent. The front was open, and inside Charlie could see all manner of oddities carefully laid out on long tables. Contrary to the tent's outer appearance, the inside was the very picture of organization and cleanliness.

"You four, bring your packs here," the Tslavar said, gesturing to Charlie, Tuktuk, and a pair of faintly yellow men with long golden hair.

Ootaki, they were called. A species of humanoid from a yellow subdwarf system. According to Tuktuk, they held no powers themselves, at least, not that they could wield. It was their golden hair that was valued.

Apparently, it could hold a "magic" charge when woven and worn by a power user, though the Ootaki themselves couldn't use it. This led to a market for their slow-growing locks, typically woven into a bracelet or choker. The truly wealthy could afford a belt or scarf of the material, but growing it would take years, and a *lot* of Ootaki. That was something few could afford.

The rarest of all––with the exception of the first cut of Ootaki hair, which always held the most power potential but was typically made at an early age––were Ootaki locks given freely. Slaves could be forced to 'give' their hair, but it lacked the basic element of free will that imparted a many times greater power than when taken by force.

These guys have more superstitions than old Chinese men eating rhino horns to get bigger erections, he had thought as the ridiculous mythology was explained to him. *Whatever floats your boat, I guess. Not my galaxy.*

"There, on the table," the Tslavar commanded as they stepped into the tent.

Charlie and the others gratefully slid the containers from their shoulders, the straps holding the packs leaving angry indentations in their skin from the weight.

"Now wait outside, and do not wander," the elfin man said, muttering a quiet word for emphasis. *"Nari pa."*

A slight zap from their collars lit up their skin. The Tslavar smiled, his point made, then proceeded to open the containers and lay out the contents on the table. Most were things with no discernible purpose, but the old trader seemed quite interested in many of them.

A lot to learn, Charlie noted. *It's like space Bedouins, or something. Trading, moving on, trading some more.*

The Tslavar unceremoniously dumped a large device onto the table.

"Hey, that's from my ship!" Charlie blurted.

The Tslavar gave him a dirty look.

Oops.

"*Binari pa,*" the alien growled. The next thing Charlie knew, he was coming to his senses, flat on his back.

"Okay, now we know what *that* does," he muttered, making note of the voice-activated remote command. *One of these days, you'll be the one in the dog collar, and then, my pointy-eared friend, you'll learn an old Earth expression about payback being a bitch.*

"You not making he angry," Tuktuk said as the blue man helped Charlie to his feet.

"Note taken," he replied.

The slave trader and strange Bedouin-like vendor haggled a while, though the Tslavar had turned off the translation devices used by the slaves, so Charlie had no idea what they were saying. The device from Charlie's ship seemed to interest the man, though it was apparent neither knew what the hell it was.

I suppose I could tell them that's a waste water impeller for the toilets, but they did want me to be quiet, Charlie thought with a little chuckle. *Wouldn't want to anger Mr. Pointy Ears over there, now would I?*

Finally, the two came to an agreement, pressing the backs of their hands against each other in what he assumed served as a handshake in these parts.

"*Impezu Ovusk,*" the Tslavar said, reactivating their translation devices. "You, come here," he commanded the taller of the two Ootaki men.

"What is he doing?"

"Shh. Just watch," Tuktuk said.

The vendor's lackeys packed up an assortment of devices into the packs, but instead of loading one onto the Ootaki's back, the Tslavar made the man kneel, then drew a deadly sharp-looking blade from his belt.

"Tuktuk, what the hell is he doing?" Charlie asked with a

newfound urgency. He didn't know the man, but he couldn't just stand there and watch a murder. "We have to help him."

"It is okay," the other Ootaki said, laying a reassuring hand on Charlie's arm. "Aaran will not be harmed. We have been through this many times since the Tslavar captured us in our youth."

Charlie watched as the yellow-skinned man's gleaming hair was held up in the Tslavar's hand, then carefully cut at a precise length, leaving the man with a bob cut instead of flowing golden locks. Coin changed hands, and the Bedouin vendor grabbed the hair, quickly secreting it in a pouch, secure within his robes.

"You three, come here. We take these with us," the Tslavar ordered.

Soon they were back walking the marketplace, a bunch of random alien junk traded for a bunch of other random alien junk, at least to Charlie's uneducated eyes. That, and a piss-water pump from his ship, the sale of which amused him to no end. He just hoped they'd turn around soon. His pack was even heavier after the trade, and he looked forward to being free of its weight.

No such luck.

They walked and looped through the marketplace for nearly two more hours as the Tslavar conducted his business before he finally steered them back toward the waiting ship. Charlie didn't want to be in his cell, but as tired as he felt, he nearly did, if only for the comfort of his cot.

But that was before things went to shit.

CHAPTER TWENTY-NINE

The blue sun's effects were surprising, to say the least. While the color is normally associated with cool refreshment back on Earth, the reality of a blue giant was that it burned at nearly four times the intensity of Earth's own sun. Charlie knew this, of course, but that didn't make the strange, radiant heat any less oppressive.

I'm just lucky it's not a supergiant, he consoled himself. Those could actually double in heat yet again, though any planet in such close proximity would be reduced to ash.

The sweat trickling down his back made the straps of the pack he was muscling back to the ship dig in even more uncomfortably. The pack itself was plastered to his skin, the moisture causing the material of his shirt to make a wet suction cup smacking sound whenever the load would shift and pull from his back.

One small bit of fortune was the small, metal flask each of the, what? Servants? He hated to be called a slave. *Porter,* perhaps? Whatever the phrasing, each of the men laboring beneath a heavy load had one, full of water. It was the foul-tasting stuff, again, but it was something.

Charlie unclipped the flask from the strap of his pack and took a swig. It was almost empty, but they were close to the ship. At least he thought they were, though the twisting aisles of the marketplace could be confusing, to say the least.

He was about to clip the container to his pack once more when a running man barreled into him, nearly knocking him over, running into several others as well in his flight.

"Hey! Watch where you're going!" Charlie growled, then felt a new dampness on his arm. "Aw, man. He sweat on me. Gross," he grumbled. Then he realized what it was, just as the man fell to the ground, immobile.

Blood.

"Oh, shit."

Up ahead the sounds of a disturbance cut through the thickness of the crowd. Some rushed to see the conflict, but far more were running the other way. Charlie, feeling the natives likely knew best, turned to follow them.

Zap. Right in the neck.

"We keep going this way," the overseer said. "The ship's close by, and the captain wants us back."

"But it sounds like—"

"Nari Pa."

Zapped, again.

"Okay, okay. I get it. We go through the chaos," Charlie said. "But what about—?"

The Tslavar held up his hands. A slaap was slid over the fingers of *each* hand. Charlie didn't think much of it, but Tuktuk and the others' eyes went wide.

"Quiet. Nothing will happen to you. Now move."

He turned to his blue friend as they closed in on the sounds of violence. "Tuktuk, what's the deal? You all seemed legit scared when he showed his slaaps."

"Is not that he has slaap, Charlee. Is that he have *two* of them at once."

"That's bad?"

"Is very dangerous for user. Only very strong can handle it, and me know this man. He not strong. For him to wear two mean him scared. There be *very* bad things ahead."

"Well, shit," Charlie said. "Just my frikkin' luck."

The jostling crowd abruptly evaporated, and Charlie realized they'd stepped into the impromptu arena. A ring of onlookers. He glanced in all directions, quickly surveying the situation.

The pale Wampeh was there, his dark hair slick with sweat. All around him over a dozen aliens of a half-dozen different species lay on the ground. Charlie couldn't tell if they were dead, dying, or merely wounded, but he was impressed by the evidence of the man's skill regardless. But more were circling him. It was an incredibly uneven fight, and the pale man was unarmed, no less.

Making one hell of a good showing for an empty-handed brawl, he noted.

A pair of attackers rushed at the Wampeh. One bore a club with sharp spikes jutting from the end, the other a pair of blades. They attacked in unison. The one-at-a-time bullshit of martial arts movies was nowhere to be seen in this fight, and the pale man moved at a frantic clip to avoid the flashing weapons.

With a fast snap of his hands, he broke the smaller attacker's wrist, sending one of his knives flying. The man's other hand still bore a weapon, however, and the Wampeh took a slice to his arm as the injured assailant spun away.

No sooner had he done so than the spiked club swung through the space he'd just been standing. Any normal man would have been dead, impaled by the weighty instrument, but the pale fighter twisted in an almost impossible way, the spikes only grazing him as they passed.

Charlie found himself rooting for the underdog, while the

Tslavar tried to lead them in the safest route around the fighting men.

From the parting crowd, a young violet-hued man with bulging muscles raced toward the Wampeh's back, a large spear preceding his speeding body. The intended target was oblivious, too busy fending off the other two attackers.

If you asked him later, Charlie would say he didn't know what possessed him to do it, and that was the truth. In the spur of the moment, he saw what he considered a dirty trick, and his sense of fairness kicked in.

"Look out! Behind you!" he shouted, hurling his flask at the running spear-bearer.

Charlie had never been a very good shot, failing at basketball and baseball alike back on Earth, but even he was bound to make a good show once in a blue moon—or blue sun, as the case may be.

The metal clanged off the attacker's head, distracting him just as the Wampeh turned, the spear narrowly missing his torso.

The pale man's eyes flashed brightly, then locked on Charlie a moment.

Is that blood on his lips? He must be more injured than I thou—

A tiny flicker of a grin tugged the corner of the Wampeh's mouth, and Charlie suddenly felt *very* unsure if he'd done the right thing. This only compounded when the pale man turned back to face the three men attacking him.

He quickly parried a series of attacks with blinding speed, then rushed backward a dozen steps, creating space.

He's got to be getting tired. Why doesn't he just run?

A fourth man entered the fight, a faint purple glow forming in his hands as he joined the armed assailants. This, it seemed, was what the Wampeh was waiting for.

He stomped his right foot, and the men hesitated.

"Tuktuk, why did they stop?"

"They just realize what kind of Wampeh they dealing with," he replied. "No so easy. This one no victim. This one hunter," he said, then hurried even faster, trying to distance himself from the scene.

The last thing Charlie saw before his group dove back into the throngs of spectators was the Wampeh clapping his hands and barking a guttural word.

"Azkokta!" he growled, and for a brief instant, a near-black blast of power flew from his outstretched hands.

The four men fell as if pummeled by a giant hammer, their bodies broken and twisted. Only the man with the purple glow had survived, but only just. The Wampeh reached down and hauled him to his feet, pulling his head to the side, exposing his neck as he leaned closer.

Charlie didn't see what happened next as the porters all rushed into the crowd, hurrying back to the ship. But he didn't need to see. He couldn't believe it, but he *knew* what had happened.

That wasn't his own blood on his lips, he realized with horror. "Wampeh," he softly said. "Sounds an awful lot like Vampire."

CHAPTER THIRTY

"Jesus, what the hell did I just see?" Charlie asked as the group of load-bearing men neared the ship.

"Was Wampeh. I tell you this already," Tuktuk replied.

"I know, but his face—was he *drinking their blood*?"

Tuktuk shuddered. "I tell you, very, very rare, but some Wampeh take power from others."

"So they drink blood. Holy shit. He's a motherfucking space vampire."

"No, no, you mistake."

"Oh, thank God," Charlie said with a sigh. "I was about to get really freaked out there for a minute."

"No, of course not. Would be impossible have a society if everyone drink everyone's blood."

"Okay, it must have just been the light or something."

"Oh, no. Now *that* one. *Him* drink blood."

"But you said—"

"I say *very* rare. I see him show true self when power man come into fight. Wampeh was holding back until then. Waiting for to see if stronger man come."

"And when he did, he took his power?"

"Yes. Good, Charlee, you learn."

Charlie was floored. A tricky vampiric alien who sucked magical energy out of others and was a pretty badass fighter regardless. And he had just stuck his nose in the creature's business.

Way to go, Charlie, he groaned to himself, adjusting the load on his back, wondering if the whole thing might just come back to bite him in the ass, the dark humor of which was not lost on him.

He increased his pace along with the others as their Tslavar guard forced them along at a brutal clip despite the size of their loads.

"Hey, Tuktuk, why doesn't anyone use wheels around here?" he asked as the straps dug into his shoulders. "I mean, it's nice to be out of the ship and all, but it would be more efficient, and a whole lot easier than us carrying all of this on our backs."

"We carry because Captain Tür no want spend for Drook-made sled."

"So, no flying carts. Gotcha."

"No. But telling me, what is wheels?"

"Round things that make carts move. You know, *wheels.*"

Tuktuk just looked at him with a confused expression. Then Charlie took a closer look around. He didn't know how he hadn't noticed before. No one had a traditional cart. Even the rabble of the marketplace were using strange, floating conveyances, powered by what Tuktuk called magic.

"No one has ever invented the wheel around here?"

"I still no understand what is wheel, Charlie."

"Well, I'll be," he said, an odd little grin spreading across his face. "I may just get to reinvent the wheel after all."

Charlie moved close to the other porter slaves as they lined up to carry their loads into the ship, quietly asking each of them if they'd seen another human, like him. A female.

He knew Rika was there somewhere. He had seen her taken

aboard the ship when he was first captured, but there'd been no sign since then.

"Oh, the new female," a stocky, short fellow with enormous hands and deep red skin said. "I've seen her. Keep her alone, they do. A cell at the far end of the ship near the rear storage. Heard her cries, I did. Late at night it was. But a tough one, she is. The Tslavars seem frustrated when they come from her cell."

Charlie was both distressed and relieved. She was still on the ship, but they were mistreating her, likely as they had done to him. But the red man was right, Rika was a tough one, and even if she hadn't bathed in the healing waters, she'd be a tough nut to crack.

"Where is your water container?" the Tslavar logging their packs into the ship's stores asked, snapping him out of his thoughts.

"Um, there was a fight back on the way here. It must have come off with all the people running."

"It is your responsibility. You lost a piece of your kit," he said, slapping Charlie across the face. "You will have reduced rations until the cost of it is recuperated. Captain Tür may opt for additional punishment as well. Now get moving with the others, and go back to your cell."

Great. Now I'm in the shit for helping a vampire. A space *vampire, no less.* The others had heard the Tslavar, and Charlie knew at least a few had seen what he did, but despite not knowing him, none, it seemed, were motivated to rat him out. The hatred of the Tslavars was a bond of mutual suffering they all shared.

Sweaty and tired, Charlie flopped onto his cot as soon as they reached their cell and fell asleep almost immediately.

It had been a several-day voyage to the next world on the Tslavar's agenda, and oddly enough, Charlie found himself getting used to the fact that he was traveling farther and faster than any human ever had. In fact, in a mere week, he had been to more worlds than his entire species, save Rika, with whom he was currently tied.

I bet she'll try to make a side deal to let her set foot on one more planet than I do, just to mess with me, Charlie mused with a little chuckle. He was missing his friend, and hoped they'd allow him to see her soon.

That wish would be granted the following day.

They landed on a planet called Oksan. The entire clutch of male labor from the ship was called out and lined up along its hull.

"Listen up. We are on a tight schedule, so we will be moving quickly to gather our loads. The payment has already been made, so you will be traveling light on the way there. I expect you to be fast. If you fall behind and cause delay, there will be consequences."

The Tslavar leading them was a different one than the other day, and Charlie had a feeling this one would be less sparing with the use of the shock collars, by the look of him.

"Okay, stay close," he said, then took off at a quick jog.

The line of slaves kept pace, unburdened by heavy loads, and Charlie almost found himself enjoying the chance to see another marketplace without the distraction of a massive weight crushing down on his back.

"No, this not Buru Markets," Tuktuk had told them when they disembarked. "This much nicer place. Buru is very tough. No want to be sold off there. Many bad people come to Buru. This market is largest on entire planet of Oksan. Good place to being."

"I suppose I'll be grateful for that, then. And they already made their transaction, so we'll only be carrying stuff one way. I tell ya, though, I really need to show you guys wheels. It'll change your life."

In short time, they arrived at a large and pristine tent at the center of the market. Obviously, someone of wealth owned it.

"Mester Binslar," the elfin man said, bowing low in greeting to the ebony-skinned man with happy eyes who stepped out to greet him.

"Dolomir, it is good to see you. You look well. Out for a bit of exercise, I see."

"Yes, Mester Binslar, the run feels good. A nice stretch for my legs after many days in the void."

"Yes, the voyage would be difficult in a craft as small as yours."

Small? I wonder what this guy is used to flying around in, Charlie wondered, but wisely kept his mouth shut.

Mester Binslar walked through the ranks of men, studying each of them. "And you seem to have very good stock this visit," he said, squeezing the bicep of another blue-skinned Bantoon. His appearance was very similar to Tuktuk, though the other fellow was far stockier. "Perhaps I shall discuss an additional transaction with your captain after I've spoken with my wife. She is always on the lookout for good help, you know."

"I will tell Captain Tür to expect your emissary, then."

"Oh, why so formal, Dolomir? I'll just contact him myself over my skree," he said, tapping a small, highly decorated device resting in a little holster on his waist.

"Tuktuk. What's a skree?" Charlie whispered.

"Is for talking with person far away."

"Ah. Alien comms tech. Got it. Thanks."

The dark-skinned man gave the ranks of porters another appraising glance, then walked back toward his tent. "My man will load your cargo around back. I'll send one of my conveyances to your ship to gather my payment shortly."

"Thank you, Mester Binslar," their overseer said, turning to the group. "You heard the man. Everyone around back. Load your packs full. We are doing this in just two trips if we can. Out and back. You got it? Now, let's go."

Charlie and the others were given massive amounts to carry, but his legs were growing stronger with every load he was forced to haul, and the walk back really wasn't so bad under the mild yellow sun.

Not a bad day, he thought, satisfied at a relatively uneventful morning.

But that would soon change.

CHAPTER THIRTY-ONE

The work team had been given a break after unloading their cargo in the Tslavar ship's hold. The smaller team of less-muscular slaves then stowed the goods and supplies in their various storage compartments within Captain Tür's vessel.

Charlie drank deeply from the water dispenser mounted near the wall. All of the men were drenched in sweat after laboring under such heavy weights, the lines of their pack straps showing clearly on their skin in the form of indented, red grooves where the load pulled hardest.

It was during this unexpected downtime that Charlie had an inspiration.

The doors seem to be on voice command, and those hand thingies the guards are wearing appear to be the remote access devices. I've never seen them push any buttons, so it must be strictly voice-activated. I wonder... Charlie stared at the guard lazily pacing the cargo hold while the slave laborers regained their strength for the next run.

Worth a try, he thought, rising to his feet and walking more toward the guard than the water vessel.

"Charlee, what are you doing?" Tuktuk hissed.

Charlie flashed his friend a little smile and kept moving. The doors on either end were sealed with the usual force field, but if the guard was facing the right way, maybe, just maybe, the device he wore was directional as well as voice activated.

With an exaggerated flourish, Charlie tripped and fell, catching himself on the Tslavar guard's arm on the way down.

"*Faramano,*" he said, uttering the word he'd heard the Tslavars say into the wrist-worn device in a hushed voice as he struggled back to his feet.

The guard yanked his arm away and shoved Charlie roughly. "Watch where you're walking."

"Yes, of course. I'm sorry. I was just feeling lightheaded from the work. May I please get some more water?"

"Of course, idiot. Captain Tür wants all of his laborers to drink well. You're of no use to him unconscious." He thought a moment. "Well, we could sell your worthless body for chum, I suppose," he added with a laugh.

"No, I'm fine. Really. Just some water, please."

"All right. Go on, then."

Charlie caught Tuktuk's look and gave a little smile as he crossed to the water dispenser. The guard had turned and wandered off the other direction, bored and pacing as he waited for orders to head out once again. This was his chance.

Slowly, Charlie filled a cup of water, then casually strolled toward the door the voice device had been pointing at when he had surreptitiously grabbed onto it. He nonchalantly turned his back to the door, surveying the men in the room with him.

All were in their own worlds, relaxing and gathering strength before the next heavy load would burden their backs. Perfect for his needs.

With a tentative hand, he reached behind him, feeling for the odd resistance of the force field tech the Tslavars used in place of actual doors. Rather than coming up against a barrier, however, his hand passed right through. The door was deactivated.

Holy shit, it actually worked! So, the device just needs either proximity or contact. Or maybe both. Whatever. From now on, I'm memorizing every damn command phrase I hear.

The realization he might have just found a way out of this place filled him with a welcome rush of adrenaline that now coursed through his body.

Only Tuktuk was looking, shaking his head slightly, as if trying to will Charlie not to be so foolish. But his human friend had a mission, and with a smile and a wink, he stepped through the door and was gone.

No telling how long I have before they notice. Better be quick, Charlie reminded himself as he raced down the corridors, careful not to rush around corners without first taking a stealthy peek, lest he bump into one of the crew.

Fortunately, their arrival on this world seemed to be like the others he had observed in his brief captivity, and despite being aliens—to him, anyway—the captain's men were like any other sailors finally on dry land. Shore leave was their only interest as soon as the craft settled into port, and they made haste in heading to town to drink, fight, and whatever other sort of mischief they might get up to, leaving but a skeleton crew on board.

They said Rika was being kept in the rear of the ship near the storage areas, Charlie noted as he oriented himself within the ship's corridors.

This was an area he was unfamiliar with, the slaves only being ferried in and out by the same bland corridor every time their brawn was needed. But this was something different. More ornate, the lines of the walls gently sloping, rather than possessing the harsher geometry of the steerage compartments he was accustomed to.

The lighting was even better. A full-spectrum light with a

warm, comforting glow illuminated the length of the ship as far as he could see.

"Right. That's the way," he muttered, taking off at a careful trot toward the back of the ship. "Rika!" he hissed as he passed what appeared to be slave quarters. The accommodations were far nicer than what he'd experienced, he noted. "Rika!" he called again, careful to keep his voice low.

A form shuffled toward the force field door and appraised him with curious eyes. A Drook, and an older one at that. He still didn't understand how these odd people managed to command the ship's drive systems, but now was not the time to play twenty questions.

"Hey, I'm looking for a woman. Human, like me. Have you seen her?"

The man looked at him a long moment, then turned and headed back into the comfort of his confines.

"Hey, I asked you a question. Hey!"

"He doesn't talk much," a young woman's voice said from behind him.

Charlie spun to find a thin woman, barely more than a girl, really, with a shaved head. Her skin was the palest shade of yellow. If he didn't know better, he might have thought she was merely jaundiced and not an Ootaki.

"You're Ootaki," he said, stating the obvious.

"Yes."

"I haven't seen you before. With the others, I mean."

"No, you wouldn't have," she said, mindlessly rubbing her hand across her bald head. "Captain Tür bought me from my former master just the other day."

"So you're new here too. And I guess he cut off your hair for himself before tossing you in there."

"Oh, no. I was attacked while fetching my master's dinner. Bad men pinned me down and did terrible things to me."

Charlie felt a knot forming in his stomach. "I'm so sorry they hurt you. If you need to talk about it with––"

"Hurt? I was not harmed. I'd have preferred that, to be honest. But no, these men were not after my body."

He knew what they had done, and from what Tuktuk had said about the Ootaki, losing their hair was a Samson-like tragedy under even the best circumstances. To have it taken by force? He could only imagine her distress.

"But it'll grow back, right? Given time."

The girl tried to smile, but the effort did not ring true.

"I appreciate the kindness," she said. "I am Neema."

"I'm Charlie. I'd shake your hand, but the force field door would make that an unpleasant experience."

"What is a force field?"

"You know, the energy field blocking the door. What's keeping you in and me out."

"Oh, the spell, you mean."

"People keep saying that. It's gotta be some sort of glitch in the translation software."

"What is software?"

"You know, the device that translates our languages so we can communicate."

"Ah, the *Ovusk* spell. Yes, Captain Tür was kind enough to give me a fairly powerful one when he brought me aboard. It has made my assimilation to my new home much easier."

There she goes with that magic talk again, he silently lamented. "Well, listen, Neema. I'm trying to find my friend, and unlike you, I'm afraid they are hurting her in far worse ways than shearing her hair."

The woman shuddered at the thought. "That is terrible."

"Yes, it is. But I was told she is being held somewhere around here, toward the rear of the ship. Have you seen another human, like me? A woman with dark hair. Her name is Rika, and she's kind of hard to miss."

"She is large?"

"What? No. Just her personality greatly outsizes her frame is all."

The Ootaki girl leaned against the doorway, making sure to stay clear of the force field. "I'm sorry, Charlie, but I have not seen another of your kind since my arrival."

"Damn," Charlie groaned.

"But I have heard a female voice crying out from far down the passageway. I could not give you an accurate location other than that it came from that way," she said, pointing down the hall.

"That's more than I had to go on a minute ago," he said, turning to leave. "Thanks. And I hope your hair grows back soon."

Neema smiled as her new acquaintance took off at a quick trot down the corridor.

He passed numerous rooms, each containing one of the Drooks that piloted the ship. Their accommodations were relatively lush compared to what he was used to, but then, if they were the ones making the ship go, it made sense Captain Tür would afford them some degree of luxury.

A happy crew is a productive crew, after all.

He was just musing that thought when he ran smack into a wiry wall of muscle exiting a room into the passageway.

"Shit, I'm sorry. I was just––"

Captain Tür's angry gaze froze him in place. Charlie had the briefest of moments where he glanced the half-clothed Drook woman in the room the man had just left. Then the captain spoke.

"*Nari pa.*"

Charlie felt the shock from his collar surge through his body. At least it was a minor one, he realized, taking minor consolation in the fact he hadn't been zapped into unconsciousness again. Captain Tür hauled him roughly to his feet and dragged him forcefully back to the cargo hold.

He threw Charlie through the open door, sending him sprawling to the floor.

The guard was stunned. Apparently he hadn't noticed his missing charge.

"Sir, I can explain—"

Captain Tür was having none of that, the swift violence of his hands quickly knocking the man to the ground. He didn't stop there. Several brutal kicks soon followed, until a thin trickle of blood dripped from the guard's lip.

"Get up," Tür growled.

The guard complied, doing his best to stand straight after his beating.

"You are on punishment rations for the next month. And no shore leave until I deem you worthy of my trust. Is that clear?"

"Yes, Captain," the man said, chided.

"Now go fetch me Targan. He will take your place."

"As you wish," the guard said, then raced off to get his replacement.

Tür turned to Charlie.

"And as for you," he said, looming over the human like a wrathful storm. "I believe you to have value, and I do not wish to diminish that value by harming my merchandise."

Thank God, Charlie thought, breathing a little sigh of relief.

"However."

Shit.

"Disobedience is not tolerated among my slaves. From time to time an example must be made to reinforce that point. Today, you shall help me remind the others why it is best not to test my resolve."

Charlie didn't hear much beyond *"Uzri ha,"* which flung him across the room, followed by *"Bandu,"* which delivered an invisible blow, knocking the wind out of him. From that point, it was one voice command followed by another, knocking him around, shocking him, and making him regret ever searching for his friend.

When the beating was over, Charlie's body showed no outward signs of the punishment, but the pain was there, quite real despite the lack of bruising.

"Now, gather your wits and prepare for your next load. You will do as you are told, and you will carry my merchandise efficiently and quickly. If you do not, you will see what I am like when *truly* upset."

Captain Tür strolled out of the room, casting a glaring eye upon all of his slaves, daring any one of them to question his will. The replacement guard came rushing in just as he was about to leave.

"You are to take these porters to fetch the rest of my goods."

"I see. Yes, sir. I will take them as soon as their rest cycle is complete."

"No. I am cutting it short. The rest period is over. Leave now, and keep an eye on that one," he said, pointing to Charlie.

"Yes, sir," the man said. "You heard him. Get moving, you worthless beasts!"

Charlie felt it was going to be a very long day.

CHAPTER THIRTY-TWO

"Cargo to the hold," the Tslavar standing at the ship's entrance said, directing the line of slave porters where to carry their loads. Given the number of them slowly filing in, Charlie realized it might take a while.

"Hey, check out that ride," he said, gesturing to the approaching vehicle, hovering on a golden cushion of air. Judging by the details and ornate design, there was little guess as to who had sent the large flying conveyance.

"Is Mester Binslar's," Tuktuk said.

"I kinda gathered as much. Looks like he's sent someone to pick up his money."

"Oh, him no take money for goods. Him trader. Barter. Binslar and Tür make trade."

"For all of this stuff?" he said, motioning to the loads on their backs. "I can't help but think maybe this Binslar guy is getting the short end of the stick, here. I mean, we don't seem to have that much good stuff left to trade, from what I've been able to see in the hold."

Captain Tür himself walked out of the ship to greet Mester

Binslar's emissary, giving the man a little bow, but nothing so deep as to give the impression of diminished rank.

"Off to the side, all of you," the Tslavar overseer commanded. "Make room. Clear the path."

It was then that Charlie saw what payment the two men had agreed upon. One by one, a slow walking procession of slaves, all clothed in basic white tunics, were being led from the ship. When they reached the two men, they would stop. Captain Tür would then hold his slaap over their collar and say, *"Ngthiri oolama tangopeh,"* at which point the collar would snap open.

The emissary would then quickly fasten his own collar in its place. Equally slender, but decorated with a different set of odd runic-looking symbols. The slave would then climb into the waiting vehicle to await departure to their new home.

"Rika!" Charlie shouted out, spying his friend in the line of sold slaves.

She didn't seem to notice him, eyes fixed forward as she trudged along with the others.

"Rika! Over here!"

"Quiet, Charlee. You make to draw attentions."

"That's my friend," he replied, dropping his load and rushing to her side. "Rika, what's wrong? It's Charlie," he said, grabbing her by the arms. She turned her head and looked at him with blank eyes. "Oh, God, what have they done to you?"

He had just a moment to notice the healing burn marks on her temples. Signs of whatever torture they had inflicted upon her. Then he heard a phrase–– *"Binari Pa,"*––and all went black.

Charlie woke up in his cell sometime later, his ears ringing and a faint buzzing in his head. Sitting up was not an option. At least, not for a minute or two, while he regained his senses.

"My mouth tastes like metal," he griped. "And I smell toast. Oh man, am I having a stroke?"

"What is stroke?" Tuktuk asked, eating a slice of toasted bread from his meal tray.

"Whew, thank God," Charlie said. Then things got really clear really fast. "Wait a minute. I saw Rika."

"Yes, your friend. I asking about her for you. She sold to Mester Binslar along with others. She to be house servant for his daughter."

"Rika's second-in-command of a goddamn spaceship. She's not some kid's nursemaid."

"But is good, Charlee. She selled to good family. Many other places, bad man try to buy. Especially in Buru Markets. Very bad mens in Buru Markets. Do bad things."

"Even so, she's no slave, Tuk. But when I saw her, it was like she was drugged, you know? She was different. They did something to her."

A troubled expression spread across Tuktuk's face. "You friend, she very strong."

"Yes, I know that."

"So strong, them no able to put compliance spell on her mind. One that make her cooperate. I hear that *all* spells not work on her. Is *very* unusual."

It was probably that water we drank, Charlie thought. *If it made me less susceptible to their weapons, then it must have done the same for her,* he realized, wisely keeping that bit of information to himself, as he was sure now that the Tslavar's were listening in to their conversations.

"What did they do to her, Tuktuk? Will she be okay?"

"Them do old magic on her. Crude. Very harming."

Charlie's mind flashed to the burn scars on her temples. The water had helped her heal faster, but there were marks nevertheless. A great violence must have been done against her.

"They burned her," he said, quietly.

"Yes. Them burn into the head, right through the side parts.

Make brain part for rebellion no more. It not been used for many, many years. Considered too risky."

"They were worried they'd hurt someone? I find that hard to believe."

"Oh, not about hurting. They worry they lose value if too much damage being made."

"So she might get better?"

"No," Tuktuk said somberly. "No one ever get better from this."

But not everyone drank and swam in the stuff that we did, so if anyone might have a chance...

He hoped he was right, but deep down, he knew that wouldn't be the case. The brain was a different thing entirely than a cut or broken bone. Tissue might heal, but knowledge, memories, they were lost.

Rika had been lobotomized. She was gone.

CHAPTER THIRTY-THREE

Things had taken a dark turn for the stranded spaceman from Earth.

He ate joylessly. He slept when he could. But in the days since his discovery of Rika's horrible fate, Charlie had found himself sliding deeper and deeper into depression.

She wasn't just his acting captain, she was also his friend. And with her gone from the ship––in mind as well as body–– Charlie was now effectively the only human in the entire freak show galaxy. He was alone.

"You need eat, Charlee," Tuktuk said, offering him a bowl of the Tslavar's gruel come mealtime. "Is no good you no eat. Work very hard. Body need food."

He turned and looked at his blue friend with red-rimmed eyes. He was a space-age Robinson Crusoe, just like Rika had said, only his man Friday happened to be blue.

Okay, maybe he wasn't *entirely* alone, but blue men with eyes on stalks aside, he was isolated. On top of that, he was still the only one of his species in the entire galaxy––at least with an unlobotomized brain––so despite having a friend to talk to, his feeling of isolation was much the same.

Tuktuk lightly shook the bowl at him and nudged him with an elbow.

"Eat."

Charlie finally did as he was asked, though the food was even more flavorless than usual. Everything seemed to have lost that shade of novelty. Before, it had been tough, and he had strived for freedom and to return home, but at least he could appreciate the wondrous sights he was seeing. Things no human had ever seen before.

Now it was joyless. The different worlds and their novel species variants were noted, of course. The technical side of his mind couldn't *not* keep track of those things. But he took no real pleasure in it. Where he would previously lie in his bunk at the end of the day, replaying the things he had seen and experienced, now he dreamed of home. Of returning to Earth. But that wouldn't be happening. Not so long as he was a slave.

I'm getting out of here, he decided several nights later. *Whatever it takes, I'm getting back to the ship. Hitchhike, steal a transport, whatever. I'm getting back and figuring out how we got here and how I can get back. Best case, I get home. Worst case, I die trying.*

He shut his eyes and lay in bed awake a long time, gears churning in his head while he worked on a plan for escape.

As Charlie ran frantically through the winding streets of a strange world a few days later––the low buildings and vendors' tents illuminated by a setting blue sun––he couldn't help but note just how far his meticulous plans had flown out the window. *This* was not what he had in mind. Far from it, in fact, but given the circumstances, it would have to suffice.

The actual plan had been a distant cry from his current flight.

Charlie had simply planned to overpower one of the guards

upon planetfall and take his slaap remote control voice-command thingy to access the rest of the ship's doors and systems. At least, that was how he hoped the device worked.

From there, he'd use the voice commands he'd memorized to open doors. Ideally, he'd be able to free and gather up the Drooks who piloted the vessel, though he was still rather unclear exactly how that all worked. He would gather them in the passageway undetected, where he would make them his proposition.

That was the easy part.

Somewhat more difficult, he would need to convince them to follow him, a fellow slave, off the ship. They were Captain Tür's property, just like he was, but given their more comfortable accommodations, a few might be reluctant to trade certainty of a decent life for the risk associated with flight.

It was a chance he'd have to take. If he could just get them to come with him to a neighboring ship in port, they could then offer their services in exchange for passage. Apparently, they were in high demand for that sort of thing.

Charlie felt a bit dirty at the thought of offering up the Drook slaves for even more labor, just as they'd been used by Tür, but if their means of escape was trading work for freedom, he thought they'd agree it was worth it, at least for a short while. Perhaps they could even help power their new ship for a few weeks to not only pay their way, but also save the captain enough money to buy her silence.

He'd have to move fast once he took out the guard. There was no telling exactly how many of the Tslavar crew would still be on board, but if he made his move when Captain Tür was off the ship on one of his commerce negotiations, he would at least stand a chance.

One lingering concern was that he wasn't sure exactly how far-reaching the restraint collar's power might be. Ultimately, he figured if he could get out of the city, or even better, off-world before the slave driver noted his absence, he'd probably be far enough away. Even if not, securing passage on a new ship was bound to get him out of range soon enough.

If that were the case, he'd just have to suck up the pain until they were clear. It would hurt like a bitch, but if that was the price of freedom, he'd gladly pay it.

After that, it would just be a matter of securing passage back to the planet he was taken from—if he could figure out exactly where that was. In any case, it would be better than life as a slave. All he had to do was carefully follow his plans, and things should work out okay.

CHAPTER THIRTY-FOUR

Sprinting around a corner, knocking a vendor flying as he ran, Charlie scanned the streets in a panic. Things were *not* working out okay.

Shit, where can I—? There!

He bolted for a narrow alleyway spied between two food stalls.

If he couldn't escape the planet, he could at least get out of sight. Maybe he would get lucky and Captain Tür would give up if he couldn't find him. Maybe he wouldn't use his collar to shock him to death.

Maybe.

Things were definitely not going the way he had planned.

Charlie had watched and waited for a half-dozen stops as they hopped from port to port, trading and loading supplies. For whatever reason, Captain Tür rarely left the ship since Charlie's failed attempt at rescuing Rika. Whether it was coincidence or him sensing some plot in the air, he wasn't certain, but it was looking like he'd have to wait a long time to execute his plan.

When opportunity presented itself in the form of one of the other porter slaves snapping his leg when his load broke free, falling on top of him as he struggled for balance, Charlie seized it.

"You all, keep moving," the Tslavar guard who had been taking up the rear grumbled as he assessed the fallen asset.

That's all they were to the elfin-looking slave traders. Goods. Assets. Not men with minds of their own. Charlie half-wondered if they wouldn't just shoot the poor man like a horse with a broken leg.

"I said, keep moving," the Tslavar growled as he pulled a skree from his hip and called ahead to his comrade leading the procession. "Dolomir, one of the porters injured himself."

"Fatal?" Charlie heard the voice ask over the communications device.

"No, just a broken leg. A cheap fix."

"All right, stay there with our goods. I will bring a fresh porter back for you once we drop this load. Keep up!" he heard the man shout over the skree device as well as faintly from the front of their procession.

This meant the Tslavar would no longer be guarding the rear, and there was still quite a long way to go back to the ship. If ever an opportunity would present itself, this was it. His original plan was not bearing fruit, but the wise man knows when to seize upon an alternative.

Charlie kept walking, careful to maintain the image of just another porter heading to the ship. But he slowed his pace slightly.

"Charlee, are you okay? You walk slow."

"I'm fine, Tuk. Just a cramp in my leg. I'll catch up with you in a bit. I just need to stretch it as I walk."

"Okay. Seeing you at ship."

Tuktuk continued on, steady in his pace, while Charlie kept dropping farther and farther back in the group, until he was the last man in line. He looked around. No one was paying them any heed. Why would they? Just another slave carrying goods to one of the many ships that came and went every day. In a galaxy where slavery was commonplace, Charlie might as well have been invisible.

Invisible except for the golden band around his neck marking him as Captain Tür's property.

Okay, Charlie, this is it. Now or never.

He halted his walk, making a show of stretching the leg he'd been pretending was cramping for the past several minutes, then moved to the side of the roadway and took off his towering load of goods. His shoulders reveled in the relief as the weight was lifted.

As casually as he could, he took a few steps away from his pack.

Then a few more.

A minute later he was quickly walking away down an adjacent street. The style of the low buildings and the assortment of vendors who had set up shop out front of them were familiar. He actually knew where he was, relatively speaking. The ship was behind him, the layout of the neighborhood providing an easy guide away from his mobile prison.

As the seconds ticked past, Charlie felt panic welling up in his chest. What if they came looking for him sooner than he expected? What if they found him before he could secure a ship to stow away on, or at least find a way to take the collar off?

He picked up his pace, rushing as he walked along the smaller side street he had veered onto. He felt as if everyone was looking at him, but he knew that was just his nerves.

Then he noticed a gray-skinned man *definitely* watching him with interest.

"Shit!" he hissed, and quickly ducked into the passing throng.

He rushed around the corner, knocking into a vendor as he ran. The small alley just up ahead beckoned to him, and he beelined his way to it as quickly as he could, tucking into the relative safety of its dim length.

"That's the one," a gruff voice said from the shadows.

"You sure?"

"Yeah. Look at the collar."

Two stocky grayish men stepped into the light. One bore a long scar tracing down from his forehead to his shoulder. Whatever had caused the injury apparently hadn't cut deep enough to penetrate his thick skull, but it had left him what was surely a very painful parting gift.

The other was a bit younger in appearance, but his eyes were equally hard. Charlie noted that both men had multiple pouches in a bandolier configuration strapped to their chests. Pouches, and weapons. Each also wore a slaap on their hand.

"Hey, fellas. I'm just heading to meet my friends."

"Friends, he says," the scarred man said. "You hear that, Looral?"

"I did, Marban. But we know that slaves don't have friends."

Charlie began backing out of the alleyway. "Hey, I don't want any trouble."

"Well, I'm sorry to be the one to tell you, but it looks like you've found it," the one called Marban said. "Nothing personal," he added, as he raised his slaap. *"Dispanus."*

Charlie hit the ground, stunned and unable to move. This was something different than his collar's shock spell. Something quite different, but equally unpleasant in its own way. He was paralyzed, trapped in his own body.

Not *quite* paralyzed, he realized as he wiggled his toes in his boots.

A new shadow joined them in the alleyway. Towering. Big. Looming.

"Did you get his cargo?" Looral asked.

"Yup," the man replied, moving closer.

"Good catch," Looral said approvingly. "A slave deserter. And not just the man, but his load as well. The captain will reward us all handsomely, I wager."

Charlie saw it wasn't a huge man who had joined them, but rather, another grayish thug. The one who had been watching him on the street. And he was carrying Charlie's discarded pack.

Charlie moved a little bit, the stun slightly wearing off.

"Better hurry up and do it, before his owner activates the collar," Looral said.

"On it," Marban replied.

The scarred man bent over Charlie and dug in one of his chest pouches, pulling out what appeared to be a thin strip of a filthy and well-worn yellow bandana. He made fast work with his hands, wrapping the cloth around Charlie's collar and securing the ends with a simple knot.

"*Firmus,*" he said, locking the knot in place. "Okay, it's secured. Now help me pick him up. We'd best get out of here and back to the ship before his owners come looking. Captain Saramin is going to be pleased with our new prize."

The shift was sudden, but Charlie realized the men's speech had abruptly changed to gibberish. Whatever they had done to his collar had also shorted out his translator, it seemed.

"Hit him one more time. We don't want the spell to wear off before we're back on the ship."

"*Dispanus,*" Marban said once more, and this time Charlie found he couldn't even move a toe.

Things went dark when the men draped a filthy cloth over his body and hefted him between them, balancing his paralyzed form on their shoulders. Bouncing uncomfortably as they walked, his new captors then carried him off to whatever fresh hell awaited him.

This, Charlie lamented, *was not what I had planned.*

CHAPTER THIRTY-FIVE

The stench of feces and old urine was sharp in the air. A pungent mix that was enough to make Charlie's stomach churn. Fortunately, he hadn't eaten in some time, so there was nothing in his belly should it decide to empty itself.

Though disgusted at the thought, he noted his gag reflex calming down as he became accustomed to the stench. It was still awful, but at least his stomach had settled into a low rumble rather than a tumultuous roar.

As the stun effects wore off, Charlie found himself gradually able to move his head side to side as his limbs slowly unfroze. This afforded him a proper look at his new confines. They appeared to be almost as bad as they smelled.

When he was taken aboard his captors' ship, he had been roughly deposited on an uncomfortable bunk in what appeared to be a single-occupant cell. At least he had that to be grateful for. No telling what horrors might befall a man unable to move to defend himself in a place like this. The smell, he learned, was coming from a waste-encrusted toilet of sorts halfway embedded in the bulkhead.

It seemed as though the device was originally designed to

retract into the wall when not in use, similar to those aboard the Tslavar vessel, but years of wear and abuse had rendered it stuck, unable to properly function. The result was an ever-present whiff of the ship's waste disposal system wafting up from the pipes.

There had been no such issue on Captain Tür's ship. Waste, once carried from the cell, was evaporated by some system that had continuously left Charlie wondering how the hell the thing worked. Tuktuk kept saying it was just a waste-removal spell, but Charlie knew there had to be a mechanism at play. He just needed to find it, was all.

No such questions sprang forth in his new confines. The problem with the broken toilet was pretty obvious. Lighting in the cell was dim, and the walls were covered in a uniform layer of grime deposited over years of rotating occupants. The only clean things at all were the window and doorway, but as Charlie had learned on the Tslavar ship, those were force fields, and nothing clung to them, leaving them perfectly clear.

When sensation had finally returned to his body enough to sit up without risking falling face-first onto the filthy floor, he propped himself up as best he could to better assess his situation.

The impromptu escape had taken a terrible turn, that much was obvious. He recalled the man carrying his pack, joining the others in the dark alleyway.

Stupid, Charlie, he chided himself. *Stupid, stupid, stupid. Making yourself a target like that. Should have hidden the damn thing and not just dropped it and run.* He let out a low sigh. *Well, too late to change it now. So, let's see. What do we know about this new mess I'm in?*

He thought back to the sounds that had rushed past his ears after he had been stunned as the men carried his inert body, bundled up in a filthy tarp of some sort.

The marketplace near the space port, he was sure of it. The

same din of voices was unmistakable, though they were now speaking gibberish rather than English. His translator had been disabled when he was captured and they wrapped that filthy rag around his collar, he recalled.

Must be some sort of Faraday material blocking the signal from Captain Tür's remote device, he posited.

Charlie tugged at the simple knot holding the material in place, but it wouldn't budge in the slightest. It didn't seem like a terribly tight knot, but he figured he was still weak from the stun blast that had taken him down.

Neat trick, that, he noted appreciatively. *'Dispanus,' I think it was. Going to have to add that to my list.*

A few times humming the little mnemonic tune that helped him remember the remote-control words and the new one was firmly fixed in his mental catalog. Now if only he one day had the opportunity to use it.

Charlie looked out the window and saw nothing but the distant stars. That meant they were definitely on a ship, not in some terrestrial hovel. A ship taking him farther and farther from Captain Tür and his slave drivers.

Voices filled the air, growing closer by the second. An angry man, and what sounded like pleading, though he couldn't make out the words.

Another gray man wearing a weapons harness full of all sorts of deadly-looking implements passed his cell, dragging a bloody Drook by a chain affixed around his neck. Unlike Charlie, the man did not seem to be wearing a control band of any sort.

The captor yanked the sobbing man roughly, making him trip over his own feet. The Drook fell to the deck, receiving a swift kick for his trouble. The words the angry gray man uttered were unintelligible, but the tone was not. "Get up, or else," sounded about right to Charlie.

Judging by the hurried manner the fallen man scrambled back to his feet, he surmised he was correct in that assessment.

The two men passed from his field of view, but a moment later Charlie heard the unmistakable sound of a body thrown onto a bunk, followed by quiet sobs as the man's tormentor stalked back down the corridor the way he came.

Ah, so that must be my new neighbor, he realized as he settled back on his bunk and closed his eyes.

His body was still wobbly from whatever they had done to him, and a cat nap would be restorative. The whimpers floating to his cell faded as he drifted off into a much-needed slumber.

"Get up when Captain Saramin is present!"

Charlie lurched awake, heart racing from the unexpected yelling in his cell.

"I said on your feet, scum!" the burly man standing in the doorway said. Charlie recognized him by the scar running down his face.

Marban, he thought to himself. Another stood just outside the door. The captain. *Wait a minute. How am I understanding him?* he wondered, fingers going instinctively to the band around his neck.

Captain Tür's band was still there, wrapped tightly in the signal-blocking material, but his fingers brushed against another band, thinner but familiar in its feel. They had put a new collar on him while he slept.

The captain watched the gears turning in his mind and smiled.

"You've figured it out, haven't you?" he asked.

"Figured what?"

"Why you can understand us now."

"You activated a new collar."

"That's just a restraint. But yes, I have wasted some precious power granting you a translation spell for the moment. All new crew need to know what is expected of them. First things first. Step outside."

Charlie did as he was told, stepping into the corridor, where an older man with thinning hair and a milky eye stood waiting.

"Now stand still while Terranz measures your potential."

"My what?"

"Shut up, scum. Captain said to stand still, so you do just that," Marban growled.

Charlie wisely kept quiet while the odd man waved his hands over him while chanting a series of quiet words.

"Almost none," he finally said. "There's a trace of *something*, but even that is not worth note."

The captain sighed. "Well, I'd hoped for another magic user, but I guess another unpowered bit of fodder will still come in handy." He pulled a signet ring from one of the pouches strapped across his chest. "Come closer."

Charlie did, and Captain Saramin muttered a few words, then pressed the ring to the skin just in front of his left ear. Charlie felt a jolt of pain and pulled back, earning him a slap from Marban.

"Hold still."

The captain grabbed him roughly by the chin and turned his head to better examine the new mark embedded in Charlie's skin.

"Looks good," he commented, then turned and walked away without giving the human another thought.

"Wait, what does all of this mean?" Charlie asked.

"It means you're part of the crew now," Marban said. "And you will be expected to pull your own weight when the time comes. Pay attention. Learn. Be useful. If you can do those things, you will prove your worth and eventually move up in the ranks. If not, your time here may well be limited."

"You'll let me go?"

At that Marban showed a rare flash of mirth as he laughed heartily. "Oh, my dear fool. That's priceless. Let you go. Oh, thank you. I needed a good laugh." He wiped the tears of amusement from his eyes and shoved Charlie back into his cell.

"Now, rest up. You'll be fed with the others in a little while. And remember what I said. Pay attention. You seem like you have a bit more brain in that head than most we pick up. I suggest you put it to good use. You'll live longer that way. Or not. The choice is yours."

Marban held up his slaap. *"Yakkan,"* he said, sealing Charlie in once more. He then followed with another. *"San ovusk."*

I know that one, Charlie realized. *He turned off my translation unit. Bastard.*

"Hey, what am I supposed to be doing on this ship? You said I'm crew, but what's my job?"

Marban smiled with amusement, then uttered a lengthy stream of gibberish, likely explaining the details of the work he was expected to do, fully aware the newcomer had no idea what he was saying. He laughed, amused with himself, then walked off, leaving Charlie alone to ponder the new developments in his already tenuous situation.

CHAPTER THIRTY-SIX

In the days following his capture and imprisonment aboard the strange, and filthy, new ship, Charlie was granted access to common areas with other captive crew during mealtimes. Each of the men, he noted, wore the same slender band around their neck. A few also sported a filtering wrap around their previous owner's control collar, but the vast majority wore just the lone device.

The guards watching them all sported similar versions of the same bandolier-style pouches, though their underlying attire varied from man to man. Also, it appeared the crew of the ship was not limited to the grayish, human-looking species he had first encountered, though they were a definite majority. Many other races were represented, and to his eye, all appeared to have one thing in common once you got past the whole alien thing. Each had a basic humanoid shape, and an apparent degree of fitness.

Studying them quickly became a pastime during meals as he forced himself to eat the unappealing slop scooped onto his metal tray.

Nutrition is nutrition, and you can't escape if you don't have the energy for it, he reminded himself at every mealtime. It didn't make the food taste any better, but his determination to obtain his freedom at least helped him keep it down.

Somehow, he had actually managed to escape his original captors, and in so doing, had found himself in an even worse situation. Charlie only hoped his next chance at freedom wouldn't turn out so bad.

The chow hall was packed wall-to-wall, and Captain Saramin had apparently not wanted to spring for sound-deadening tech to keep the noise to a dull roar. As a result, the cacophony of a dozen disparate languages was a rumbling buzz in his ears at mealtimes, and while the dozens of other captives had languages in common with one another, Charlie was the lone human. A situation that he had accepted would not be changing.

Amid the whirl of voices, trying to single out any particular language from the mix was almost impossible.

Almost.

One language, however, stood out. The 'magic' words used to control the voice-activated devices aboard the ship. Those had a very distinct sound to them. And for whatever reason, those words sounded the same whether he had a translation unit functioning or not. It was something of a boon for Charlie, as his previous captors had been careful with such language around their slaves, whereas this new bunch were either careless, or simply didn't give a damn.

In either case, he paid close attention whenever one of those strange words filtered its way to his ears, eager to learn a new voice command. His sing-song trick to remember them all was getting longer and more complicated, so he started breaking them into chunks of words memorized to a short tune, rather than one long one. He didn't know what every one of the commands did, exactly, but the basic gist was enough for now.

The pattern continued for over a week, the ship hopping

from planet to planet, various men captured and collared on each world, forced to become part of the reluctant crew. In short order, the craft seemed to have reached capacity, with nearly all of the cells now occupied by new residents.

Despite his dislike of the gruel fed to them, Charlie had more than once been forced to fend off a would-be bully trying to muscle in on his food. It was like a prison yard in that respect, he reasoned. Everyone trying to be top dog and take advantage of those weaker than them.

Of course, the guards held the real power, and if anyone *really* acted up, they'd be put down with one of a number of voice commands, each of which Charlie took care to note.

Interestingly, it didn't seem as though the slaap had to be pointed at the intended target to function. A design quirk that caught Charlie's attention. If it worked that way, somehow sussing out the command speaker's intention, then perhaps he didn't even need to be facing the doors he wanted to open when speaking the command. Should he ever get his hands on one of the devices, that is.

After their meals, the ship's grimy galley crew would perform the most basic of cleanups. Not so much cleaning the space as moving dirt from one place to another. It was for this reason Charlie selected the same seat at every meal. He would, without fail, wipe down his section of table and seat every time he ate, and after a full week, though the surface was still discolored with age, his little zone had at least finally ceased feeling sticky to the touch.

The Tslavar ship he had first been imprisoned on was so much different by comparison. With the aesthetic choices of Captain Tür and his demand for cleanliness, one area where expense was not spared was maintenance and upkeep. *His* ship was spotless, and a mess was not tolerated.

Captain Saramin's craft, on the other hand, was the polar opposite. Spills were mopped up, but only just. And the waste-removal systems were horrid in most of the cells from what Charlie could see every time they walked the corridor to the galley.

It was an odd realization to have, but Charlie found himself actually missing the comparatively clean imprisonment he suffered while Captain Tür's captive. And there he was afforded a translator at all times, though it may have been a poor-quality one.

As his captivity stretched on, much to Charlie's pleasant surprise, he found himself learning the different sounds of each species' language, even picking up a few words of several of them overheard in passing. He still felt like an alienated foreigner surrounded by locals, but it was a start.

The other prisoners, while lacking translators, at least were not the lone representative of their species on board and tended to congregate in groups of their own kind, sticking with those they could easily understand. It made sense, of course, but it was also a problem in Charlie's eyes. A weakness they could address, but wouldn't make the effort.

They're all so dependent on their translation tech that they don't even bother to learn one another's language. What if there were a power outage or something and the translators stopped functioning on their worlds? They'd be stuck, unable to communicate with people other than their own, just like we all are here.

It was a familiar bit of tribalism he had witnessed back on Earth throughout his life. Even while building the *Asbrú* he had seen the different disciplines fracture from the others, grouping together even during meals and social break time, regardless of whom they worked with.

Engineers ate with engineers. Flight crew ate with flight crew. Lab techs, and ground support, and the list went on and on. All the while, Charlie observed them from his own little nook away from the others. It wasn't so much that he was a loner, nor that he was antisocial or a crippling introvert. He was simply engrossed in his work, and the constant gossip and chatter was more of a distraction than a pleasing social engagement for him.

He liked to call himself an extroverted introvert during his military service, gregarious when need be, but opting to skip the more raucous outings with the others. That followed into his civilian training and subsequent jobs. Sure, he enjoyed a good party as much as the next guy, but if his head was busy working a problem, the stimulation of a loud room could quickly become overstimulation, leaving him exhausted.

But he could smile and put on a social face as good as the next person if need be. He just chose to avoid those situations when possible, opting to focus on the current task his engineering mind was running through at high speed. He could always step away from the work if he wanted to socialize and be a part of the club. Suddenly, he realized perhaps he had been taking that for granted.

He was the lone human aboard a ship full of aliens, none of whom he could understand or communicate with, light years from his home world, and without a soul to talk to. On top of that, even if his translator device was functional, he doubted he had much to talk about with this new band of ruffians and thugs.

Didn't think I'd miss the guy, but what I wouldn't give to have to listen to another one of Tuktuk's little pep talks right about now.

Charlie's thoughts were interrupted by a klaxon alarm and the lights within the ship turning a reddish hue. The guards jumped to their feet and began yelling, either forgetting, or simply not caring, that the men couldn't understand what they were saying. The arm gestures were clear enough, though. 'Come this way' the waves urged them.

The assembled captives hurried from the galley, leaving behind a mess of food and trays. Someone would have to clean it later, but that didn't seem to be a priority at the moment. With great haste, they were hustled back into their cells, only a handful kept out and directed to follow the guards once the others were locked up safe and sound.

A great shudder rumbled through the ship as it sharply increased speed.

Oh, please don't let me die in a filthy, shit-stained cell in deep space, Charlie muttered to the walls. The craft bucked, then pulled some serious Gs, which meant a particularly harsh maneuver given the lack of gravity in space. Charlie saw spots before his eyes when the pressure suddenly let up. He strained his ears but heard nothing. Thumps on the hull, however, he could feel. But what the unsettling rumbles meant, he could only guess.

CHAPTER THIRTY-SEVEN

Rough hands shoved and herded the prisoners down the dank corridor. The faint smell of smoke, ozone, and something else Charlie couldn't quite place, wafted to their noses, growing stronger as they walked.

"What's going on?" the lone human asked the guard nearest him.

The man just looked at him and motioned to keep moving. It seemed the translators worked for the ship's crew just fine, so it was only the prisoners who couldn't understand one another.

A blast of air suddenly created a vacuum, sucking the men off their feet en masse before abruptly ceasing. They crawled off of one another and stood up, the guards urging them forward. The smells, Charlie noted, had vanished momentarily.

What the hell was that? he wondered. *Felt scarily like a decompression.*

In space, that was always a concern. And with no EVA suit to protect him from the vacuum, unconsciousness and death would find him in minutes if that were the case. It was cold in space, sure, but asphyxiation would kill him long before he froze, since the only way to lose heat in a vacuum is by radiant cooling, and that would take over a half hour, if not longer.

Of course, there was also the painful possibility of death by embolism as the air in your lungs tried to exit your body to the no-pressure environment of space. You wouldn't explode, as old-timey science fiction loved to depict, but your lungs could rupture, and, if not, deadly air bubbles could be forced into your bloodstream, causing a most painful demise.

Whatever had just happened, however, had been rectified almost immediately. For that, he was grateful. Captivity may have been bad, but death was a far worse option.

The smell of sweat and tangy smoke grew strong as the group of men were guided down a corridor Charlie had never seen before. Up ahead a door was open. A door that seemed to lead to what appeared to be an adjacent vessel. A large ship of some type that was floating no more than ten meters from their craft.

The lead guard stepped right out the door into the seeming void, but he kept walking. Some invisible force was creating a walkway from one ship to the other. He turned and motioned for the others to stop gawking and follow him. The prisoners did as they were bade and made their way, single-file, out of the open door.

"I'm stepping into space," Charlie muttered, experiencing what no human ever had.

An unprotected spacewalk. Technically, he was surrounded by an invisible protective bubble, but the effect of the experience was that of being in space with no suit yet no death.

"Okay, maybe this isn't entirely bad."

A roughly human-looking man ran screaming toward them from the far end, rushing toward the open hole in the other ship's hull.

"*Hokta!*" one of his gray captors shouted, aiming his slaap at the approaching man.

He crumpled to the ground in a pile. Dead.

From within the other ship, a pair of prisoners Charlie recognized from mealtime rushed into the force field passageway and dragged the man's body back into the other ship, clearing the way for the arriving reinforcements.

And reinforcements was what they were, he realized as he unglued his eyes from the door ahead of him and let himself take in the scene before him.

The ship they were boarding was riddled with holes, the hull torn open in several areas where the boarding parties had breached it. Bodies floated in the space nearby where force fields were not in use, either sucked out or thrown out before the openings had been sealed with the strange alien tech.

Bandolier-wearing men from his own ship were fighting their way through the other craft, he could see through the jagged holes. Fighting with not only slaaps, but also short swords, knives, and clubs. They were taking over the crippled vessel by force.

"Pirates," he gasped as realization set in. "I've been shanghaied by fucking alien space pirates."

The guard nearest him glanced at his astonished face and laughed, then pushed him through the hole and aboard the other ship.

The craft was beautiful. Or, it had been before the invading force had taken it by storm. The walls were smooth and flowing, a distinct lack of sharp angles making it feel almost organic, as if it had been grown and not built. The lighting was warm and bright. That is, in the parts that were not shattered and ruined by the force of the invaders' weapons.

The smoke he had smelled had come from one of those attacks. A handful of bodies lay smoldering against a dented wall, where some form of weapon had ended their resistance with brutal efficiency. But that would have been the initial boarding. Now that the pirates were scrambling through all levels of the ship, they'd have to switch to close-quarter tactics.

At least, that's what he assumed they would do. But Earth was a long, long way away, and he had no idea how these strange men would carry out their plunder.

The prisoners were quickly herded down a long corridor, the lights flickering from unknown damage to their power source. Bodies littered the way, and the cries of close battle could clearly be heard. And it was getting closer.

Charlie nearly jumped back when they rounded a curved section and came across an enormous hole in the hull. He instinctively grabbed for anything he could to not be sucked out into space, drawing laughter from his captors.

Of course. It's sealed, he realized as he forced his hands to release their grip on the bent section of a doorway he had latched onto in his panic. *But this isn't like the others. This is bigger. And it blew from the inside out,* he noted as he studied the blast pattern.

He'd seen similar-looking damage on vessels back home, typically caused by a fatal decompression inside. This, however, appeared intentional.

They tried to scuttle the ship, he realized. *That was the pressure change we felt. They knew they were losing and tried to take us with them.*

The nearest guard shoved him along. No time for sightseeing. They had work to do, apparently, but what it was, he didn't know. His feet slipped momentarily on the slick ground, but he knew better than to look. They'd been passing bodies for a while, and that wasn't spilled water he was walking through. The hole had sucked out most of the dead and dying before the pirates could seal it, but the blood remained.

He only hoped the force field the pirates had put in place was strong enough to hold. If not, his next spacewalk wouldn't be as pleasant as his first.

CHAPTER THIRTY-EIGHT

The bright sound of clashing blades rang out as the prisoner work group entered a large cargo area. As fighting raged all around them, the screams of men dying hung in the air. They had finally caught up to the main body of the invading force, the pirate ship's top fighters. Men who were dismantling the resisting crew with brutal speed and efficiency.

Damn, these guys are good, Charlie gasped as he watched the pirates clash with the defenders.

Using their strange force weapons was a no-go in the tight confines of the battleground. Too high a likelihood of hitting your own men. So it was short swords, clubs, and knives doing the work, and despite their grubby appearances, his captors were very skilled in their profession.

The scarred man called Marban he recognized immediately. His other captors were there as well, working as a team, the three of them fighting twice their number but quickly reducing those odds as their blades flashed through the opposing crew members. Spinning and dodging, the trio covered each other's flanks while they engaged the enemy, denying them an exposed target.

They'd spent a long time fighting by one another's side. That was obvious by the fluid way they fought, each of them instinctively knowing where his friends were, the three working as a single, deadly unit, slashing and stabbing their way through those foolish enough to stand against them.

The other pirates fought similarly, utilizing unconventional techniques that seemed to confuse their opponents. They fought hard, and they fought dirty, because at the end of the day, survival was what they cared about. Honor had no place in this battleground.

Charlie and his fellow prisoners were guided to the area of the cargo hold that had already been cleared. Bodies littered the ground. Most wore the sleek uniform of the invaded ship, though a few of the pirate crewmen lay dead or dying as well. The guards paid them no heed.

"Impezu Ovusk," the pirate leading his motley band of men said, activating the prisoners' translators. "Okay, you lot, listen up. You are to carry as much as you are capable of back to the *Rixana*."

So, that's the name of the ship, he noted. A rare piece of information in a captivity that had been devoid of any.

The pirate gestured to the fighting. "Steer clear of the fight. If you get injured, you will be left behind. Now load up and form a line. You only stop when I tell you, and that's not happening until there's nothing left to take. You got that? Now, get moving," he growled, then canceled out their translation once more with a single command. *"San ovusk."*

All the chatter and yelling assailing his ears immediately switched back to gibberish.

What if my old collar weren't dampened? Maybe that one's translator still works, Charlie wondered as he shouldered an enormous load.

The pirate guard took note of the particularly heavy burden he had lifted and nodded approvingly, then gestured for him to get moving back to their ship. Apparently his brief stint carrying heavy loads as a porter slave for Captain Tür was doing him some good in his new circumstances. The one good thing to come from that whole ordeal. Of course, he wondered why they didn't deactivate the artificial gravity to make it easier to transport their captured goods, but Charlie wisely kept that thought to himself.

He kept his head down and silently followed the others back to their ship, returning via a parallel force field connector, allowing a more efficient transfer of plundered goods. Say what you will about the pirates' hygiene and living conditions, they were very efficient at what they did.

Charlie followed the others to the *Rixana's* cargo hold and handed off his load, then turned back to gather the next batch. As he walked, he tugged at the fabric covering his collar. The knot had not once budged, but for some reason, this time it seemed to be slightly more pliant to his efforts.

Whatever they did to this, it seems to be wearing off. Maybe too much other stuff going on that it's interfering with it.

He continued to pull at it as he walked back to gather his next two loads, the knot gradually easing, if only fractionally. He had stumbled over a body on the second trip, drawing the laughter of the guards as he scrambled back to his feet. What they hadn't seen was the small piece of sharp debris he had hidden in his hand, snatched up from the blood-soaked ground. Charlie hid it carefully in his clothes, then continued his labors. There would be time to put it to good use later. This was not the moment.

On his third trip back to the captured ship, the sounds of combat had finally ceased. The vessel, he gauged, was a loss, given the amount of damage done to it, both by the invading pirates as well as its own crew as they desperately tried to scuttle the ship. Victorious, the pirates were ransacking the craft for smaller valuables, while the prisoners carried the cargo back to their own craft. Fortunately, that task was near completion.

What he saw as he gathered up his final load was that instead of fighting, a line of a dozen bloodied crewmen now sat kneeling in a line in the nearly empty cargo bay.

Captain Saramin paced in front of them, placing a thin collar on those he deemed worth keeping, executing those he found too weak or injured to be of use.

Several Drook captives were also present, he noted, and they all still wore the collars of their ship. Captain Saramin pulled a wounded man who was wearing a more ornate uniform than the others to his feet and led him to the captive Drooks.

Probably an officer of some sort, he guessed.

They exchanged words, and after what appeared to be a very lopsided negotiation, the wounded man was handed a thin golden band. Captain Saramin never took his hand off of it, though. He merely allowed the man to touch it.

Charlie couldn't hear the words spoken from that distance, but he saw the effects of them when the Drooks' collars briefly glowed, then clicked open, falling to the deck. The injured man had said the release phrase.

That's why they used that Faraday material, or whatever it is, on my collar, Charlie realized. *They don't have the release word for it.*

Captain Saramin smiled and affixed his own collars to the Drooks, then turned back to the wounded man. They exchanged a few more words. The officer gestured to the remaining captives. Captain Saramin nodded his agreement and uttered something to his crew. The injured were not killed, but rather, pulled to their feet and assisted to the *Rixana*.

The captain and officer watched them leave. Saramin paused a moment, until the spared men were gone, then in one swift motion, drove a dagger straight into the man's heart, killing him instantly.

CHAPTER THIRTY-NINE

Back in his cell, Charlie washed the traces of blood from his garments in his crusty sink. He'd tried to steer clear of the more gruesome battlegrounds, but even so, he had brushed against a few bloody bulkheads during his labors.

Charlie put his fingers to work on the knot again as he replayed the brutality he had witnessed in his head over and over, pulling at the material tightly bound to his collar as he did.

"So, this is a pirate ship," he muttered. "I guess that explains a lot, actually. So now I'm part of a pirate crew, I guess."

He sat quietly a moment as his sore fingers tugged and pulled at the stubborn knot. It had moved, but only a fractional amount. The shard of sharp debris he had secreted back to his quarters had proven useless against the seemingly delicate fabric. Every time he attempted to cut or fray it, he would receive a hand-numbing shock for his trouble.

He tried wrapping the end of the shard with his shirt, but that provided no insulation. Pretty much whatever he did, if he attempted to cut the material, he would wind up on his ass, and facing a ten-minute wait before sensation would return to his hand. It took three attempts and their subsequent unpleasant results before he finally decided maybe it would be better to forego the piece of metal in favor of his hands. His fingers ached from it, but at least they were functional.

"If I could just get this stupid thing off, maybe I could understand what's going on around here," he grumbled to himself. Quietly, though. His translator may not have been functioning, but that didn't mean the guards' units weren't operational.

Not long thereafter, the new captives were ushered down the corridor to their waiting cells. Fresh bodies to replace the ones lost in battle. Charlie realized that was probably an ongoing pattern aboard the ship. Fight, capture, dispose of the dead, and replace them with new fodder. And that's what he was. Fodder.

Not if I can help it.

For the better part of the next hour, Charlie worked at the knot around his neck with raw fingertips. Amazingly, after all of that effort, it seemed his labors might finally pay off.

A shadow filled his doorway, and before he could pull the loosened knot free, Marban opened the force field door and dragged him out to join the others queueing up for mealtime. The scarred man then moved on to the next cell before finally rounding up the newest captives.

It was interesting to watch now that he had a different understanding of the dynamics at play. The men who had been aboard the longest were served first, while the newest ate last. It was Alpha Dog territory, but with prisoners instead of canines. It made sense, though. Those who had survived long enough to start at the front of the line had earned that privilege. This was not an easy life.

Charlie gathered up his plate of slop and made his way to his favorite seat, eating by himself as he always did, unable to communicate with the others. The food was unappetizing, as usual, but he had learned to force it down quickly, before his tongue and brain could argue over whether or not it belonged in his belly. The weak tea they were served actually wasn't all that bad, and he found it washed the residual taste from his mouth quite effectively.

The new prisoners were a mess of bruises and other minor injuries, the walking wounded staring wide-eyed at their new surroundings. Unlike Charlie, they knew full-well what fate had befallen them. In that, at least, they were starting their imprisonment with a slight advantage. Even so, without translators to aid in their conversations, they, too, split into the usual divisions based on species and tongue.

The pirate crew seemed to have thinned a fair amount, but as he scanned the men's faces, Charlie realized he knew several of them. That, in and of itself, was to be expected after his time aboard the ship, but the faces he saw wearing pirate garb had just the other day been prisoners like him.

The most senior ones, he realized. *They're fleshing out their ranks with the ones who have been aboard the longest. The ones who are institutionalized and used to this life.*

Charlie took new interest in the newly minted pirates, picking at the knotted material wrapped around his collar absentmindedly as he noted the attire and accoutrements afforded the newest members of the crew.

They had the same basic uniform as the others. Plain clothing, often what they had already been wearing as prisoners, but now with bandolier pouches strapped across their chests and heavier boots on their feet. They also bore arms, though from what he could see, the new pirates didn't seem to be sporting any of the power-wielding items. Only knives, clubs, and short swords adorned their belts.

Of course, he didn't know what was in those pouches, but he suspected they would become filled with tools and plunder over time as they proved their worth.

A strange sensation tingled across his fingertips as the knotted fabric around his neck slowly slid loose in his grip.

Holy shit. I finally got it! he silently exclaimed. *And it's about time. Now let's see if that translator is still functional.*

Charlie undid the rest of the knot, then pulled the fabric free from his collar. For a moment, he felt nothing. Then the collar Captain Saramin had put on him touched his original one, and the world ignited in pain.

Charlie dropped to the filthy floor, writhing in agony as the collars fought for control of his body, shocking him mercilessly in the process. He thought he heard one of the guards swearing, but with the pain, he couldn't be sure if it was his old collar translating, or if it was all in his mind. What he did know was he would do anything to make the pain stop.

Marban crouched over him, an annoyed look spread across his scarred face.

"Idiot. Now look what you've done."

There it was. Confirmation. He could understand.

The old collar still worked. Charlie almost felt a flash of excitement at the realization, if not for the continuous charge shocking his neck.

Just as when he had first captured him, Marban took the fabric Charlie had worked free and quickly wrapped it around Captain Tür's collar once again.

The pain ceased nearly immediately once the knot was affixed, held firm with whatever verbal command he mumbled. Then his world went black.

CHAPTER FORTY

Once again, Charlie woke to the horrid stench of his cell, only this time he had one hell of a whopper of a headache to go along with the nasal assault. He couldn't tell what time it was—the lighting in the corridor outside was always the same—but they had been kind enough to dim the light in his cell at least.

Judging by how relatively quiet it was, he figured it was either night time or mealtime, but during the latter, there was always a bit of a ruckus.

So, night it was. Or more appropriately, 'off shift,' seeing as night and day were relative in the constant dark of space.

"Oh, my aching neck," he grumbled as he pushed up to his elbow.

Apparently, it wasn't only his head that had taken a bit of abuse. The dueling control collars had made his body their battlefield, and ground zero for them both was just above his collarbones.

He gingerly touched the skin beneath the two bands, expecting blisters at the very least, but was pleasantly surprised to find everything intact. Whatever the collars had done, it had spared his dermis from harm.

"Score one for Charlie," he said with a little chuckle. "But hot damn, I feel like I was on the wrong end of a pissed-off rodeo bull."

He moved a little more, forcing himself to sit upright though his body wanted nothing more than to just lie there and melt into the lumpy bunk. Some of the soreness, he reckoned, was from the heavy loads he had carried from the ruined ship. Lots of twists and turns, stepping over bodies and debris to and from the *Rixana*. He'd been without any form of exercise for days, so it was logical that the unusual motions would leave him sporting a bit more lactic acid in his muscles than usual.

He didn't want to do it, but Charlie knew he needed to move if he didn't want that preliminary ache to develop into full-on delayed onset muscle soreness. The pirate crew were somewhat unpredictable, and he didn't want his reactions slowed around them if at all possible.

With a grunt of discomfort, Charlie forced himself up to his feet.

"Great, now I'm making the old man groan," he lamented. "Not good, Charlie. Don't let yourself sound like a geezer. Get your shit together."

He peered at the door, realizing he was talking to himself out loud.

And use your inside voice, for fuck's sake. No telling if they're listening to everything you say, he silently reminded himself as he began to move and stretch. *There we go. Get the blood flowing. Loosen everything up.*

For ten minutes he limbered his tight muscles, working up to pushups on the edge of his bunk––no way he wanted his hands on that floor––and bodyweight squats, his knees and hips popping as fluid in the joints gradually worked free. Gravity, at least, would help with that.

It was something mentioned briefly in training before their ill-fated mission, and as the one with medic training, though from many years past, Charlie found the detail interesting and quite logical. In space—or a low-to zero-G environment—the body had a hard time healing from trauma.

While fluids normally worked their way out of a wounded area on Earth, without proper gravity, they would pool and stay put. This not only made swelling last longer, but greatly hindered healing times. And worse yet, injuries that would normally not be too big a deal back home could be life-threatening sans gravity.

He quietly thanked his captors for the small comfort of the artificial environment that allowed him to heal, though he was quite sure it was unintentional, then finished his little workout with a set of bicycle crunches on his bunk. He was hoping to loosen his hip and lower back while getting some blood flowing, but it was more than his hips he loosened up.

"Oh shit," he said, lunging for his filth-crusted toilet as his stomach painfully rumbled.

He desperately tugged at his waist fasteners, knowing full-well his captors would likely just leave him wearing shit-stained pants if he soiled himself. Fortunately, he managed to push them down just as his bowels lost control and voided explosively into the basin.

It felt as though his guts had been run through with a pipe-cleaning device, then the lone cork holding it all in was abruptly pulled free. In seconds he was empty, but that didn't stop the cramping.

The automated bidet-like cleaning blast hit him as he squatted there, doubled over in pain, thighs burning from holding himself above the disgusting device. He still hadn't figured out exactly how it worked, but at the moment he really didn't care. Charlie just hoped it would finish its cycle quickly.

Just as he accepted that his quads couldn't take any more and he'd probably have to live with soiled bedding, the cleaning cycle ended, and none too soon. His legs gave out as he threw himself onto his bunk and curled into a ball. He was clean, so there was that to be thankful for, but the cramping continued for a full two minutes before finally easing up.

After that, he just lay there for a good ten minutes before finally mustering the strength to pull his pants back up.

Damn. Shit my brains out so hard, I think I lost some IQ points, he grimly chuckled to himself.

The toilet had—as per usual—finished its auto-flush cycle then rocked back and forth a few times before giving up and staying put. The waste in the bowl had cleared, thankfully, but with all of the cells full of new occupants, the system it fed into was operating at high capacity. That meant the stench of dozens of prisoners' bowels wafted up through the bowl.

Charlie, exhausted as he was, felt a burst of anger flood his system.

"Okay, fuck this," he said, getting to his feet.

He retrieved the sharp piece of metal he had secreted off the pillaged ship from under his bunk and began tracing the lines of the wall panel around the toilet system.

If I can just get in there, maybe I won't have to keep smelling this shit all day. I'm a goddamn engineer. If I can build a spaceship, I sure as hell can fix a stinking toilet.

Charlie paused and shed his shirt and pants, carefully folding and placing them on his bunk, ensuring they would not become filth-coated from the work. His body he could wash far easier than the material, he figured. It was disgusting to even think about, but with all he'd been through, his tolerances were shifting regularly.

Ten disgusting minutes had passed before he finally managed to work free a panel after scraping off the years of crusted buildup over the seams.

What the hell?

The workings were unlike any he had ever seen before. The mechanical aspects were clear. A few pivot joints to allow the unit to retract into the wall, and a simple tube leading into the depths of the ship, where waste was stored for eventual disposal. The rest, however, was, well, *alien*.

Where he expected circuits and wires, Charlie found only small, ornate, embedded metal squares, no thicker than his little finger. Those, he quickly learned, would not budge.

Okay, so these must be alien circuit boards of some kind. I guess it makes sense their tech would be totally different than ours, but still, this is just weird.

He traced the different moving parts with his piece of metal, scraping crusty grime from the frozen parts as he did. He might not be able to access the circuit system––whatever they tied into, he had no way inside that flush-mounted piece of bulkhead–– but he could at least see about getting the moving parts moving again.

Charlie rinsed off at the sink for the umpteenth time since beginning his task, then carried a handful of warm water back to the system and began using it to help loosen whatever it was that had fouled the joints. It took hours, but after a lot of elbow grease, he had restored them to a functional, if not beautiful, degree of operation.

He stepped back from the toilet and watched as the unit retracted into the wall. He moved closer and it swung out again, ready for use.

"Now that's what I'm talking about," he said with a triumphant smile.

Just one problem. The toilet itself was still filthy.

He looked at his hands, already soiled from his labors.

"Fuck it," he grumbled, then set to work with his modified tool, manually breaking free the hardened shit and grime with his bare hands. Once that was done, he let the toilet flush away the debris. Then he carefully washed his makeshift tool and used it to cut a strip from his blanket, which he then soaked in hot water and used to scrub the remainder of the toilet until it was clean.

He looked around. The cell wasn't that big, and he was already dirty, so why not?

For another hour, he scrubbed the floors by hand, gradually lifting years of grime, revealing the dull gray surface beneath. There was no waste disposal bin, so he cut another strip from his blanket and wrapped the foul cleaning cloth in that. He'd just dispose of it at mealtime, he figured, not wanting to risk clogging the toilet with something so large after all that work.

Charlie then rinsed off in his sink, scrubbing and washing his entire body as best he could. There would be a communal shower soon, he figured, seeing as they'd all just worked hard emptying the captured ship of its wealth. But the pirate captors were unpredictable on that front, so it could just as easily be a few days.

And if he'd once shied away from the group showers at the base on Earth, he had now been forced to see enough alien private bits to last a lifetime.

With a clean body and a clean cell, Charlie finally lay down on his bunk and breathed a deep breath of satisfaction. The lingering smell was still there, but it would just take time to fade. With the toilet functionally retracted now, he drifted off to sleep, the constant assault on his nose having, at long last, come to an end.

CHAPTER FORTY-ONE

Despite the relatively unappetizing smell of the slop fed to the prisoners, those with more sensitive noses turned their heads in an attempt to suss out where the foul stench wafting through the galley was coming from.

Charlie––carrying his wadded up, shit-stained rag as covertly as possible––noted the searching eyes and anxiously watched the line move ahead of him. Once he had his food, he could easily make quick work of his meal, then toss the offending matter into the waste receptacle with the other trash.

After so long with the constant smell of his living space, Charlie had almost learned to tune out the malodorous fumes, but now, surrounded by the others, he realized perhaps this wasn't the best idea. He might be used to it, but no telling who might notice the odd human carrying a shit-smelling bundle into their eating space.

He made it to the front of the line and collected his food with no trouble, then hastened to his usual spot, wolfing down his meal so as to throw his load in the trash as quickly as possible and finally be done with it once and for all. And he almost succeeded.

Almost.

A guard, a man Charlie didn't recognize from before, stepped in front of him, placing a firm hand on his chest as he walked toward the waste disposal receptacle.

"What the hell are you doing coming in here smelling like that?"

Charlie had no idea what the man said.

"Answer me," the guard demanded, smacking the tray from his hands. The waste-soaked rags fell to the ground, unwrapping and unleashing their full stench. "You disgusting little shit. What were you thinking, bringing that in here?" the guard demanded.

Charlie smiled and shrugged. He couldn't understand a word the man was saying, but the gist was clear enough. A meaty hand swatted him to the ground, then yanked him back to his feet.

"Think you're so clever? You answer when you're spoken to!"

Again, Charlie was struck, but this time he managed to stay on his feet. An unfamiliar urge flooded his chest, and when the next blow fell, he found himself very much wanting to strike back.

Be smart, Charlie. They'll kill you, he reminded himself, forcing his fist to loosen.

The guard had struck him yet again, demanding answers of the prisoner, when Marban entered the galley and saw the commotion.

"What's going on?" he demanded.

"This one. He's carrying around a wad of shitty rags and won't tell me what the hell he was doing with them. So I'm reminding him who's in charge."

Marban slapped the man. The dull roar of the galley's mealtime chatter went silent.

"You're an idiot, Durral. The translation spell is not active. None of them know what you are saying."

A slight blush rose to the gray man's cheeks. "Well––uh, I suppose. But I thought––"

"You didn't think. And that's a problem. Now, you know I'm up for a good beating as much as the next man, but if you damage our goods for no reason, and right after we lost so many on a raid, no less, the captain will not be amused. And you know what happens then."

"I do," he replied, the blush in his cheeks replaced by a far paler shade than he had sported previously.

"Good. Keep that in mind and *think* before you start beating on our merchandise." He turned his gaze to Charlie. "Now, let me find out what is actually going on here. *Impezu ovusk.*"

The whispering voices in the galley suddenly snapped into clarity as the translation spell took effect.

"What were you thinking, bringing your shit-stained rags into the galley? We may not be high-class men, but we eat here. This sort of thing is not only not allowed, it's just plain stupid."

Charlie locked eyes with his captor. The scar running from his head to his shoulder seemed a deeper shade. Perhaps his anger made it darken. But that wasn't important at the moment.

"I needed to dispose of them," Charlie finally said. "There's no trash bin in my cell, so I rolled it up as best I could to throw away in the big receptacle we use at mealtime."

"That explains why you brought it here, but not why the hell you have those shitty rags in the first place."

"I used them to clean my cell after I fixed my toilet."

Marban looked at him oddly. "You did *what?*"

"I cleaned my cell."

"No, the bit before that."

"I fixed my toilet, then used these to wipe everything down. I figured since I had already gotten dirty, I might as well clean the whole space. Really, I didn't mean to do anything wrong, I just wanted a clean––"

"Shut up," Marban interrupted. "Pick up that filth and throw it away," he commanded.

Charlie complied.

"Good, now come with me."

The pirate ushered Charlie out of the galley and down the corridor back to his cell.

"Show me," he ordered.

Charlie stepped up to the clean panel where his toilet was retracted. The unit swung out and locked into place. It still moved a bit jerkily, but it was nothing a little oil couldn't remedy.

Marban pushed him aside and examined the spotless basin. He then looked around at the rest of the cell. The walls were still grimy, but the entire floor was the cleanest he'd ever seen it.

"You did all of this?"

"Yes."

The pirate stepped back from the toilet and watched it retract back into the wall. He took a small device from one of his chest pouches and held it to his mouth.

"Captain Saramin, this is Marban."

The captain's voice replied. "Yes? What is it?"

So that's a comms unit of some sort, Charlie realized. *Probably similar to the skrees Tür's men used.*

"Captain, one of the prisoners did something to the waste disposal system in his cell. I think you may want to see this."

"Very well. Which cell?"

"Section three, cell nine."

"I'll be there momentarily," the man replied, then the comms went silent.

Less than two minutes passed before the captain strode into the cell.

"Look at this," Marban said, gesturing toward the clean floor, and more importantly, the retracted toilet.

The captain stepped up to the unit and watched as it swung into place.

"Fascinating," he said, then unfastened his pants and relieved himself in the spotless bowl.

He can just pee on command. Well, that's an unusual skill, I guess, Charlie mused with a little grin.

No sooner had he finished, than the unit emptied and swung away once more, sealing itself within the walls out of sight. Captain Saramin turned to Charlie.

"You did this?"

"Yes, sir."

"How? You have no means to carry out this kind of work."

Charlie decided it was best to come clean. It was a gamble, but he hoped one that wouldn't bite him in the ass.

"With this," he said, slowly pulling the sharp piece of debris from under his mattress.

Marban snatched it from his hand immediately, but the captain seemed more amused than annoyed.

"This one shows some spirit, eh, Marban?" he said with a laugh.

"Yes, Captain, that he does."

"Such initiative. Acquiring a weapon––that was your intent, was it not? I don't think you took that planning on using it to clean a waste disposal system, did you?"

Charlie nodded, silently.

"I thought so. And yet here we are. And you have somehow done what none of the idiots on my crew have been able to accomplish. And with a useless little bit of metal, no less. You see this, Marban? All of those spells wasted, when a simple little piece of scrap could have solved our problem."

The captain tossed the shard back onto Charlie's bunk.

"I-I don't understand. Am I in trouble?" he asked.

"Not at all," the captain replied. "In fact, you've just earned yourself a promotion."

How do you promote a prisoner? he wondered. "Promotion?"

"Yes. You have a new job. Marban, get him what he needs to fix the others."

"Yes, sir."

"Wait. *Others*?"

"Yes. Many of the waste disposal units have similar problems as this. It makes for a rather unpleasant odor on those levels, but if the units do not retract properly, we can't purge the waste into space. Without it sealing, the spells don't hold and we'd suck out our air in the process. So, your new job is to fix them."

The captain walked out of the cell, an amused grin on his face.

"Wait!"

The captain turned, eyebrow raised questioningly.

"I'm sorry, sir. No disrespect intended. I was just wondering, if I'm to fix the other toilets, could you at least have the others clean them first? It would make the job much easier. Uh, and faster, I'm sure."

Captain Saramin looked at Marban and laughed. An inside joke, apparently.

"Why not?" he said, thoroughly amused. "Though I'll say this, it won't make you any friends."

He then nodded to Marban and walked away.

"Okay, what do you need to do your work?" the pirate asked.

Charlie told him what would be useful in effecting the repairs, now that he had a basic understanding of how the system worked. He also made a point to request some oil or grease to make the mechanisms move smoother as well. With that, he felt he could do as the captain asked.

"I'll get what you need," Marban said. "You'll start in the morning. *San ovusk.*"

With his translator off once more, Charlie lay back on his bunk and pondered his new situation. He was still a captive and in a world of shit. Only this time, it was literal.

CHAPTER FORTY-TWO

For the better part of a week, Charlie spent his daytime hours wrist—and sometimes elbow—deep in all manner of foulness as he toiled over the broken toilet mechanisms plaguing the ship. He hadn't realized it at the time, but his own personal commode was just a much smaller symptom of a far larger problem.

With the system unable to properly close and seal, the pirate craft was forced to haul around the waste of the entire crew until they entered the atmosphere of a planet with breathable air. Only then could they open the purge and dump the accumulated mess, likely to the great horror of any unfortunate enough to be located beneath them.

To attempt the maneuver in space with so many toilets stuck open would have killed most of the crew from rapid decompression.

Charlie had asked how it was that they could form a force field over holes in a hull, but couldn't seal off a simple toilet. The answer made his head spin a little. Apparently, when the ship was built, it had a robust 'magic' design powering all systems. The residual 'magic' ensured toilets stayed unobstructed from the bowl all the way to what had been intended as a temporary holding tank.

Of course, now that tank was regularly put to far more use than it had been designed for.

The cells he worked in constituted a good sixty percent of those on the ship, though at least there were several of them that were a quick fix. Others, however, required far more work.

The prisoners had been required to clean their toilets prior to his working on them, as he had requested. Some complied without complaint, but others were decidedly annoyed by the disgusting task. All knew who was to blame.

They would do it, of course. To not would incur the captain's wrath. But once Marban had inspected the unit to ensure it was ready for Charlie to work on, several of them made a point to leave a smeared and still-warm greeting for him on every surface they could reach.

Charlie could have complained, and Marban would certainly have made an example of the men responsible, but he felt it was far wiser to simply get the job done and get on with his life. And once their toilets all functioned perfectly, who knew? Maybe those upset by the inconvenient cleanup job would come around and even be thankful.

Or at least not hold too much of a grudge.

He hoped.

The week had been grueling, but another benefit Charlie had reaped from his new job was a bit of special treatment from Marban. A few days into the project, Charlie had impressed him with the progress he had been making, and that night Marban sat with him during dinner and activated his translator. None of the other prisoners received that treatment. Charlie, however, had piqued the pirate's curiosity.

"Okay, you've got to tell me. How did you know how to open the panel? Only a select few know repair spells, and even fewer can wield them without a slaap or konus, but you're unpowered."

"I don't know about slaaps, or konuses, or spells," he had replied. "I'm just using my engineering experience and applying it to a new type of technology, is all."

"What is 'technology?'"

"It's the mechanical processes by which things function. In your case, voice-activated devices woven into your society's daily life."

"Magic, you mean. Power."

"Well, you call it that, but that's got to be a translator glitch. It probably actually translates to wireless power or something," Charlie replied. "Regardless, once I figure out the underlying principles of the system, from there, it's just backtracking the mechanism until I find the fault."

Marban studied the unusual human with great curiosity as they ate. It was almost a friendly meal between equals, rather than guard and prisoner. And then there was the fact that Marban had been one of the men who had captured him, though truth be told, he didn't really hold it against the pirate. Sure, it wasn't pleasant, but it was the life they knew, and for a pirate, he seemed to be a decent sort.

Somewhat surprisingly, they wound up chatting about things other than waste disposal repairs as well as they finished their meals. Charlie's homeworld, the mechanical issues with the *Rixana*, how the crew was replenished from captured vessels.

"Rather like the Roman Legion," Charlie said.

"The what?"

"A great army from my world, thousands of years ago. They spread far and wide, amassing an enormous fighting force. But the thing was, when they would vanquish an opponent, rather than kill or imprison their men, they offered them the option of joining their ranks as legionnaires."

"It makes sense," Marban said. "It is a waste of manpower to constantly execute prisoners."

"Exactly. So in a sense, your operation here is sort of similar to the Romans. I mean, it's different, obviously. For one, you're space pirates. But the general idea is the same."

They shared a few more tales, and Charlie actually found the company improved the taste of his food. It had been a long time since he'd simply talked with someone. Tuktuk was a friend, no doubt, but their stilted discussions had been cut rather short by his impromptu escape.

"Come," Marban said at the end of their meal. "Drop off your tray and follow me."

Charlie obliged, following the man through the ship until they reached a familiar chamber. The communal showers. Only, at this time of night, they were empty.

"You've worked well and hard. Others would have complained the entire time, but you just put your head down and got the work done. The captain may not always show it, but he appreciates your efforts. Go ahead and get cleaned up. You have the facility to yourself. I'll see if I can procure a set of clean clothes in your size from one of the dead's belongings. That way you can rinse the day's clothing as you bathe and start the next day fresh while the damp ones dry."

"Thank you, Marban, I don't know what to say."

"Say? There is nothing to say. You have performed well, and on the *Rixana*, those who carry their weight are rewarded."

The scarred pirate then left him to bathe in peace.

As the warm water flowed over his body, washing clean the past several days' grime and smell, Charlie found himself almost feeling content. He knew it was just the relaxing heat loosening his tense muscles and steam flushing out his poor sinuses, but for a moment at least, he allowed himself to feel at peace.

But soon enough, he knew with certainty, things would undoubtedly shift. For now, however, for the first time in too long, he soaked in the heat and felt, well, *human*.

CHAPTER FORTY-THREE

A week had passed since the completion of the toilet system repair job, and Charlie was back to the daily grind of prisoner life. Their ship did capture and board a smaller vessel, so at least he got to head out and see something other than the walls of his cell. Better yet, that particular action had been bloodless.

Apparently, Captain Saramin wasn't as bloodthirsty as he led people to believe, though he'd kill you if you suggested it. However, Marban had been activating his translator at mealtime somewhat regularly now, and during one of those conversations had mentioned that a lot of the time the captain would essentially play chess with his prey. Once he positioned them for checkmate, he would offer them the opportunity to surrender without needlessly causing the deaths of their crew.

Alive and captive was still better than free but dead, he argued.

Quite often, that point was persuasive enough.

So Charlie lugged pillaged supplies while the captain sorted through the crew, selecting those he would take, but leaving the weaker ones to go their way. After he had taken everything of value, that is.

That evening as they ate, Charlie asked Marban why he didn't take the ship as well.

"Goods are easily moved, but stolen ships are really hard to sell in most systems. Plus, we would have to make landfall in this system to release the crew the captain didn't want to take on board."

"So why not do that?"

"Because we survive by doing what we do and *not* drawing unnecessary attention to ourselves. In space, we are masters of our realm, and able to simply jump to another system if a fight we don't want shows up at our doorstep."

"But I've seen you guys in action. I can't see you backing down."

The scarred pirate laughed. "Oh, believe me, there are some we have no desire to fight. Council ships, for example. We could take on several at a time, no doubt, but if we did, we'd have the rest on our tail so bad we'd have to flee to the most distant systems for any peace. Nope, we have a good thing, so the captain doesn't push his luck."

"I suppose there's logic in that," Charlie replied. "But what are council ships?"

A brief look of worry flashed across the pirate's face. "The Council of Twenty. The group of systems and their representative warlords, all powerful vislas, far more power-hungry than any regular men. They control the systems. They dictate the laws. Collect taxes. Guide and control both business and war. To run afoul of the Council is to see your life expectancy shorten by a good margin, no matter who you are."

"Fascinating."

Marban hastily jumped to his feet as the captain entered the galley. For a pirate, he seemed to have a thing for military protocols that made Charlie wonder what his prior history might actually be.

"Captain," the men greeted in unison.

"Marban. Charlie," he replied. "I see you've spent power on translation spells for our friend here," he noted.

"I'm sorry, sir. I just thought it could be useful to understand how he managed such an unusual repair feat. I'll deactivate it at once."

"No, that's fine, leave it. I was actually coming to do the same myself. Plus, one other thing," he said, pulling a small bandolier strap with a pair of pouches on it and dropping it on the table. Prisoners took note, especially the ones with the most seniority.

Marban's eyes widened. "Already?"

"Our numbers have thinned in recent engagements. And besides, now that we no longer have to make planetfall to empty our waste system, I think Charlie's earned it, don't you?"

"I do, sir," Marban agreed, a hint of a smile on the corners of his lips.

"Then there it is. Congratulations, Charlie. You are no longer a mere laborer. You've earned yourself a higher position aboard my ship."

Charlie picked up the bandolier and studied it. Others had far more pouches on theirs, but he figured that likely came with experience and seniority. A small knife and a short sword were clunked down on the table as well.

"You've been promoted to the lowest of the low among my men. But that's a world better than being a toilet-scrubbing prisoner, wouldn't you agree?"

"I'm sure it is, Captain," Charlie replied, still a bit unsure what had just happened.

"Marban will go over the fine points of your new position with you, but in my book there is just one true rule. Fight or die. If you are caught hiding or running from the face of the enemy, I'll end you myself, is that clear?"

"Yes, Captain."

"Good. Marban, you fill him in on the rest," he said, then walked out of the galley.

Once the captain had cleared the doorway Charlie spun back to his unlikely friend.

"What just happened, Marban?"

"Well, little brother, you have just joined the illustrious ranks of the crew of the *Rixana*," he said, flashing him a jolly smile.

"I'm a pirate now?"

"That you are."

Charlie picked up the short sword from the table. It was lighter than he expected, but seemed deadly enough. He looked over the weapon and noticed the fine rune work etched into the pommel.

"Ah, you've already noticed the *gallen*, I see."

"The what?"

"*Gallen.* It's a specific spell worked into the material of the weapon itself. They're used to prevent a fallen man's gear from being captured and used against his own comrades. Here, I'll show you," the scarred man said. "Try to strike me with your sword."

His hands were empty. Marban had no means of defending himself.

"No, that's okay," Charlie said.

"Oh, don't be a baby. Just take a little swing," the pirate urged.

"Fine," he relented, halfheartedly attempting to swat the larger man with the flat edge of the sword.

Marban didn't move an inch, nor did he utter a word, but when the sword came within a few inches of his body, Charlie felt a blast of energy discharge into his arm, throwing him back several feet into the wall.

"Oops, I didn't think this one was that strong," Marban said as he helped Charlie to his feet. "Sorry about that."

"Fuck. You could have warned me."

"Yes, but that isn't the point of the lesson."

"Which is what? Don't hit your own team? I think I could've figured that out without the shock, thank you very much."

"No, it's much more than that, Charlie," he said. "Look, I like you, so I don't want you to die our first time out if you suddenly decide to do something stupid like run and fight your own comrades."

Must've been reading my mind, Charlie mused. He had, in fact, wondered if now with weapons and a bit more freedom, he might manage to effect an escape.

"The thing is, we're just playing around, and the *gallen* recognizes your intent. If you had swung with the aim to kill me, you wouldn't be standing here right now."

"Hang on. You're saying whatever I try to do to my own 'team' this thing will do to me instead?"

"Not quite like that, but if you were to try to harm one of us in any serious way, then yes, you would be struck dead."

Charlie dropped the sword to the table, rubbing his sore hand. "I'm not so sure I'm cut out for this."

"None of us were our first day. Well, almost none of us. A few had other, uh, *experience* that prepared us for this sort of life."

"And what was your experience, Marban? Who were you before all of this?"

The scarred man's smile faltered just an instant, but Charlie noted the brief look in the man's eye. There was a story there all right, but tonight was not the night he would hear it.

"Plenty of time for tales of adventure later," he finally answered. "Anyway, rest up. The captain's been tracking a cargo transport and thinks we may be able to approach and disable them before they can jump away."

"Jump away? That's an option?"

"If their Drooks are well trained and powerful enough, yes. It doesn't happen often, but we've lost our prey a few times when their Drooks surprised us. Now the captain tries to hit them with a disrupting spell as soon as we make contact. It doesn't knock them out, but it plays merry havoc with their powers for a minute or two. More than enough time for our men to board," he said. "You'll see. But now, rest. Tomorrow the fun begins."

CHAPTER FORTY-FOUR

Charlie had begun his first day as a space pirate desperately dodging the frantic swings of a young man with a long knife. It took every bit of his attention and energy to avoid being sliced open by the dangerous-looking blade.

This is what he calls fun? he silently grumbled as he parried yet another assault with a piece of debris, then landed a hard right on the point of the man's chin. He crumpled to the deck, unconscious.

They had managed to board the ship in pretty much the manner Marban had laid out. The captain flashed in quick and 'cast a spell,' which to Charlie meant he activated a voice-triggered EMP or some such device that kept the other ship from jumping away. With its drives incapacitated, the pirate crew quickly breached the hull from several points and swarmed into the ship.

Charlie saw several other men, who had also been prisoners until recently, join in the fray. He wasn't the only one newly promoted, it seemed.

One of them sprayed blood from his mouth as a long sword pierced his torso. It appeared their numbers would need to be added to again, shortly, and he had no intention of his own space needing to be filled.

He recalled the captain's warning--*fight or die*--as he followed the others deeper into the vessel.

Well, he didn't say kill or die, he thought, looking for some wiggle room. Charlie had no desire to take anyone's life, and if he could avoid it, he certainly would do whatever it took.

Fighting was heavy around him, but he kept his weapons secured, instead relying on his old martial arts close-quarters combat training from so many years ago. He hadn't practiced in what seemed like forever, but the basic moves were still there, and apparently were a style of fighting the crew of the boarded ship were not accustomed to.

A burly man nearly twice his size charged at him, a bloody club in hand. As he moved, however, Charlie realized he could take him.

He's relying on brute strength, he thought as he used the man's momentum against him, disarming him and flinging him into the nearby wall, while avoiding injury himself. The man was taken totally off guard, and the wall he hit so very hard did the rest of the work for Charlie, dropping him to the ground in an unconscious heap.

Two down.

And so it went, though for far too long. Charlie would punch, kick, and even choke opponents into unconsciousness, but despite taking a few hits and suffering a cut or three, he did not fatally injure anyone.

They were mopping up, the prisoners from their own ship already carrying out the plundered cargo, when the young man with the dangerously long knife leapt out of nowhere, swinging wildly at Charlie. Apparently, he'd recovered prior to being taken by the other pirates, and now Charlie had to deal with him once more.

The others all had clear angles of attack, but held off. This was his initiation, of sorts. A fight to the death in front of his new brothers. He only hoped neither of them would have to meet that fate.

A glancing blow cut his arm, but it was shallow, and Charlie barely noticed it in the heat of battle as he and his opponent circled one another.

"Get him, Charlie!" someone shouted.

"Kill him!"

"You can do it!"

Cheers from his fellow pirates, urging him to violence. But that simply wasn't his way. Exhausted from so much combat, Charlie realized his younger opponent would likely outlast him if he kept dancing around rather than actually fighting. A decision had to be made, and soon.

The young man lunged, but rather than jumping back as the attacker expected, Charlie leapt forward, taking a small cut as he passed the blade but effectively cutting off the man's angles of attack. With a sharp crack, he head-butted his opponent, breaking his nose in a bloody spray. The concussive effect made the man's eyes water and balance waver.

Charlie took that opportunity to grab his knife arm and spin him into a modified wrist lock, then drove him down to the ground, his arm locked out above him. His fellow pirates looked on with amusement as he casually removed the knife from the pinned man's hand.

"Kill him, Charlie!" one urged.

Charlie tossed the knife aside and hauled the vanquished youth to his feet. "No. There's been plenty of that today."

"But he cut you."

"We just boarded his ship. Can you blame him?" he replied. "Put him with the other prisoners and let's get on with it," he said, shoving the young man to his waiting colleagues.

Ten minutes later Captain Saramin was walking the line of captured men, as Charlie had seen him do before. Terranz, the milky-eyed man, was with him, reading each of the new prisoners, seeing if they might possess any power of their own.

The captain's hands were still a bit bloody from the fighting, Charlie noticed. Unlike so many 'leaders,' this one believed leadership was setting an example. Leading his men in battle. Two words reinforced his role as their commander. "Follow me." And his men would, with no questions or hesitation.

Captain Saramin stopped at the young man Charlie had spared, Terranz whispering in his ear. He nodded slightly, then moved on to the next man. At that moment, the youth pulled a small blade the others had missed and lunged at the captain.

Saramin easily stepped aside, catching his wrist and ripping the blade from his grasp before plunging it into his chest. The youth was dead before he hit the deck, a puddle of blood leaking from his pulseless body.

The captain looked across the collected pirates, pausing especially long on Charlie.

"This is why mercy is weakness. This is why we do not spare our enemies. Those who would surrender, we gladly accept into our service. Those who would rather die than be enslaved will have that desire fulfilled."

He looked at Charlie once more, his point clear. "Bring them," he said, then walked back to the *Rixana*.

"You heard the captain. Prisoners to the cells. The rest of you lot, we've got a ship to pillage!"

A cheerful cry erupted among the pirates as they set out to find whatever remained of value to be taken. Charlie, however, was tasked with escorting the prisoners, as was the newest members' traditional role.

He was missing out on plunder, but didn't really care. He was just glad to have survived one more day.

And that was how he would continue to survive. Living like some bastardized space pirate motivational poster cliché. Taking it day by day.

CHAPTER FORTY-FIVE

Charlie was a pirate.

A space pirate.

A space pirate on a ship of aliens.

Every time he paused to assess his situation, the ridiculousness of what his life had become evoked a painfully amused laugh.

'Look at me now, Ma,' was one thought he had on repeat, though with all of the amazing things he was doing as a full-fledged space pirate, the sarcasm in the statement was only partial.

It had been many days, or maybe even a few weeks. He wasn't sure anymore. Once the ship got into fighting trim, they happened upon a largely unprotected trading route full of tempting prizes, the daily tasks of invading, pillaging, and surviving took up most of his time. They'd been relatively fortunate in their hauls, the ships targeted being pushovers, mostly.

Mostly.

A few, however, put up one hell of a fight, and there had

been a several-day gap in action as Captain Saramin was forced to jump to the particularly tough world of Etren to recrew with veteran fighters.

He would slowly fill his ranks with prisoners as they became seasoned, but for the immediate jobs at hand, he needed experienced men and simply couldn't wait. There was a tiny bit of friction with the other crew at first––many had a sense of seniority due to the way they had come up in the ranks––but after seeing the new additions in combat, they quickly gelled into a cohesive team.

The new guys, it seemed, were certifiable badasses.

It was a crash course in pirating and space combat for Charlie, and he studied the fighting techniques employed by the different men with great interest––when not frantically trying to save his own life, that is. Through all of the raids, he stuck true to his personal ethics, never killing anyone, though he did suffer a few minor injuries for his trouble.

Fortunately, the healing powers of the waters he and Rika had discovered seemed to have lost none of their potency, and his wounds healed with astounding speed. This durability was one trait he did his best to hide, not knowing what the captain might have him do if he were aware he had a crewman with such a gift.

Now, this is not saying he did not harm anyone. Far from it. In the heat of battle, fighting for your life, you don't really have the choice of simply not laying a finger on anyone. Fortunately for Charlie, it seemed Earth's martial arts styles were unfamiliar to pretty much everyone they encountered. A few had interesting techniques of their own, but most seemed focused around the power devices they were suddenly unable to wield in close-quarter combat.

Charlie left more than a few men with concussions that would leave their heads aching the next day, but at least they would live. Likewise, survival was the result for those he choked out, rendering them unconscious with a well-placed squeeze of the arms.

Except for the few alien species who apparently had diverse enough physiology for his choke-out techniques to not work on them. Hence the concussion option.

One aspect his scientific mind took in with great interest was the layout and function of all the different manner of ships they descended upon. Breaching their hulls was a fairly straightforward process, but once inside, the differing designs and built-in functions of each craft were a wealth of novelty for the human engineer.

And all of the systems were voice-controlled. No matter whose craft they invaded, it seemed that in every single system they traveled to, all tech was voice-activated. And all ran on the same odd language, no less.

Charlie continued to add to his mnemonic song, making a point to keep his ears open for any new command words he had not already committed to memory. Unlike his previous experience with the Tslavar crew, the pirates seemed far looser in their use of the words, and though he lacked their voice-activated devices, Charlie nevertheless began amassing a decent amount of command words for all manner of things.

"Marban, I noticed something about Captain Saramin," he mentioned as the two ate dinner one evening.

"Oh?" his friend replied.

Friend. How unlikely that the very man who had captured him, then hauled him off to a life of labor and piracy, would become his friend. But oddly enough, the men had developed a mutual respect the more they talked. And the older pirate was clever. *Very* clever. Marban would never discuss his past life from before he joined Captain Saramin's crew, but given his articulate nature and intellectual ways—especially compared to his comrades—Charlie was certain there was *quite* a story there.

One day, perhaps his friend would tell it to him.

"Yeah," he continued. "These past weeks, I've really watched him, both on the *Rixana,* as well as when we board other ships."

"Good. You can learn a lot by simply observing," his scarred friend noted. "The captain is one hell of a leader. Always in front with his men, never shying from a fight. *That* is why he has the loyalty of his men. He may be our captain, but he's also truly one of us."

"Yeah, I've seen him fight. It's almost like he enjoys the risks."

"Well, you didn't hear it from me, but there's talk that the captain was once a gladiator in his early days."

"A gladiator? Are you serious? Like fighting in arenas? People actually still do that?"

"Of course," Marban said, as if it were the most normal thing in the world. "It's an immensely popular sport. Anyway, rumor has it the captain was captured in a pirate raid that took the ship he was being transported on. Realizing what was happening, his owners freed him and gave him arms to defend the ship along with the crew. He killed a *lot* of men, but at the end of the day he simply couldn't fight off all of the attacking force. He wound up pretty badly injured, and was the only survivor, but apparently the captain of *that* pirate ship was so impressed with him that he let him live, fixing his hurt and making him part of his crew."

"And the rest is history."

"Precisely."

It explained a lot about the captain, actually. But whatever his combative life had been in the past, he was a learned man now as well.

"The thing is, it seems Captain Saramin does nearly everything himself. Like, we board a new ship and he is diverting systems, opening sealed compartments, overriding power controls. From what I'd seen up until now, that's pretty unusual."

"It is," Marban agreed. "Nearly everyone specializes in their field, learning the spells specific to their tasks. Pilots learn all the maneuvering spells, repairmen learn the repair spells––"

"Chefs learn the chef spells."

"Don't be silly, Charlie. Chefs learn to cook," Marban said with a funny little grin. "Well, okay, and maybe some kitchen spells too," he laughed. "The thing is, there are thousands of spells––"

"Voice commands."

"*Spells*, Charlie. Call them what you like, but they're spells, controlling unseen power, bending it to do a specific task."

That was one area he and his alien friend had a never-ending difference of opinion on. It was clearly more than just a semantic issue. It was almost a religious one, though none seemed to deem this 'magic' as an actual deity. Rather, it was a power, an invisible force that was present in all things. To Charlie, it was ludicrous, though he kept that opinion largely to himself.

"So the captain is a learned man, is what you're saying."

"I'm saying he has prepared himself, as one would expect of a gladiator, to be able to overcome and be victorious in a wide range of situations. Most are so specialized, they wouldn't know what to do outside of their own narrow spectrum of skills if something went wrong. Why, even some of the most powerful users, from mesters and emmiks, all the way to vislas, are limited once they step outside their chosen skills."

"Seems like a dangerous way to live. I mean, what if they lose their pilot or something?"

"Men like that have resources, Charlie. *Vast* resources. They'd just get another. In fact, most have a few redundancies on hand. The truly wealthy ones, at least. That's what slaves are for, after all."

The slavery discussion was one they'd had many times. Marban found it quaint that in Charlie's world slavery had been abolished many centuries ago. The idea that no man could own another was quite novel in his eyes. *Here*, however, it was not only alive and well, it was an accepted part of society, though, obviously, none wanted to become enslaved.

The only positive Charlie could see of their system was that at least there seemed to be no restriction on who might find themselves an unwilling servant. Race and species was not the driving factor at all.

Sure, certain species, such as Drooks or Ootaki, held more value than others, and as such, were often taken if they strayed from their own systems where they were protected by numbers, but otherwise, it seemed *anyone* could wind up a slave. Even a former gladiator or a space engineer from another galaxy.

"You know," Marban said, a curious look in his eye. "The captain is not a fool."

"What do you mean?"

"He knows what you've been doing."

Shit, how can he know I'm memorizing the control words?

"I don't know what you're talking about," Charlie said with a straight face.

"Well, he knows. And one of these days he's going to call you out on it. Consider that a friendly word of warning," Marban said, downing the last of his meal. "Anyway, it's been a long day. I'm going to get some rest. Word is we've got a juicy prize waiting for us tomorrow."

He rose and cracked his back with a big stretch, then wandered out of the galley, leaving Charlie in his usual spot, pondering what he'd said.

The captain knows. Somehow, he knows. Charlie looked at the others in the galley. All were either engrossed in their meals, or in conversations with one another.

Then he saw him.

Captain Saramin stood at the far end of the room, leaning

against the doorway as he surveyed his men. His eyes locked on Charlie's a moment and he smiled. Then he turned and was gone.

I am so screwed.

CHAPTER FORTY-SIX

It was just after lunch when the captain sounded the call to arms.

"We've got a juicy prize, boys, so gear up and get ready. It won't be an easy one, but the rewards are great," he said to his assembled men.

"Number of enemies?" a man asked.

"Expect at least forty, if not more," the captain replied.

"We can handle that."

"Yes. But my sources tell me the captain of that ship is one of the older caste. He is highly unlikely to surrender without a bloody fight, and there's a very good chance he may try to scuttle the ship. We need to put up barriers at every major structural choke point to ensure we maintain atmosphere if he tries to blow the hull on us."

Charlie looked at Marban. This was beginning to sound a lot more challenging than their usual smash-and-grab brand of piracy. This was an actual battle, and careful attention to tactical details would come into play, lest they be unceremoniously evacuated into space.

"Don't worry, little brother. I've got your back," he said, noting his friend's worried look.

Then the rush of preparation began in earnest. They were heading into harm's way, and more than a few might not come back.

Time flies when you're having fun––or facing a number of potentially unpleasant ways to die––and before he had time to get into his own head and overthink the whole thing, they fell upon their target.

The ship was much larger than any they had taken since Charlie had been aboard the *Rixana*. Its long, multi-sectioned design seemed rather akin to the way a wasp's abdomen pinched and separated from its thorax. Only this craft could be far deadlier than a wasp, with many means of defense and a half-dozen sections for the pirates to board.

The narrow segments were apparently designed to make it easier to segregate sections in the event of a catastrophic decompression. In other more hostile circumstances––like pirates, for example––they would also create multiple choke points. Bottlenecks that hindered any invading force.

Charlie noticed all of this as they hurtled toward the craft, Captain Saramin's Drooks applying reverse thrust only moments before impact.

The *Rixana* made hard contact, and Captain Saramin immediately unleashed his disabling 'spell,' rendering the ship incapable of jumping away.

"Go, go, go!" he shouted to his men as three narrow force field tubes deployed, the sharp crack of shattering metal ringing out as they made contact with the hulls of three of the six sections, sealing instantly and providing the pirate invaders with a breathable atmosphere as they boarded.

They wouldn't need it for long. The pirates may have been rough and uncultured individuals, but when it came to the work of piracy, they were unparalleled, swarming into the ship as fast and efficiently as a crack commando team. Utilizing portable force field devices, they poured through the holes, quickly taking out any resistance and securing the path.

"Clear! Let's go, lads!" the first through cried out with glee.

A few of the crew perhaps enjoyed their job a little too much, Charlie noted. He was, nevertheless, glad they were on his side.

Section by section, the pirates flooded the disabled craft.

"This one's ours," Marban said, scanning the dwindling resistance as he pulled his short sword free from the chest of the man he'd just impaled. "We need to get moving to the next section before they try anything cute. We've already blocked two attempts by their captain to scuttle the damn thing."

The threat of violent decompression did not sit well with Charlie.

"Well then, let's get moving," he replied.

Marban smiled broadly. "Now you're getting into the spirit, little brother!"

They joined the handful of men charging into the next section and ran headlong into a fierce fight. The captain was already there, efficiently working his way through all who stood in his way. If any had considered challenging him for control of the pirate ship, seeing him in action would immediately quell any such ambitions.

Charlie ducked and dodged a pair of attackers, breaking one's knee in passing as he moved to choke the other one out. Marban finished the man on the ground with a quick blow to the head. Charlie flashed an annoyed look, then realized the seemingly finished man had pulled a dagger from his belt and was about to push off with his remaining good leg, aiming to put an end to Charlie's pirating days.

He gave a grateful nod to Marban as the man in his arms slid into unconsciousness. He quickly trussed him up for the others to retrieve, then moved forward.

The fighting continued, but it seemed as if the next section was theirs for the taking, the defenders having fallen back in panic. A pair of men eagerly charged through the short corridor into the unprotected section.

"Wait!" Captain Saramin called after them, but it was too late.

There was no time to save the men. As it was, the captain only barely managed to utter the command while there was still atmosphere to carry his voice, quickly placing a force field across the doorway. A doorway that now opened into the vacuum of space. The last two sections of the ship were broken free, falling into the nearby planet's gravity. In short order, it would pass into the atmosphere, eventually plowing into the ground below.

"Idiots. Never charge in like that," he growled, then turned back to his men. "Okay, you lot, we're done here. They've scuttled the rest of the ship, so gather up whatever cargo there is and send the laborers to carry it back to the *Rixana*." He turned to Marban and Charlie. "I need volunteers to go to the surface of that planet and see if anything useful survived the impact. You two are it. Go gather some muscle and get to it."

"Yes, Captain," Marban said, then took off for the cells on their craft, Charlie following close behind.

"Shit, that was close," the greenhorn human said.

"That's why the captain warned us. Those idiots tripped the spell that scuttled the rest of the ship. If the vacuum and reentry didn't kill them, I'm sure the captain would have."

The two men quickly made their way through the bustling ranks of men ferrying their plunder back to the *Rixana* and pulled a half dozen of the strongest prisoners from their cells. They then loaded into the ship's cargo shuttle with its contingent of a handful of Drooks and separated from the larger craft.

Finding the scuttled ship was easy, Charlie realized. Just

follow the smoke, flames, and debris. And of that there was plenty.

As their shuttle grew closer to the crash site, he found that despite the greenery crushed and shattered in the crash, as well as the vast, verdant landscape around the wreckage, he nevertheless couldn't help but feel a sense of deja vú.

He had arrived in this galaxy in much the same fashion. The crew of this particular ship, however, had most certainly not fared as well as he had.

CHAPTER FORTY-SEVEN

The two sections the hapless ship's captain had chosen to scuttle, rather than allow to be captured, had apparently possessed some sort of automatic safeties that kicked in when they neared the planet's surface. Their rapid descent had not been fully arrested, but the impact had lessened enough that whatever protective shielding had turned on somehow managed to keep the structures largely intact.

The only problem was, they had buried themselves deep under the loamy soil when they crashed.

Unlike the hardpack Charlie's ship had encountered, causing a long slide as it gouged the surface, this world was *softer* in that regard. As a result, the speed and angle of approach turned out to be just right for the craft to burrow like a tick on a dog. Only, unlike a tick, this time the entire body was underground.

"Okay, you know what the captain expects of you all. Get digging," Marban said to his crew of prisoners as they disembarked the shuttle.

He and Charlie surveyed the crash site as the men labored

below. It was going to be a long day. "That thing plowed in there good," he noted.

"Yeah, that it did," Marban said with a little laugh. "On the bright side, that means we'll have an extended bit of fresh air down here on the surface, right?"

"But won't Captain Saramin be a bit anxious for us to get back with our salvage?"

"He will be, but the captain and I have a history. Been with him a long time now, and he knows how I love the more quiet worlds. And just look at this," he said, gesturing to the vast expanse of utterly quiet forests and fields. "And better yet, once they dig their way underground, even the sounds of their labor will be out of earshot."

Charlie looked at his unlikely friend with amusement and a bit of wonder. Marban looked the part of a rough and tough pirate, but there was an underlying tranquility the others seemed to lack. Whatever his past life had been, he was definitely far more than merely a thuggish pirate, despite his scarred and rugged exterior.

"You think we'll find any survivors in there?"

"Nah. Not a chance, little brother."

"But the ship seems pretty intact. Maybe––"

"Trust me on this one. I've seen this sort of thing before, and believe me, it's not pretty. The ship was scuttled, which means violent decompression. Now sure, maybe some were in sealed compartments away from the breach, but then you have a mostly unshielded atmospheric entry, the temperatures of which would fry most beings, powered or not."

"That must be horrible."

"To say the least. Now, suppose those poor souls somehow survived both of those things. Unlikely, but for the sake of argument let's just say they did. Well, these two segments here were not individually powered by Drooks, which means what slowed their impact was an embedded safety spell, likely put in place by either the ship's designer, or the party paying for the cargo being transported. In either case, the concern was preserving the ship and its contents. Not the crew."

"So the deceleration——"

"Would have crushed them to death well before they impacted the surface. All protective spells target the ship's hull and the cargo. Anyone unfortunate enough to be rattling around inside would be on their own."

Marban fell silent as he watched the workers below. The only sound in the air was that of the constant digging and a faint wind rustling the leaves of the nearby trees. Despite the horrific details he'd just heard of the crew——and his fellow pirates'—— deaths, Charlie couldn't help but feel some of the stress of captivity seeping out of his body.

He took a deep breath. Then another.

"That's the way," Marban said with a tranquil smile. "We have to enjoy these moments of tranquility when we can. It's a nice respite from the cacophony of our daily life."

"You really are surprising," Charlie said. "And I mean that in a good way."

"Thank you, little brother. As are you. And though I'm sorry for the manner in which you came to join our little group, I'd be lying if I said I wasn't glad for it."

The two men took a seat and watched the prisoners labor in the sun. The system possessed a yellow dwarf star, and the intensity of the sunlight was relatively mild. If not for the gray complexion of the man next to him, or the far more alien-looking aliens laboring in the dirt, Charlie could almost have felt like he was on a picnic back home.

"You know, this would be so much faster if we had our survey mech," Charlie said after watching the work for a while.

"Survey mech? What manner of thing is that?"

"Wow, how to explain? Uh, I guess calling it a giant robot wouldn't help."

"What is a robot?"

"Yeah, exactly my point. Um, let's just say it's like a big metal thing, as tall as those trees over there, that's in the rough shape of a man."

"A statue, you mean? Yes, I've seen many of them at the estates of powerful vislas. Usually tributes given to them by those within the systems under their rule."

"No, not a statue. A mech *moves*."

"Moving statues? I've never heard of this magic."

"It's not magic, Marban. It's technology. A combination of hydraulics and gearing, all linked together by a bunch of solid-state components and heavily shielded wiring."

"Your words make no sense, Charlie. This technology-magic that moves statues."

"Not magic. Just tech. It's a power system that runs off of a battery charge. We were actually working on developing a fusion-based power cell, but that's years from even being tested. Too hard to make them small enough, you see. That kind of power system is pretty much reserved for full-sized ships and whatnot."

"So you say it *is* power."

"Not like you mean. Not your people's 'magic' stuff––and I still don't know why this translation thingy always uses that word. It's maddening."

"Magic is magic. I don't see the problem."

"Well anyway, our mech is designed for hard work on Mars––that's where it was meant for. It's a planet with an unbreathable atmosphere––we're talking like ninety-six percent carbon dioxide––plus some pretty drastic temperature and weather conditions."

"Carbon dioxide?"

"A gas. It's what we're exhaling."

"Ah, I see."

"So the mech, it has tools built into its arms. Digging

implements, drilling augurs, things to move a lot of dirt and soil if needed. If we had that with us, we'd have those access ports uncovered in no time."

Marban laughed merrily. "Oh, little brother, you have the most amusing stories. Metal men as tall as a tree, moving by tech-magic. Such a vivid imagination. It would be a marvel to see, if only such a creation actually existed."

"Just because you haven't seen one, doesn't mean it's not real."

"A valid point, Charlie. But in absence of proof, I shall remain skeptical."

The better part of several hours passed before the prisoners finally reached a functional accessway into the buried sections of the scuttled ship. Marban rose to his feet, stretching and cracking his back.

"Well done. Get yourselves some water, then join us inside. Whatever is left to salvage will need to be transferred to our shuttle," he said to the sweat-and-dirt-covered men. "You ready to take a look?" he asked Charlie.

"Might as well get it over with," he replied, not anxious to dig through more death and dismemberment.

They descended into the wreck, and amazingly enough, the lights were still functional.

"Part of the designer's features," Marban explained. "Not dependent on the rest of the ship's functionality. It'll likely still be illuminated long after we're done with it."

The angle of descent into the craft was somewhat close to level, but still rather steep, but that was to be expected given the way it had come to rest there in the first place. Carefully, the two pirates climbed through the outermost wreckage, making their way into the internal cargo hold.

As Marban had foretold, drying red stained the walls where

unsecured crew had been flung into them during the crash. It was a telling crimson confirmation that there would be no survivors.

"Now that's going to make the captain happy," the scarred pirate said when they finally reached the innermost stowage area. "Nice and safe, and all intact."

"What is it all?"

"Not a clue," Marban said. "But so long as we bring the containers to the ship in one piece, that's enough to put him in good spirits. He always enjoys the opening part. Finding out what exactly we captured. I mean, we know the basics of most shipments from their records, but there are always surprises."

"And what kid doesn't like surprises?" Charlie said. "It's like Christmas, but in space. And with blood, and pirates, and aliens." He smiled to himself. "Okay, maybe not that much like Christmas. But still."

"Christmas?"

"I'll explain it later," he replied with a chuckle. "Shall we?"

"Let's get to it."

The labor team was called in and joined them a few minutes later to begin the long process of hauling the cargo to the surface and back to their shuttle.

"Shall we go deeper and see what's in the other section?"

"Lead the way," Charlie said as the pair of pirate spelunkers ventured farther into the metal cave.

CHAPTER FORTY-EIGHT

"You've done well," Captain Saramin said, eyeing the haul retrieved from the surface.

"I'm sorry we weren't able to salvage as much as we'd hoped from the frontmost section, but it looked like the protective spells simply weren't strong enough for the intensity of the impact."

"It's to be expected," the captain replied. "Now go clean up and get some food. You've both had a long day of it."

Marban and his human friend nodded and left the captain to survey his booty.

"He didn't seem to take the loss of part of the cargo very hard," Charlie said as they walked to their respective quarters to shed their dirty garments and gather clean ones.

"He's a practical man. Sometimes ships simply don't hold together as well as we expect them to. In this case, he was able to keep the majority of the cargo safe and intact, and he got a fair amount of prisoners in the deal as well. It was just the sections that were scuttled that proved troublesome. Hell, he had probably already written them off and was happy there was anything worth salvaging."

"And there was quite a bit, in fact."

"Yeah. Fortunate bit of business, that was. All right, I'm going to grab some food. You coming?"

"I'll catch up. I need to grab a quick shower first."

"Suit yourself. I'm grabbing mine after. I'm starving. I'll save your spot. Just don't take too long. You don't want the new prisoners to eat before the crew, after all."

"Of course not. Pecking order and all."

"Exactly."

"Cool. I'll see you down there, then."

Marban peeled off, heading for the galley to fill his belly. Charlie, on the other hand, freed himself of the uncomfortable pirate raiding gear, grabbing his regular clothes before trotting off to the shower compartment. He was thrilled to find the others had already cycled through hours before. He may have been one of them now, but there was something deeply unsettling about watching the red swirls of blood flowing into the drains––the blood of the men and women they'd killed in their raid, gradually washed from their bodies.

Alone in the hot water, however, Charlie could feel the strain of the day gradually ease from his shoulders and neck. In no time, he was clean, refreshed, and ready for a bowl of whatever the hell that mystery stuff they were serving was.

Clothed in his own attire, he felt surprisingly good as he walked to dine with his friend and recount the day's adventures. He'd even properly explain Christmas to his alien friend, though the idea of a magical fat man on a flying sleigh would probably seem more rational to him than that of a giant robotic man.

"There you are. I was going to wait, but I figured you wouldn't mind," Marban said, tucking into what appeared to be his second bowl of slop. "I got you one, but it was getting cold, so––"

"It's okay. I'll go grab a fresh one," Charlie said with a little grin as he diverted and headed toward the mess line.

He felt his stomach rumble with anticipation as he grabbed a heaping serving for himself, slipping to the front of the line ahead of the prisoners, as was his prerogative now that he'd been promoted to actual crew. Amazingly, the mystery food he had so recently barely been able to get down had become almost appetizing.

Almost.

Just needs some hot sauce, is all, he mused. *Going to have to see if a reasonable facsimile exists on one of our next stops.*

He carried his metal tray back to his usual spot, a few of the new prisoners throwing a healthy amount of stink-eye at the man who had just cut in line. In his regular attire, he figured it was to be expected. He didn't look much like a pirate minus the usual accoutrements. It was just one more thing he'd learned to take in stride.

"You see the new batch?" Marban asked.

"Yeah," he replied as he took his seat. "Seems to be a pretty rugged crew, compared to the last few."

"Agreed. And they fought well. I know the captain holds that in high regard, despite losing a few men."

Charlie observed the new group as he ate. It was still an odd feeling, surveying the 'fresh meat' joining them on the ship. Captured fodder to replenish the ranks of those killed in the course of their piracy. It was an efficient system, he had to admit, but it was still strange, thinking he was just a labor prisoner a few short weeks ago.

And even though Charlie was officially a part of the crew now, he still wore the collar of Captain Saramin. No matter what anyone said, he was a slave. Just a slave who was afforded a great deal of freedom so long as he was in his owner's service.

Some of the pirates, however, were not wearing the telltale collars. Truly free men who were living the life of piracy of their own volition. Some had joined up when the captain required specialized crew and offered them enough coin. Others had gained their freedom after years of labor and service, though none would tell him exactly how long he might have to fight for Saramin before he too might earn his for himself.

What fascinated him was that most of the men were glad participants in Captain Saramin's piracy. Given the choice between death or a pirate life, they had chosen the latter and not looked back. It was, as Charlie had mentioned to Marban, similar to the way the Roman Legion on his home planet had functioned.

"Join or die, eh? It seems our captain would have gotten along well with your Romans."

"It would seem so," Charlie agreed.

Across the galley, one of the new captives––a thin young man with faintly yellow skin and a close-shorn head––stumbled and fell as another captive from his ship shoved him out of the way. The young man's shoulders slumped, but he took the abuse, quietly rising to his feet, only to be shoved down again by another of the captured crew.

Marban's gray face flushed with anger.

"We are pirates, not cowards. Attacking the defenseless has no honor. It is beneath us," he said, rising to his feet. "I'll be back in a minute," he said, crossing the room to have words with the newcomers.

The abused man may have been subject to mistreatment aboard their ship, but they were *all* captives now, and none, save the captain, would be beating on them.

A shadow loomed over Charlie.

"You're in my seat," a stocky man said.

He looked up calmly. No one would be foolish enough to start trouble on Captain Saramin's ship.

"Sorry, you must be new. I always sit here. But you're welcome to join me."

The man shoved him hard, sending him falling to the deck, then swiped his tray off the table and onto the floor. "I said it's *my* seat."

He was not sitting down.

Oh hell, the guy wants to get in a pissing match, Charlie silently bemoaned as he got to his feet, picking up his tray and placing it back on the table.

"Look, I can see you were just captured. And I get it, you're angry. But the thing is, the captain doesn't like disruptions on the ship, so why don't you just——"

The man swung hard, but Charlie had seen the telegraphed roundhouse coming a mile away, easily dodging the blow.

"Listen. I'm serious, the captain won't put up with any——"

The man dove at him, tackling him in a rage. *That* Charlie had not seen coming. The two rolled on the ground, the larger man throwing heavy-handed punches, but not managing to land any of consequence.

"Stop it!" Charlie growled, bucking the man off and scrambling back to his feet. "You're going to get us both in trouble!"

No respite was given. Instead, the attack continued and increased in ferocity.

Shit, of course. He's new here. The captain didn't give him a translation spell yet. He doesn't understand me.

Charlie did his best to avoid the onslaught, but until someone with high enough rank decided to activate his attacker's shock collar, he would be forced to defend himself. And from the look of things, his assailant had more than just a beating in mind.

This one was out for blood.

Faster and faster the attacks came, and Charlie was already somewhat cornered by the location of his favorite table, far away from the others and close to the wall. It had prevented him from being taken by surprise when he first arrived, but now he saw the one flaw in his seating choice. He had no easy avenue to evade the unlikely assault.

A pair of sturdy metal mugs swung at his head, the improvised cudgels swinging hard in the enraged man's hands. Charlie desperately snatched up his tray to block the onslaught, but the force snapped the cheap metal in half, leaving him gripping two jagged fragments of his improvised shield.

The man smiled, wicked intentions in his eyes, and pulled a small knife from his waistband. Somehow, the others had missed it when processing him into the ship. And now Charlie would die because of it.

The knife flashed out, and Charlie slapped it aside with a piece of tray, but the attack persisted, the man pushing his advantage. A small cut opened on Charlie's arm, a hot pain shooting through his nerves.

Shining metal was about to find a new sheath in his chest when Charlie acted out of pure instinct. He slipped the attack and spun, his hands moving without the need of his brain's input.

Moments later he was the lone man standing, a sticky warmth dripping from his face and arms where the dead man's arterial spurt had splashed him.

He looked at his hands, stunned, replaying what had just happened.

One of the jagged tray pieces jutted from the unblinking man's neck, the metal driven deep, first with his hands, then followed up by a quick kick to the dull edge, driving it deep and nearly severing the man's head from his neck. It had happened so fast Charlie didn't even know what he did until it was over.

The onlookers were likewise shocked. Everyone knew Charlie would not kill. And now, here he was, a dead man at his feet, and by his own hands.

Charlie turned and threw up, mortified.

"Everyone out!" a voice bellowed.

When Captain Saramin used that tone, no one dared hesitate.

Charlie straightened up, waiting for the attack that never came. Instead, the captain studied him, a curious little grin on his lips.

"Nicely done," he finally said, looking at the body on the ground. "First-rate improvisation, avoided most damage to yourself, kept the fight short. Yes, nicely done, indeed."

"You're not angry?" Charlie quietly asked.

"I've watched you these past weeks," the captain replied, ignoring his question. "You have far greater skill than most of the others. A highly unusual fighting style you choose to use to run away and avoid harming others, but nevertheless, the potential was there. And now you've proven me right. I think you may have substantial value to me yet."

Charlie realized what had just happened.

"This was a setup. A test."

A little smile curved Captain Saramin's lips. "Clean up this mess and have that arm bandaged. You need to be presentable when we make planetfall."

He left Charlie alone with the dead man.

"Presentable?" Charlie quietly repeated. "What have I gotten myself into?"

CHAPTER FORTY-NINE

Captain Saramin walked the marketplace of the new world, a dozen of his men accompanying him, as well as another dozen prisoners. When Charlie had shown up wearing his pirate gear, the captain had told him that wouldn't be necessary. As a result, he was walking this strange planet wearing nothing but the clothes he'd originally arrived in. Entirely unarmed.

After weeks of pirating, the sensation was rather unsettling.

Of course, Charlie was still somewhat in a daze after taking a life. He knew it was his or the other man's, but all the same, he had never killed before. Never even thought about it, even during their multiple pirate raids. But the cold, hard reality was he was a killer now, and nothing would change that. He just had to accept it and move on.

Marban was among the men accompanying them through the streets, but on this occasion his demeanor was all business. He didn't say a word to Charlie as they walked, though Charlie could have sworn he saw a note of sadness in his friend's eyes.

"Okay, you lot. Stay here until I return with the buyer," the captain said. "That group of five will be sold together," he said, gesturing to a handful of prisoners. "Keep them right there. These others will follow to the next buyer I have lined up."

The captain disappeared into the tent, emerging a minute later with a thin woman with violet scales on her skin and no apparent ears, save a small hole on either side of her head. She was wearing layers of close-fitting robes, each a different sheer material that had an opalescent glow to them. The way the woman carried herself as she walked, Charlie couldn't help but wonder if she was some sort of royalty or dignitary.

"These are the ones I contacted you about," the captain said. "As you can see, they are all in perfect condition and will serve your needs, as specified."

The violet woman walked the line of slaves, examining each of them closely. For Charlie, watching the meat market nature of the transaction was surreal. On Earth, slavery had been abolished for centuries, but in this galaxy, he had been a slave recently.

Technically, he still was, though he felt far more secure in his life now that he was part of the crew. A real pirate and not just a laborer. And he didn't even have to wear his pirate gear on this outing. The captain must have been truly pleased with him to offer him the luxury. A reward of sorts. Things seemed to be looking up. It wasn't freedom, but it was a start.

"Yes, I'll take them, Saramin," the woman said. "I'll have my men deliver the cargo to your ship, as agreed."

"Excellent. Shall we, then?"

"Of course," she replied, pulling several gleaming collars from the folds of her robes. She placed them on the slaves' necks one by one, uttering a quiet phrase, making them seal seamlessly, but making sure to hold the metal away from the other collar, avoiding contact.

The captain then grasped his collar and *very quietly* whispered his release phrase. So quietly that Charlie couldn't hear the words. The collar's glow dimmed as it unsealed and fell off into his hands. They repeated the process until the transfer of all the slaves was complete.

"A pleasure doing business with you, as always," the captain said, giving her a gracious bow.

"Impezu Ovusk," she said, activating her new slaves' translators. "You will all follow me."

The slaves did as they were told, disappearing into the tent behind their new owner. The whole transaction left a bad taste in Charlie's mouth, despite his becoming familiar with the uncomfortable truth that slavery was alive and well in this entirely alien place.

Two more stops were made, and the remainder of the slaves sold off for supplies. Captain Saramin had taken on an excess of prisoners in the last raid, and with his ranks full, he was merely thinning the numbers to sustainable levels ,while replenishing necessary items.

"Well, that wasn't so bad," Charlie whispered to Marban as they walked.

His friend said nothing, but gave him an odd look.

A few minutes later the sounds of weapons clashing rose through the din of the market.

"Sounds like a fight," Charlie said, suddenly wishing he had his weapons and gear on him. He felt almost naked without them with apparent violence nearby. The men with him didn't react to the noise, almost as if they had been expecting the sounds of combat.

"This is the place," Captain Saramin said, stopping outside a tiny arena build at the edge of the central marketplace. "Wait here."

He stepped inside and was gone for several minutes before returning with a sturdy, heavily muscled man covered in the scars of battles long past.

"Which one?" he asked.

"That one," the captain said, pointing to Charlie. "He may

not look like much, but I know talent. That one's got real potential."

"I don't know," the man said. "I trust your judgment, Saramin, you know gladiators better than most, but he just looks so, I don't know. Weak."

"Trust me on this one," Captain Saramin said. "Let us go inside and discuss it over a drink. I brought a bottle of the finest Savloki liquor."

The man's eyes lit up. "Trying to ply me with my favorite drink?"

"Of course," Saramin said. "But pleasantries aside, with the right training, and a strong hand overseeing him, I am confident this one can be molded into a *very* profitable gladiator."

Charlie felt the color drain from his face.

"A what? Wait, what's going on?"

Captain Saramin glanced at him. *"San ovusk."*

Suddenly the voices surrounding him were all speaking gibberish once more. Charlie had a fully-] functional translator for so many weeks, he had forgotten how disjointed it felt being awash in a sea of undecipherable babble.

The captain pulled a bottle from Marban's pack and walked into the depths of the building. Given the way the two carried on, Charlie couldn't help but think they'd be a while.

"Marban, what the hell's going on?" he asked his friend.

The scarred pirate gave him a pitying look and put his hand on his shoulder.

"I know you can't understand me, little brother, but I hope you know how sorry I am this is happening to you."

Charlie didn't understand the words, but he did understand the tone. He was being sold into slavery once more. And there was nothing his friend could do about it.

In a flash, four of the dozen pirates had abruptly fallen, blood spraying from their corpses before the remainder realized what was happening.

A pair of lithe green men brandishing wicked blades and slaaps charged them. The two were easily tearing through the entire band of pirates with almost tangible fury.

Blood spewed, the dirt street quickly staining red from the men wounded, dead, or dying on its surface. Marban shoved Charlie behind him and joined the others in the fight. It was eight against two, but the Tslavars did not seem concerned at all.

Shit. Captain Tür? And is Saur with him?

Indeed, it was the men who had first captured him, and by the looks of things, they'd be his captors again soon enough.

In his close combat experiences with the pirates, Charlie had thought the rough and tumble men were top-notch fighters, but he had never seen the Tslavar crew in action. The gap in skill would have been almost comical, if it weren't so horrifying. His former crewmates were now being slaughtered wholesale, Tür using both his blade and his slaap to rend them limb from limb. And the knife, Charlie noted, seemed to be faintly glowing, slicing through everything in its path with ease.

Powered blades? he wondered. In this galaxy, anything seemed to be possible, so he didn't rule it out as he watched the captain and his sidekick work their way through the pirates like so many matchstick men.

Marban took a glancing blast from Tür's slaap and was thrown back on top of Charlie, while the other fighters still on their feet tried desperately to stave off the attack and fetch their captain for backup. It was a logical choice, but the door to the arena was simply too far.

Saramin would find nothing but his dead crew by the time he came outside.

"Marban, you have to run," Charlie said as he pushed his dazed friend off of him.

The scarred pirate's vision slipped back into focus as he regained his wits. Instinctively, he grabbed for his sword.

"No, don't," Charlie said, clutching his hand. "I know you can understand me. Only a fool throws his life away for no reason. This is not an honorable death, and you *will* die. These are the men you stole me from, and they will kill you without hesitation. You cannot defeat them. Not on your own. It is already too late. Please, you have to run."

Marban was torn. His was a life of combat and honor, but he could see the bloody truth of the situation. Charlie was right. He and his fellow pirates were no match for the Tslavar fighters. He locked eyes on Charlie and squeezed his shoulder, then rolled free and scrambled to his feet, darting for a nearby alleyway.

Tür shouted a curse after him, but didn't pursue, his bloodlust sated by the carnage all around him. He stalked over to Charlie instead, roughly yanking him to his feet in his fury and holding a bloody, glowing blade to his throat. He stared at him, unblinking, for several seconds, studying him, then noticed the dual collars on his neck.

The raging Tslavar captain's grip loosened and dropped him to the ground. He then reached down, one hand sliding around the second collar.

"*Yama harazan toora,*" he said over and over, his voice wavering with concentration. The collar heated to the point of sizzling on Charlie's skin, but he knew he had to hold still, unsure what the green man might do in his state if he moved.

A loud crack echoed through the street as the collar shattered and fell to the dirt. Captain Tür then uttered the same phrase as he tugged at the knot around the remaining collar. Moments later, the binding slid free.

Captain Tür unwrapped the collar, and Charlie felt a familiar sensation wash over his senses. He could understand again, though the translator Tür had given him had always been a pretty mediocre one.

"Ootaki hair, Saur," he said to his companion, showing him the cloth. "They blocked my collar with goddamn Ootaki hair."

He turned the filthy cloth over in his hands, studying the

scrap before folding it and slipping it into his pocket. "Still intact, and possessing a little power, yet. Though the piece is of mediocre quality," he said dismissively. "Bring him."

Saur roughly pulled Charlie along.

"Hear me!" Captain Tür said, standing among the bodies of the dozen fallen men. "I am Captain Tür, right hand to Emmik Yanna Sok. This is what will befall any who dare steal what is mine! Spread word of what happened here today, and who dealt this death. Do not forget it, lest the same happen to you."

He then spun on his heel and stormed after his lieutenant and recaptured slave.

CHAPTER FIFTY

"They wanted to sell *you* as gladiator material? Ridiculous!" Captain Tür was beside himself with amusement as they boarded his ship.

Amused, *after* he had gotten over his fury at his property being stolen, that is.

That he had taken so much time and tracked Charlie down across all of those systems really spoke to just how seriously he took his reputation. And now, with a dozen formerly dangerous men lying in pieces, rotting in the sun, that reputation would only strengthen.

As to the question of Captain Saramin coming after him for payback, that was highly unlikely. He was a pirate, but one who knew when to leave well enough alone. It was a simple calculus. On this one occasion, he had been out-pirated, and it made no sense throwing good money after bad, wasting even more lives to recapture a stolen slave.

Saur ushered Charlie through the familiar corridors of the Tslavar ship. He marveled at how clean everything was. How bright and organized. He'd become used to the run-down state of the pirate craft, nearly forgetting the seeming luxury he had lived in previously.

The Tslavar guided him to a room he had not been in before.

"Strip," he commanded in a bored tone.

Charlie obliged. Showering with the motley crew aboard the *Rixana*, he'd quickly gotten over his prior shyness.

Saur looked him over from head to toe, examining him for injuries or illnesses, while also gauging his level of fitness and likely ability to return to his labors. The Tslavar lieutenant straightened as Captain Tür strode in.

"As you were, Saur. You did well today."

"Thank you, sir. It felt good to put those filthy animals down."

"Which you did with great efficiency," Tür said with a grin before turning to Charlie. "You know, at first, I thought you had run from me. That would have been a very, *very* bad outcome for you. But then your collar went dark and I was unable to track you, and that was something you simply do not have the requisite skill, knowledge, or power to accomplish. That was when I knew someone had been foolish enough to steal my possession."

"Yes, I was captured by the pirates you killed. They took me when our group was forced to thin out, stunned me with some paralysis device."

"I figured as much," he said, looking his returned slave over. "He appears to be in good condition."

"Yes, sir. I see no injuries, though there are a few new scars and marks healing up. They must have abused him a bit aboard their ship."

"Pirates," he said with an annoyed sigh. "It is to be expected of them, I suppose. In any case, he is returned to us now. See him to his cell. We will put him back to work tomorrow."

The green-skinned man turned to walk out, but Charlie felt this was his one opportunity to gauge his situation.

"Captain Tür?"

"Yes?" he said, looking back over his shoulder.

"Thank you for saving me from the pirates," he said, neglecting to mention he actually was one of them until just that very day.

"It is not wise to steal from me," the captain replied.

"Well, I appreciate your coming for me regardless. But one question, if I may. What would have happened to me if I actually *had* run away?"

A cold smile spread across Captain Tür's lips. "Simple. We would not be having this conversation right now, and I would be selling your corpse for Zomoki food."

Saur let out a low, rumbling laugh as his captain walked away. "He didn't come after you because he cares, you know. He did it to teach any and all who would dare cross him what would happen to them."

"Given the carnage, I think everyone will get the message," Charlie replied.

"And that was the intent. Now come along. Back to your cell."

"Charlee!"

The lone Earth man in the galaxy found himself wrapped up in a joyful hug by a large blue man, and he was perfectly okay with that.

"Hey, Tuk. Good to see you, man. It's been a while."

"Been too long! Tuktuk thinking you dead!"

"Nope, I'm still here, though there were moments I wondered if I would be."

"Is it trueness? That you were being take by pirates?" Tuktuk asked, his eyes wide with curiosity on their stalks.

"Yeah, pretty much," he replied. "Got kidnapped and

dragged off on their ship. They had me doing slave work until Captain Tür came and saved me."

He wanted to tell his friend the truth of his adventure. How he was only spared because he happened to not be wearing his raiding gear, and that was only because he was about to be sold to a new owner. But Charlie already knew the captain eavesdropped throughout the ship, and if Tür discovered that he had indeed fled––and then become a pirate himself on top of that––his days would either be full of torment or numbered.

That also meant he couldn't unburden himself of the guilt over killing that man in the *Rixana*'s galley. It had been self-defense of the most understandable kind, but nevertheless, he had taken a life, and that was not sitting well with him.

Eventually, he found some comfort by discussing it in the third person, as if they were events he witnessed, not ones he participated in.

Tuktuk listed intently to the stories. Adventure aboard a pirate ship––even as a prisoner––was fascinating to him.

"Is their way of to living, Charlee. Killing is normal."

"Maybe, but it just seems so unnecessary, ya know?"

"I being pacifist. Believe me, I know. But also know that when it is your life or someone else, no choice, there is. But only those who enjoying taking life are evil. Sounding like the man you seeing only defend because him have to."

"Yeah, I guess I hadn't thought of that," Charlie said after a moment's reflection.

Charlie didn't so much see the door force field open as sense it. All that running around ships, looking out for traps and ambushes had attuned his senses somewhat, it seemed. Captain Tür strode in.

"Come here," he commanded.

Charlie did as he was told. "Yes, Captain? What can I do for you?"

"You can hold still," the green man said as he roughly

twisted Charlie's head to the side, brushing the hair from his ear. "As I suspected. They tagged you."

"Tagged?"

"Crude. Primitive. Stupid, outdated system," he spat with disgust as he dug in a pouch on his hip.

"What is?"

"This is an obsolete means of marking livestock, separating them and ranking them based on their power capabilities. Worse yet, it's not only old magic, it's often terribly inaccurate," he replied, slipping a lightly glowing ring onto his finger and pressing it to the mark. "Now hold still. This is going to hurt."

It was not so much a warning as merely a statement of fact, as moments later an electric sensation pounded into Charlie's ear. It took all of his willpower to hold still. The pain was extreme, feeling almost as if something was being ripped from his body. Something tied into his very being. Deep within himself, through the waves of pain, Charlie felt something else. Something stirring inside. Then, as quickly as it started, the pain was gone.

"There. Got it in one try," Captain Tür said, examining his handiwork with satisfaction. "That'll heal in no time, and a good thing, too. Those markings reduce value."

Gee, thanks, Charlie silently grumbled to himself.

Captain Tür walked out and sealed the door once more. "Oh, and in case you were wondering, your ranking was the lowest possible."

Charlie sank down onto his bunk. It was clean, and the food would be worlds better, but he was already wondering if he might have been better off aboard the *Rixana*. Of course, he was going to be sold off anyway, so that wasn't even an option.

Exhausted from the day's ordeal, Charlie curled up in a ball and fell into a deep sleep almost immediately.

CHAPTER FIFTY-ONE

The next two weeks passed in a blur, all blending together as the Tslavar ship jumped from one world to the next. They visited different-colored suns, and with them more people imbued different types of 'magical' powers. It had taken some getting used to, but Charlie was slowly coming around to accepting that this truly was some sort of 'magic,' and that technology––at least in the traditional, human sense––was not coming into play as he had formerly thought. The revelation was a bit of a mind fuck.

He had also witnessed the Drooks doing their chanting thing a few more times when he was sent on an errand within the ship. Apparently, they all had the ability to power devices or actually make a vessel fly, but for all that strength, they couldn't break free of their own slender restraints.

After so many worlds, he came to realize that most aliens in this galaxy were quite human in appearance. Sure, some had pointy ears, or violet skin, or golden hair, but aside from the truly alien bits, like Tuktuk's eyestalks, they were pretty easy to think of as almost human after a while.

The differing powers endowed by certain suns were widely varied, and it seemed that, despite his original skepticism, some of these power-wielding people were in fact able to 'charge' devices with their magic. It was, actually, the principal means of operating almost every piece of equipment.

Some devices were fairly common, and were actually more akin to multi-tools, where the weapons aspect was just one of many. They could control ships, open locks, even remotely guide smaller craft if adequately charged.

The slaaps, however, were far more military in nature. They somewhat resembled something akin to large brass knuckles, though sliding over a bit more of the hand than their human counterpart.

Then there was a much rarer weapon. The claithe, looking like a more robust slaap that extended to the back of the wearer's wrist, was something that was purely a tool of violence. Charlie hadn't seen one in use yet, but he had spotted one carried by a bodyguard of the wealthier traders they encountered as they passed from solar system to solar system.

They had landed just outside yet another planet's commerce center. This time a brown dwarf cast a rusty hue over the skies. It was a brutal world, and everything about it felt oppressive, from the light, to the heat, to the dusty refuse stench hanging in the air.

"I hate this place," he grumbled as he and Tuktuk lumbered along under their heavy loads.

"Is not pleasant. No," Tuktuk agreed.

There was a relatively thin crowd in the markets that day, so at least they had less careless foot traffic and wandering drunks to get in their way. Stopping suddenly while carrying a massive pack was quite trying on the knees and back.

Carrying shit around again. Oh, how far I've fallen, he laughed to himself, thinking back to his buccaneering life just a few short weeks ago.

Nearby, sounds of a crowd cheering would occasionally rise over the constant din of the marketplace. Something was up, but Tuktuk didn't seem to know what it was.

"Excuse me," Charlie said to a turbaned man who happened to be walking the same direction as their porter team. "What is all the cheering about?"

The man looked at the slave with distaste, but answered him nonetheless. "The festival of Yondar, celebrating the twelve victories over the Booran invaders."

"So, it's a party, then?"

"Of sorts. Some speeches from the mayor and regional patrons, then the good stuff. Many bouts, lasting all week."

"Bouts?"

"Yes. Our arena is one of the largest outside of the Buru Amphitheater on Gilea. Many will fight this week. A spectacle worthy of the Festival of Yondar." The man seemed taken by his own sales pitch and swerved in the direction of what Charlie now knew was the local arena.

"You hear that, Tuk?"

"I hear. Is season for fighting, then."

"It sounds like gladiators, he was talking about."

"If that means slaves who fight each other for their owners, then yes, it is very much like that. Wait until we reach Buru Markets on Gilea, Charlee. The arena there is very big sight to see."

Charlie let out a grim laugh. "Gladiators and slaves. I'll say it again. How very Roman of them."

"Less talking," the trio of Tslavars leading their group said as they casually negated Charlie's translation spell as they passed.

"*San Ovusk,*" one said, and suddenly, all were speaking gibberish.

Why the hell did they do that? Charlie lamented. *Bastards, that was totally uncalled for.* The rest of the walk he was forced to hear all of the languages in their native tongues, and the sheer quantity of foreign sounds made his head spin. *Imagine being stuck here without a translator permanently,* he mused. *I wouldn't even be able to ask for water or where the bathroom is.* He thought on it a moment. *Well, I could, but I wouldn't have a clue what they were telling me.*

As he was shoved back into his cell, Saur and Captain Tür stood nearby, watching curiously. They spoke their incomprehensible language to one another, and something in the way they were looking at him made Charlie very uncomfortable.

Saur called out some random sounds. Charlie just sat on his cot.

"*Impezu Ovusk,*" he barked, and Charlie felt a slight shift in his ears as the translator spell reactivated. "I said, come here, slave."

By this point, Charlie had learned it was far better to go along with things and not rock the boat. The Tslavar could make things very uncomfortable if they wanted.

"Give me your hand," Saur said.

Ugh. What this time?

Charlie extended his hand, and before he could pull back, the Tslavar had pulled a small knife and made a shallow cut on his forearm.

"Back in your cell," Saur ordered, then walked away with his captain.

"What the hell?" Charlie said, wrapping his arm with a scrap of cloth.

Tuktuk leaned in close, pretending to look at his arm. "Them forget to cancel my translator spell. I hear it all, Charlee."

"Oh yeah? So, what's their problem?"

"Shh. No speak loud. Them listen," he said, pointing to the eavesdropping walls of their cell.

"I know," Charlie replied in a whisper. "But what's going on, Tuk?"

"Captain say he may sell you to fighting school for to make you gladiator."

"Deja fucking vu. But I don't want to fight."

"Not your choice, Charlee. Them say you heal fast. Make them more profit."

"So that's why he cut my arm? To test how fast I heal? Dick move. And what if I just pick the scab so it heals slower? That'll screw up their plan," he said defiantly.

"Is true, would be bad for selling to be fighter. But Captain Tür, him say if you no good for fighting, maybe you be worth something as Zomoki food."

"Zomoki?"

"Is big animal. Many teeth."

Charlie blanched at the thought of ending his days on the receiving end of a mouth full of fangs. "You know, Tuk, maybe fighting would be better than being fed to a Zomoki, whatever that is."

What the hell has my life become? he grumbled to himself, imagining some ginormous hairy beast having him for dinner, then settled into his bunk and drifted off into an uneasy sleep.

CHAPTER FIFTY-TWO

Charlie, much to his surprise, had not dreamt of being an appetizer for a massive Zomoki beast. In fact, he slept better than he had in days. Whether it was the exhaustion finally catching up with him or an acceptance that he would never again see his Earth friend and was truly on his own, a feeling of simply not giving a shit had settled in.

Whether that was a good thing or not was up for debate.

They had stayed within the brown dwarf star's system, making a tiny hop to a neighboring planet. Unlike the previous day's oppressive feel, this one was a cooler climate at least, being located at a slightly more distant orbit of the sun. It was still a brutal world, but the creature comfort of not sweating excessively from every pore was a welcome one that lifted everyone's spirits a bit.

Everyone except Charlie.

To be sure, he was glad for the cooler temperatures, but after hearing he might be sold yet again, he found himself still firmly wrapped up in his fuck-it attitude. He'd had it up to here, and his last bit of patience was worn thin. Tuktuk saw the look in his eye and worried about his friend.

The planet was a fertile one, and plentiful food was readily available at a fraction of the usual cost of restocking the ship's rations. Even the cheapest of slop normally fed to the slaves on board the ship still came at a much higher price.

Captain Tür, always looking to save some coin, arranged for his ship to disgorge its slaves into one of the many feed houses in the area used for precisely such instances. It was a supply hub of some importance, and the amount of traffic flowing through the region was significant. Every ship at one time or another seemed to settle in for a meal and restock.

Having selected an establishment, after a suitable haggling session, of course, the captain was treating his crew to a sizable feast in the upper halls of the building. The slaves, on the other hand, were cast into what could only be described as a prison yard buffet from hell.

Long tables filled the vast space, while serving slaves continuously replenished the family-style chafing barrels along one wall. A feral vibe permeated the place, more like a bull pen holding area you'd lock up your toddlers while you tried to get a moment's peace over a meal. Only these weren't toddlers, and there was no ball pit to play in. Just a bunch of prisoners, slaves, and low-tier crewmembers all vying for a less picked-over plate of food.

"You've got to be kidding me," Charlie grumbled as they fell into the long line with the others.

"Is no very good food, but at least is fresh."

"Thanks, Tuk. I can always count on you to see the bright side," he said as he scanned the slowly approaching piles of unappetizing food. Fifteen minutes later, they finally reached the front of the line.

Nutrition is nutrition, so eat up, Charlie boy, he told himself with a grim smile, then proceeded to load up a plate with a healthy amount of food. If they were eating off-ship, he was going to make it count.

He stepped out of line, food in hand, and a hungry rumble in his belly when a tall, pale blue thug stepped in front of him. There was no collar around his neck, Charlie noted. He was some ship's crew, though if he was eating down here with the rabble and slaves, one had to wonder how good a ship it was.

"That's mine, slave. Give it to me," he said, reaching for the tray.

"Wait in line like everyone else," Charlie shot back, twisting away from the man.

Heads turned, and several gasps could be heard.

"You are a slave. You must do as you are told," the man growled.

"You're not from my ship, so this stupid collar doesn't make you my boss, asshole. Now piss off. I'm not in the mood." Charlie would have blanched at his words if he'd had a moment to realize what he had just said, but before that could happen, he found himself roughly grabbed and spun around.

The man wound up to throw a looping punch.

He's actually trying to throw a haymaker? Charlie found himself wondering in astonishment. *My God, could he telegraph it any more?* He almost laughed as the scene unfolded in comical slowness.

Charlie casually ducked, letting the punch fly over his head, the force behind it sending the man spinning.

"Shit," he said as the crewman lunged at him again.

Well, I can always get more, he figured. *And this will be so damn satisfying.* He didn't hesitate, slamming his metal tray right into the attacking man's face.

The impact took him right off his feet, and before he could get any ideas about making yet another go of it, Charlie put his hand-to-hand training to good use, wrenching one of the attackers' arms into a painful wrist lock.

"Now, are you quite done?" he yelled at the man. "Because I just want to eat my fucking food without assholes like you getting all up in my shit. You hear me?" He twisted the man's wrist for emphasis.

"Yes, I hear you, I hear you!"

Charlie eased up on the pressure, still controlling the man's wrist. "I could break this, you know. Right now. It wouldn't take much. But I *choose* not to. But if you mess with me or my friends again, you'll be wiping your ass with your other hand for a long time. Is that understood?"

"It is. I'm sorry."

"Good. Now get the hell out of here," Charlie said, releasing the man's aching wrist.

"Charlee, that was amazing," Tuktuk said, watching the vanquished attacker slink away cradling his wrist. "Unwise, but amazing, yes."

"Thanks, Tuk," he replied, picking up his spilled tray. "Aw, sonofabitch," he said, looking at the line.

Charlie headed toward the rear to wait all over again. Unlike Spartacus movies and feel-good tales, he may have beaten the bad guy, but the others weren't about to let that slow them in their pursuit of food. Or so it seemed, until a very large and very muscular man with a jeweled slaap on his hip and long, greasy hair elbowed his way through the crowd, straight to Charlie.

Oh, great. Here we go again.

"You. Slave. Come here."

Reluctantly, Charlie walked to the man.

"Come," he said, clamping a meaty hand on his shoulder and pushing him to the front of the line. "Get food," he instructed. Not a single person in the line said a word, Charlie noted as he piled his tray again. "Now, come with me."

He steered Charlie to a table—which rapidly vacated at his arrival. "Sit. Eat."

Charlie did as he was told. "Thank you," he said between mouthfuls.

"You deserve it," the man said. "You fight well. Sloppy, yes, but there is some skill. Good instincts. You have trained, yes?"

"Yeah, a bit," Charlie replied between bites. "Some Krav Maga, a bit of Jiu Jitsu, a little Silat." He realized the words meant nothing to the man. "Yes, I had instructors in my training program on my homeworld, but long ago," he said, then quietly shoveled more food into his mouth.

"You have spirit," the man said, sizing him up like he was a horse at the market. "I think you have gladiator potential. With proper training, you could perhaps win me some coin. I wish to inquire your price. Who is your master?" he asked, then roughly grabbed the collar around Charlie's neck. "Ah, Tür. He is a savvy haggler, but I think he'll see reason."

"I appreciate the kind words, but I don't want to be a gladiator," Charlie said. "I've never had any desire to fight. What just happened here? That was weeks of stress finally piling up, that's all."

Without warning, the man slapped him across the face.

"Do not speak to me of wants and denials. You are a slave. Open your mouth for more than eating again and I will feed you to a Zomoki and be paying restitution for burial costs instead of a purchase price."

Charlie wisely did not utter another word.

"Good. Now, go about your business, *slave*. I shall go speak with your master."

CHAPTER FIFTY-THREE

The Tslavar ship stayed on the planet an additional day, the captain allowing his men some rare R&R shore leave to relax and unwind. For most, that meant either gambling or women, but a few of the crew—those with the most years spent aboard the ship—opted for the open fields surrounding the city, where they set up a small campsite and relaxed in nature, sleeping beneath the stars.

For the slaves, however, it was a continuous burden of work, though it felt as if Captain Tür was more showing them off to potential buyers than conducting trades of any significant value. Sure enough, early in the afternoon, a sturdily built woman in ornate robes handed the captain a stack of coins, at which the captain nodded to one of his men, who pulled a particularly muscular greenish-hued man named Oglar from beneath his load.

"You are to go with Denna Purna. She is your new owner," Tür said, intoning the words, *"Ngthiri oolama tangopeh."* Oglar's collar snapped open, and the captain quickly locked Denna Purna's in its place.

"Come, Oglar," the woman said with an enigmatic grin.

Oglar followed along, content enough, but Tuktuk and several of the others seemed particularly distressed by the occurrence.

"What's up, Tuk? It looks like Oglar just scored an easy gig working for that woman."

"Is easy, yes," his blue friend said. "But no worth the price."

"What are you saying? Captain Tür was ripped off?"

"No that price. The one Oglar pay."

Charlie watched the burly man follow his new master into the crowds. But Oglar hadn't paid anything. The slaves had no possessions, and he said as much.

"You no understand, Charlee. Him go to work in woman house."

"Yes, I saw her."

"No, him no going work in Purna's house. Him go be guard and servant for the women in her house."

"Um, okay. But I don't see what's so bad about—"

Tuktuk cupped his crotch. "They no allow *whole* man to work this job."

Suddenly the situation became crystal clear.

"Eunuchs?" Charlies blurted. "They're going to cut off his junk?"

"Do not know what is oonoch, but yes, they make him less than man. Safer for women that way."

Charlie decided at that moment that there were far worse things than carrying large bundles to and from the Tslavar ship.

That evening they were sitting at one of the long tables, enjoying an early meal after a long day's work. After the prior day's incident, Charlie was given a wide berth by the other men. At least, most of them.

One particularly greasy-looking laborer with a thick band around his neck kept giving him some pretty intense stink-eye.

"What's with that dude?" Charlie muttered between bites. "He's been mad-dogging me since we got here."

"Most likely is him wanting to make show of how tough he is. After yesterday, beating you become the best way to prove himself."

"Oh, for fuck's sake, I just want to eat in peace."

"Seeming you not getting the chance, Charlee."

He looked up from his plate. Sure enough, the greasy man was making his way toward him, clearly looking to start something.

"Hey, man. Look, I just want to eat in peace, okay? You're the toughest guy in the yard, I concede. Everyone hear that? This guy is the toughest man here."

The hard-eyed man didn't sway his course, but instead walked right up to him. Charlie, not about to be taken out while sitting on his ass, rose to his feet to meet him head-on.

"I don't want a problem," he said.

The man merely smiled a rotten grin, then reached out a filthy hand and grabbed a fistful of Charlie's food from his plate.

No slaap on his hands, he noted. *And he's not that big.*

"Okay, enough of this," he said, hoping to intimidate the smaller man. "Take a hike back to your table and let's call this a draw."

Yellowing teeth shone like a tainted sun from the man's mouth as he let out a menacing laugh. Charlie thought that was the end of it, but the man then threw the handful of food in Charlie's face. He felt a surge of adrenaline shoot through his veins.

Fine. You want a piece? You got one.

Charlie wiped the food from his cheek and threw a quick jab followed by a cross. The greasy man was quick, but he didn't completely dodge the blows.

"Yeah, not so tough now, are you?" Charlie said as he struck again.

This time, however, the man did something Charlie wasn't expecting.

"Kika rahm," he blurted, throwing his hand up, open palm toward Charlie. For a moment, he glimpsed a fine band around the man's wrist, but that was brief, as he was immediately thrown off his feet, as if hit by an invisible punch.

"What the hell?" Charlie wondered aloud as he scrambled back to his feet. *But he isn't wearing a slaap.*

The man moved on him again and this time Charlie moved aside, on the defensive.

"Uzri ha!"

Charlie felt himself abruptly lifted from his feet and thrown to the ground, as if by some giant, invisible wrestler. A quick series of additional attacks left him dazed and bruised, sprawled out on the ground and wondering what the hell manner of fighting this was.

"No fair, you have magic," he grumbled.

The man looked up into the crowd then back at Charlie. He flashed his yellow smile once more, then turned and walked away.

Charlie's gaze went to where the man had looked. There, in the observing crowd, stood Captain Tür. At his side was the enormous man Charlie had encountered the prior day. The man looked disappointed. Captain Tür, however, looked disappointed and *angry*.

CHAPTER FIFTY-FOUR

"Failure," the elfin captain said, the disappointment clear in his voice.

Charlie had, upon his humiliating beat-down in the eating hall, been summoned before the slaver boss, and Tür was not pleased.

"I didn't want to get in a fight." Charlie rubbed the sore spot on his shoulder where the ground had done its best to remove his arm from his torso. "He attacked me. What else was I supposed to do?"

Captain Tür fixed him with a long, unblinking stare.

"You were supposed to fight better," he finally said. "You were supposed to win."

"Better? The guy was cheating. That wasn't a fair fight. He had magic. It wasn't a slaap, but he had something."

"He did not *have* magic. He *used* magic. There is a huge difference between the two." The green-skinned man pushed up his sleeve, revealing a slim bracelet, similar to what his attacker had worn. At first glance, it was nothing of note, but then Charlie saw the fine symbols etched in the metal.

"This is a konus. It is what defeated you today."

Charlie squinted his eyes, but the writing refused to make itself any clearer for his human mind.

"So it's like a slaap?"

"Not unlike one, but while it can be charged with magical energy, much as a slaap is, the konus is a focusing device. For gladiator trainees with a potential of power in their bodies, it can help them tap into that magic. The man you fought, he possessed the tiniest amount of magic in his body, yet it was the konus that held his edge. A slight bit of power stored in the item. It was that, not his own middling powers, that he wielded against you, a much larger opponent, to devastating effect."

"Okay, it wasn't *his* magic, but it was still an outside advantage."

"And if you were a gladiator you would have known the counter-spells to negate that advantage."

Charlie suddenly realized what was happening.

"That wasn't a random attack, was it? I saw you with that man. The one I spoke to yesterday. He said he wanted me to be a gladiator."

Captain Tür did something he rarely did. He smiled.

"Very observant. It is your sharp wits that led me to believe you would perform better when faced with an asymmetric attack. I was mistaken, and it cost me a great deal of money."

A flash of anger flooded Charlie's veins, but he wisely kept it inside. So long as he wore that collar, he was at Tür's mercy.

"The whole thing was a setup. A test."

"Yes. And you failed quite miserably."

"Well, good. You were going to trade me off to some guy to be a punching bag for a bunch of muscle-headed lunks?"

"No, I was going to make a hefty profit off of you, and in turn, you would learn to wield a konus, and possibly a small slaap as you developed into a more skilled fighter. It is a good living for those who excel."

"And that's not going to be me," Charlie said firmly.

Captain Tür smiled. It was not a warming expression.

"You have proven to be a disappointment, a financial drain, and more trouble than you are worth," Tür said with a tired sigh. "If you will not fight, then you will find value for me, one way or another."

Charlie didn't like the sound of that one bit.

Their ship took off late that evening. Whatever deal had been in the works had gone south, and Charlie had a sinking feeling he knew what the cause of that was.

They traveled for several days, and though there was no vibration to tell just how fast they were going, it seemed to him that the Drooks were working overtime. Wherever they were going, Captain Tür seemed to be in a hurry, though not so much of a hurry that he'd spend power jumping to the next planet.

Gradually, the light outside the ship from the new star system made its way in through the window, and the reaction from Tuktuk led Charlie to believe it was a bad omen.

"What is it, Tuk?"

The blue-skinned man quietly rocked on his bunk, his eye stalks darting about in fear. "We going to dark place, Charlee. We going to where Wampeh come from. We going to black sun system."

Charlie had seen what the one Wampeh he'd encountered had been capable of many worlds ago. He had terrified Tür's men, and *they* were exceptional fighters. He knew the same man wouldn't be on this random planet, but the thought that there were more deadly creatures like him out there was unsettling, to say the least. And they were going to a world where they thrived.

A heavy, oppressive feeling crept into the ship, despite whatever magical shielding they had in place. The black sun's powerful rays penetrated one and all, the light passing ultraviolet spectrum. When they touched down on the small planet, they stepped out into a dark world illuminated entirely by magical light.

Tuktuk may have been exaggerating when he said magic users were a rarity on such planets. Fully powered Wampeh, perhaps, but there were myriad other varieties of aliens with abilities not seen on other worlds. The planet was thick with magical energy, and it hardly seemed you could walk ten feet without stumbling into another enchanted device or system.

Even the sewage control was handled by magic, some creature's powers being used to vanish waste from the toilet systems, perhaps teleported to some distant––and likely very upset––land.

The porter slaves all lined up at the usual spot near the ship's exit, ready to hoist their big loads to their backs. One by one, they set out into the market, following Saur and Dolomir. Charlie, however, was given a much smaller pack, which was still sizable, but not nearly as immense as he'd grown accustomed to.

They set out into the market, and Charlie noted Captain Tür himself was accompanying the group.

"Kika rahm!" the captain grunted, violently blasting a group of ruffians from their path before they could draw their concealed weapons. "Keep moving," he growled, keeping his slaap ready. Charlie realized Saur and Dolomir also had their slaaps firmly in hand.

This planet was not a friendly one, and the bazaar they were heading into seemed just the sort of place one would go if looking for trouble. Conscious of his surroundings, Charlie kept pace with the others, staying close to the safety of the group.

"Kika rahm," he quietly muttered to himself, wondering what exactly it meant as he committed the word to his mental list with a helpful tune. The little school trick he used with most of the magical commands he had learned thus far was doing the trick. A good memory and a knack for mnemonic phrases had served

him well, and now he had quite the collection of little tunes compiled in his head, each full of dangerous magic words.

At least I won't forget them, he thought gratefully.

"Ngthiri oolama tangopeh," he whispered, but his collar stayed firmly attached. In all likelihood, even if he had a slaap he couldn't have made the band release.

Well, it was worth a try.

Deeper they traveled into the bazaar, and heavy magic was everywhere. Goods and wares illuminated by spells, and castings of a dozen types of magic could be had at any one of the stalls and marketplace tents. Charlie even saw what could pass as a flying carpet, though the airborne conveyance was more of an upholstered sled than an actual woven rug.

"Stop gawking," Tür said. "We're not here for sightseeing."

But there were so many varieties of pale alien life to see. Wampeh were plentiful, though none had that menacing look of the one Charlie had encountered many worlds back. These seemed to be normal people, albeit very pale ones, with slightly protruding spinal ridges.

Other types of aliens were there as well, most of which he had seen on other worlds. What was interesting was he found it relatively easy to spot the expats who had taken up residence from the mere visitors. It was in the skin. The skin and the eyes. The former becoming paler and paler, the latter wider of pupil from the endless darkness.

A sharp, invisible tug on his collar pulled him from the others.

"Tuktuk! What's happening?"

His friend turned to look, but was hurried along with the other porters by Saur, who shot a dark smile Charlie's way.

"We have a different destination." Captain Tür looked around, then, once his bearings were straight, headed farther into the market, the invisible tug on Charlie's collar urging him to follow.

He quickly fell in just behind the wiry alien, ashamed at himself for feeling the need of his captor for protection, yet involuntarily flinching as he heard unworldly shrieks and bellows from the mid-sized arena looming ahead.

"Where are you taking me? And what was that noise?"

More screaming cries that sounded like a beast had swallowed broken glass filled the air. A chorus of them, he realized, accompanied by a high-pitched buzzing sound like a swarm of flies.

Tür regarded him with a contemptuous look, then smiled. "Where I am taking you, is to your new owners."

"Wait, new owners? What are you talking about?"

"Precisely that. I tire of you, and your unwillingness to be of greater profit to me has left little option." He looked ahead to the building from which the shrieks were emanating. "As for what made those cries, you will see soon enough."

CHAPTER FIFTY-FIVE

Knives, swords, and clubs lined the tables set up along the high stone walls of the arena. The building had a heaviness to it. A weight of centuries of use, years steeped in magic and power, and not all of it good. Charlie felt a little lightheaded just being near it, yet Captain Tür was dragging him even closer.

"Enchanted sword, sir?" a vendor called out as they passed.

"Enchanted, you say? What is it capable of, then?" Tür inquired.

"Oh, it is a powerful weapon, brave sir. Guaranteed to cut the hand of all enemies who try to wield it."

Tür picked up the blade and swung it a few times, testing the weight. "A decent weapon, but the enchantment is but a middling one that would wear off after its first use," he said, showing the konus bracelet glowing around his wrist.

He slid the lightly glowing blade from the sheath on his hip. "*This*, I can assure you, is *not* underpowered. You would be wise to keep that in mind when next you attempt to sell knock-off enchanted weapons."

"So sorry, sir. So sorry," the man groveled.

Captain Tür paid him no further heed and walked away.

"There are *actual* enchanted weapons here?" Charlie found himself asking, his curiosity outweighing his discomfort and anger for a moment.

"Not true powered weapons, but temporary enchantment that will do the trick in a bind. With a strong enough casting, you can achieve something close enough to the real thing for those less knowledgeable."

With all he had seen, call it what you will, a special form of tech, or magic, or something in between, it was finally clear that there was a power at work in this most unusual galaxy that was unlike anything Charlie had ever even hypothesized to exist.

They rounded the structure, heading toward a large tent just ahead. A small gate, just big enough for a man to pass through was carved into the stone. Heavy metal bars, dark with age and something he didn't want to even try to identify blocked all from entry.

Or exit, he realized.

Captain Tür unexpectedly allowed him to pause a moment, amused as his slave peered through the bars into the vast holding area within.

"What the actual fuck?" Charlie couldn't believe what he saw. His shock was broken when the bellowing shriek of one of the massive beasts within pierced the air.

"Ah, the cries of the Zomoki. They are haunting, are they not?" Captain Tür said, watching his terrified slave with great amusement.

"*Those* are Zomoki?"

"Yes. Though I thought Gramfir had a larger collection on hand."

A plume of smoke wafted out the opening as one of the beasts spewed a stream of hot flame and stamped its feet.

"Zomoki are fucking *dragons?*" Charlie blurted, stumbling back in shock.

"I've never heard of a '*dragon*' before, but that's what I get for this mediocre translation spell, I suppose. Now come along. You don't want to be late meeting your new master."

Charlie felt the collar tug and quickly moved his feet to keep up, all the while his mind racing from what he'd seen. Dragons. And not little piddling lizard pretenders. These were Grade-A, big-as-a-house, fire-breathing dragons.

"Who is this Gramfir?" Charlie asked, already knowing and dreading the answer.

"He is your new owner. He procures and breaks Zomoki for domestic use. Of course, they are wild creatures, and ever so violent, so the process tends to be rather labor intensive."

Tür nodded to the heavily armed man at the entrance to the tent, then entered, Charlie in tow.

"Gramfir!" he called out in greeting to the rotund, heavily bearded man with pale orange skin and jet-black hair. "It is good to see you, my friend."

"And a pleasure it is to lay eyes upon you as well, Tür. It has been a long time."

"Indeed, it has."

"So, I received your skree message. You say you have a troublesome one you're looking to offload?"

"Yes. This one has proven most stubborn. I had hoped to sell him into the gladiator schools, but he simply will not fight."

Gramfir looked Charlie up and down, assessing him as one would a horse or pig. "Well, he's got some meat on his bones, and he doesn't appear diseased. You say he's strong?"

"Yes, quite, in fact."

"Hmm, well, I suppose I have been in need of a few more slaves to feed the Zomoki. Your usual fee?"

"Plus ten percent for his belongings," Tür replied, pulling open the pack on Charlie's back and removing several items.

"Hey, those are mine!" he blurted, recognizing his med scanner, sampling probes, and survey goggles.

Gramfir cuffed him across the head. "You do not speak

unless spoken to."

"Like I said, a difficult one," Tür said.

"Well, since we are old friends, I'll take him off your hands for the standard rate, plus five percent."

"Ten."

"Seven, and I throw in dinner and a woman."

Tür laughed heartily. "Now *that* is what I call making an offer I cannot refuse. Very well, seven it is."

The two men shook hands and the deal was done.

Charlie looked around the area. It was stocked with weapons and what appeared to be stretchers, but nothing edible so far as he could tell.

"Excuse me. You said I was to feed the dragons. But I don't see any food."

Gramfir and Tür stared at him a moment, then burst into laughter.

"Come here, slave," the green man ordered. "I have to tell you, Gramfir, it's been slim pickings lately," he said as he raised his hand to the collar.

"I have heard similar from other traders, my friend. But it should pick up soon enough."

"One would hope. *Ngthiri oolama tangopeh.*"

The collar snapped open and Charlie felt his neck free of the weight for the first time in what felt like ages. The two men continued chatting away, but Charlie again found that he now understood not a word of what was said.

Gramfir pulled a slightly heavier collar from his belt and snapped it roughly around Charlie's neck. The metal grew warm a moment as the seam sealed, then rested coolly on his skin.

"There we are," Gramfir said, the new translator functioning. "Collar on. Deal done now. Go, we eat, get you woman," the large man said to the captain.

"Is good. Happiness to seeing you again, friend."

He must be even cheaper than Captain Tür if the translation spell is this bad, Charlie lamented, looking around what was to be his new home. But what were his duties, exactly? And how much of his kit had just been sold off along with him? Did a man's possessions go with him upon transfer? Was that normal?

A cacophony of shrieks filled the air.

"Zomoki hungry. Nava, come take new one for feeding," Gramfir called out to one of his men.

"I'm sorry, did you say feeding?" Charlie asked, a sinking feeling in his gut.

The lackey grabbed him roughly and hauled him out of the tent, across a small patch of dirt leading into the walls of the arena. Charlie fought back, thrashing in the man's hands as hard as he could.

"Stop, fool!"

Charlie spun from his hands, smashing hard into the jagged edge of the wall, opening a nasty slice in his arm for his trouble, and just as the one the Tslavars had cut had finally healed completely. With his adrenaline spiking, he didn't even notice.

"Fuck you. I'm not about to––"

"Binari pa," the man said, ending the discussion then and there.

Charlie woke some time later laid out on a small cot. He had been washed, clothed in simple attire, his injured arm wrapped in a piece of cloth, though blood had begun to seep through.

It isn't broken, he noted, moving his fingers. *Should heal fast with the water still in my system.* He sniffed the air. *Is that spice?* He sniffed again. It most definitely was. A sinking feeling grew in his gut as he put his nose to his skin.

"Aww, shit," he said with a defeated sigh. *He* was what smelled good. They'd bathed him, put him in clean clothes, and even spiced him to make him smell nice. After all, they wouldn't want to serve a dragon a smelly meal.

CHAPTER FIFTY-SIX

Scars were abundant among the staff in the arena. Nearly all bore the signs of their work with the deadly beasts. Some were missing limbs, while others had jagged pink flesh where a claw or tooth had done damage. Still others looked partially melted, unfortunate survivors of dragon fire.

And Charlie was one of them now. The new guy. Looking around, he realized there weren't any old slaves to be seen. It made sense, he supposed. Older means easier to catch. Only the young and spry might hope to survive a while.

Contrary to his initial impressions, their job actually was to bring food to the beasts.

"We food bring," a one-armed man said with a morbid laugh. "But sometimes, they still hungry."

The others laughed as well. Gallows humor of the short-lived.

Enormous metal trays, rent with gouges and dents, were piled with food. It seemed the dragons were omnivorous, based on the hodgepodge assortment stacked high.

"Here. We put on stretcher. Carry for to eating," a moderately burned man said, motioning toward a rickety old conveyance made of wood and cloth. Gramfir was too cheap to even spring for a basic hovering platform despite the short distance it had to be carried.

"Seriously? We go out there with food and nothing else?"

"Is how it done."

"But why? I mean, couldn't they just throw it into the arena instead?"

"Oh, that. Them make wagers who eaten. Is popular game."

Charlie felt hysteria creeping up on him. *This is it. This is how I die. Eaten by a goddamn dragon in some distant galaxy, no less. Look at me now, Ma! Dragon food. If only my friends could see me, they'd never believe it.*

"Food slaves, pick up and go," their overseer commanded. He was, Charlie noted, a Wampeh.

"You don't happen to drink blood, do you?" he asked casually as they passed him on the way into the arena.

The horrified, offended look on the man's face said a lot. Namely, that even among the Wampeh, those who drank blood were frowned upon.

"I take that as a no?" he said to the pale man. "Well, that's good to know."

Charlie and his litter-bearing partner cautiously made their way out into the open space of the arena. Large boulders dotted the landscape, some inked with the dried blood of whoever had the misfortune of being smashed against it by the flick of a mighty tail.

"Holy shit, these guys are *big*."

The smaller dragons were perhaps as big as a garage. The larger were the size of a small house. All of them were lounging along the edges of the arena, watching the tiny creatures entering their space with mild interest, like a lion might observe prey it wasn't sure if it really felt like chasing and devouring.

They seemed benign enough, but that could change in an instant.

At the sight—or smell—of food, the dragons roused themselves. That was when Charlie saw the heavy golden collars affixed around their necks. The runes were constantly shifting, aglow with an internal flame. Judging by the size, the metal rings were insanely powerful. To require that level of control, he figured the creatures wearing them must be immensely strong.

The others quickly gathered up trays of food and began approaching the dragons, the meals held out like an offering before them. A smaller black dragon eagerly chomped down a tray of food, servant and all, then searched for more, while a yellow dragon waited until the blue alien carrying its meal was close before lunging and making the man drop the tray out of fear. It then ate the food slowly, amused at terrifying its prey, like a sadistic cat might toy with a mouse.

There were over a dozen dragons in all, and the strange buzzing sound they gave off that filled the air was driving Charlie to distraction. One particularly large dragon, its scales the color of deep rust mixed with dried blood, sat farther back, not seeming very enthused about the goings-on. Of course, that was the one he was tasked with feeding.

Well, if I'm going to go, I have to admit this is one hell of a way. He strained his muscles and picked up the last tray from the litter, then carried it right to the looming animal. It was even larger than he first thought, he realized as he grew near. A pair of golden eyes watched him with intelligent curiosity as he placed the tray on the ground before it, sliding the tray closer, keeping eye contact the whole time.

"Here ya go, fella. Hope you like it," he said, flinching in spite of himself as he heard a scream as another hapless alien was devoured somewhere in the arena.

The dragon shifted its enormous mass and leaned down to sniff the offerings, food and human alike. It moved oddly, he noted, and after building up enough courage to look away from the enormous teeth that could be his end, Charlie saw the problem.

The end joint of the dragon's wing was broken. Whether it was injured fighting another dragon, or had happened during its capture, he couldn't quite tell, but the injury seemed quite fresh.

Suddenly, it wasn't a dangerous beast. It was a creature in need, albeit a creature that could devour him in a single bite. It felt a little crazy, but he figured he was a dead man either way, so Charlie started talking to it as his plan developed.

"Hey, buddy. I can see your wing is hurt. I studied emergency wilderness first aid training, and I'm pretty good at setting broken bones, especially after my ship got blasted to this God-forsaken galaxy and crashed in that stupid Balamar Wasteland."

The dragon paused a moment, then continued eating, watching him as he talked, but making no move to take a bite out of the delivery boy. At least, not yet.

"So, I know you can't understand me, but if you'll let me, I think I can help you." Charlie walked closer, the dragon shuffling back slightly at the totally unexpected act. People ran from it, not the other way around. This was most unusual.

Gently, he reached out for the injured wing. It was massive, unlike anything he'd ever splinted before, but bones were bones, and the anatomy was starting to make sense.

His hands touched the leathery skin, and the most incredible rush of energy shot through his body. It was incredible. Orgasmic, almost. Suddenly, with that one act, all the suffering leading up to that moment almost seemed worth it.

The dragon twitched a little, but nothing more.

"Okay, look, I can't just leave you injured like this. I'm going to try to fix your wing, if you'll let me. I'd really appreciate it if you didn't eat me while I did."

Charlie trotted over to the discarded litters he and the others carried the food out on and dragged them closer to the dark red dragon. He then began disassembling them.

"What's he doing?" someone in the stands shouted.

"Is it letting him go?" another asked in confusion.

"Nah, it's Old Red. Five to one he's eaten in under two minutes!" another yelled, and with that, a new betting frenzy was underway.

Charlie ignored them and lay the bits near the curious dragon. The creature was watching him with the curiosity of a seemingly lazy cat that could quickly swat a mouse at any time if it wanted to.

"I'm just going to talk you through this, even though you don't speak English," he said, chattering more to soothe his own nerves than anything else. "What I'm going to do is use these pieces of wood to hold your broken bone in place so it will heal straight. But to do that, I'm going to need to align the break first. It's going to hurt, but please don't eat me."

As quickly as he could, Charlie began tying lengths of strong wood in place, laying the foundation for the big moment.

"Okay, now, here it comes. It's only going to hurt a second," he said, then yanked and pulled, jamming the crooked bone back into alignment.

The dragon shrieked and spat a stream of fire into the sky, but miraculously, it didn't harm him.

Cautiously, Charlie turned to look at the dragon. It was watching him with great curiosity, but suddenly, he didn't feel any fear. It was as if they had come to an understanding, of sorts.

"Well, all right, then. Let me get you properly wrapped up here," he said, admiring his handiwork. "Yeah, I think this should heal just fine, though I don't know how fast you guys mend."

The wound at the break wasn't too deep, but the blood flowed anew once the bone was set, splashing on Charlie's arms as he worked fast to not only tie off the splints, but also staunch the flow. In just a few minutes, both tasks were complete.

"Ow, that stings," he griped as he wiped the iridescent red

blood from his arms with a leftover scrap. It stung particularly badly where his injury was wrapped, but if a little infection was all he got out of this, it was worth it. "Okay, you should be all right, now. Just don't flap your wing for a few weeks."

Charlie felt amazing as he backed away from the dragon, his adrenaline running high and his spirits even higher. And the dragon felt something too. After finally being shown kindness after a lifetime of ill-treatment, the enormous beast held back and merely watched as he walked away, letting him go free without biting off so much as a nibble, much to the dismay of the betting public.

CHAPTER FIFTY-SEVEN

"He's burning up. Feel his forehead," the man said, touching Charlie's head.

"I did. What should we do?"

"I lost a lot of money on him. I don't know why the beast let him live."

"That's why they call it gambling, Linook."

"Whatever," the man grumbled. "I say we let him die."

"Look at his arm. It's red. Maybe infected. If he got even a drop of Zomoki blood in that wound, he won't survive the night."

"We have to tell Gramfir. He'll want to know why his newest purchase is taking up cot space when he should be filling a dragon's belly."

"But if he *is* infected, no Zomoki will touch him. That would explain your loss. You know how they are about sickness. They can smell it."

The gathered overseers and facility managers charged with keeping the operation running smoothly huddled over Charlie's immobile body a while longer, quietly debating his fate while he lay in a fever state, oblivious to the world.

After weighing the punishment for having an illness on their shift versus not reporting it to their boss, the trio finally drew straws to select the unlucky soul who would inform their employer.

"Sick, you say?"

"Yes, sir. He is running a high fever, and his arm is inflamed. An infection, I'm sure, though one of the others thinks he may have gotten a drop of Zomoki blood in his wound."

"Oh?" Gramfir asked, suddenly interested in the new development. "But he isn't dead yet?"

"No, not yet. He's hot, and his arm is red, but he's still hanging on."

"Then it's definitely just an infection. He'd be dead, otherwise. Still, fascinating. A fighter, then, this one."

"Time will tell, sir."

"Indeed, it will. But how did he come to get Zomoki blood on himself? Was one of my beasts harmed during the feeding?"

"No, sir. It was the damnedest thing, actually. You know the injured Zomoki? The one people call Old Red?"

"Yes, a recent acquisition, that one, and quite a difficult catch."

"Well, he was feeding it––"

"Ah, I see. He approached the beast and its blood flew on him when it flapped its wings in rage?"

"Uh, no, sir."

"No? Then what?"

"Well, he, uh, mended its wing. That's when it got on him."

His master's silent pause hung heavy in the air.

"I'm sorry, did you say he *mended* its wing?"

"Yes."

"He actually touched the beast?"

"Yes, sir."

"And it *let* him?"

"Yes."

Gramfir stroked his long beard, his brow furrowed. "*Very* interesting. There is bravery there. Or stupidity, often one cannot tell the difference. See that he has the care he requires. If he survives, this one may be of great value to me yet."

Charlie did survive, though for a few days that was in question. The fever rash spread to his entire body, turning him somewhat red for a time before gradually receding. At the end of a week, though, he was well enough to sit up and take fluids, and even a few bites of solid food.

"What happened to me? I feel like I was hit by a truck."

"Ah, you're awake," the overseer said. "I must tell Gramfir. We've all been most expectant, wondering if you'd live or not."

"Gee, thanks. Did you win the betting pool?"

"Sadly, no. I did not bet on your survival and lost a small sum."

"Shit, man. I was kidding about there being a death pool on my head. That's not cool."

"In any case, you are on the mend, and Gramfir wished to see you as soon as you regained consciousness. He will be most pleased." The man quickly exited the room to fetch his employer.

Hang on, they upgraded my translator, he realized. *What's going on?*

Charlie rose unsteadily, swaying on weakened legs.

Exactly how long was I out for?

He looked around the room. It appeared to be a small medical facility of some sort, though lacking in what he would consider traditional equipment. Having come face-to-face with an actual dragon, Charlie was forced to accept that this galaxy really was fueled by magic, and if that were the case, their healing tech would be no different.

There were some crystals on rods hanging from mounts on

the wall, all varying in size and color. What resembled an operating table lay in the far end of the room, another set of odd implements laid out beside it.

"Surgery by magic," he said, shaking his head in disbelief. "I am most definitely *not* in Kansas anymore."

Cries and cheers of a crowd met his ears, reminiscent of the merriment of the men and women watching him and the others feeding the Zomoki. But this sounded different. Louder. And there was the faint clang of metal on metal and the grunts of men. Fighting, he realized. But where and why was the question.

A slight breeze was blowing in from the window, and Charlie found himself smelling far more of the strange world than he had upon first arriving. Scents were clearer, crisper, and he seemed almost able to tell them apart from each other within the overwhelming stench of sweating bodies, refuse, and death. With a bit of effort, he suppressed the odors, making himself only smell the planet's vegetation on the breeze.

"Now that's downright odd," he muttered as he looked out the window.

He was in a higher window. Likely the third floor, if he gauged the distance correctly. Not too far in the distance, he could see what appeared to be the edge of the bazaar, where a small space port welcomed new arrivals.

He'd never seen ships landing from this vantage point. He'd always been either locked within a cell aboard the Tslavar craft, or hunched over, carrying some massive load through a dense crowd. But this, this was fascinating.

Drooks of varying abilities controlled the approach and descent of the various ships, glows of differing colors enveloping the craft, depending on the origin of their magical propulsion slaves. The ships, too, were many in shape and design, though despite his time with Captain Saramin, Charlie still couldn't tell which ship was from what system just by looking.

Shrieks and bellows cut his contemplation short. The

Zomoki were restless, it seemed, though unlike previously, it sounded as if someone was hollering back at them equally loud.

"Let me look at you!" Gramfir said, his robes flowing behind him as he breezed into the room.

He was dressed in far nicer attire than when Charlie had first seen him. This, he realized, was his non-public image. The bearded man put on quite a show for the rabble, but in the comfort of his own walls, he was actually surprisingly refined. For a slave trader, at least.

"How do you feel?" he asked with genuine interest. "Do you have pains? Do your ears ring? How about your eyes? Can you see better than before?"

"I-I don't think anything is different," Charlie replied as the man grabbed his arm for a closer inspection.

"Look!" he exclaimed. "Nearly entirely healed, and despite the possible contamination. Oh, you, my boy, are a strong one indeed. You are strong, and you heal *fast*. Most promising, indeed!"

"I'm sorry, what's promising?"

"Why, you are the most fortunate of slaves. With some luck, you may even live long enough to achieve true glory. And win me a lot of coin in the process. And if you are truly exceptional, maybe even your freedom one day."

"I don't understand."

"You will. Bring him," he commanded, flowing out of the room like a man of half his mass.

"You heard the boss. This way," he was ordered, then led down a long corridor to a staircase leading down to the ground level.

Once outside, they steered his fever-weary legs around the building until they reached a large pen full of men in wild and varied costumes. Only they weren't costumes, he soon realized. They were wearing armor. Strange, alien armor.

The men were pacing with nervous energy, the heavy bands

around their necks glowing with power. Charlie noticed they were wearing slender konuses on their wrists, and many had slaaps dangling from their hips.

Some had power, too. Not as much as the captain or his new owner, but there was magic there. That explained the stronger control collars. They were deadlier by design, but still needed to be controlled. These were men preparing to fight. Fight for the pleasure of a crowd.

Gladiators.

"Ah, I see you recognize what is going on," Gramfir said happily. "I lost several of my better fighters in the last bouts. Unfortunate, and completely avoidable. But you, my boy. You will help replace them."

"But I don't want to be a gladiator."

"Yes, Captain Tür told me as much," he said, stroking his mighty beard. "But despite the kindness I am showing you today, you should know, I am not nearly as gentle and understanding a man as your former owner. Now, you heal quickly, and you even survived the Zomoki, and that makes you a valuable asset. However, I do not suffer fools, and if you think even for a minute to refuse your training, you will quickly find your world to become one of extreme discomfort."

A bruised and injured man groaned slightly from the cot he lay on. Welts covered his body as if he'd faced some terrible foe and barely come out the other side.

"You see him?" Gramfir gestured toward the man. "This is what will happen if you hold back. You will train with the best of them, or you will be used as a practice dummy." He fixed Charlie with a steely stare. "One choice seems to be the obvious one, don't you agree?"

CHAPTER FIFTY-EIGHT

The ship carrying Charlie to his new training camp left the very next morning, whisking him off to yet another world, only this time he wouldn't be someone's pack mule. His work would be grueling, no doubt, but as a gladiator-in-training, he would be afforded at least a modicum of respect. Or so he hoped.

Only two others accompanied him on the small craft—gladiator hopefuls who had volunteered to be trained in hopes of bettering their circumstances. It was a rare thing, a non-slave entering the profession, but when times were tough, tough men sometimes resorted to unusual measures.

Bini and Gok were the men's names, the former a slender greenish species, likely a close cousin of the Tslavar, while the latter was pinkish, and nearly indistinguishable from human. They were both in excellent spirits for men who were about to be beaten and forged into hardened fighters, though given the scars each bore, Charlie had a feeling they'd both already seen their share of conflicts.

"Hey, Charlie. How much longer do you think it'll be before we get there?" Bini asked.

"I told you an hour ago, Bini, I have no idea when we'll get there. Jeez, next thing you'll tell me you have to pee."

"Well, I do, but I didn't think that was relevant."

Charlie grinned. In the short time he'd known them, he dared hope he could one day call his two companions friends. They were both of excellent spirit and jest, and were fairly articulate as well, though he also chalked that up to his new owner providing him a far better translation spell than Captain Tür.

And then there was that. The magic. Spells and powers, running everything from the toilets to spaceships. Charlie had slowly, but finally, come to grips with the notion that what they called magic was––whatever its source––their version of technology, completely normal and integrated into all aspects of daily life.

For that matter, Charlie figured his technology and science would probably seem akin to magic to the denizens of this galaxy, though a rather inelegant variant, from what he'd seen of their sensibilities.

"I hear Baruud is one of the greatest fighters ever to stain the arena's sands," Gok commented, idly picking his teeth with a gleaming dagger. "If we can achieve even half of what he has, we will be living like kings."

"Famous, beloved kings."

"Yes, Bini, that too," Gok said.

"And women. Don't forget the women."

"Yes, Bini, of course there will be women," he replied with a deep laugh. "And food, and wine, and all manner of good things."

"I was going to say––"

"I know, so I said it for you. Now, didn't you have to pee?"

"Ah, yes. Thanks for reminding me," he said, trotting off to the head.

"He's a good friend, but I swear, some days I can't help but wonder if there isn't a little something off up here, you know?" Gok said, tapping his head.

Charlie chuckled and shook his head.

"You *both* signed up for this of your own free will, Gok. I'd say there's something wrong with *both* of your heads."

"Funny, Charlie. But you wait and see. If we excel, glory is ours for the taking."

"I'd settle for a quiet life back home right about now. No adventure, no dragons and aliens, just me and a porch, quietly watching the world do its thing."

"But where's the glory in that?"

"That's the point."

He lay back and closed his eyes, resting and regaining his strength. He was nearly at one hundred percent, and from what he heard about his soon-to-be home, he'd need it.

It turned out to be a fairly long flight to the planet he learned was called Habogad. It was a small world covered in dense forests, thick swamps, and rugged mountains. The air was crisp, and the gravity was only slightly heavier than Earth-normal. It was there he would come under the tutelage of the great Ser Baruud, survivor of hundreds of contests, and now head of his own training center.

Their arrival was not greeted with fanfare or attention, but rather, a lone man of average height and build, dressed in a plain tunic, waiting to show them to their quarters.

"But where's Ser Baruud?" Gok asked. "I thought––"

"Oh, you'll meet him soon enough," the man said with a knowing look. "But for now, you are to go to your new lodging and become situated. You may walk the grounds, but do not venture outside the compound unattended."

"Why? Are there animals out there?" Bini asked.

"Because it is what Ser Baruud wishes," the man answered

plainly. "Now, please, follow me. You will receive your novice tunics in the morning. Training begins at sunrise. I suggest you eat heartily and get a good night's sleep. You will need it."

"You hear that?" Bini chirped with excitement. "We're going to begin training tomorrow. We're going to learn to kick ass!"

Their guide merely smiled and quietly led them to their room.

"This sucks," Charlie said, standing atop a slender pole on one foot, balancing a meter above the ground, holding a tiny cup of water in each outstretched hand. "Tell me again how this is going to be fun. How we're going to learn to kick ass."

"Shut up. I didn't know they'd make us do *this*," Bini grumbled.

"Quiet, both of you," Gok said from his adjacent pole. "Don't give them any reason to make things worse."

"What could they possibly--"

"You! Bini! Come here!" a burgundy-clad man called from the training field.

"You hear that? Now we get to the good stuff!" he said, jumping down from his pole and trotting over to the training assistant.

A flurry of swift fists and kicks greeted him upon his arrival, knocking him to the ground.

"Did I tell you to spill your water?" the man barked.

"No, but you said come--"

"Back to your pole!"

Bini's species didn't have tails, but if they did, it would have been planted firmly between his legs as he trudged back to his pole and climbed up. Once he had regained his balance, the man in burgundy walked to them and eyed them all with steely intensity.

"Do see that you don't spill them this time," the man said,

then walked away, leaving the trio perched atop their poles.

Thirty long minutes had passed, and their shoulders were crying out in pain, when a middle-aged Wampeh with broad shoulders, his hair pulled into a neat ponytail, casually strolled up to them, looking them over like one assesses a horse at market.

The three men wisely said nothing, focusing instead on remaining balanced, and not spilling any of the water.

"I am Ser Baruud," he informed them. "You are here to learn to be better than you are. Stronger, faster, tougher."

He began pacing around the poles, the three wondering if he'd lash out at them. He did no such thing, but, rather, gave them a speech he'd undoubtedly given hundreds of times before.

"You will learn the ways of combat here. The fist. The foot. The sword, and spear." He paused, lightly kicking the poles the men were standing on, making them shake. "You will also learn the ways of power weapons. The slaap, the konus, and, if you show true skill, the claithe. But before you are allowed to handle a power weapon, you must first learn to control them. To that end, you will each memorize a specific set of commands. I recommend you learn them. Those who do not will be returned to their homes or owners with an unsatisfactory performance report. Any questions?"

No one uttered so much as a peep.

"Good. When the sun sets, you may descend from your perches, but not a moment sooner. To do so is to court fate." Without another word, Ser Baruud spun on his heel and walked away, leaving Charlie, Bini, and Gok to their own devices.

Charlie silently sang his mnemonic song of magical words to himself, accepting their situation as best he could. The three men didn't budge until the sun was well down, finally climbing to the ground in the dark with the horrible realization that this was going to be far more difficult than they'd imagined.

CHAPTER FIFTY-NINE

Charlie dodged the heavy staff swung at his head but was a little slow in his reaction. The tip of the pole caught him above the ear, knocking him to the ground.

"Had this been an actual bout, you would be dead," Ser Baruud said to the assembled gladiator trainees watching the demonstration. "And if you are dead?"

"You cannot achieve fame and glory," they replied in unison.

"Exactly."

Charlie rubbed his head as he climbed back to his feet and checked his fingers.

No blood, he was pleased to note. He had bled often in the first months of training, but he healed exceptionally fast—which had caught Ser Baruud's attention early on, making him a favorite sparring partner for full-speed demonstrations. As his reflexes improved and his training began to sink in on a muscle-memory level, however, the bleeding occurred far less frequently.

"Do you know your error, Charlie?"

"Yes, Ser Baruud. I was watching the staff and not your

shoulders and hips. Your body will telegraph the strike more than the staff will."

"Very good. But there are exceptions to that rule, are there not?"

"Yes. You can feint and misdirect, using false movements to give the impression of one attack, while actually launching another."

"So it is," the master said, pleased with his pupil.

There were students who had been training with Ser Baruud for years, many of whom were actual gladiators now, returning to hone their skills further between bouts. Charlie, on the other hand, was as green as they came in the ways of their gladiatorial games. However, his completely blank slate gave Ser Baruud something he had dreamed of. An untainted mind with which to work.

The others had watched the bouts since childhood and knew the moves and spells from years of observation. Charlie, on the other hand, was an open book, and quite willing to do as his master taught, even if it didn't entirely make entire to him. For that reason, as well as his already-present skills in some rather unconventional hand-to-hand combat that he brought along from his homeworld as well as his brief stint with the pirates, he had quickly become a favored pupil.

"Everyone, partner up and run the drills again. Charlie, come with me."

The students took up their weapons and set to their assigned task, while Charlie followed Ser Baruud to the gardens.

A chessboard sat as they'd left it, the game half-completed. Charlie had crafted it for his master after discussing the Earth game often called the game of kings. One that taught strategy as well as patience. It was the one thing Charlie could best his master at, though he had suspicions that advantage would be very short-lived.

"Tell me, Charlie, you fight well, and you are more of a

thinker than most who pass through my doors, so why are you still not living up to your potential?"

Charlie took a deep breath and studied the board, finally sliding his rook into position. "I don't know, Ser. I want to do well. Hell, I *need* to do well if I don't want Gramfir to have me killed when I return. But I'm not supposed to be here. I have a life. A life on a planet where slavery was abolished centuries ago. And now here I am, someone's property, with no free will."

"There is always free will, Charlie. Even for those bound in servitude. It just presents itself in different ways than you expect." He moved his bishop. "Check."

"Maybe it does, but I'm just not getting it," he replied, sliding his queen and taking a knight.

"Use your circumstances to your advantage. Do you believe I was always as you see me now?"

"No, of course not. You were once a slave, just as we are."

"But the others, they fall prey to the myth of the man rather than the reality. To them I am this infallible guru, but you, Charlie. You realize the truth. Even a teacher has to rise from the mud and be formed into his final shape. Check."

"So you're saying I'm mud? I feel so much better now," Charlie said with a wry grin.

"You have it in you. The potential. I can *feel* it. You just need to stop holding yourself back."

"I'm trying. It's just hard, is all."

The black-haired Wampeh studied him with his unsettling eyes. "I believe you think too much. You need to think less, and *believe* more."

"I'll try harder," he replied, moving a single pawn. "Oh, and that's checkmate."

Ser Baruud studied the board, pleasantly surprised. For the great master, it was a pleasure rather than an annoyance to be defeated, for with every such loss, he learned that much more.

"I wish you to try something, Charlie," he said, reaching into his pocket, removing a very slender golden band. Charlie recognized it. A konus, though an incredibly slim one. "Put this on and come with me."

He accepted the device and slid it over his wrist, a low tingle settling into his skin where it rested, then followed his teacher back to the training grounds.

"Hurzahan, come here and power yourself," Ser Baruud called to one of his senior students.

"Um, what are we doing, Ser Baruud?" Charlie asked.

"*We* are not doing anything. *You* are going to use your konus in live combat."

"Did you say *live*?"

"Do not worry. Your device is very weak, and Hurzahan has excellent control of all gladiatorial weapons. You may be sore after, but no real harm will befall you."

Charlie wasn't so sure about the whole idea, but he stepped into the training circle just the same.

You've got this. You know the words. Just remember what you learned.

He had spent many hours memorizing the relatively short list of spells given to him many weeks prior and felt confidence building inside of him as he was finally getting the hang of keeping them separate from the list of other words already rattling around in his head.

With the konus on his wrist, he couldn't help but wonder if it wasn't a magical ability deep within him now triggered by the device resting on his skin. The folly of a man from a world with no powers.

"Prepare," Ser Baruud ordered.

Both men settled into their fighting stances.

"Begin."

"*Nari Pa!*" Charlie shouted, hoping to quickly stun his

opponent. His konus did nothing. *"Nari Pa!"* he said again to no avail.

"Uzri ho," Hurzahan calmly said. The spell lifted Charlie into the air and flipped him once before unceremoniously dumping him to the ground.

He jumped to his feet and rushed the more-skilled opponent, hoping to catch him off guard.

"Kika rahm," the man said, sidestepping the attack and landing a gentle, but firm, magical slap on his face.

"Eefanguley!" Charlie shouted, trying to bowl his opponent over. Again, nothing happened, but this time he at least felt *something* tingling in his wrist. Hopefully it was the konus trying to work.

Damn thing doesn't have any power, he griped silently, while Hurzahan landed spell after spell on him, sending him tumbling to and fro.

The fight continued, yet the novice human could not land a single blow on his opponent, while at the same time he took a beating. It was a relatively gentle beating, but a beating just the same. Over and over, Charlie was knocked to the ground, but each time he forced himself back to his feet. The spell commands just weren't coming to him, and all the hours of practice seemed for naught.

Frustrated, Charlie threw out his hands. *"Azkokta!"*

A dark energy began to pull from his chest and into his arms, building in strength as it moved toward his hands. Ser Baruud leapt in front of him. *"Vafangoolvavia!"* he shouted as he snatched the konus from Charlie's wrist.

The feeling in his chest immediately dissipated just in time for him to feel the blow of a full-force *"kika rahm"* send him flying. When he came to, he was still lying in the dirt, but all of the others had left. All but Ser Baruud, who sat looking at him with a strange and frightening look.

"Where did you learn that spell?" he finally said, a calm yet angry energy in his voice. Charlie knew, somehow, that his very life depended on the answer.

"A Wampeh. Someone I saw in one of my first days as a slave. He was fighting a group of men. He said it then, and I remembered it. It was one of the first spell words I heard."

"And do you know what this word is?"

"A powerful blow."

"No. It is far worse. This word is a death word. One of the forbidden, known only to a handful of the Wampeh Ghalian."

"The what?"

"They are an ancient order. Men and women of my race who possess great power, but who also use it to cause harm to others. They are assassins of the highest degree. For you to have been allowed to hear this word and live was a mistake they should never have made."

Charlie thought back to that day, to his saving the man's life just before the spell was cast. "Are you going to kill me?" he finally asked.

Ser Baruud thought long and hard, staring at him until the silence threatened to unsettle his mind. "No, Charlie. I will not. Not today, anyway."

He rose and began walking away.

"Wait. Will you still train me?"

A pause.

"You still wish to learn?" Baruud asked.

"Yes. Please. Help me understand this. Why was the only spell I could even start to make work one of the worst imaginable? Am I cursed?"

"You show a willingness to learn from your mistakes." A long silence hung as the Wampeh master considered his pupil. "I will continue to train you, Charlie," he finally said. "And what you should really be asking is not why you were unable to tap into the lesser spells, but why you were able to even come close with one of the most potent ones. And using an underpowered konus, no less. Now, your training is over for today. Eat. Build your energy."

"Yes, Ser Baruud."

"Clear your head, Charlie. We renew this training tomorrow. Now go eat. Find me when you are done."

CHAPTER SIXTY

The Wampeh master was sitting tranquilly in the small meditation garden adjacent to the training grounds. It was outside the main walls of the facilities, and animals and curious wanderers periodically disrupted the order of things, occasionally making a bit of a mess of the vegetation and overturning the low seats.

Ser Baruud, however, seemed almost pleased by this, taking the time to put things back in order as just one more form of meditation. An opportunity to calm his mind through simple actions that required little thought.

Today he had no such work to do and was sitting tranquilly beside a large, weathered rock, one small section of it polished to a high gloss. He looked up at Charlie with a calm and assessing eye as he approached.

"Come, sit with me," he said, offering a cup of tea.

"Thank you, Ser Baruud," Charlie said, taking the offered seat.

They sipped tea in silence a few moments, the Wampeh master slowly rubbing his hand across the smooth part of the rock, as if stroking a cat.

"Do you know why you have such difficulty with casting spells, Charlie?" he asked.

"I think it's my pronunciation. When I got flustered, I must not have been saying things right."

"And the killing word you attempted to use? How was it that particular spell nearly worked?"

Charlie hesitated. "Well, to be completely honest, there are some commands I've known for a while. Since I was taken captive. A lot, actually. I sing them to myself to help remember them. Because I've repeated them out loud and in my head so many times, the words are easier to say."

Ser Baruud looked at him with a curious expression.

"You have learned other spells, you say? Yet no one taught them to you?"

"That's right. I..." he hesitated. "I learned them in hopes of one day using them to escape. Please don't tell Gramfir. He'll sell me for Zomoki food."

The great gladiator let out a low laugh.

"Oh, I will not see you fed to the animals, Charlie. But now my suspicions as to your problem are confirmed. You keep talking of these spells as though they are mere words. Your mind will not allow you to accept that this galaxy is different from your own. I admit, I, too, found it difficult to accept that a world such as yours could exist. One where not magic, but this thing you call 'tech' ruled the lands. But once one accepts that there are places ruled by laws of nature far different from any we understand, then all one must do is learn to work by those new rules, no matter how foreign and illogical they may seem."

"What are you saying? You believe me about technology?"

"Yes, Charlie, I do. The concept, at least, though the actual function still evades me."

"Everyone else calls it tech-magic."

"It is what we know in this galaxy. But magic for us is a term for things of power, just as you use the word technology. Consider them interchangeable, at least conversationally."

"But the Tslavars said they could feel no power in my tech. No one could. They don't understand how it works, and that makes everyone uncomfortable."

"I know. Just as I know where your mind is stuck in these matters. We have discussed many things during our chess matches. You open up more than you realize as we play those games."

Charlie hadn't thought about it much. He assumed the Wampeh had simply been absorbed in learning the new strategy game from another world. But as he reflected back on their games, he supposed they actually did have a bit of a psychologist's couch feel to them as well.

"You used the game––something from my world that made me comfortable––to dig around in my head."

"I wouldn't put it quite like that, but yes. And I see your problem. You witness magic around you every day, Charlie. Our entire galaxy functions by it. Yet you still call it 'voice command,' as if it were technology from your world despite accepting it for what it is."

"Right, different tech for different galaxies."

"No, that's not what I'm saying. In *this* galaxy, there are hundreds of billions of stars, and of those, there are hundreds of millions of planetary systems. And of those, there are hundreds of inhabited worlds, though many speculate there could be tens of thousands of them, and exploration is constantly occurring. As you've seen, different species possess different abilities, though those who can wield power without external aid are extremely rare."

"Hence the konus, the slaap, and the claithe."

"Exactly. Tools that store power for those without, as well as focusing that of those who already possess it. These powers evolved over millennia, you see. The radiation of a tiny handful of suns in this network of systems interacting galactically, creating a solar harmonic between the worlds. It is an invisible force of immense power, able to be stored in some devices. And some evolved to be far more attuned to it than others."

"That sounds more like a superhero origin story than magic," Charlie noted. "Makes me expect to find a big chunk of Kryptonite laying around somewhere."

"You use humor to hide your confusion and fear, and that is normal. But I want you to try to understand that magic is not voice command of a technology device as in your world. Magic is *power*. Power in the air. Power in the void of space. Power that certain sound combinations tap into."

"So, voice control."

"No, Charlie. The voice is only the smallest part of it. The trigger, if you will. It is the visceral feeling, the *intent* and will within the caster that ultimately makes a spell work."

"And these words, they just stumbled upon them across all those systems?"

"Actually, yes," Ser Baruud replied. "What you hear now are the combined learnings of hundreds of worlds, the knowledge pooled as contact and alliances were formed. The spells themselves are not true words, in the sense of language. They are sound combinations that *transcend* language. You may have noticed that even without translator spells these words sound the same, yes?"

"I was wondering about that, actually."

Baruud smiled. "Good. You *have* been paying attention. These spells were discovered by accident. Sounds and thoughts uttered causing things to happen. And even then, only for the smallest fraction of beings. That power is incredibly rare. Those who possess that kind of internal power move on to become mesters, emmiks, or, for the truly powerful, vislas. These beings dedicate their lives to training, gaining more control of their power, while pushing the boundaries of spells, expanding our magical knowledge. That was how the Council of Twenty was formed."

"The what?"

"A group of the most powerful vislas and power users from twenty key systems. They rule the others, keeping order. Once, they promoted peace, but now they focus on amassing more power and control, though with every new power-using planetary system discovered that is not under their rule, their power seems to weaken. It is the unusual way of the galactic network. Contact triggers a connection and ties the worlds together in mysterious ways mere men cannot fully understand."

"But what about the Ootaki? Or the Drooks? They have power, as you describe it, yet they are sold off as animals, essentially. Where's the upside for them?"

A sadness flashed across Ser Baruud's face. "Those who possess power but either not the ability to use it––such as Ootaki––or are limited by a single use for their power––such as Drooks––were seen as tools. Organic versions of slaaps, konuses, and other devices that store or control power."

"That's horrible."

"That's how it has always been," Baruud replied.

"But I still don't understand how these spells came to be. Even if people stumbled upon sounds and feelings that made these solar-spawned powers react, a full-fledged magic-based society would take centuries to evolve."

"Millennia, actually," the pale man replied, stroking the smooth area of the rock beside him. "Do you see this, Charlie? A massive rock, jutting from the ground. Rough, hard, set in being exactly what it is. A rock. But time alters things, with a little help. This spot was as rough as the rest of it when the first builders broke ground here thousands of years ago. One of the master builders took to sitting in this very spot, absentmindedly stroking this very rock as he pondered his next designs. When he died, his apprentice adopted the habit. Over time, all of the masters of this estate have been drawn to this place. This innocuous rock. And all have caressed its surface."

Charlie looked at the polished area. He had thought it had been made that way by tools, though for what reason he was unsure. Now he realized the truth of it. Hundreds of hands, over thousands of years, had slowly worn it down, transforming it over lifetimes.

"You're saying thousands and thousands of years of trial and error evolved your galaxy's magic system?"

"Yes. And now you too are a part of that system. I've sensed something in you. It's small for now. Just a tiny spark. But magic is like a muscle. The more you use it, the stronger it gets and the easier it is to wield and control."

"I don't have any magic in me. I'm human. It's just not possible."

Ser Baruud cocked his head slightly. "But you do, and one day that spark may be fanned into a flame." He sipped his tea and caressed the rock beside him. "Think of it like walking. To an infant the task seems utterly impossible, yet that same child will one day run and jump, not even thinking about their former state. So it is with magic."

"But I can't even do anything with a slaap, let alone without one."

"The konus and slaap are among the devices most often used by those with no power. They can be charged, like the 'bahtrees' of your world you've spoken of. This allows all to wield magic. But others use them to focus and enhance their own internal gifts."

Ser Baruud finished his tea and rose to his feet. "You have potential, Charlie. A power within. That is why the killing word very nearly worked. Your anger was visceral. And while anger is a terrible place to cast spells from, you have shown you *do* have the ability to cast. It's not the words alone. If it were, any fool could use magic."

He gathered up the cups and pot and turned toward the compound walls.

"I'll leave you here to consider all of this. I know it is a lot for your mind to handle at first," he said as he walked away.

Charlie rose and took his master's still-warm seat. Without thinking, he found his hand slowly caressing the glossy groove in the rock as he thought about what living in this galaxy truly meant.

CHAPTER SIXTY-ONE

Charlie was given a konus to wear at all times from that day forward to help him *feel* the power and become accustomed to it. Only it wasn't just any konus, it was the weakest, most underpowered one on the entire planet. Perhaps the entire system.

It was the magical equivalent of training wheels, elbow and knee pads, and a giant helmet, but if that was what it would take to let him safely train, he was okay with that.

What he quickly learned as well was the konus he wore was also restricted from all but a handful of rather benign spells. Ser Baruud knew his secret. His list of spells running through his head. So it was he was limited to the basics. A simple pushing spell, designed to move an opponent, or object, should the need arise. Its counterpart, a pulling spell, to accomplish the opposite. Things of that nature.

There were also a handful of what he considered borderline cheap trick spells. Tripping spells, itching spells, blurry vision spells, any of which seemed ridiculous against a trained opponent, but Charlie persevered and practiced them every day, finding some pleasure in at least pestering those he could not defeat.

Soon, his unconventional sparring sessions took on a different feel, and despite being clobbered by his opponents constantly, Charlie learned to apply his rudimentary defensive spells to minimize the damage.

One in particular, the *"Konus magusi"* spell, had an unexpected effect. He learned this when he accidentally cast it while touching his restraint collar. The spell was designed to weaken whatever attack an opponent had cast, but in casting his purely-defensive spell with his hand on the enchanted collar, he found he had unintentionally fed the spell into the charged metal.

The result was a crackling of energy in the slender metal band, followed by a surging of his own power, as if in reducing the neutralizing effect of the band, even temporarily, he was suddenly free to use far more of the magic at his disposal.

Of course, Charlie was a non-magical being, and from a different galaxy, no less, so that was obviously impossible, but he found the sensation intriguing nevertheless.

Weeks upon weeks of training passed, and the previously perceived handicap of having access to only a handful of spells began slowly turning into an advantage of sorts, as Charlie was forced to rely on agility, deception, and misdirection to drain his opponents' weapons of their energy before launching a counterattack.

Outside the arena, Ser Baruud and he continued to play chess daily, and while the martial master was now winning as often as not, Charlie felt his abilities growing simply by the casual, unguarded conversations they had during those rare moments of downtime. In the arena, it was all about combat, but over the chessboard, his training tended toward the more philosophical.

"You have learned some interesting things about yourself

these past weeks, have you not?" Baruud asked during one such game.

"I believe so," Charlie replied. "The less I force the spells, the more the konus seems to react. It's almost like as casting becomes second nature, the lack of conscious effort is what makes the device work."

"But you know it's a magically charged tool. Its powers are fixed by what it was imbued with by its creator. So how do you improve on what cannot be improved?"

Charlie had already been thinking long and hard about that and had formed a rough hypothesis. "It's kind of like a limiter on an engine. I mean, you don't use engines here, but the principle is the same. Something used to restrict the gas flow so a vehicle can only reach a certain top speed. Only, in my case, the limiter was myself. It's not so much that I'm outpacing my konus, it's that all this time I had been underutilizing it with my own internal limiter."

Ser Baruud smiled. "Very good, Charlie. You have learned a lesson it takes some students years to comprehend."

"Well, you did say I was an empty vessel."

Baruud chuckled softly. "Yes, though I must admit that was not entirely intended as a compliment at the time," he replied with a wry smile. "Give me your arm," he commanded. Charlie immediately complied, and his teacher gently touched the slim metal ring around his wrist.

"Is everything okay?"

"Yes, I believe it is," the Wampeh replied. "I am going to teach you a new spell. It is only barely within the capabilities of this konus, and you will have no time to practice it, but I want you to utilize this tool in this afternoon's training."

"I'll do my best."

"Good," Baruud said, taking off his own konus for the moment. "Now, repeat these words. *Klaatu endatha.*'"

"*Klaatu endatha,*" Charlie repeated. He felt the slightest of tingles in his arm, but no more. "Was that supposed to do something?"

"It is a combination spell. A block and counterattack. But you're thinking the words. They are brand-new to you. You need them to flow as second nature, like you described earlier. Strive for that state when you fight this afternoon, and perhaps you may finish a match with your feet on the ground, instead of your rear."

"Gok. Charlie. In the ring," Teacher Fazool commanded.

The two men stepped into the combatant's arena. Ser Baruud sipped tea, watching from his seat on the sideline. The master slipped his slaap onto his hand and touched the outline on the ground. "*Invario doman ubantunu,*" he said, charging the arena with a protective dome, as he did before every session. The spell, while preventing stray castings from injuring bystanders, would not, however, keep the fighters' physical bodies from passing. Magic was the only thing it held at bay.

He nodded to his assistant.

"Begin," Teacher Fazool ordered.

Gok was Charlie's friend, and the two had grown reasonably close during their time in the gladiator camp. In the arena, however, they fought without reservation. They were not enemies at that moment, but neither were they friends. Regaling one another with jokes and stories would come *after* the fight. *During* was a whole other story.

"*Yap zina!*" Gok hissed, launching a sneaking attack, low at Charlie's legs, the spell designed to upend his opponent.

Charlie dove to the side, conserving his energy, dodging with physical prowess rather than magical.

Gok smiled. He knew the extent of his opponent's abilities, and given their limitations, it was only a matter of time before he landed a solid spell. In the meantime, he moved in close, peppering him with annoyance spells as a boxer would throw a flurry of jabs––not to cause damage, but to create an opening.

"*Bandu,*" he quickly blurted as Charlie frantically evaded the attack.

Charlie grunted hard as the magical blow sent his feet sliding back in the soil. He had been prepared, but it still nearly took the wind out of him.

"*Yapzi,*" Charlie countered, releasing one of his least powerful spells.

Gok wasn't expecting that one, and the surprise sensation of flies swarming his face threw him off his attack, buying Charlie much-needed seconds to scoot clear of his next bombardment. He smiled at the success of his little trick.

"*Dipangu,*" he followed up, Gok wincing from the sudden, and totally overwhelming stench of feces.

I've got this, Charlie allowed himself to believe. Maybe this time he really would come out ahead. Spells were flowing easily, like Ser Baruud said.

That moment was shattered when Gok kicked him square in the chest, knocking him into a backward roll. Charlie had become so enthralled with the magical aspect of the fight, he had neglected the physical.

A series of punches and kicks flew his way, but Gok couldn't do any damage. When it came to hand-to-hand combat, everyone knew Charlie was better. All the years of training, which he had always considered just another part of his service requirement back on Earth, had left him outclassing those who had always relied heavily on magic.

Ducking a looping hook, Charlie threw a quick jab to Gok's midriff, followed by a Muay Thai kick to his thigh, nearly dropping him to one knee.

Gok flung a disabling spell at him as he lurched back upright, but Charlie slipped the attack, putting himself in the clear, and with a wide-open shot. Gok realized his mistake and blurted out a quick stun spell, but Charlie had already begun casting.

"Klaatu endatha," he said, the new spell popping into his head and out of his lips without even thinking about it.

A blast of power flowed down his arm and out through his hand, channeled through his konus. Gok's spell was pulverized, but unlike most counter-spells, this one took the shattered energy and reconstituted it, throwing it back at its sender with additional force.

Gok grunted hard as his own stunning spell hit him full-force and then some. He shook on his feet a few seconds, then dropped to the ground, groaning from the blow.

"Oh, shit, are you okay?" Charlie said, rushing to his friend.

Gok looked up at him from the dirt with a pained smile. "Where in the worlds did you learn *that* move?"

From his seat on the sideline, Ser Baruud sipped his tea contentedly, the hints of a smile teasing the corners of his eyes.

CHAPTER SIXTY-TWO

Charlie had experienced a breakthrough, and with it came a rapid improvement in his combative skills. Spells flowed fast and easy, even more so when he stopped trying to figure out why only those words were not altered at all by his translation spell. Apparently, the sounds were *beyond* translation, as Ser Baruud had said, so he finally just let go and accepted that fact.

It was as if a mental block had been removed. The words controlling the power contained in his konus were connecting with the magic-imbued device with increasing ease, and his sparring sessions were ever-improving. His spell arsenal, while still limited, was put to increasingly clever use.

More often than not, he was keeping up with his gladiatorial comrades, matching them, and sometimes even exceeding them, in one-on-one combat. Part of that was due to his improved use of the magical device, but just as much was his physical fighting skill. It was one talent Ser Baruud had him focus on with grueling exercises, often performed long after the others had retired for the day.

"You are not from a naturally magic-wielding galaxy, Charlie," he told him. "Yes, you have the use of a konus. And one day you will be trained in the slaap, and perhaps even allowed to attempt a claithe, rare as they are. But at your core, you are not of this realm, though you do appear to have some unusual power connection I still cannot quite place."

"But I'm learning. I can cast spells proficiently now," he said, tapping the slender band of his konus.

"Yes, you can. But what if your konus fails? What if you're suddenly left without magic to defeat your enemy? The others, they do not organically think in terms of strictly physical combat. For them it requires conscious effort to transition, and that is a weakness. You, however, do not possess that flaw. I think it is precisely that which could see you become one of our greatest students yet. If the training doesn't kill you, of course."

"Well, yeah, there's that, naturally," Charlie said with a laugh, limbering up for his daily post-training training. "So, tell me, Ser. What would you have of me today?"

The Wampeh slowly untied his overcoat and placed it on the nearby chair. "Today, you fight *me.*"

Charlie kept his face calm, expressing none of the sheer panic that had flooded his veins at the utterance of so simple a sentence. *'You fight me.'* Words that sent a blast of adrenaline through his body, and rightly so. Ser Baruud was a legend, his skills second to none. He had used Charlie to demonstrate techniques plenty of times, but now, Charlie was to face him in single combat.

I hope he was just kidding about the training killing me.

Baruud, he noted, had foregone his usual weaponry, leaving his slaap and even his konus on the low table. He would be fighting Charlie as an equal. At least as far as magical assistance went. Unsurprisingly, that didn't make him feel much more confident.

"Place your konus on the table, then let us begin."

Charlie did as he was told, sliding the band from his wrist. It was strange, he had grown so accustomed to wearing it that he felt almost naked without it. Underpowered as it was, the device gave him a sense of confidence, knowing he could call on its stored power if the need truly arose.

The pale Wampeh shifted his center and seemed to almost fly across the soil with barely a movement, the force driving from his hips and legs as he planted a solid palm in the center of Charlie's chest, sending him toppling over backwards.

"Why didn't you block the attack, Charlie?" he asked as his pupil rose to his feet and dusted himself off.

"Because I wasn't ready. I had only just taken off my konus, so I thought—"

"Never think your enemy will abide by any archaic rules of decorum. You are engaging in combat, and someday it may be to the death. If you can achieve that end with a single stroke, even if it does not fit your sense of fair play, all the better. It would serve you well to remember this."

"I will, Ser—"

Another flash of his pale hands, but this time Charlie twisted away from the blow, throwing a parrying block while launching his own counterattack, a low leg kick snapped out from his front leg. Baruud easily avoided the blow, but Charlie felt his foot just barely graze the man's pants. This earned him a small grin from his master.

"Better," Baruud said. "Now, let us train in earnest."

For the better part of a half hour, Charlie was basically pummeled by the inhumanly fast grandmaster. He was, however, holding his own much of the time, despite the blows cascading off his body. A few months prior and he would have been unconscious on the dirt in the first twenty seconds.

Other pupils, as well as several of Ser Baruud's teaching assistants, gathered to watch the contest, and with the feeling of critical eyes on him, Charlie dug a little deeper, pulling out all of the stops, calling up the unconventional combat tactics drilled into him all those years ago when he had been moving up in the ranks. He hadn't forgotten them, per se, but lack of use and the diminished physical capability that came with a more sedentary existence had pushed it from his mind.

Now, with months of physical labor and martial training whipping his body back into peak condition, those old lessons came almost subconsciously as his hands remembered what his mind did not.

Faster they went, the pale warrior's blows unrelenting. Charlie nearly kept up, but couldn't quite match his speed. Then, in a counterintuitive move, Charlie leaned into a blow rather than away from it, absorbing the impact in the manner of a Russian Sistema fighter, using the recoil to launch his own flowing combination attack, both faster and more surprising than either had expected.

"Enough," the Wampeh said, stopping the exercise.

Ser Baruud stepped back, a grin on his face where a dot of red blood spotted his pale lips.

"Oh my God. I'm sorry, Ser," Charlie blurted.

Baruud smacked him on the head with a laugh. "Do not apologize for striking your opponent in combat. I have suffered far worse, you know."

The onlookers were murmuring amongst themselves. Charlie had landed a blow on the Master. It was like a pigeon flying at Mach one. It just didn't happen. And, yet, somehow, it did.

The smiling Wampeh put his arm around Charlie and began walking.

"You see what happens when you let your mind flow with your body?"

"I think I finally do."

"Good. Now, let us get something to eat. I know I could devour a full-grown gramundi! Tomorrow, we begin your next phase of training, so eat well. You'll need the energy."

CHAPTER SIXTY-THREE

They didn't have telephone poles on the planet. That would be silly. Not even Earth had telephone poles anymore. Those outdated bits of lumber had vanished as wireless transmission took over the globe. And on Ser Baruud's world? They would serve no purpose whatsoever.

What the Wampeh teacher did have, however, were dozens of logs, stood on end and looking an awful lot like the telephone poles of old to Charlie's eye. The students had trekked through the woods all morning to reach the distant clearing. What they found upon arrival looked like some sort of alien obstacle course, so far as he could tell.

The assistant teachers quickly divided the students by skill and seniority, then set them to work on a variety of drills, ranging from simple balance training at ground level, all the way up to what could best be described as pole hopping.

It was exactly as it sounded—the men would take turns climbing a pole, then balance atop it before jumping to the next. They were only five meters high, so while egos would bruise every time someone took a fall, no bones had broken. At least, not yet.

Charlie had scampered across the poles faster than most, his reflexes sharp and his legs strong.

"Good. Now the water," Teacher Azman instructed, leading Charlie to a much lower pole, no more than a stump, really. "Climb up," he commanded.

Charlie did as he was told, while the teacher filled two small buckets with water. They were tiny things, perhaps a liter each at best, but far larger than the tiny cups he and his companions had been forced to hold on their first day of training.

"Wrap these around each bicep," Azman said, handing him two straps made of prickling thorns.

Charlie did as he was told, twisting the ends to secure them, then holding his arms up and out to avoid jabbing himself.

"Now take these."

The buckets felt light in his hands, and their grips were padded and comfortable. Not what he'd expect for such small vessels.

"Ouch!" he exclaimed as a thorn stabbed his side.

"Arms extended," Azman ordered.

Charlie held the little buckets out, his arms feeling strong and solid after all of his labor and training.

This is it? Piece of cake.

Teacher Azman looked him over as he balanced atop the stump, buckets in hand, nodding approvingly. "Good. Now stay this way until I return."

He then walked away, leaving Charlie on his own to watch the others train. After a minute, the buckets seemed to be getting heavier. By five minutes, sweat was beading on his forehead. At ten minutes, his shirt was drenched, and several fine pricks of the thorns had left tiny crimson blossoms spreading on his shirt.

"Breathe, Charlie," Ser Baruud said, walking by as he surveyed his students. "Your energy flows through your arms, and that is what holds the water, not your muscles."

"Ser Baruud?" Charlie said, hiding the strain in his voice as best he could.

"Yes?"

"May I ask a question?"

"What is on your mind?"

"You are a free man, but you were once a slave, like me. If it is not inappropriate, I wondered how one gains their freedom."

The Wampeh smiled, an amused look on his face as he recalled something from long ago.

"A slave rarely earns his freedom, Charlie. It is simply not the way of things. But a gladiator––well, we are different in that regard."

"How so?"

"If a gladiator is brave and true. If he shows exceptional skill and cunning. If he puts on a truly spectacular performance in front of the right crowd with the right, powerful people present––*then*, if he is lucky, he may be granted his freedom. It is exceptionally rare, but in those circumstances the act of granting it earns that owner great renown for their show of largess to their slave. And the gladiator so freed finds many opportunities to put their fame and skill to use as a free man, such as what you see around you."

"And how did you win your freedom?"

Ser Baruud merely smiled and left it at that.

For nearly an hour after Teacher Azman finally let him down from his perch Charlie's arms refused to function. His shoulders, though strong from his training, felt like lead weights were strapped to his arms every time he moved. Gradually, however, they loosened up. Had he attempted the task right after crashing in this galaxy, he doubted he'd have been able to use his arms at all for a week.

Things change, Charlie boy, he mused as he sipped a cup of water.

"Charlie. You are to run to the top of that peak and retrieve the konus hidden atop the tallest tree," Azman instructed. "Then you will return here for the rest of your day's training."

Charlie nodded once and took off at a quick run. The peak wasn't that far, really, and he felt confident he could make it to the top and back before nightfall. After using his arms and shoulders to such a great extent, putting his legs to use felt quite refreshing.

He made good time up the hill, cresting it well before the sun began to set.

Now where is that thing? he wondered as he scanned the trees.

All of them seemed tall, but one stood out, not because it was taller or bigger, but because of the slight disturbance of the ground at its base.

Gotcha.

He scaled the tree with ease, his arms fully recovered. At the top, there was a konus tied to a branch, as he'd been told. He claimed the slender band and slipped it around his wrist, then climbed down and began the run back to the others.

No one was there when he returned to the training grounds just as the sun went down.

"Hello?"

Silence.

"Oh, that's just great. Y'all went and forgot about me. Not cool, guys, leaving me out here in the dark."

Charlie scanned the training grounds and looked up at the emerging stars. It had been a long trek there, but he felt he knew the way back.

"Better save me some dinner, is all I can say," he grumbled as he began the long trek through the woods.

He'd only been walking an hour when he sensed he was not

alone. It was not that he heard anything, but something was tickling that warning bell in the back of his mind.

Cute. They're messing with me now, he grumbled to himself.

He had walked another ten minutes before the attackers fell upon him. There were three of them, all dressed in ragged cloaks. In the dark, he couldn't tell who exactly it was attacking him, but from the way they moved, he guessed the teachers had sent some of the less experienced students.

Fine. I'll show them what I've learned.

Charlie spun in the dark, using his ears and senses rather than his eyes. With a konus on his wrist, he even used a few minor disabling spells, which seemed to land with great effect. Then two more men rushed from the darkness. And that pair had more skill than the previous trio.

Charlie found himself hard-pushed to avoid their blows, fists and staffs swinging at him in the darkness. The glancing crack of wood across his head made a loud report that echoed through the woods.

"Sonofabitch. That hurt!" he shouted, his anger leading him to retaliate with a bit more force than he'd intended, the spell cast by his konus shattering the staff in the man's hand. The attackers quickly realized they were outclassed and scattered into the night.

"That's right, bitches. You better run. And we're going to have a little talk about this when we get back to the compound," he called after them.

Charlie felt his head. No bloody wetness, so that was good, but there would be a nice bump come morning. *Just great,* he groaned to himself and walked the rest of the way back.

"There you are," Ser Baruud said as Charlie walked into the eating hall. The others looked up with curiosity, their meals nearly finished. "I was beginning to wonder if you had gotten lost on the way back."

"You left me in the dark, way out in the middle of nowhere."

"Yes. And?" the Wampeh said plainly.

"And? And luckily it was a clear night and I could use the stars to find my way back."

"As I knew you would."

"And which of you thought it would be fun to attack me in the woods, huh? That was not cool."

Ser Baruud's smile took on a slightly serious air. "Charlie, they've all been here. You must have encountered the local ruffians who roam the outskirts."

"Wait, what?"

"They are the reason we mostly stay within the compound. Not out of fear, mind you, but it would be annoying having to constantly fight them, and none of us really wants to kill the poor fellows to make a point."

Charlie digested what the Wampeh had just said.

"You left me out there with bandits? I could have been killed!"

"Yes. But you weren't," he replied serenely, an amused look in his eyes.

"Was that a lesson?"

"Of sorts," Ser Baruud replied. He then returned his tray to the wash bin and strolled out of the room.

Charlie took a deep breath, then let it go. The Wampeh had challenged him, and he had come out the other side intact. That was all there was to it. He grabbed a tray of food and sat down at the nearest table.

"Don't take it so hard," Teacher Fazool said. "That he is confident enough in you to allow such a test speaks of his respect for you."

"An unusual teaching style," Charlie said.

"And an unusual man," Fazool replied.

The two ate in silence before Charlie spoke up.

"Teacher Fazool, what did Ser Baruud do to gain his freedom?"

The older man smiled at the thought. "Oh, that was one for the ages, let me tell you. And I was there to see it. Mind you, I was much younger and not in that fight. It was a massive death match. A dozen men with only one survivor. I was not fit to participate, thank the gods, but watching, oh, what a performance."

"So he fought well against a dozen highly trained men? That *is* impressive."

"Oh, it was far more than that. You know Baruud. He's a Wampeh, but possesses none of the 'unusual' gifts a few of their type are known to have."

"Yes, I've seen one such man," Charlie said. "It's horrifying."

Fazool seemed surprised by that news. "Yes, it most certainly is," he continued. "Well, Baruud, as you know, is a gifted fighter, but he is still just a man, and against a dozen fierce opponents, the risk of defeat was very real. However, being a Wampeh, he realized he had a secret weapon."

"Oh?"

"Yes. You see, he put the legends surrounding his people to good use."

"How?"

A big grin spread across Fazool's face. "It was amazing, really. He had a false set of fangs made in secret. Only the *others* of his species possess the ability to grow them at will, but Baruud was a savvy fighter. He knew it would be his toughest fight yet, so he started spreading the rumors early. Leaking news that he actually *was* one of the few deadliest Wampeh. That he actually *was* able to take the abilities of other men. To drink their blood and steal their power."

"But he can't."

"No, that he cannot," Fazool said with a laugh. "But his

opponents did not know that. Not for sure, anyway, and the false fangs he flashed just as the fight began threw the whole thing into such delightful turmoil. It was chaos, I tell you. He got into their heads, you see? Seasoned fighters, some of the best, and he had defeated them before they even began. And I tell you, it was a bloodbath, that bout."

"A dozen men all going at it at once? It's no wonder."

"Yes, it was brutal. But Ser Baruud was so very clever. After the first pointy-toothed smile, the others avoided him as best they could, but he would race through the arena and crouch over every fallen man and pretend to drink their blood. He even wiped some on his lips for effect. The others didn't know who among them possessed power of their own and who didn't, but with his act they were so scared of his potential stolen magic building up that they began casting wildly."

"And if they were relying on slaaps and konuses instead of their own power, those charges could run out."

"Exactly. All Baruud had to do was avoid their spells, which he did easily. Panic makes you sloppy, you see. And when he did get close enough to engage, he used conventional weapons, totally the opposite of what was expected of a power-filled Wampeh."

"He psyched them out."

"Yes. And at the end of the bout he was the only man standing. Not only that, he had not cast a single spell the entire match, yet had taken out nearly all of the dozen opponents. It was incredible. Something never before seen, and the crowd went absolutely wild. And with such fervent support—and the fact that his trick would soon be known among the top gladiators, leaving him vulnerable in future bouts—his owner seized the opportunity, playing up the victory and freeing him there on the spot. It greatly enhanced his fame and reputation, while cementing Ser Baruud as something of a legend."

Charlie couldn't help but feel an even greater respect for the man. Yes, he was a great teacher, but he now realized there was so much more to learn from him. Lessons he hoped the great Wampeh would one day share with him. For now, however, he would keep his head down and work hard.

Any gripes about being left to fend for himself in the woods melted away. He was being trained by a legend, and he would make the most of it.

CHAPTER SIXTY-FOUR

For three months Charlie trained harder and harder with the scarred and grizzled assistant instructors, each of whom had joined Ser Baruud after winning their freedom in the gladiatorial arena. Some were men the Master had fought with in group events at one time or another. Some he had even battled against in the past. Now they were bonded. Friends and peers.

All were cut from a cloth that Charlie had only seen among the most elite of the fighting forces his space teams occasionally had the fortune of crossing paths with. And even then, only a few of those men lived up to that high a standard.

With each lesson, his skills sharpened. No longer was he training with only his friends and other lower-level students, though he still bunked in the dormitories with Gok, Bini, and the others. Now, he learned from the most knowledgeable of the higher-ranking within the grounds, and every day his skills grew.

But it was in his absorption of the Master's more cryptic lessons that he had surpassed them all. Watching him progress, Ser Baruud would occasionally pull him aside for private instruction, the human listening intently, absorbing every word with sharp attention.

"How do you feel, Charlie?" Ser Baruud asked him one evening about six months into his residency within the school's walls.

He had been performing better and better, and no longer did he wake in pain from the prior day's beating as before.

"Good," he replied, honestly assessing himself. "It all feels like it's finally coming together."

Earlier that day he had disarmed three separate opponents in both magic and unarmed combat, though greatly underpowered in his konus, and outweighed in size.

"Your progress is heartening, but I worry you still need a push to reach the next level. To overcome your own insecurities."

"Master, what would you have me do?" Charlie asked.

"Eat. Sleep. Prepare. Tomorrow, you will be tested."

Charlie had no idea what "tested" entailed, but knowing Ser Baruud's proclivity for pushing his students to the limit in order to achieve breakthroughs, he didn't know how well he'd sleep.

Well, I suppose given how hard we work, at least it can't be that much worse than our normal training.

"This is going to be much worse than our normal training," Charlie said as the small ship rattled and lurched its way through the atmosphere. No Drooks powered this craft, but rather, a layered series of spells, carefully applied by powerful emmiks and even a visla who owed Baruud a favor after he rid him of a troublesome priest stirring up the locals in his realm.

The ship, therefore, flew under the guidance of one pilot, a single man controlling the craft. While Ser Baruud was unequaled as a fighter, his piloting left something to be desired.

"You know, I might be able to help with that, if you like," Charlie offered.

"No. I am fine."

"Okay. It's just, I trained to be a pilot before I side-slipped into engineering and—"

"I said I am fine. Just relax and prepare yourself mentally. This is no trifling matter. You must not embarrass me, young apprentice."

Charlie couldn't help but take note. It was the first time he had called him anything other than a student, which already a step up from his original title upon arrival: *burden*.

Ser Baruud was taking Charlie and a pair of other students from the training facility off-world to a nearby solar system. It was his first time out of the training center's walls since his arrival, and now he was off to another planet. And not just for a supply run. A tournament was being held, and Ser Baruud had seen fit to enter a few of his pupils as combatants.

Charlie, much to his surprise, was one of them.

When they finally landed after a long day of space travel, the first thing that struck him about the new world was the odd, burnt umber tone the sun cast on everything. It was a little unsettling after so much time on a verdant planet.

The next thing that struck him was the smell, which assaulted his nose like a wet fist thrown with stinking malice. The denizens of the city were not the most cleanliness-oriented of people, he noted. He only hoped the man he would be fighting at least bathed more often than they did.

"Give me your konus," Ser Baruud commanded as they stepped inside the walls of the small arena. Charlie handed over the device as he looked about the facility. They stood inside a small preparation area, where all of the combatants shared a common space.

"Shouldn't we all be separated?" he asked. "Isn't there too much risk of violence like this?"

Ser Baruud looked over the assembled gladiators and nodded with satisfaction. "No, this is not a concern here. Not one of these men is your enemy, Charlie. But one of them is your opponent. Learn that difference, for only a brute animal treats his fellow gladiators with disrespect and anger. This is not a high-level event. There will be no fighting to the death. You are here to entertain the locals for the magistrate's birth month celebrations. You will fight, and you will fight hard, but you will not kill. It is far too costly to train a gladiator to waste their lives with every low-level bout."

"And if my opponent ignores standard practice and tries to kill me?"

"Then I suggest you do not let him. Now, give me your arm," he said, then pulled a larger konus from his pocket and slid it onto Charlie's wrist.

The konus was at least three times the size of the one he had been used to training with, and Charlie could feel the power coursing through the enchanted device. Suddenly, he didn't feel so unsure about the fight.

"That is your opponent," Baruud said, pointing out a hulking man with a studded club, as well, Charlie noted, as a rather sizable slaap.

"Um, he has a slaap."

"Yes. And a club too," Baruud pointed out with a chuckle. "You disappoint me, young one. Have you forgotten your training so soon?"

"No, of course not. And this konus is much more powerful than my old one, but he has a slaap. That's easily more powerful than my konus, and he has a club."

"Yes, he does. And those things will be his undoing."

"I fail to see the logic in that assessment."

The Wampeh sighed and shook his head. "Charlie, he may appear to be better armed than you are--in fact, he *is* better armed than you--but *you* are better prepared. Use his

345

confidence to your advantage. Leverage his reliance on stronger weapons against him. Think of this as a chess game, not a punching contest. Brute force will not win you the day."

Charlie took a deep breath and recited the spells in his arsenal, quietly singing them to himself. Oddly, he felt the konus powering up before he meant it to.

Whoa. This thing is on a hair trigger compared to the last one. And a lot stronger too.

Crashing and shouted spells filtered into the holding area until a great roar sounded from the crowd, then simmered to a dull murmur. A few moments later, the prior combatants returned from their bout. One walking, the other carried on a magically floating litter. He was alive, but with his injuries, it would be some time before he would fight again.

"You're up," Baruud said, pointing him to the arena entrance.

"All right. Wish me luck."

"You possess the *skill*. You have no need for luck."

Charlie hoped he was right.

CHAPTER SIXTY-FIVE

The waiting had been excruciating. Charlie's nerves were on fire with anticipation when he finally entered the floor of the arena to find himself greeted by the yells of thousands of spectators, all cheering for the pending battle. It was one hell of a rush.

Looks like they're jazzed about the fight, he noted. *And speaking of which, where is my—?*

A tingling on the back of his neck made him dive immediately to his left, the studded club whiffing through the space he'd just occupied.

"Sneaky bastard," he growled through clenched teeth. "Ser Baruud was right about that at least."

"*Hazookar! Moraxia poona! Effian!*" the man shouted, his slaap throwing a trio of spells at him back-to-back-to-back.

Charlie had no idea what those spells did, so he launched the most broad-reaching counter he knew as he rolled clear of the path of whatever the burly gladiator was hurling at him.

His counter-spell, thrown in haste, was nevertheless many times stronger than ever, thanks, he realized, to his new konus. The attack spells dissolved––barely––but that did nothing to stop the steam train physical assault of the much larger man. He landed a kick square in Charlie's chest, sending him flying backward onto the ground.

Charlie rolled back to his feet, using the momentum of the impact. Surprisingly, he realized he remained unharmed. The training worked.

He combined physical and magical attacks, he noted. *So, he's not just a brute. Going to have to be creative, here.*

Charlie charged the larger man, throwing the limited spells at his disposal as fast as he could manage. His opponent canceled them out, his slaap swatting them aside as easily as a grown dog toyed with a pup.

Changing it up, he opted for a physical attack. Charlie landed several blows, even managing to briefly stun the man with a firm elbow to his chin, but his opponent was made of solid stuff, and once again, Charlie found himself flung to the ground.

He rolled frantically to the side, the large club denting the ground where his body had just been. Charlie swept at his legs, forcing the man to step back, giving him time to regain his feet. The club whistled through the air, barely missing him as he faked a move to the left, opting instead to duck and go right, landing a quick punch to the man's ribs before jumping clear of another massive swing.

Once again he used all of his defensive spells to stop the onslaught of attack spells. A few made it past, however, and Charlie was dazed for a second before his head cleared. Fortunately he saw the man's shoulders and hips move even through blurry eyes.

The thing was, the man's club was deadly, but it was also almost comically large, requiring more time and muscle to wield than the man realized. That gave Charlie an idea, and the fraction of a second he needed.

"Yapzi uzri ho!" he said plainly, relying on his intent rather than the power of his vocal cords to direct the konus's power.

It was a combination of linked spells, and the first time he had ever attempted to do such a thing. In fact, he wasn't sure if it would even work, but the tandem effect of swarming flies in the eyes, combined with a throwing spell, took the off-balance man right off his feet.

Charlie wasted no time, jumping atop him, pinning his slaap hand with a knee and aiming his palm at his face. "Submit, or I'll cast at point-blank range, right between the eyes," he commanded.

The struggling man reluctantly relaxed and held up two fingers. The sign for surrender. The crowd applauded the combatants, then a casual murmur rose as they waited for the next bout.

Sliding from the mount position, Charlie reached down and helped his opponent to his feet. "Thank you for a good contest," he said. "You fought well and honorably."

The larger man was obviously upset at his defeat, but the gracious expression of sportsmanlike conduct by the victor sat well with him. "And you, little man. You possess surprising power for such a tiny adversary."

Charlie couldn't help but laugh. "I guess I am pretty small, compared to you. I mean, look at those muscles. I bet you worked hard to grow so strong."

"Many, many years," the man said, then held out his hand in friendship. "I am Korban. It was an honor to fight you."

He clasped the man's hand tightly, the crowd cheering the show of good sportsmanship as the two walked out through the arena's tunnel, back to the gladiator preparation and holding area.

"I am Charlie, and the honor was mine, my friend. I hope to see you again, but hopefully next time not on the opposing end of the field of combat." He looked around the sea of burly men camped out. "Hey, I'm seriously thirsty. There's gotta be something to drink around here. You want to get a drink?"

"Follow me," Korban said.

They proceeded to sit and share tales of their ordeals and training, bonding over a common lifestyle. Ser Baruud watched from afar, a pleased smile touching the corners of his lips.

"You fought well," Baruud said on the flight home. "And I see you made a new friend in the process."

"Yeah. After he was through trying to bash my head in, it turns out Korban is actually a pretty nice guy."

"I met Teacher Azman much the same way."

"Oh?"

"Yes. Though ours was a fight to the death."

"Yet he lives."

"Indeed. He was on the losing end, but he fought so bravely that the lord of the region halted the match and granted him a reprieve. That was the bout in which I received this scar," he said, lifting his tunic to show a jagged line across his flank. "A deadly fighter, Azman."

"And despite nearly killing you, you are now friends and allies."

"Yes, so it is. The way."

"Which way?"

"Of life. Things are not always as they seem, and only a fool assumes to know the difference at a glance."

They talked at length the rest of the flight home, discussing life and the danger of death, but also the glory in facing it. "I hope that one day you will be prepared enough to face that challenge and experience it for yourself," Baruud said.

Under his guidance, Charlie was feeling confident he might, indeed, become prepared, even if he had no desire to ever kill another man. In any case, he would train hard and make his teacher proud.

And so he did for the next two years. And Ser Baruud kept entering him in increasingly difficult tournaments as he improved. The strange human from a distant world who somehow, against the odds, kept winning bout after bout after bout.

CHAPTER SIXTY-SIX

A few years older and many fights wiser, Charlie was at ease as he prepared for what promised to be his most challenging bout yet.

"I'm okay," Charlie said, adjusting his short sword strapped to his back.

"But it's a team bout. And to the death," Bini said, tightening the straps of his protective leggings. "Ser Baruud has never let any of us fight in a contest like this."

"And from what he said, there has never *been* a bout like this," Charlie replied, slipping on his heavily charged konus. "The marriage of a regent, joining two systems as one, called for something special."

He slipped a heavy slaap into the secure pouch on his hip. A deadly device, but only to be used as a backup in the most dire of circumstances, per Ser Baruud's orders.

As Charlie's skills increased, so had the strength of the weapons he was allowed access to, but for today's match, his teacher had deemed it dangerous enough to warrant fully powered weapons. His konus could do incredible damage, if wielded properly. And Charlie had learned to wield it like an expert.

As he did before every bout, he once again quietly sang the dozens of spells at his disposal to himself, a musical mnemonic that had served him well, making their casting almost second nature.

Gok stood nearby and was anxiously bouncing on his feet, agitated and full of nerves. "I don't know how you can be so calm. This is *it*. The big time. Today we fight our best or we die."

"And, apparently, there will be some surprises as well," another member of their team said. They didn't know the man. He came from a different world, but for this event, anyone wearing the green of their side was a brother, at least until victory or defeat.

"Yeah, I heard talk, but what are we looking at?" Bini asked.

"Not sure. My master said the last time there was anything close to this kind of event, there were wild Yatzar beasts loose on the field of combat. They were painted with team colors and assigned to each side, but those razor-backed bastards paid no attention to color or allegiance and took down as many fighters as the gladiators did that day, from what he said."

"Whatever they are, we stick to the plan. Fight intelligently, as a team. Protect one another and we live. If they thin our ranks, the remaining men will be sitting ducks."

"What is a duck, Charlie?" Gok asked. "Is that some kind of pacifist who sits rather than fights?"

"What? No, it's––never mind, okay. It just means they'd be an easy target. Now, let's go over the plan again. We won't have many chances to reach the golden ring, so we have to make them count."

The main event was a battle royale, a chaotic melee with three teams, each with a dozen fighters per side, all engaging at once. There were only two ways to win the bout. If a gladiator somehow scaled to the top of a tall, greased pole in the center of the massive arena and grabbed the golden ring sitting atop it, they would be crowned champion and the fighting would cease. The winning team would feast like royalty, while the vanquished would be whipped, then sent packing.

Whipping, however, was preferable to death.

And that was the other way out. If two sides were annihilated, the surviving team would be declared victors. While they would not bask in the full glory obtained by capturing the ring, they would still have a great feast and pleasure women—or men, if they preferred—provided for them.

Charlie didn't much care about any of those things. He simply wanted to prove himself worthy of his teacher's trust and efforts. He had been taken from a mere slave and elevated to an established, and popular, gladiator. So much so that Ser Baruud had made the unusual request of his owner to allow him to remain in his compound to train year-round rather than see his skills lessen by returning to live in Gramfir's camps.

His bearded owner agreed, so long as Charlie continued to win. The betting against the off-worlder from a distant and unheard-of world was always profitable, and Gramfir had earned considerable coin from his impulsive purchase.

Upon their arrival to the planet, the gladiators had stepped from their ships into a caravan of small conveyances that carried them from the arrival area through the bazaar to the waiting arena. As they passed through the winding streets, Charlie thought he recognized the bustling world.

"Hang on, I think I've been here before. But the bazaar seems bigger," Charlie noted.

"You've been to Gilea?" Gok asked.

"Wait, this is *Gilea*? We're fighting in the Buru Arena?"

"I thought you knew. It's the biggest in a dozen systems."

"I guess I did. I just didn't think we were going to be fighting *here*," he said, taking in the sheer size of the arena as they drew nearer. "Dear Lord, that's one big building."

"Yes, and the place is going to be filled to capacity," Bini said, with an excited giggle.

"Calm down, Bini. You're going to make a spectacle of yourself."

"Right, okay," he said, forcing himself to stay planted in his seat.

They were hustled through the crowds to the waiting preparation area within the arena, then the gladiators from all across the systems were grouped together with their teammates to spend the day learning each other's strengths and weaknesses, while preparing to fight as a slapped-together team.

The following afternoon they would either fight together, or they would die. And they only had one day to form a bond that would very literally be the difference between life and death.

CHAPTER SIXTY-SEVEN

The men were as varied in shape and size as they were in coloration and species, but all of the gladiators gathered in the three waiting chambers––be they clad in blue, red, or green–– were alike in one regard. They were about to take the lives of other men.

It was something that would have troubled Charlie as little as six months prior. He was fighting and winning, yes, but he had excelled in the tricky defensive spells, utilizing them to gain advantage and take down his opponents in the least violent manner possible. He had hurt many, and crippled a good few, but he did what he could to avoid killing.

Today, however, there was no room for such mercy, because he was quite certain none would be afforded him.

"I hear word that we are to have beasts assigned to our teams, though the reliability of each holding loyalty to any particular side is in doubt," a muscled Wampeh named Roph said as he readied himself for combat.

"So we avoid them and force our opponents within striking range," Charlie suggested. "Roph, wasn't it?"

"Yes."

"Okay, did you hear anything further? Like, are they chained or otherwise bound? What I mean is, how much do we need to worry about watching our backs?"

"I do not know for certain, but the servant girl I spoke with said they had forged special restraint collars for the event," the pale man said, touching the band around his neck. "For that, the beasts must possess quite a fearsome power."

"Let us hope these spells at least keep them loyal to our side," Gok said. "If they do not attack us, we can steer our opponents toward them. Perhaps thin their numbers without getting our hands dirty."

"A good idea," Charlie said. "But it's likely one of the other teams already thought of that. Remember, we are fighting men very much like ourselves, and they will be just as cunning and devious and do whatever it takes to survive. Now, Phamli, you're the lightest of us. Are you sure you can scale the pole should we clear you a path?"

The Tslavar bore the scars of many battles on his pale green skin, but the wiry muscle beneath rippled with anticipation of action. "Oh, yes," he said. "Just get me to the center and I'll have that ring for us in no time."

He tucked a pair of small daggers into the straps of each boot, but these were not meant for combat. They were tightly bound on the inside of his ankles, the points barely reaching the ground. Not of use for fighting, but excellent for climbing a greased pole.

"Five minutes!" a herald shouted into the room.

The gladiators checked each other's gear and psyched themselves up as best they could. Calm strategy would win the day. Berserker rage would just get you killed all the quicker.

The minutes ticked down until at long last the door to the tunnel leading into the arena's dirt floor slid open.

Here we go, Charlie thought as he steeled himself for a brutal fight to the death.

.   .   .

"Zomoki!" someone shouted as they reached the mouth of the tunnel.

"Dragons? Here?" Charlie asked, hesitating a moment. "Are they collared and on our side?"

"It appears so, yes. There is a splash of green on the side of this black-skinned beast."

"Well, then, there's nothing else we can do about it. Let's go."

The dragon turned its head and tried to spit fire at the men in green, but the thick collar around its neck glowed brightly, snuffing its flames when it tried.

"It's working!" Bini said with glee. "It can't hurt us!"

"Can't *burn* us," Charlie said. "It might still be able to step on you, or eat you. So be careful!"

Each side had not one, but *two* Zomoki fighting with them. Normally this would have made for an incredibly short bout, but the magical restraints placed on the beasts effectively hobbled them, adding a deadly surprise element to the affair.

A spear from the red team had apparently already wounded the blue team's smaller dragon. A poor throw gone lucky, finding a seam between its armored scales, though it seemed to have pissed off the dragon more than harm it.

"Follow the plan and fight together. Get Phamli to the pole and maybe we will all go home in one piece," Charlie said. He didn't believe his own words. Many of them would not go home at all.

The men raced for one another, a fierce battle among some of the best gladiators of the day. Of course, there were only so many available for the event who had true skill. As such, many of the men fighting were more fodder than predator.

Charlie's friends fit that category, but he multi-tasked as best he could, peppering their opponents with defensive spells that used little energy, buying them some time while he fought his own attacker.

The man charging him was incredibly fast on his feet, and his spell casting was just as speedy. Charlie found himself quickly on his heels, diving and spinning from the man, waiting for an opening.

It finally arrived in the shape of a small puddle of blood, conveniently deposited from the perforated body of one of the red team's men. Charlie positioned himself just past it and feigned a slight injury, hoping his attacker would take the bait.

Overzealous, the man did just that, rushing in when he should have been cautious. That would be his downfall.

A terrible shriek filled the air behind him as one of the blue team's Zomoki had its heart pierced by the blade of a thick-necked orange man. He was one of Charlie's green team allies, but he would have no time to celebrate as a gush of iridescent blood sprayed him from head-to-toe.

He didn't even have time to scream as his life was snuffed out in an instant by the toxic blood. Moments later, the dragon succumbed to its injury and collapsed on top of him.

But Charlie didn't have time to worry about that. He rushed to his slipping attacker's flank and moved as if casting a spell, but when his opponent cast a counter-spell, Charlie dove forward, his short sword flashing from its sheath and embedding firmly in the man's chest.

The sword had no power of any kind. A non-magic weapon in a battle of magic users. It was the one thing his dying foe hadn't prepared for.

But Charlie couldn't savor his brief victory as two blue-clothed gladiators raced toward him.

Shit!

He turned and ran. There was no dishonor in gaining a moment to regroup, and he was doing just that, one quickly falling foot after another.

As he fled, he saw that Phamli was at the base of the pole, but given the rapidly pumping wound in his side, Charlie doubted he'd be able to make the climb, let alone survive the day. It looked like they would have to win the hard way. By taking out all the other fighters one at a time.

Their black dragon lunged out, snatching an opposing fighter from the field and tossing him into the stands. The dead man's body passed through the enchanted shielding with ease, but his weapons caught on it, the one thing keeping him from landing in the rapt audience.

Now the Zomoki were being seen as the real threat, and the men on the field, as if by unspoken agreement, turned their attentions on the beasts, determined to wipe them from the equation before they returned to trying to kill one another. A raging bellow caught Charlie's attention, but not just his ears. He felt it in his whole body.

He turned and saw the source of the sound. An enormous red dragon, its scales the color of old rust and dried blood, was spewing flames against four attackers as they charged it with both spells and weapons. Charlie saw the lighter coloring of a scar on its wing. A scar where he had healed it years prior.

The dragon sensed him as well, turning its gaze on him, locking eyes a moment before dodging another violent attack. The blue team were hectoring the creature, and by the looks of it, had it cornered.

Without thinking, Charlie raced toward them, sword in hand as he drew his slaap from his belt. If there was a time to use it, this, he decided, was it. It was four on one, not counting the dragon, and Charlie didn't know which of the many spells racing through his mind would be the most effective. He dodged a stun spell, then stumbled through his own incantation, accidentally singing two spells together as his melodic memory device tripped up his tongue.

"*Floramar Ivanti Necctuzriha!*" he blurted, unintentionally mixing the Drook propulsion spell with a magical throwing one. The results of his combined konus and slaap's power with the strange spell was immediate.

And violent.

Two of the men were crushed flat to the ground, while the others were flung high into the air until they bounced off of the enchanted barrier.

What the hell was that? he marveled at his unexpectedly effective spell.

Movement caught his eye, and Charlie spun to the great fanged creature, ready to fight if need be, but held his hands up, palms open.

"Hey, fella. I'm the guy who fixed your wing. You remember me?"

The dragon gave him what looked suspiciously like an amused smirk.

"For one, I am not a fella," a female voice said, reverberating in his head. *"And remember you? Of course I remember you. You were kind to me, though I could smell your fear. Now, however, I can smell no such cowardice."*

"Wait a minute, are you actually talking to me?"

"I thought that was obvious. It is rather interesting, though. Not for a very long time have any of my kind been able to speak with a non-Zomoki like this. The only one who had that ability is long dead."

"You mean Visla Balamar, I assume."

"How did you—?"

A poorly-cast spell crashed into the soil beside them.

Their moment of grace had passed, and several men were racing toward them with the aim to do violence. The crowd didn't know what to make of what happened next. A man and a Zomoki, fighting side by side, and not even from the same team. The gladiator in green was not magically protected from the red team's beast.

The dragon spat flame and slapped with her tail, while

Charlie threw defensive spells from his konus to protect her, then went on the offensive with his slaap. The speed at which spells were flying from his lips seemed almost unnatural. But then, he was an astronaut from another planet, fighting alongside a dragon and using magic. Unnatural was just a matter of opinion at that point.

Two of the attackers fell to stun spells, another succumbed to the dragon's fiery breath, but the strongest of them landed a shot on Charlie, sending him tumbling to the ground, clutching his arm.

The dragon bellowed and charged the man, foregoing defense, opting for brute force. She was going to run him down, he realized, and quickly turned and ran away.

Her ruse worked, and the dragon quickly circled back to the injured human.

"Quickly, climb onto my back and hold on tight."

"What are you going to do?"

"If a fighter claims the ring atop the pole, the combat ceases. Now, hurry!"

She dropped flat, allowing Charlie to scramble to her shoulders as best he could. The crowd was abuzz with utter shock.

With nothing to hold on to, he slid his hands around the shining band around her neck and held on tight. With a few flaps of her great wings, she launched into the air, but the protective dome pushed her back lower, where a Wampeh and two red aliens Charlie had never seen before all threw spells at her in hopes of bringing her down.

"No!" Charlie shouted when he felt one fly true, stunning the Zomoki.

She managed to stay aloft, but only just.

"Konus Magusi!" he barked, the defensive spell draining the incoming ones of their potency.

As he cast, something unexpected happened. The band

beneath his hands lost its glow, and as it did, Charlie felt an immense power surge from the creature beneath him.

"Oh, my," she said, flapping hard, driving toward the towering pole. *"Grab it and end this,"* she said, but seeing another on the verge of defeating them, all of the opposing gladiators turned their spells skyward, driving her back with a ferocious onslaught.

"Enough!" Charlie bellowed, feeling the energy from the Zomoki flowing around him. *"Banduzriha!"* he shouted, drawing power not from the konus or even the slaap, but much to his shock, from the Zomoki herself.

A blinding flash burst out, the accidentally modified spell stunning every gladiator on the arena floor, knocking them to their knees. But it didn't stop there. The spell blew right through the enchanted dome protecting the arena seats, sending the spectators flying.

Nothing like that had ever happened in all the years of contests, and no one knew what to do.

A startled hush fell over the crowd. Then they went absolutely wild, cheering with gusto as the dragon and its rider swooped in and grabbed the ring from the pole just as the powerful vislas overseeing the event frantically uttered the emergency spell, activating every collar to its fullest, knocking every last man and beast unconscious.

Charlie and his mount somehow sustained a moment longer than the others, but the glow of power around them faded quickly, and they too dropped to the ground.

The stands were pandemonium. It was the most amazing thing any of them had ever seen. This would go down as one of the greatest bouts ever, and they had borne witness. A pale man in the stands was particularly impressed with the chaos he had just witnessed, his pointed canines barely showing through his curious smile.

From his seat on the lower-tier sidelines, Ser Baruud's brow was furrowed as he surveyed the scene. *This* was not normal, and for once, the great master didn't have the slightest idea how to handle things.

In one of the private boxes high above the field of combat, someone else took great interest in what had just happened.

Charlie was on the radar of someone very wealthy, and very powerful.

CHAPTER SIXTY-EIGHT

"Hey. Hey!" a female voice called out to him.

"What? Let me rest, I'm tired."

"You are *resting,"* the woman noted. *"And I'm tired too, you know."*

The voice was familiar. He couldn't place it. Not at first, anyway. But as she spoke, the burning under his skin began to grow, spreading to a tingling fire itching across his body.

"What are you doing to me?"

"I'm not doing anything."

"Then why does it burn like this?"

"Burn?" she asked. *"What sort of burn?"*

"My body. My skin. It feels like thousands of tiny flames are dancing across it."

"Does it? Hmm. Interesting," she said. *"Use one of your spells to reduce the sensation."*

"I don't know how to do that. And besides, I have no konus."

"You don't need a konus. And what do you mean, don't know how? You possess great power. Something like that should be simple for you."

"I have no idea what you're talking about. And who are you? You

seem so familiar. Are you come to carry me to the other side? Is this what death is?"

"Hardly."

"Life, then. Freedom, perhaps?"

The mysterious voice tried to speak once more, but her words faded into the darkness as they drifted apart in the void of a dreamless slumber.

CHAPTER SIXTY-NINE

Charlie stretched in the soft sheets of his bed, the fine material smooth against his skin. From somewhere nearby, the smell of baked goods wafted to his nose, gently pulling him from his slumber.

Wait a minute—

He lurched through the layers of grogginess, forcing his eyes open in the well-lit room.

This isn't the compound. How did I—?

The memory of falling flashed through his head, his last conscious thought being that he hoped he wouldn't be crushed to death by the enormous dragon plunging down beneath him. Then blackness.

"Where the hell am I?" he croaked through a dry throat.

A glass of clear water sat beside his bed. He lifted it to his face and carefully sniffed it. No foul odor. Took a sip. Fresh and clean. He shrugged.

If they wanted me dead, I already would be, he reasoned, greedily drinking it down. From the hollow splash it made in his empty stomach, he figured he had been unconscious for a fair amount of time.

His senses returning, Charlie slid from the light blankets and gingerly rose to his feet, which were met, he noted, with a curiously warm stone floor. He found he was wearing a light pair of sleeping trousers, akin to his old pajamas back on Earth, but was, however, shirtless.

The konus and slaap were gone from his hand and wrist, he realized, and he felt a little naked without them. He'd been using his konus for so long now, magic had become as natural as technology had been before he was first thrown into this powerful realm in a distant galaxy.

A light tunic was draped over a nearby chair, beside which a clean pair of sandals awaited him. He quickly dressed himself, then walked to the window to see just where it was fortune had taken him this time.

The smells floating in through the open window were of a sort he had not experienced in ages. There had been plenty of greenery at Ser Baruud's compound, but there was always a faintly clinging musty odor in the air from the planet's swamps bordering the lush forests, if you paid attention to such things. Here, however, the air smelled almost like home. Fresh grass, blooming flowers, a breeze flowing through clear skies.

My God. It's a paradise, he gasped. *What did I do to deserve—?* Memory of the bout flooded back. *Could I actually be free?*

It was hard to believe, but given his performance, the possibility was definitely there. No one had seen anything like that before, he was sure of it. And when he and the dragon had stunned the other combatants and snatched the ring, the crowd had gone absolutely wild.

"It worked for Ser Baruud," he mused, a contented smile growing on his face. "I can't believe I actually did it. I won my freedom."

He would never see home again, but he had resolved himself to that years prior. Now, however, Charlie felt on top of the world as he filled his free lungs with the air of this new world.

Freedom. His prize. A reward for magnificence in combat. And what a treasure it was. Spread before him were rolling hills in the distance, and beneath his window—on the third floor, it appeared—were well-manicured grounds of a sprawling estate rivaling any palace on Earth.

Holy hell, I'm pretty high up. How did I wind up here, anyway? And where exactly is 'here'?

Charlie gripped the thick stone windowsill and leaned forward to better see the structure he was in. Long stone walls, each piece intricately fitted so well nary a sheet of paper could pass through the seams that made up the lengthy structure. It truly was like a palace, though the lines had a decidedly alien lay to them, just a little different than anything you'd find on Earth.

Water features dotted the walls at lengthy intervals, magically controlled, obviously. Their output fanned out until a mist formed at the base, casting small rainbows along the lower portion of the building. But no mold had formed on the stone. Carefully crafted spells kept the walls free of condensation.

Likewise, greenery sprang up at the base of the structure, lush and healthy, but it too did not climb the walls. It was as if a beautiful yet impenetrable barrier had surrounded the estate.

The overall effect was something akin to an elfin castle, where the shortcomings of man's seeming excellence in architecture were laid bare with the subtlest of tweaks to what had previously seemed a perfect design. The palace was perfection in stone and glass and magical enhancements.

Peering up, Charlie observed a lone, yellow sun. This was what gave the planet such a familiar hue. It almost felt like home. Almost.

He stepped back from the window and slowly paced the room, taking in his surroundings with a gladiatorial eye despite his newfound freedom. There were no weapons of any sort, nor anything that could be hastily crafted into one. The chair was hewn of stone, and the bed was a magically supported mattress with no actual frame holding it aloft.

Someone spent a lot of coin on this place, he realized. *Especially if they put up an off-worlder in this kind of lodging.*

But what if it wasn't coin at all? What if the lord of the manor was a powerful wizard himself. Wizard. He had spent years learning to call them by their local names according to power and rank.

Visla. Emmik. Mester.

And now that he was on an Earth-feeling world, he so easily slipped back into his old way of thinking. Charlie allowed himself a moment of amusement at his slip-up. He had survived by assimilating as best he could, and from that moment on, he would redouble his efforts to fit in and not draw attention.

But he *had* drawn attention. He had impulsively joined forces with a dragon. A *dragon!* And he had done it in the presence of tens of thousands, and it had earned him a new life.

What happened to her? he wondered, remembering the amazing feeling of flight atop her deep red back, the wind racing across his skin. They had made quite an impression, he was certain, and they had won the bout in a heretofore unseen and entirely unexpected manner.

A bright glimmer from the nearby table caught his eye. The ring. His prize from the bout, threaded on a golden chain. He picked it up, admiring the simple, yet beautiful lines of the metal. Something tingled in his fingers.

The ring has a bit of power, he realized. *But what kind, I have no idea. It feels strangely familiar, though.*

Charlie slid the chain over his head, dropping the ring against his chest just as a knock at the door made him spin, his hand instinctively coming up to cast a defensive spell.

No konus, he silently reminded himself with a chuckle.

"Yes?" he called out.

The door opened without waiting for further prompting and

a stout, curly-haired woman with dark orange skin flowed into the chamber, her apron and underskirt flowing around her shins.

"Good, you're finally awake," she said, quickly surveying the room. *"Yona ha."* The sheets and covers on the bed rustled, then slid back into place, the corners tucking neatly, leaving a perfectly made bed.

"Neat trick. '*Yona ha*,' is it?"

"Yes," she replied. "A basic cleaning spell. Makes beds, sets tables, folds laundry. But you are without a konus, so it won't do you any good casting it, and besides, that's not your job."

"Oh, I know. I just try to learn as much as I can," he replied. "I'm Charlie, by the way."

"Oh, I know. We *all* know who you are. My name is Magda," the orange woman replied. "I oversee Visla Maktan's housekeeping."

"Visla? So, the lord of the house is a powered man?"

"Visla Yoral Maktan is one of the most powerful vislas on the Council of Twenty, and he is the man who saved you from the arena on Gilea. You've found yourself in a position men would kill for. A new favorite of Visla Maktan. When he brought you here, he was most excited. You should be thankful."

"Oh, I am, believe me," Charlie covered. "It's just all so new to me. This place––it's just the last thing I remember was frantic combat, and an enormous red dragon. And then, nothing. And now, here I am, in this place."

"Visla Maktan brought you straight home after the tournament," Magda informed him. "And what is a '*dragon*'?"

"Sorry. *Zomoki*. I don't know why that word doesn't translate. But, do you know what happened to her?"

"I don't know about that sort of thing. But what I do know is the master wanted you bathed, clothed, and fed while he was away on his business. The first two are done, now come with me and let's see to the third."

Charlie followed the woman from the room, wondering exactly what this new life would entail. After the previous places he'd lived, it certainly seemed to be an improvement thus far. If he was lucky, maybe he'd even find a sponsor of sorts in his new friend.

CHAPTER SEVENTY

"Charlie!" a familiar voice bellowed as he entered the kitchen.

He had to consciously hold back his gladiator-trained reflexes as the big blue man lunged forward and wrapped him in a bear hug.

"Tuktuk? What are you doing here?" he asked when the overjoyed Bantoon finally released him.

"Visla Maktan bought me over a year ago when Captain Tür happened to be passing through the system. It was blind luck, really, but the visla needed kitchen help and happened to hear me when I blurted out that I could cook. Good thing, too. Captain Tür would have whipped me for speaking publicly to someone like that. But Visla Maktan seemed amused by me and bought me off of Tür right on the spot."

"That's fantastic news," Charlie said, looking his friend over. "And you look well."

It had been more than two years, but Tuktuk seemed well cared for and very well fed. His species' naturally loose skin was somewhat tightened on his larger frame, apparently fattened up from a substantial diet of rich foods. On top of that, he bore the look of a contented man. The chef's clothing, Charlie thought, suited him well.

"Yes, and now I finally get to use my talents rather than toiling away, carrying cargo like a mere pack animal. Visla Maktan treats us all so well here."

"It seems that way. But what happened to the way you speak?" Charlie asked. "I mean, no disrespect, but you're actually literate and understandable now."

The blue man laughed merrily.

"Oh, I told you when we first met, don't you remember?"

"Vaguely?"

"Liar. That's okay, though. It was a rough time for you, I know. But the thing was, the Tslavars had given us all such cheap translation spells, it was a miracle we could communicate at all. But Visla Maktan is a *very* powerful man. For him a proper translation spell was a simple thing. *Everyone* here has the best spells available, and it makes everything flow so much smoother."

"So, everyone is articulate?"

"Illiteracy is offensive to him. And he's a patron of the arts as well, so we are all expected to keep things aesthetically pleasing to the eye as well as the ear. It really is impressive, the resources he gives the staff."

"I saw that Magda was outfitted with some interesting housekeeping spells."

"Yeah, she's great, isn't she?" Tuktuk said.

Charlie thought he sensed a little more than friendly interest. He looked around and saw that Magda had walked out of the kitchen for a moment, leaving the two men alone.

"Yeah, she seems to be," Charlie replied. "But weren't you married back home?"

A brief shadow crossed Tuktuk's face, then passed.

"You remember correctly. I even managed to have a message secreted to my wife not long after you were sold to Gramfir. But our lives were hard work, and we were never rich. She simply couldn't raise the funds to buy my freedom," he said. "But I hear she is happy now. Met a new man, and I really can't blame her for it."

"So, this is your life now? No hopes of freedom?"

"Honestly, this is better than freedom in many ways. My job is now doing what I love, and I am well taken care of, living in an amazing estate I could never afford earning even a substantial wage, working with all of this amazing food. It's not freedom, per se, but it's a life I can appreciate, and far better than any job I've ever held."

Charlie tried to imagine being a slave once again. That life had been so tough, but as he looked around the pristine kitchen, he could see the appeal to his friend. Like everything he had seen so far, it appeared Visla Maktan spared no expense in any part of his home, be it servants' quarters or the kitchen, all were well stocked and spotless.

A plate of some sort of savory biscuit caught his eye. They were still steaming, fresh from the oven.

"Ah, I see you eyeing my pastry. Well, they're best when they're hot. Why not have a few?"

Charlie's stomach rumbled loudly in the affirmative before the man himself could speak. Tuktuk laughed as his friend plucked one from the pile and took a bite.

"Oh my God, this is wonderful," Charlie said through his full mouth.

"I'm glad you like it. But you need something to drink. I just made a fresh batch of yonda cooler, which I think you'll like. The yonda are grown right here on the grounds, and it's something of a restorative as well as a rather refreshing drink."

He crossed to a refrigeration unit that, like everything else, was powered by a series of spells, keeping each of the contents within preserved and cooled at precisely the right temperature.

He poured a tall glass of a cloudy, violet-colored beverage and handed it to his feasting friend.

"Tuk, this is fantastic!"

"I thought you'd like it. This is going to be so much fun. Finally, I have a new person to test my recipes on. Magda likes them, but she says she has to think about her figure," he said with a laugh. "Personally, I like a woman with a little more to hold on to."

"Are you going to fatten me up, Tuk?"

"Not likely. Look at you. You're all lean muscle these days. Not that you weren't fit before, but the years have been kind to you."

"Well, there was also a lot of intense training pretty much every day."

"Yeah, that too," Tuktuk chuckled. "But now you are here, and for our reunion day, let me feed my old friend. Sit, I'll prepare you something more substantial to fill your stomach."

Charlie ate well, and the two sat and talked, swapping stories of their trials and adventures over the years since they'd last met. He may have been blue, and with eyes on stalks, no less, but Charlie still felt that Tuktuk was one of his dearest friends in this strange part of the universe. The man who helped get him through those horrible first days and weeks.

"We just heard! The Master is coming home!" a dark-eyed servant girl said, rushing into the kitchen. "He will be back by the end of the week at the latest."

"Excellent! I'm sure you will like your new master, Charlie. He's a good man," Tuktuk said, rising to his feet to clean the workspace.

"I'm sorry, what did you just say?"

"I said he's a good man."

"No, the part before that. The *master* part."

"What? I just said I'm sure you'll like your new master."

"But-but I'm free. I competed bravely and earned my freedom in the arena."

His blue friend fixed him with a sympathetic look. "Oh, my friend, I'm so sorry, but you're not."

Charlie's fingers reached up, brushing the band around his neck. He hadn't even noticed it before, being so taken with the surroundings and so accustomed to the feel that its weight didn't even register anymore. His fingers traced the metal. It was much thinner and lighter than his old one, but a great deal of power went into its creation, and traces of it now tickled his fingertips.

"No. No, this can't be happening."

He stepped to the nearby reflecting panel and said the simple words to enable the enchanted device. *"Occulo."*

His reflection appeared, but as he would be seen by others, a difference in this galaxy that had taken him a little time to become accustomed to. The only place he would see himself reversed in a truly mirrored reflection was in calm waters and other naturally reflective surfaces he encountered in his travels. Mirrors, as he had known them on Earth, simply did not exist.

There it was, plain to see. A collar on his neck.

New. Bright. Golden.

And though it had the look of a decorative piece, with all of the inscribed runes and symbols, it was, he noted, somewhat more robust than his prior one.

So many runes, he marveled. *But if he saw me at the arena... Given what the dragon and I did, I suppose it freaked a lot of people out. Overkill would be a natural response.*

"Are you okay?" Tuktuk asked, resting a hand on his friend's shoulder.

"Yeah," Charlie replied, more than a little crestfallen. "I had just thought––Well, it doesn't matter, I suppose," he said, allowing himself a moment to really consider his new surroundings. "It's not Earth, but compared to my last several homes, you're right. This *is* a life of luxury."

"Yes, it is. I'm sure you'll enjoy yourself once you settle in."

Charlie looked out the small door leading from the kitchen. The world was bright and warm, and no one was trying to kill him for a change. All things considered, it wasn't a bad place to be. He had survived, somehow.

Crashing, fighting, all of it. And now he would live a good life on a beautiful estate, even if it wasn't as a free man.

"I suppose it's just like any other job," he said, echoing Tuktuk's sentiment. "And if this Visla Maktan is truly such a good guy and patron of arts, this might wind up being better than any gig I'd ever have on Earth anyway."

Charlie took a deep breath, the last remnants of stress in his body slowly releasing and drifting away in the warm breeze. It wasn't Earth, but the realization was finally setting in. This life might be even *better* than Earth.

After years of struggle, Charlie was home.

EPILOGUE

In the dark of night Charlie lay wrapped in dreams, his mind's eye flying high among the clouds, soaring free. From altitude, he took in all of the visla's expansive grounds. In the distance he saw a beautiful ship silently gliding through the skies, descending toward an open landing space to the side of one of the outer buildings. A few other ships sat there as well, but this was a work of art by comparison.

That must be his, he thought. *The visla's ship.*

He strained to see more, but his dream was disrupted as an encroaching blackness pulled his sight from him, plunging him into the dark.

All was still and silent.

"Hello?" he said, his voice muffled by an oppressive weight. It was as if he was ensconced in a dense fog, blocking all light and sound.

Two enormous golden eyes flashed open, their blazing irises fixing on the tiny man before them. Charlie could feel the invisible heat radiating from the unseen beast that owned them.

He tried to run. Tried to scream. But neither his lungs nor legs would function.

Slowly the eyes moved closer, dropping down to his level for a clearer look.

"Hello, my little friend," a woman's voice said, her words penetrating his head like a firehose of thought. *"You and I have much to discuss."*

BUT WAIT, THERE'S MORE!

Follow Charlie on his continuing adventures in the second book
of the Dragon Mage series: *Space Pirate Charlie*

THANK YOU

Reader word of mouth is an independent author's lifeblood. So if you enjoyed this book and have a moment to spare, please consider leaving a rating or review on Amazon or on Goodreads, or even sharing it with a friend or two. Your support is greatly appreciated.

Thank you!

~ Scott ~

ALSO BY SCOTT BARON

Novels

Living the Good Death

The Clockwork Chimera Series

Daisy's Run

Pushing Daisy

Daisy's Gambit

Chasing Daisy

Daisy's War

The Dragon Mage Series

Bad Luck Charlie

Space Pirate Charlie

Dragon King Charlie

Odd and Unusual Short Stories:

The Best Laid Plans of Mice: An Anthology

Snow White's Walk of Shame

The Tin Foil Hat Club

Lawyers vs. Demons

The Queen of the Nutters

Lost & Found

ABOUT THE AUTHOR

A native Californian, Scott Baron was born in Hollywood, which he claims may be the reason for his rather off-kilter sense of humor.

Before taking up residence in Venice Beach, Scott first spent a few years abroad in Florence, Italy before returning home to Los Angeles and settling into the film and television industry, where he has worked as an on-set medic for many years.

Aside from mending boo-boos and owies, and penning books and screenplays, Scott is also involved in indie film and theater scene both in the U.S. and abroad.